THE YEAR OF THE
LIEUTENANT

JOHN HARRINGTON

ARCHWAY
PUBLISHING

This is a work of fiction. All of the characters, names, incidents, organizations, and dialogue in this novel are either the products of the author's imagination or are used fictitiously.

Archway Publishing books may be ordered through booksellers or by contacting:

Archway Publishing
1663 Liberty Drive
Bloomington, IN 47403
www.archwaypublishing.com
1 (888) 242-5904

ISBN: 978-1-4808-3414-9 (sc)
ISBN: 978-1-4808-3415-6 (e)

Library of Congress Control Number: 2016911340

Print information available on the last page.

Archway Publishing rev. date: 7/27/2016

DEDICATION

To my dear, departed friend, John "J.B." Steplen,
who could have written a much better story.

ACKNOWLEDGMENT

Thank you, Eileen, for giving me the time and freedom
to write the story and encouraging me to revisit it.
The greatest wife, mother, and grandmother.

PROLOGUE

September 1974

I received a Christmas card from Bob Saunders this year, the first one in four or five years. It had been forwarded several times from my last Air Force address to Connecticut and finally arriving in New York. He must have been reassigned to a new base, lost his regular Christmas card list somewhere in transit and used an old one. It was one of those photo-type cards, his wife sitting, blond with a toothy grin, her glasses off, and a little girl, new to me so probably not more than three, in her pajamas and holding a Raggedy-Ann doll. Behind them in his Air Force blues, now a captain, stood Bob. His face was expressionless, his mouth held in a short flat line. It is a manner that military people seem to find so appealing. "I am a professional, just a no-nonsense guy with a job to do." The photographer's flash reflected too brightly off Bob's glasses, and he was not wearing a hat. It was just as well as they never fit him correctly and usually fell down on his ears. Across the bottom of the card it said, "Captain Robert A. Saunders and Family." No other message.

I placed the card on the mantel piece along with the others, and occasionally during the Christmas season my eyes returned to it and caught Bob's flashy stare. The season is now past, the cards long ago put away, but I can still see Bob, his face grimly locked in its forced ferociousness. I have begun to realize how much time I have spent in the past few years thinking about him. It took his image to make it clear. From the picture, it appears he has changed very little, still trying to be and seeing himself as something his is not. And of course, if he were to look at his own picture, he would see the epitome of military toughness, a real air commando. Some thoughts of him have always brought laughter to my mind, and with a few drinks, I can tell some old stories about him guaranteed to get a few laughs from everyone.

Yet, there was a time, despite all I knew was absurd about him, that I found myself extremely envious of Bob Saunders, for he, it seemed at one time, had found something which I was clumsily and unconsciously seeking. No matter that he soon lost it, and worse, that he never considered himself a seeker nor a finder nor a loser. Yet today, if I think of it—say look at the Christmas card—I can quickly summon up that sharp, painful anger I once felt towards him.

I am not a maker of events. Things seem to happen to me. So it was then in 1967 and 1968. There were just over one hundred airmen in Nakorn Sarang, a United States

Air Force radar site in Thailand when I arrived. Bob was already there, and he left before I did, but somehow it always seemed I had been there long before him. When I signed in, I shared a bungalow in town with him, filling the spot of another lieutenant who had just rotated back to the States. Bob's idea of welcoming me and acquainting me with Thailand was to read me letters from his wife. Out of politeness, for the first few evenings, I sat and listened. Then I began to ignore him; I would have a beer, read my own mail, take a shower, change, and go into town for something to eat.

His reaction never changed. He would sit in the living room in his underwear in a large rataan chair underneath the overhead fan, drinking a beer or a soft drink and call out, "Hey, Jim, listen to this. 'Daddy says, (her father was a retired colonel) that a year over there with those people will do you a lot of good. Kind of teach you to appreciate America more, you know. Also, you'll have a chance to win some medals and help your career along.'"

Pulling himself forward in the chair and seeking my whereabouts in the bungalow, he would call to me, "What medal do you want to get out of this war, Jim?"

Since I had developed the habit of ignoring him as much as possible, I would have to ask him to repeat the question.

"I said, what medal do you expect to get out of this war?"

"I won't settle for anything less than the Medal of Honor."

Nothing was beyond Bob's consideration, so he would lean back, sip at his soft drink or beer, and perhaps contemplate the blue ribbon with the white stars being ceremoniously placed around his neck. After a moment, and with his eyebrows drawn closely together, he would lean forward again and say, "I don't think there's much hope of that here, since we're not being shot at. I'd say a bronze star is our best bet. Of course, I'd settle for nothing less than a commendation medal. Heck, they're giving them out like they were good conduct ribbons."

Other nights, while I would be enjoying a cold shower (there was no hot water in Nakorn Sarang), I could hear, "Hey, Jim! Listen to this. 'Daddy and I went to the football game up at State (Bob and Betty had both gone to Michigan State where he had majored in finance), but they lost.'"

Then he would pull himself forward in the chair and search me out. Finding me in the shower he would yell a little louder. "How'd your school do last weekend?"

Of course I would ask him to repeat himself, and after he had, I would say, "Lost to Radcliffe, two to one."

Leaning back in his chair, sipping on his beer and addressing the whole room he would ask, "How the heck do you get just one point in football?"

After changing, I would go into Nakorn Sarang and eat. Occasionally I would ask him if he's like to join me for some fried beef with vegetables, rice and a few Singha beers.

"Oh, no!" Head shaking. "I do all my eating on the site or stuff I buy in the BX. You never know what these people put in their food. Betty's dad warned me about that. He said, 'Son, stay away from that brand X.' Besides that, I've heard these people eat dogs."

After two months of this, I came home one evening, packed my clothes and moved out. Bob stayed there for nine more months and in that time shared his bungalow with three other new arrivals, each of whom repeated my abrupt departure procedure within a similar length of time.

Bob reacted to my leaving in much the same manner that he reacted to my lack of attention to his evening letter readings; in other words, he reacted not at all. After I had moved, he would seek me out in the mess hall and pick up conversations that had been left suspended at the bungalow. When I finished my food, and in the middle of his stories about Betty and Daddy and State and medals, got up and left the table, he again took no offense and would resume his tales the next time we met.

When I moved out, I went to share another bungalow with a junior captain named Joe Stacy, who was a tall, heavy-set man with a broad grin. Joe arrived in Thailand at about the same time I had, and, like me, had been hustled into sharing a house with someone he found himself unable to bear over any length of time. Joe stayed on in Thailand for six months after I left, and had, in fact, been stationed there several times earlier in his service career. We became close friends, and, unlike Bob Saunders and me, we have kept in touch with each other through visits and letters over the years.

In the evening, before dark, Joe too would sit in the living room of our bungalow, the sweat running off his huge, hairy and bare stomach. Seated on a rataan couch with a paisin—a Thai sarong—loosely hanging around his hips and legs, he had more than casual resemblance to some of the statues of Buddha.

Drinking Singha beer from a glass, he would say, "There's no sense, Jim, in showering before dark," when I suggested we clean up and go into the village to eat. "You'll be sweating just as much in a few minutes."

From a plate on the table, he would pick up a handful of the nuts that Ewan, his girlfriend, had prepared for us. She would sit at the far end of the couch, out of reach, rarely saying a word. Joe had met her in Bangkok several years before, and now she came and went with a frequency that defied any identifiable pattern. Sometimes for several weeks she would be with us, and then one evening she would come and stand before Joe in his chair and say, "Joe, Evan go Bangkok. See Mama-san." It would always be quiet and unassertive, yet so flat and blunt you knew there was nothing that would change her mind.

"Are you," Joe would ask, "Going tonight, or are you going to get the morning train?" not using the Pidgin English that so many of us affected when speaking to a Thai.

"Ewan go morning." The next day Joe would be late coming to work because he had seen her to the train where he had tipped the conductor to insure she was sent some fried rice during the ride, and stuck one hundred dollars in Thai baht into her purse.

And then, as quietly, on an evening when I arrived at home, she might be there. A quick smile crossed the light brown skin of her face, and, looking down, she slipped into the kitchen to return seconds later with a beer and some nuts.

"Sawadee, Jim," and then she sat down in the chair across from me and began to wait. She seemed perfectly comfortable and prepared to sit there silently all night.

I felt as if I should be saying something, and at long last asked, "How is Mama-san?"

"S'okay."

I drank my beer and waited with her, after awhile reading a letter I had received that morning. Suddenly, without any warning or expression on her face, she stood up, walked to the front of the room and peered through the screens searching the walkway that led to the road.

"Jim, Joe come by home soon?" She turned her head slightly but kept her back to me, and I could see nothing in her face.

"Yes, he just had to work a little late." And she would say, "Oh".

When he came home, she would stand and greet him with a wai, her hands held together at a respectable position in front of her face. Joe would beam and return the greeting and add a little bow, but he never touched her. Then the evening would be like the others. After dark we would shower, and the three of us would ride in samlows into town for dinner.

That night after dinner, I left them and went to the Argo Bar while they came directly back to our bungalow. Later, when I came home, I could hear Joe snoring, and if I had looked in I'm sure she too would have been sleeping, her head resting on his chest.

"Joe," I said one night as we both sat in the Argo Bar, Ewan being in Bangkok. "Joe, do you really think Ewan gives that money you give her to her mother?"

He laughed some and drank more beer. "Of course not. She has a bank account in Bangkok. That's where most of it goes. Maybe some of it goes to Mama-san."

"You don't feel like she's taking you for a ride?"

Still smiling he turned and looked at me. "Well," he began, "Now I guess you could say she is. She does have a mother, just like you and me, but she doesn't give her all the money she earns, and then neither do we. And she likes to put her extra baht in the bank so she'll have something when she has to stop working. Now that seems like a reasonable idea. I do it myself sometimes."

He turned back to the bar and drank some more of his beer. Without the smallest part of a smile on his face, a rare thing for Joe, he said, "Besides, in the three or four years I've know her, I think I've given her maybe twenty-five or twenty-six hundred dollars. She sure isn't going to get rich on that."

As for the both of them, Bob and Joe that is, I think that if not for me, each of them could have spent the year stationed together in Nakorn Sarang and never have considered the other. To Bob, Joe was an anomaly, an imponderable, like the one-point in football or the Medal of Honor without being shot at. And Joe, he certainly did not find Bob worth considering.

SEPTEMBER 1967

CHAPTER ONE

THERE WERE TWO PLANES A week into Nakorn Sarang, both of them from Takhli, a larger U.S. Air Force base about a hundred miles to the south, which provided Nakorn Sarang with supplies. (There were occasional flights directly from Bangkok, but they were irregularly scheduled.) It was on one of these supply flights that I first arrived in NSG which is what the Air Force seemed to prefer calling Nakorn Sarang. My duffel bag and I had been placed between NSG's weekly supply of food and a large carton, which claimed to hold 400 cans of paint, olive drab.

From the air, the town of Nakorn Sarang could not be seen, but the radar site of a dozen or so buildings with aluminum roofs spread around a small trapezoid shaped area of a few acres could be clearly made out. It lay at the far end of a runway. At the other end, where the plane rolled to a stop, was a white building with a tower. This was the Nakorn Sarang Airport.

Around the rear of the C-130 aircraft, as the supplies and I were being lowered by the hydraulic lift to the runway, there were standing about some dozen sergeants and airmen. Above the roar of the idling engines, one of them yelled to me, "Hey, Lieutenant, are you part of the supplies or you going on up the line?"

"Is this Detachment 8 of the 519th Tactical Air Control Squadron?"

"It ain't fucking Disneyland."

"Then I'm part of the supplies."

I rode, still in my place between the food and the paint, on the back of a large truck along the pot hole marked dirt road that led to the radar site. When the truck stopped in the center of the site and was being unloaded, one of the sergeants, at my request, pointed out the orderly room as, "that little fucking building by the fucking gate."

Toting my duffel bag toward the orderly room, I became aware of the tremendous heat and humidity. A thermometer off the porch of the orderly room indicated it was, in the sun, one hundred and eleven degrees. I tried to remember if I had ever been so hot.

As I reached for the door handle, the door swung open quickly and a short, pudgy, burr-headed, blond lieutenant crashed into me and my duffel bag. The crash joggled me a little, but it knocked the other fellow's cap and glasses off. He groped about and I helped him recover them. After putting them back on, he turned to me and saluted, then hustled off; I noted he had placed his cap on backwards, his little silver bar trailing behind.

Inside the orderly room, when I entered, two sergeants and an airman were laughing about something. I introduced myself. "Hello, I'm Lieutenant Doyle, the new administrative officer," an announcement which certainly did not appear to strike any great degree of awe into the group. The senior of them, who introduced himself as Master Sergeant Sutton, the First Sergeant, mentioned something to the effect that they had been expecting me and my desk was to one piled under with bed sheets and blankets..

"We, uh, been using that desk sort of, uh, to hand out supplies to, uh, the new personnel," explained Sgt. Sutton, at the same time stroking his pencil-line moustache.

I placed my duffel bag next to the desk, took off my cap, and began to look around the room. It, aside from my desk, was an orderly enough place. There were the usual cases full of Air Force regulations and manuals, also the usual pictures of the chain of command, working its way down from President Johnson to a craggy faced major I assumed to be the site commander. The far wall featured a large map of the site; on it, a red X and some words were lettered, "You are here!" Next to it was a large National Geographic map of Thailand, this one with a red X placed in the north central area, also inscribed, "You are here." The wall by the door carried several charts and listings featuring the usual Air Force conglomeration of initials and acronyms—AFSC, DOR, DOS, EDSCA, TPS-27, UPA-35, MPS-14, GPS-16, TACC, CRC, CRP, etc., etc., some of which I eventually came to know and others which I never had the slightest idea about. Two small rooms led off the main room, one marked "First Sergeant" and the other, "Commander." The chair behind the desk in the latter room was empty.

When I pulled on the top drawer of my desk, it was stuck. With both hands, I yanked at it. It gave some and opened about an inch. It was empty except for some dust and an empty wrapper for a prophylactic. The other drawers, which opened easier, were also empty, completely empty.

"Say, Sgt. Sutton, did the last admin officer use this disk?"

The airman, whose name was Burnett and was now filling in some forms at his desk with his back to me began to laugh. Sgt. Sutton came out of his office. He had a firm wide stride and held his back ramrod straight.

"Well, uh, you see, Lt. Doyle," he spoke deliberately, still stroking his moustache, his eyes just missing mine, aimed at about my left ear. "You see, uh, we've never had no, uh, administrative officer before. In fact, according to the, uh, UMD..." He drew these letters out, "yewww emmm deee." It was a mannerism, I came to note, he often used when reciting Air Force initials, assigning a certain degree of reverence to them.

"UMD?"

Sutton paused and caught my eyes momentarily, but quickly continued, "Yes, Sir. The unit manning document, the UMD does not, uh, authorize an administrative officer for the,uh, site."

"It doesn't what?"

"Yes, Sir. Uh, that is until recently." Airman Burnett, who was now laughing quite hard, got up, put on his hat, and asked if he could take a break. Sgt. Sutton waved his hand at the airman, "Sure, Smiley, go get a coffee."

When Sutton's attention seemed to return to me, I said, "I'm not quite sure I understand what you're talking about."

"Well, uh, you see, Sir, like I said, that is till, uh, recently. In fact, approximately one month ago. At which time, I, uh, we, uh, received a new yewww emmm deee." He reached and pulled a slim volume off one of the shelves. It was enclosed in a plastic cover. He opened it, and holding it in front of me, pointed to a line which read: "OFF ADMIN 1/LT 7024."

"Now we have not, uh, previously been authorized such a position." From the same spot on the shelf, he produced a similar looking document, except each page had been stamped, "superseded." Sure enough, there was no mention of, "OFF ADMIN 1/LT 7024." Sutton looked at me more directly with this, removed his hand from his moustache and placing it on his hip. I could hear the very regular clacking of a typewriter and noticed that the other sergeant, a staff sergeant named Chance, was working away at a monotonous pace, seemingly oblivious to the discussion Sgt. Sutton and I were holding as regards the vagaries of the Air Force personnel assignment system.

"As I understand it, Sarge, you have only recently been authorized an admin officer, and I'm the first one to be assigned as such."

"Yes, Sir."

"So, despite the confusion of the past, I am now here and it seems as if there is really little to do except get on with the job." I was afraid from the constipated look that settled over Sutton's face that it was not quite that simple.

"Well, uh, uh, yes, and no, Sir." Sutton was stroking his moustache again and boring in hard on my left ear. He had both the superseded and current copies of the UMD in his hand and began waving them about in an inconclusive manner. "You see, Sir, we, uh, that is the Major and me, had originally, uh, requested a change in the yewww emmm deee." As he began, he ceased stroking his moustache and put one copy of the UMD in his left hand and the other in his right. During his explanation of my situation, he would raise the pertinent document and lower the other in the manner of a scale. Up the left, down the right, and vice versa. Also at some time during our conversation, I'm not sure when, he pulled over a straight-backed chair and swung a leg over it, cowboy style, sitting on it backwards, resting his arms on its back.

"Now this requested change in the, uh, then current yewww emmm dee, uh, reflected our need for additional, uh, weapon's controllers and, uh, the new, or, uh, proposed yewww emmm deee so, uh, reflected this proposal." The left hand went quickly up at this point and the right hand down, and I thought I may have identified them.

But I still had other points of confusions. "What, Sarge, is a weapon's controller?"

Judging from the pause my question generated, and the blankness of his stare, I may well have asked what is an airplane. After a rather lengthy pause, Sutton went into a definition of young officers trained in the art of communication with airborne vehicles while assisting in selection of proper routes of air passage and aerial rendezvouses, to put it in the sergeant's language.

"You mean 'scope dope?'"

He quickly emitted a somewhat garbled, "Oh, yeah," and continued on with his explanation of my presence in Nakorn Sarang.

"So, you see, we, uh, that is, the Major and me had originally requested an increase in our, uh, allotment of, uh, weapon's controllers from nine to twelve. What with the, uh, air war heating up, our workload has, uh, increased considerably. However," (while saying this, both of his hands dropped wearily to his sides), "the new yewwww emmm deee, which we, as I have, uh, previously stated, uh, received approximately one month ago, uh, maintained our current level of controllers at s, uh, level of nine personnel units, and authorized us, uh, an administrative officer."

A sense of deep dejection settled across Sgt. Sutton's face, and I found it uncomfortable to look at him very closely. But he soon picked himself up and, throwing both UMD's back to the shelf, went on. "Now next, the Major and I, uh, reinstituted our request for an increase in our authorization of weapon's controllers. In the, uh, meantime, we received these." At this he got up and went over to the black binder which was marked "PCS Order", and turned pages till he came upon what must have been my orders, saying, "Which, uh, read, '1st Lt. Doyle, James M." which of course is you." He returned to his position in the chair. "Now, that, uh, complicated things to a certain degree, but the Major and me was, uh, confident that our request, when seen in the, uh, proper prospective, would be approved." He spread out his hands, palms up, apparently indicating some sense of finality, a feeling that certainly escaped me.

"But it wasn't, right?"

"Well, sir, no, that is, we, uh, didn't know. The Major and me, that is, we heard nothing. That is, uh, until today."

"And I showed up, right?"

Sutton paused to smirk and shake his head with its weary smile; this poor little looie will never quite understand, will he? "Well, yes, you, uh, did. but the main thing is, uh, that on the same plane that transported you was this transmittal from personnel." He went back into his office abruptly. While he was in there, Smiley Barnett returned from his coffee break and sat down at his desk. He began to fill in some forms again, but occasionally I could hear him laughing to himself. The clicking of Sgt. Chance's typewriter continued away at its monotonous pace.

Sgt. Sutton returned with a letter which he showed to me. The body of it read, "Request refused. See previous correspondence this subject." It was signed by someone at the personnel office in Takhli.

"So, I'm here and I'm supposed to be here."

"Well, uh, yes Sir, as you can see. That is obvious." Was anything obvious? I looked at the piles of sheets and blankets on my desk. Where would that stuff go? Christ, I couldn't even figure that much out, how the hell could I understand what this mad mustache stroker was

telling me?

"Sgt. Sutton, now that I'm here, what the hell do I do?"

Standing up and pushing his chair back against the wall, he looked down at me, again with that wearied little smirk. "No problem, the Major and me have, uh, provided ourselves with a contingency plan in the event of this, uh, event."

The door opened and a major entered. I assumed him to be the commander since he bore some resemblance to the picture on the wall. He strode by without seeming to notice me. "Sarn't Sutton, 'at plane bring mail?" Sutton answered that the plane had brought the mail and that the Major's mail was waiting for him on his desk, so the Major, whose name was Hudson, continued into his office. Sitting behind his desk, he reached into the top drawer and pulled out a letter opener, the handle of which was a wood carving of a cobra with its neck spread out. He opened each of his letters and began to read. I got up and went to knock on his door, but Sgt. Sutton motioned me with his hand, indicating with a slow shake that I should wait. Behind Sutton I could see that Sgt. Chance had stopped typing and was now affixing a rubber stamp to the upper left hand corner of a pile of forms with the same regular motion that he demonstrated while typing. Smiley Burnett was now typing and giggling.

It took Major Hudson about ten minutes to get through his letters. As he read, he would occasionally go, "hum." When he was finally through, he looked up and saw me sitting in my chair which was directly in front of the door to his office. I smiled and waved, he blinked; after that he got up, walked around his desk and closed his door.

His voice was more urgent than clear, but I thought I understood him to say, "Sarn't Sutton, come innuh my office." He had a low, gravelly voice to match his craggy face. I could hear them through the louvered doors although I wasn't always sure what Hudson was saying.

"Who 'zat Lootinin'?"

"That's Lt. Doyle, Sir!"

"Who?"

"Lt. Doyle, the uh, administrative officer." There was a pause, and I could hear someone moving about. by the shadows on the louvers, it was clear that someone was trying to peer through them and get a better look at me. The shadow disappeared, and the seat of Hudson's chair squeaked as he sat back down.

"Wha's 'ee doin' here?"

"Sir, our request for another, uh, reappraisal of our yewww emmm deee has, uh, been denied. This is a copy of the, uh, transmission from CBPO." There was a shuffling of papers and Hudson asked, "Is'isuh copyov'is orders?" Stg. Sutton replied in the affirmative, in fact that's exactly what he said, "Affirmative!" to which Hudson requested that I be shown in.

Although I had been sitting right outside the door, and it seemed apparent to me that I must have heard the conversation, Sgt. Sutton approached me as if I had been on the dark side of the moon, and with the formality of an engraved invitation. "Lt. Doyle, Major Hudson requests your presence in his office."

When entering, I snapped to attention, clicking my heels, and saluted with my best precision. "Lt. James Doyle reporting for duty, Sir!" Major Hudson seemed to wave at his forehead, and then in the same motion signaled me to sit down.

Elbows resting on his desk with his hands directly in front of his face, Hudson seemed to be focusing on a spot somewhere on the wall about six inches above my head. his hands started to move in small twisting circles before he spoke.

"Yuhhav'uhguhd trip?" What the hell was that? I asked him to repeat it, and his hands began to turn in a rather grotesque fashion, one of his wrists bending violently back.

"You have a guhdtrip?" The last two words clipped off the end of the sentence, as if the struggle to enunciate and separate the earlier words had drained him. I replied in the affirmative, although my words were the more conventional, "Yes, Sir."

By the motion of his hands, I could tell he was about to speak again. "'IdSar'ntSuttonesplainuhproblem?

I paused and tried to make sense of the sounds he had just emitted. When I felt relatively confident that he had asked me if Sgt. Sutton had explained the problem, I said, "Yes, Sir."

"Good." That was very clear, but then he added, "Hopeyuhhav'uhguhdyeah. Tha'sall." With a little abrupt waving motion of his hand he seemed to be indicating that I was dismissed.

"But Major Hudson, he only explained the problem to me, he didn't tell me what my job is or anything like that."

"Hudson's eyes met mine for the first time (they didn't appear to be quite in synch with each other), and his hands froze in mid-air. "Oh."

He must have thought, for a moment, that my orders carried some explanation because he stared at them so deeply and so intently as if he expected to see one emerge. His hands spread out and up in front of him as if he were holding the solution so I could see it more clearly. "Oh, well." This was said relatively distinctly, but when he continued, his regular speech pattern returned, "Wha'I'mgonnuhdoiz..." His sentence was broken off in the middle and he waved towards the right corner of the room, where stood Sgt. Sutton. How the hell long, I wondered, had he been there? The two offices were adjoining, and Sutton had entered through a sliding door that divided them. he had probably been there the whole time I'd been sitting with Hudson.

"What the, uh, Major has decided," Sgt. Sutton began, picking up Hudson's line without a pause, "is that you, that is, Lt. Doyle, which is, of course, you, being well aware to the, uh, normal situation on a small site, that, we are, uh, according to the pertinent Air Force regulations and manuals, uh, not authorized many of the officers and positions that are, uh, more common among the bases of a, uh, larger nature." I puzzled over his tortured sentence structure, but Hudson seemed to be signaling agreement; at least that's what I took "hum-uh" to mean. The fact that he would sometimes raise his right hand above the table in the "thumbs-up fashion also noted some form of accord.

"Now, as you are well aware, uh, what is done, in such a, uh, situation is to assign these responsibilities as, uh, additional duties." Sutton was stroking his moustache. "For instance, in our, uh, situation, where we are assigned nine radar officers and one maintenance officer, we have, uh, assigned each of them other, uh, responsibilities. Now, uh, Capt. Sheets, who is, uh, the operations officer, is, uh, also the security officer—in charge of perimeter safety that is—and Lt. Akles, who is, uh, one of our weapons controllers—an item we have, uh, previously noted—is the BX and, uh, supply officer. Uh, Lt. Saunders is the morale officer." Sgt. Sutton went on to explain the additional duties of Captains Gunn and Stacy and Lieutenants Crawford, Simpson, Gallo, and Alvarez. Major Hudson was the tenth officer, and, as I understood it, I was the eleventh and newest officer.

"Now, uh, what the Major proposes," (Hudson nodded and added a "hum-uh") "is that all of these duties and, uh, responsibilities be assigned to you, Lt. Doyle, that is. Uh, sort of to, uh, fill out your job, since there isn't really much for an admin officer to, uh, do." Sutton removed his hand from his moustache and spread both hands out, again with their palms up. Hudson's head jerked quickly towards Sutton and he said, "Uh-uh, 'member Sheets."

"Oh, yes, uh, Capt. Sheets will, uh, remain security officer, since, uh, this is an area in which he had demonstrated great, uh, expertise. And he is, of course, well versed in all of the, uh, applicable Air Force regulations and manuals, uh, dealing with security."

I looked up. "Sgt. Sutton, I mean Major Hudson, I've tried to jot this down, and I'd like to review it. As I understand it, I am, in addition to being the admin officer, am to be the supply officer, the library officer, personnel officer, dispensary administrator, theater officer, club officer, transportation officer, vehicle maintenance officer, engineering officer, athletic officer, BX officer, mess officer, fire warden, information officer, Thai liaison officer, grounds officer, USO liaison officer, and morale officer, but not security officer."

Hudson said, "Hum-uh"; Sutton, "Affirmative, Sir."

"That's a lot."

"Uh, Major Hudson thinks an excellent officer such as, uh, yourself can handle it." (I noted to myself that for such a short observation period, their judgment was remarkably accurate.)

Hudson made another noise and seemed to nod his head at me, then he stood up. "Sar'ntSuttonandIhav'tuhinspeckuhhooches." Sutton added, "Yes, Sir." With that they both walked past as I was rising and into the orderly room. I followed.

"Lt. Doyle, this is, uh, Sgt. Chance." Chance looked up from a pile of forms he had been placing a check mark in the upper right hand corner of, and after seeming to inspect my extended hand, without getting up, unenthusiastically shook it. When I released his hand, he went back to his forms.

"And this is, uh, Airman Burnett." Burnett stood up and accepted my hand with less apprehension than had Chance. When Burnett sat down, he suppressed a short laugh.

Hudson was waiting for Sutton in the open doorway seeming to be quite impatient. The hot, humid air immediately filled the room. They quickly left, heading in the direction of the hooches, which were open, screened barracks. Both of them were wearing fatigue outfits of olive drab, but Hudson's cap was a small baseball type, its brim crushed and broken from having been folded into his pocket. Sgt. Sutton wore an Australian bush hat, the left side of the brim folded up, and the entire hat tilted forward at a jaunty angle.

I turned my back to the door window and looked around the room taking in the charts and personnel listings hanging on the wall. One of them I recognized as a listing of all the site's personnel. I searched until I found my line; it had already been filled in: "7024 Admin Off 1Lt J. M. Doyle FV3178808." Really make you feel at home quickly here, I laughed to myself.

"You know," I said out loud, but not specifically directed at either Chance or Burnett, "I forgot to even ask what the mission was here."

"The what?" asked Chance without looking up from the new pile of forms he was initialing in the lower left hand corner.

"The mission, you know, why we're here."

"Listen, Lieutenant," Chance said looking up at me for the first time, some passion in his eyes for the first time as well, "No matter what the fuck those fuckin' assholes tell you, don't ever forget this: there ain't no fuckin' mission. Only reason we're here is so some fuckin' majors and captains and senior NCO's can get some fuckin' medals. The rest of us just hope our peckers don't fall off from the fuckin' clap!"

CHAPTER TWO

NEAR THE END OF THAT day, after I had been shown around the site by smiley Burnett, after I had filled my name in on what seemed to be several hundred forms, even after the sheets and blankets had been cleared from my desk and I had been issued an "in" and an "out" basket, it was brought to the attention of the powers that were that I did not have a place to sleep. Airmen and junior NCO's lived in the hooches, but officers and senior NCO's lived in the village in rented bungalows.

When I reminded Major Hudson of my lack of quarters, he said, calling through the sliding door to the first sergeant's office, "Sar'ntSutton, who'zgottuhempteeroom?" Sutton replied to the query about available quarters to the effect that he was not sure, but Capt. Sheets usually knew who was living where and he, Sutton, would call him, Sheets,, and ask who I, Doyle, could live with, which is how you ended up talking and thinking after spending any length of time around them, Hudson and Sutton.

"Uh, Capt. Sheets, uh, Sgt. Sutton here,...Yes, Sir, fine, fine, good day for fighting,...Uh, yes, Sir, uh, good day for that too." Sutton turned a little red on those words. "Say, uh, Capt., we've, uh, the major and me, have got a new, uh, administrative officer over here, Lt. Doyle,...Yes, uh, that's affirmative, we didn't know for sure if he was coming, uh, but he's here now,... Well, uh, we, Major Hudson and I, uh, are assigning him most of the additional duties,... Oh, no, Sir, you're still, uh, the security officer,...Yes, Sir, that is, uh, an important job." While Sutton was trying to find out from Sheets who I could live with, I heard the orderly room door open.

"Hi, I'm Joe Stacy." His large hand was already extended, and his grip was firm. "New, aren't you? When'd you get in?" He had a large round face, which was split by a wide, pleasant grin. His fatigues were well tailored, but stained with large blotches of perspiration. On his head, he was wearing a blue flight cap which was not authorized to be worn with the fatigues, and was decorated by a set of captain's bars.

"Jim Doyle, yes, I got in on the Takhli plane this morning."

"Takhli trolley, hey?" He turned to Burnett. "Hey, Smiley, did you get those separation request papers for me? While Smiley was searching through his desk for the papers, Joe turned back to me.

"How about going for a cold beer?"

That sounded good, but I remembered that I was waiting to find out where I was to live. "Be great, but I've got to wait for Sgt. Sutton to get me a place to live."

"Well, meet me down at the club in a little while."

With that, Sgt. Sutton emerged from his office to say, "Uh, Lt. Doyle, Capt. Sheets says, uh, Lt. Saunders has an empty room in his, uh, bungalow. He's on his way over here to, uh, escort you to his place."

Joe Stacy was folding the papers Burnett had given him into his pocket, and he looked over. "Lt. Saunders, hey? Jim, we'd better plan on catching that beer later." He was immediately out the door, shaking his head, a faint grin on his face. Smiley Burnett had turned away from us again and had his hand over his mouth to hold back a laugh.

Of course, Lt. Saunders turned out to be the stubby, blond Lieutenant whom I had crashed into outside the orderly room door. He entered the room and stood by the door, blinking his eyes, his cap remained on, pulled down tightly on his head, nearly reaching his ears. He was wearing his light tan 1505 summer uniform with a single row of ribbons over his left breast pocket. Wearing the ribbons was an option normally exercised only by old-timers with four or five rows of them. When he stopped blinking his eyes, he began to look around the room quizzically, so I walked over and extended my hand.

"Hi, I'm Jim Doyle."

He started to salute, but caught himself, then shook my hand. "Yes, Lt. Saunders here."

"What's your first name?"

"What?" He seemed more confused than indignant. "Oh, Robert A. Saunders."

"Bob?"

"Oh, yes, if you want." He seemed disappointed.

After some more words in the orderly room, a stop in the mail room—where Bob picked up a handful of letters and stuffed them into his breast pocket beneath his ribbons—a visit to the small BX—where after deliberating, "Hmm, now 100 for $1.50 or 60 for $.90, Jin, do you have a pencil?' Bob bought the smaller box of stationary—and a quick rest from the heat in the club—where we both had a beer (Joe Stacy joined us to Bob's discomfort)—we got on the bus that made the rounds of bungalows in town where the senior NCO's and officers lived.

A large, old blue bus, with the name, "Bluebird" painted on the side, it barreled over the dirt access road that led from the site across the runway, past the airport and to the main road that led into town. Since driving in Thailand is British style, on the left hand side of the road, and the bus was standard American style, a large portion of the left side of the rear of the bus had been cut away so that boarding the bus could be done without standing in traffic. It was a fine idea, but when the driver, a grizzled old staff sergeant named Hunnicut raced across the dirt access road, the inside of the bus filled up with dust coating everything.

When the bus reached the main road, the driver slowed up and began to make his way through the normal Nakorn Sarang traffic of small cars, samlows, bicycles, motorcycles, vegetable carts, mini-busses, garishly colored trucks and buses, chickens, dogs, ducks, pigs and water buffaloes. For several minutes at one point we had to wait at a railroad crossing while a slowly moving freight train made its leisurely way across the road. Outside the bus the collage of people, machines, and livestock sweated, beeped, squeaked, quacked, and farted, and I thought, edged itself perilously close to the passing train.

Bob began tut-tutting the entire scene, "You'd think these people would build a bridge here." I looked away from him and out the window where my eyes caught a little girl wearing only an undershirt. I stared at her and the child suddenly broke into a beautiful smile, all the features of her face working together. Bob saw her also and said, "It's embarrassing the way they dress children around here."

Bob's bungalow was the last one on the route, at least we were the last ones to get off the bus. I followed Bob down a driveway bordered on both sides by water to a pleasant looking yellow bungalow built on stilts and surrounded by water as well as by an eight foot high metal fence. It took Bob at least five minutes to open the many locks that had been placed on the gate.

"Kamoys," Bob said and nodded to emphasize the sound he had just made.

"What?"

"Kamoys." He nodded again. "That means thieves in Thai. It's a great problem. Everybody's always getting robbed, but this house is one of the most secure in town. That's why I've never been robbed."

Inside was a large central area, two bedrooms leading off it, along with a bathroom. Each of the rooms contained a large overhead fan, and there was a small refrigerator in the main room. I dropped my duffel bag on the floor and sat on it sweating like hell. Bob turned on the fan and the circulating even if still hot air felt good.

"Which room is mine?" I asked.

"What's your DOR?"

"My what?" ("what," I came to learn, is something you say a lot when you're around Bob Saunders.)

"Your date of rank."

"Oh, June 30th. Why?"

"Oh." Bob appeared a little nonplussed, and then he got up and looked into both of the bedrooms. "Do you mind if I keep the big room. It's all made up, and it would be a big job to move."

"No, of course not. Why the hell'd you ask?"

"Well, my DOR is only 30 July, and so you're senior man and should have the choice." I still elected to stay in the smaller room.

After I unpacked my things, I came back out to the central area. Bob was sitting in one of the large easy chairs in his underwear reading one of the letters he had picked up in the mail room. I got a beer out of the refrigerator, sat down opposite him and said. "Thailand seems like a pretty interesting place, doesn't it?"

He looked up and stared at me through his glasses which were slightly off tilt. He held up the pile of letters and said, "Letters from my wife. She writes twice a day."

"Oh, well, that's nice."

"Won't your wife write that much?"

"I'm not married."

"Oh." He paused and was apparently considering this new twist, then said, "That's too bad."

"It is?"

Bob went back to reading his letters, but after some time, he looked up again and asked, "Jim, would you like me to read Betty's letter to you?"

"No, thanks." But he started in to read, and I being new there and still regarding myself as something of a guest in the house, sat and listened. But I think I've mentioned this before.

* * *

The next morning on the bus back out to the site, I asked Bob how well he knew Joe Stacy.

"Oh, not well. He's new here too, got here last week." Bob paused to adjust his glasses and then continued, "A strange person, goes to town a lot, eats things there.

"Things?"

"Food, rice, and that stuff. The stuff these people eat."

"That's strange?"

"Yes, oh yes!" He nodded his head vigorously. "Oh, yes, it's not clean, you know."

The bus continued to fill up as we got closer to the site. "Good morning, uh, Lieutenant." I said hello back to Sgt. Sutton, however most of the riders were quite uninterested in my presence. When the bus stopped in front of a small dirty looking building with a crudely written sign that said, "Argo Bar," Sgt. Chance got on. I said hello, but he didn't notice me either; rather he slumped quickly into one of the back seats and closed his eyes.

"Yes, he's very strange." Bob started in again, and I turned to listen to him.

"Who's very strange, Chance?"

"No, No. Well, yes, he is too, now that you mention it. But I mean Capt. Stacy. I was in the orderly room the day he got here, Capt. Stacy that is. He seemed to be standing there waiting for Airman Burnett to fill in some papers, and he looked up at the pictures of the chain of command. He looked right at the picture of President Johnson, right at it, and then he said out loud so anyone could hear him while he was looking right at the President's picture, 'Hey, hey, LBJ, how many kids did you kill today?'"

CHAPTER THREE

THE DARK ROOM IN RADAR operations was the center of the site's activity, and on my third day in Nakorn Sarang, I was advised by Major Hudson that if I ever wanted to find out what we were doing in Thailand, I should ask Capt. Sheets, the ops officer, to show me the dark room.

So I did.

When I entered the office of the operations building, Sheets was seated, his feet up on the slide-out from his desk talking to a master sergeant named Pivarnik, who was at his desk which was butted against Sheet's desk. Pivarnik was listening intently, a faint smile on his face. On Sheet's desk were two framed pictures, one of a mildly attractive American woman with some inscription in a corner; the other was of two boys in their teens, smiling, well-dressed, and with their hair wetted down for the photographer.

"So after Joy makes dinner, you see, and we eat, so she goes and gets this handheld fan, and so she opens up the front of my robe, heh heh, and starts waving the fan in front of my pork." At this point Sheets shifted his feet to the floor and began to wave a magazine slowly in front of his fly. When he removed his feet, I could see several photos taped to the slide-out of his desk. The consisted of various nude poses of a Thai girl, Joy, I later learned. "So, heh heh, it doesn't take long before I've got a full-fledged hard-on, and heh heh, Joy puts down the fan and starts tugging on my tap like it's a chain. Heh heh, leads me right off to the bedroom like I'm a puppy dog." He shifted his feet back to the slide-out and put his hands behind his head looking up at the ceiling and said, "Heh heh, oh yeah, oh yeah,"

"Hi, Jim. What's up?" It was Joe Stacy entering from another room, a notebook in his hand.

"Oh, Major Hudson suggested I come over here and find out what the place is about. My last assignment was with a supply squadron, and I don't have the slightest idea what's going on here."

Joe turned to Sheets. "Hi, Russ. Wake up." Sheets looked over at us and saw me for the first time. "This is Jim Doyle. Hudson sent him over to get some idea about what the hell we do here."

Sheets got up and smiled. With one hand he reached to his crotch and shifted the erection he had just conjured up. "Hi, ya, Doyle. good to see ya. First let me introduce ya around." He waved around the room.

"This here's Capt. Stacy, the deputy operations officer and the training office." Joe bowed. "Cut that out, Joe."

"This here's Sgt Pivarnik, operations NCOIC." Pivarnik stood up. He was a big man, six-two or three and in very good shape, no waist and big arms and chest.

As he nodded his head, he said curtly, "Lieutenant."

I thought it was a prelude to something more and said, "Yes?" but he silently sat back down.

Sheets continued on. "This over here is Sgt. Reade, the training NCIOC." Reade was a technical sergeant who paused long enough from some charts and graphs laid out in front of him to nod in my direction.

"And this is Sgt. Pol, the Thai operations NCOIC." A very small Thai sergeant stood up in the corner, saluted me, and introduced himself in a rapid, high-pitched, sing-song voice, "Sgt. Pol, detachment two, sixth air control squadron, fourth air group, third air wing, fourth Air Force royal Thai Air Force," and sat down.

"Thank you, Sgt. Pol," said Sheets. Then turning to me, he went on. "Our prime mission here is to train the Thai Air Force in proper use of radar. Capt. Stacy, Sgt Reade, and Sgt. Pol work very closely in developing programs to expedite the eventual takeover of all operations by the Royal Thai Air Force." Sgt. Pol stood up and saluted me again.

"Are there any Thai officers here?"

"Oh, yes, two fine officers, heh heh, Major Boonthorn, the base commander, and Lt. Nopodol, the operations officer. However, they're presently in Bangkok on business." (I should mention that in the subsequent year I spent in Nakorn Sarang, I never met either Boonthorn or Nopodol. Queries concerning their whereabouts were always met with the response, "They were in Bangkok on business.")

Sheets moved me towards a small room with a "Top Secret" sign hanging on its door. "This is the message room, where we break frags each day." He opened the door and we entered. It was a very small room, with one desk, a cot, a teletype, and a set of file cabinets with a combination lock. A top secret marker was stuck in the file's draw handles. Seated at the desk, his back to us as we entered and staring at the teletype was Bob Saunders.

"Lt. Saunders, this is Lt. Doyle, the admin officer." Bob jumped up and started to salute, but he caught himself. I mentioned to Sheets that we had met, in fact, we shared the same bungalow, and Bob nodded in affirmation. "From here," Sheets said, "I'll turn you over to Lt. Saunders, one of our finest controllers, who is also the T/S officer. Bob, show Doyle the rest of the operation, the dark room and all."

Bob nodded again, but then asked if he could see the Captain outside the message room. A moment after they had stepped out, Sheets stuck his head in and asked, "Doyle, what's your clearance?"

"Top secret, Sir." The Bob came back in appearing a little more at ease and asked me to follow him into the dark room. I noticed he was addressing me as "Lt. Doyle."

Before he left the room, however, I stopped. "Bob, just a minute, but so I don't look too dumb, tell me, what the hell are frags?" I didn't feel embarrassed about asking such questions of Bob.

He seemed thrown off by my question, as if he couldn't believe I was asking it. It always seemed to amaze bob when others did not share his knowledge of what might be a somewhat arcane matter. But at last he answered. "They're fragmentary orders."

"Fragmentary orders?"

"Yes, or orders received in segments."

"You mean they're your orders for each day's work, then."

"Each day's mission."

"And when Sheets said 'break frags', he meant decoding the orders?"

"Yes, of course, what else could it mean?" He turned and started out, but I stopped him again.

"And when he referred to you as the T/S officer, that meant the Top Secret officer, right?"

"The what?" A new blank look emerged.

"Top secret, T/S, you're the top secret officer."

"Well, yes, I guess I am. T/S, top secret. Yes, yes, that's right. I'm the top secret officer." Bob, proud of his newly defined title then led me into the dark room.

The dark room was just that, the walls and ceiling painted black, it was illuminated only by the light from the radar scopes and small lamps that were adjacent to each of the scopes. They were arranged on three daises, rising like steps to the rear of the room from where we entered. I saw Joe Stacy walking back and forth on the top dais with a headset on. At the front of the room, where we stood, was a ceiling to floor Plexiglas wall behind which several Thai sergeants and airmen moved about. When they saw Bob and me, they stopped what they were doing and saluted. The wall contained an outline map of central and north Thailand, Laos, North Vietnam, and parts of southern China. Spread around the map were about two dozen arrows of blue and yellow. Every so often, one of the Thai airmen would wipe off one or more of the arrows which were marked in grease pencil and then make a new one in a slightly different position.

"Our primary mission here," began Bob as we stood at the foot of the lower dais, "is support of the 355th Tactical Fighter Wing at Takhli." He pointed to a spot on the map. "We hook up the fighters with the tankers before they take off for the north."

"Why do we have to do that?" Bob gave me his "Oh, not that again," look.

"Why? Well, naturally because the fighters can't take off with a full load of fuel. They're too loaded down with bombs. So when they get to altitude, the thuds rendezvous with…"

"Thuds?"

"F-105's", Bob explained. "They rendezvous with the KC-135's, they're tankers, and fuel up before they head out on Rolling Thunder."

"On rolling what?"

Bob seemed even more nonplussed by this question, and he stood up on his toes to whisper in my ear, "Rolling Thunder!"

"Yeah, yeah, I heard that, but what the hell does that mean?"

He looked around, most specifically at the Thais behind the wall—one of them saluted us again—and then he put his mouth to my ear again. "Rolling Thunder is the code name for the bombing of Laos and North Vietnam."

I looked up at the map. It was, to the north, only about sixty miles to Laos, and on beyond that, only four hundred or so miles to Hanoi. Before coming to Nakorn Sarang, I had had some idea of what radar sites did, but I was beginning to see how direct my involvement was going to be.

Bob noticed my staring at the map. When he spoke, he nodded in a manner that suggested we were sharing a common feeling. "Yes, it gives a great deal of satisfaction to be here helping someone."

"Helping them?"

"Yes, of course."

"You mean by bombing them?"

"Oh, no, I don't mean the North Vietnamese. No, no, we're destroying their will to resist. It's the South Vietnamese we're helping. We're protecting the independence of the modernization process." He nodded again.

"Oh."

I turned away from the map and asked more about the dark room operations. Pursuit of dialogues on the purpose and nature of the war, I felt, were wasted on Bob. "So after we guide them together, the fighters take off and drop their bombs. And that's it for us, huh?"

"Oh, no, we also do recoveries." Bob did not seem to think that required any explanation and motioned me to follow him as he headed around the edge of the daises. I caught him by the arm and asked what a recovery was. His face indicated that there was no limit to my ignorance. "When the thuds return, we help guide them back to Takhli. A lot of times they've caught a lot of flak and their instruments are out or heavily damaged. So they really need us. We also conduct post-strike refueling."

We moved onto the upper dais where Joe was standing in front of a radar scope. Two other scopes were on the same dais, and they were being manned by two lieutenants I recognized as Crawford and Gallo. Joe yelled down the length of the dais, "Stan, pick up Olds flight, Ben take Buick, I've got Cadillac."

Then sitting down at the scope, he picked up a compass and began measuring the distance between two bright spots on the scope. He spoke into his mike, "Cadillac, Cadillac, this is Atlas control, Atlas control. Take up heading of zero five zero, zero five zero, over."

Bob began whispering to me again. "Capt. Stacy is the senior controller. He's taking the lead flight." Joe was advising the pilot to maintain the same heading, when Bob began to explain something more about the wall. "The Thais are in charge of the vertical plotting board. The blue arrows are the thuds, the yellows are the tankers. If they ever use red, it's enemy aircraft."

Joe looked back at us, "Lt. Saunders, will you shut up!"

Turning to me and raising his finger to his mouth, Bob went, "Shhhhhhh!"

Joe continued to speak to Cadillac flight. "Roger, Cadillac, that's him at zero niner zero. Roger, Cadillac, That's him, zero niner zero. Roger, Cadillac. Close enough for government work." Signaling Bob to come over, Joe stood up and said, "Here, Lt. Saunders, mop this one up. I'll take care of Jim from here." Bob leaped into the seat putting on Joe's headset over his cap and picking up the compass to make a measurement. "Lt. Saunders, give Green 31 a heading of one niner zero and send him home." Then Joe reached over and removed Bob's cap from underneath the headset and placed it on the work area in front of the scope.

"Thank you, Sir."

"Jim, you ever been in a radar dark room before?" When I said "no", Joe went on to tell me more about the operation. There were three principal operations planned for; rendezvouses, recoveries, and intercepts. The first two had been adequately if crudely explained by Bob. The third, intercepts, were designed for aerial combat, and the aim was for the radar operator to guide one of our fighters into a position directly behind an enemy fighter where it would be easiest for him to score a kill. At Nakorn Sarang, we didn't perform any intercepts since our radar coverage didn't extend far enough north to where there was any MIG resistance. In fact, even in the more northern radar sites, this was rare since most resistance was anti-aircraft fire. Of course, as Joe noted, "That doesn't stop us from spending half our goddamned training time working on intercepts."

We moved down to the lower dais and around the front of the room. From the bottom dais, I could see Bob intently leaning over his scope, his tongue sticking out the side of his mouth.

"For the most part," Joe went on, "there's not a hell of a lot of work here. We're only busy when the flights go out in the morning, and we have to be ready when they come back. If they've run into a lot of flak, that can make for a rough time too. Some clown said that it's twenty-two hours of boredom and two hours of sheer terror. He was half right, twenty-two hours of boredom. The rest isn't that bad, at least not here. When I was in Nakorn Phanom, there was so much fucking air traffic it was really a bitch. Of course, that loony son-of-a-bitch Sheets talk this was the same. It's a crock of shit!"

Joe leaned over and took a red grease pencil away from one of the Thai airmen who was about to start plotting on the board with it. "Maidee, kop." The airman saluted. Joe smiled and handed him a yellow one. "If there was ever an enemy aircraft close enough to plot on the map, you'd hear the controllers screaming. I think red is just that guy's favorite color.

"Where was I? Oh, yeah. On the whole there's not a hell of a lot to do here. The only problem is some fucking lunatic at seventh Air Force headquarters schedules all of our goddamn flights for about six in the fucking morning. That really cuts down on my fun."

We went back into the operations office. There was now another captain there talking to Sheets. He was dressed in jungle fatigues with dark rank and insignia, a uniform designed for jungle combat. By looking closely, I could make out his name as Gunn. I heard the last words of his conversation, "The willingness to accept sacrifice, that's the key to an effective fighting machine."

"Hiya, Guerrila," shouted Joe when we entered. "Have you met Jim Doyle, the admin officer. Jim, Guerrilla Gunn, maintenance officer."

Gunn's hair was thin and gray, and he cut it in a flat-top. He had deep lines on his face, and he held his mouth in a short, grim little line. Shaking my hand with one very firm motion, he said, "Doyle, good to have you aboard." And then to Joe, in an aside not intended to be heard by the rest of us, "Capt. Stacy, I think it best if in front of junior officers," he turned and looked over his shoulder at me, "and enlisted men, you called me Captain Gunn."

Joe responded, "Right, Guerrilla."

When Gunn left, Joe pointed out some charts on the wall. "These are our training charts. When a controller reports in here, it takes about three to four weeks to get him qualified on the scope. See, here's Lt. Saunders. He's been here just a month. We should have him fully qualified in a few days." Sgt. Read began coughing and Joe smiled.

Across the room Sheets and Pivarnik were talking again as Joe sat down. "Well, I guess that's enough to know, probably too much. Jim, when are we going to get together a couple of more beers, tonight?"

Yeah, that sounds good. "Well, thanks for the time. I guess I ought to get back to the orderly room. Sgt. Chance's probably got several hundred forms for me to sign." I turned and started for the door pausing to say to Sheets, "Thanks for the time, Capt. Sheets."

His feet still up on the slide-out of his desk, Sheets did not look over, but he continued to talk to Pivarnik. "You know what I'd like to try tonight, heh heh, is that thing with the beads, heh heh, how's that work Sarge?"

"Oh, yeah," Pivarnik answered, "you see, you get your girl to shove a string of beads up your ass, then just as you're about to blow your fucking rocks, she pulls…"

"Yeah, yeah, heh heh, oh boy." I left without repeating my thank you.

OCTOBER 1967

CHAPTER FOUR

THE BEERS WITH JOE TURNED into a regular feature. The hot, crowded club that served as both officer and NCO club became a place where we met each day after work to enjoy the clean, clear taste of a cold beer down a hot, dry throat. After four or five beers, we would usually go home to change, then meet in town for something to eat. It was through Joe that I became acquainted with the Hoa Far and Tipalow's restaurants, the Mitrinakorn night club, and the Argo Bar.

Joe, it turned out, had been stationed with Sheets somewhere in Florida prior to coming to Nakorn Sarang. When Joe arrived in NSG, he found Sheets had saved a room for him in the giant bungalow that he lived in with Joy, his teeloc, or girlfriend (not quite an accurate translation).

"As if that wasn't enough, goddamn it, when that fool Russ meets me at the plane and takes me directly to the bungalow, there, waiting in my room for me is this girl, Cann, Joy's sister, or mother, or something like that. Cann is short for Can-do."

Joe lifted his Singha beer and drew deeply on the glass, before signaling the waitress at the Hoa Far to bring us another large bottle. "I gave her twenty dollars and asked her to leave. She starts yelling at Joy, throws the money down on the living room floor, spits on it, jumps on it, and yells some more at Joy. Joy in turn starts yelling at Russ. Her sister is worth more than twenty dollars. Number one girl used to live with some big colonel, comes all the way from Chiang Mai. And on and on. So ever since, Russ is pissed at me. He keeps saying, 'Gee, Joe, what's the matter? We used to have a lot of fun in Orlando. Goddamned, we have a nice place here. You aren't going to ruin it, are you?' Anyway, Cann left. I think it cost Russ some more money, and on top of that, I never could find the damn twenty dollars she threw on the floor."

This was Joe's third tour of duty in Thailand. Previously he had been assigned to Bangkok and Nakorn Phanom. After each return to the States, he would soon find himself making his way over to the personnel office to fill out the volunteer forms for Thailand. He could lose himself there; avoid most of the service rituals. In Thailand, if Joe did his job well, which he did, then the brass would look the other way when he didn't wear his uniform correctly, if he drank with the enlisted men, or if he spent a lot of time with the Thais, and, in general went his own way. Back in the States, with no real work to do, the Air Force spent much of its time being the Air Force, which meant harassment for Joe.

"This time, Jim, I'm extending for an extra six months, save some money, then getting out of the Force altogether. Go back to Missouri. Things are getting out of hand. You know, when I was in Bangkok in '63, there were only about ten thousand GI's in the whole country. What're there now, fifty thousand? Shit, you know, back then, we really did train the Thai Air Force, worked on Air Defense, did a lot of intercepts for them. Fuck it, now all we do is give them some colored crayons and let them mark on the plotting board."

The two of us chewed on some curried shrimp, and I listened as Joe talked on. "Even when I was up in Nakorn Phanom two years ago it was different. Lots of small craft then, the Thais flew some of it, even a few Laotians. Now, fuck it again, we're working with these fucking 105's, F-4's, tankers, that shit. Never even see them. They sail off and bomb the shit out of some poor little bastards I don't even know four or five hundred miles away. Shit!"

Joe reached across the table for the bottle of Mekong, ("That's enough beer") the Thai whiskey, mixed some of it in his glass with soda and slice of lemon, swallowed a large mouthful of it to wash down the last of the shrimp, and went on with his story. "Christ, now they're getting it down so fucking pat that anyone can do the goddamned job. No work to do, even that little wimp you live with, Saunders, will be able to hack it soon. You know what that means, don't you? Means they're going to start getting on my ass, going to start wanting me to shine my shoes, wear the right uniform, start saluting. Fuck 'em. Jim, I ain't going to have much fun in the future."

Rising from the table and leaving sixty baht to cover the meal, Joe said to me, "Let's go over to the Argo." I had not been there before, but I certainly knew about it. It was a dirty little place that the bus stopped in front of each morning and picked up one or two tired and angry looking airmen, Sgt. Chance more often than not being one of them. Joe often mentioned going there, but I had usually demurred and went home, the idea of a whorehouse a little unsettling to me, but on this night, about two weeks after arriving in Nakorn Sarang, I went.

From a closer view, it was still a dirty little building built close to the ground and sitting on cinder blocks. Behind it was a string of small rooms, these built on considerably higher stilts. The room closest to the main building was much larger than the others and had a window as well as a door. This was Papa-san's room and office. Inside the main room, the Argo Bar was a little cleaner than it appeared from the outside. It was about the size of the average American garage, two-car variety. There were screened windows, and overhead, three slowly rotating fans moved the air about. Six girls sat at one table at the far end of the room. In the middle, four airmen sat, without girls, at a table. At another table near the door, three airmen sat with two girls. One of the men was Sgt. Chance, and I said hello when I saw him.

"Hey, Lieutenant, getting much?"

Papa-san, who was sitting behind the bar eating some fried rice from a banana leaf saw us as we entered, gave Joe a big smile and waved us over to the bar where he had two bottles of Singha waiting for us. Behind him was a radio which was playing Thai music. He turned it down when Joe introduced me.

"Sawadee, Lootenin' Jim, friend Captahn Joe me, my friend you." He grinned and shook my hand. I mentioned to Joe that he seemed to be quite well acquainted with the place for only having been in Nakorn Sarang three weeks.

"Papa-san is a sergeant in the Thai army, stationed over on the other side of town. But he used to be one of the guards at the Air Operations Center in Bangkok four years ago. When he heard I was in town, he sent a note, personally inviting me to stop over and check out his girls."

Joe and I sat there for several hours, drinking the Singhas and trading stories. Occasionally one of the girls would come over and joke with him, laughing and patting his fat stomach. One of them sat down on the chair next to me, and Joe introduced her as Supatra. She was short and had prominent teeth with a gap in them, but she had a rather nicely proportioned body which she wore in a tightly wrapped paisin. She asked me to buy her a drink which I did, and then she reached over and began to play with my wang.

"Hey, cut that out," I yelled more in surprise than anger.

"Hey, what's amatta, no like Supatra? Supatra like you." She laughed and looked over at Joe who laughed back at her. "Hey, wha's amatta him, hey Captahn?"

"He's a crazy GI, Supatra. Everybody calls him Crazy Jim."

When she finished her drink, a Coke, Supatra reached over and flicked her finger at my crotch, hitting me right on the head of my pecker. "Ow!"

"S'okay, neva'mind, Crazy Jim. Supatra like you, friend Captahn Joe." Swinging her rear end about in an exaggerated manner, she walked back over to the table where the six girls had been sitting. On her return they began to chatter, and when Supatra had apparently finished describing what had taken place, they all broke into giggles.

As the evening wore on, the crowd in the Argo began to dwindle. Shortly after Supatra had talked with us, Sgt. Chance staggered up the back stairs to one of the rooms leaning on a short and very fat girl. Just before he went out the back door, he looked over at me and said, "Hey, Lieutenant, don't stick your dick in the wrong hole."

By midnight, the only people left in the Bar were Joe and I, and Papa-san and Supatra, although she had made one trip up the back stairs with an airman. Papa-san opened his refrigerator and said there was only one bottle of Singha left and did we want it? Joe decided to switch back to Mekong, so I took the beer.

Our conversation was not much by that time; in fact, I was getting quite drunk. "Papa-san," Joe said, "Where's Malee tonight?"

"In room, Malee rest. Before, go by home Maja' Hudson, come back now."

"What?" I blurted out. "Major Hudson had a girl sent over to his bungalow?"

Joe didn't bother with me. "Ask her to come down for me, okay, Papa-san?"

Papa-san disappeared out the back door and ran up the steps to the short-time rooms. In a few minutes he was back followed by a very tall—about five six or seven—girl I figured must be Malee. By far the best looking girl I had seen in the bar, she had long, straight, black hair, a delicate smile, and she wore a short American style dress.

"Oh, Captain, my numba' one GI. I almost go sleep, Papa-san come say Captahn want Malee, I come layo-layo go with you." She took his arm in both her hands and put her head on his shoulder.

After giving Papa-san five dollars for Malee, and another dollar for a bottle of Mekong to-go, Joe left with her in a samlow. Like Chance, Joe also stopped in the door to say something to me. "Jim, take Supatra home with you. It'll do you a lot of good."

When I turned back to the bar, Supatra grinned at me showing off her teeth, although not in a particularly unpleasant manner. She said, "S'okay, huh, you, me, go bungalow you?"

"I don't think so."

"Hey, wha's amatta you? You cherry, ching-ching?"

I assured her that was not the problem. In fact, I did not know why I wasn't interested in taking her home with me. Papa-san came out from around the bar and said, "Supatra very good girl. No have VD."

"Maybe Loootenin' fairy, yes?" Supatra laughed and held her hand in a limp-wristed fashion. I started toward the door to get a samlow and go home. Standing in the doorway, I thought of Joe stopping on his way out to tell me it would do me a lot of good.

"Okay, Supatra, let's go," and opening my wallet, I went back to the bar to give Papa-san his five dollars.

"Hey, Crazy Jim, you okay!"

Back at my bungalow, Supatra strutted about the place, inspecting it like she was thinking of buying. "Hey, very numba' one bahn. Supatra come live you, s'okay?" She crashed into Bob's room and turned on the light. He was curled up in a ball, the covers off him, and his glasses still on, but fortunately sleeping very soundly. Turning off the light, I slapped her fanny and shooed her out of the room.

"Hey, Jim, who's uh little man?"

"Ssssh, over here, come on," and I whisked her into my room, locking the door and pulling the curtain across the screen. I didn't want Bob poking his head in before he left for Sunday morning breakfast at the site.

Drunk as I was by then, I didn't really expect to be able to get an erection, but Supatra reached down once we were naked and in bed and began to softly fondle me. I felt my muscle swell and became hot, so I rolled over onto her. She guided me into her, and we began to thrash about. Surprised at my own energy, I came too quickly, and began to let my whole body go limp, expecting to be pushed off and told to sleep.

"Hey, wha's amatta you, no stop! Supatra wanna come too." A little ashamed, I began to thrash about again before I went soft. She put her legs around my back and moved with me. From her throat I could hear clacking noises, groaning, and her shaking became more vigorous. I even felt myself beginning to stir again as she yelled, "Oh, oh, kop kop, kop kun kop!"

When she was through, I did then slide off her and roll over onto my back. She followed me and put her head on my chest. After lying there awhile, I nearly drowsing off, she said, "Jim, do again, s'okay?"

"Tomorrow," I said, just before falling asleep.

In the morning, after Bob left (he had knocked on my door first yelling, "Jim, Jim, are you all right? Why is the door locked?" Supatra's head jumped up, and she looked at me wide eyed. I raised my finger to my lips and went "Sssssh," before telling Bob, "It's okay, but I want to sleep some more. I'll see you at the site later."), we did it again.

Supatra left the bungalow about two hours later. I walked her out to the road, hailed a samlow for her and helped her into it. I gave the driver five baht, and on an impulse put twenty baht in her hand. Her face broke into a grin, she laughed and said, "Hey, Supatra like you, Crazy Jim. Jim like Supatra, s'okay?"

"S'okay."

The samlow started down the street as I waved and then headed back down the driveway. It was already very hot and humid, and when I reached the house, I began to peel away my clothes so that by the time I got to the shower, I was naked. The cold water felt great. I lathered myself up several times and rinsed again and again. I even began to sing nonsense words babbling away, very exuberantly. When I finally turned the water off, I went over to the sink to shave. Even with the cold water, my beard cut away very easily, and when I rinsed my face, I examined it in the mirror. My eyes were not red as they had every right to be. I broke into a smile. "Hey," I yelled out loud at my reflection, "That did me a lot of good."

CHAPTER FIVE

A FEW NIGHTS LATER, I brought Supatra home with me again. I had gone to the Argo alone after reading in my bungalow till nearly ten p.m. The place was much quieter than it had been on Saturday night. Sgt. Chance was coming out the door as I was entering. He was sober and seemed startled to see me.

"Hey, Lieutenant, what the fuck you doin' in this fuckin' place?" I didn't bother to explain that I had been there to better part of the previous Saturday night, or that I had seen him being helped up the rear stairs by the short, fat girl. Instead, I offered to buy him a beer if he had the time.

"Shit, yes, I'll drink your fuckin' beer. I was just goin' back tuh thuh site cuz I was outuh fuckin' money." So he came back in, and we sat at one of the tables near the rear door. Supatra saw us sitting there when she came through the door with an airman. "Hey, Crazy Jim. You come back, me live you, s'okay?" she said before going off to sit at the girl's table at the far end of the room.

I'm not sure if it was befuddlement or some form of respect, but Sgt. Chance evidenced a changed attitude towards me after realizing that I had been to the Argo before. "Shit, most of you goddamned officers are uh bunch of fuckin' candy asses. Either you pay sum fuckin' whore uh lottuh fuckin' dough tuh live with yuh, or yuh sneak aroun' this fuckin' place and take thuh whores out thuh back fuckin' window."

"I'm not sure what you mean about the back window."

"Fuck it! Like fuckin' Hudson. He comes down early innuh night and walks aroun' like he's givin' uh fuckin' inspection. Then he sneaks over to ol' Papa-san, and innuh stupid fuckin' whisper, he says..." Chance went into a poor imitation of Hudson's mumble. "'Hey, Papa-san, sen'uhgirlovertuhmybungalow.' So Papa-San does it, but he don't fuckin' unnerstan' Hudson wants tuh keep thuh whole fuckin' thing quiet, so he tell everyone. That's what I mean about fuckin' officers, unnerstan'?" I said I did, and, of course it explained what Papa-san had meant on Saturday when he said Malee had been to Hudson's bungalow.

Chance and I sat together for about an hour until he leaned across the table to ask me, "Hey, Lietenant, how about loanin' me five fuckin' fucks so I can rip off uh piece of ass?" After I had handed him the red hundred baht bill, he turned and yelled to the bar, "Hey, Papa-san, how about sendin' Nitnoy down?" Nitnoy in Thai means little.

When Papa-san returned from upstairs, he was followed by the short, fat girl Chance had gone with on Saturday. She entered laughing, ran over and grabbed

Chance around the neck squealing, "Oh, Lafayette, my numba' one teeloc!" (Yes, his first name was Lafayette.)

Again, before he went out the back door, Chance paused to say something to me. "Hey Lieutenant, let me tell yuh somethin', somethin' my ol' daddy tole me. Said, 'Son, nevah pass up uh piece of pussy, Son, cuz, your nex' one may be your last fuckin' one.'"

But the point of this passage is that I brought Supatra home with me again. She was more casual about it this time, but it was still pleasant. She did not give the bungalow such an inspection, but she did ask about Bob.

"How's nitnoy poochi?"

The bathroom in our bungalow had no divider between the shower and the toilet or the sink for that matter. The next morning, Bob was on the seat rereading a letter from his wife when Supatra walked in to take a shower. She waved her hand at him and said, "S'okay, Supatra take wash," and turned on the water.

From the edge of my bed where I sat pulling on my uniform pants, it being a work day, I could hear the cold water running for several seconds before I heard Bob screaming.

"Whoa, ohhh, help! Help, help! Jim!"

By the time I got to my feet, he was standing in my doorway soaking wet and completely naked except for the shower clogs he wore everywhere in the house and his glasses which were covered with water. The letter from his wife was in his hand, and I could see the ink was starting to run.

"What was that?"

"Did it have two arms and two legs?"

Still not recovered from his unexpected cold shower, Bob answered me in all seriousness, "Yes, yes, it did."

"Then, unless you also brought a girl home from the Argo Bar, I'd say it's Supatra."

"The Argo Bar," he said, his face curling into a vision of repulsion, "Why, I'd never go there."

"That clinches it, it's Supatra." I continued to dress. While I was looking around the room for my shoes, Bob remained standing in my doorway a puddle forming around his feet. When Supatra was through in the bathroom, she came back in the door drying herself with a towel.

"S'cuse again," she said as she entered, looking at Bob who stood dumbstruck. "Hey, GI, you wet!"

Before Bob could move, she reached out and with a towel in her hand began to dry off his pecker. After a few moments, Bob started screaming and ran out of my room. Laughing to herself, Supatra picked up her dress and began to put it on, saying, "Him one crazy GI, hey?"   While I was looking through my closet for a clean uniform shirt, Supatra began to tug at my arm. When I looked at her, she said, "Hey, Jim. Jim give Supatra baht for samlow, s'okay?"I went over to the corner and picked up the pair of pants I had been wearing the night before. In one of the pockets, I found some bills and change. As I was handing her a five baht bill, I heard Bob yell out, "Ohhh, my letter's all wet and the ink's run."

It was lunchtime when I next saw Bob. He sought me out in the mess hall where Joe and I were, and sat opposite me. I looked up from our regular Wednesday fried chicken.

"Hi, Bob, how's the scope?"

His eyes flicked a little, and his voice took on his "this-is-the-gravest-subject-matter" tone. Pursing his lips and clenching his teeth, he said, "Not good, we lost two birds today." He looked down at his chicken.

"Oh, that's too bad."

"Yes," he went on just as grimly, "We can't afford to lose good men like that."

Joe looked over at Bob. "Say, Saunders, was one of those pilots your brother?"

"No, why?"

"Then fuck'em. They get flight pay."

Bob seemed startled, his eyes looked back and forth at Joe and me. Joe said, "Do you know any pilots?"

"No, but…"

"Well, on the whole they're an obnoxious bunch of loudmouths. I don't like to see anyone die, but I'm not going to grieve over every egomaniac pilot that gets his ass shot down." With that, Joe got up and left, Bob staring after him.

"Do you see what I mean about him being strange?"

However, Bob did not sit with me to discuss the air war that morning. His mind was on more carnal matters. Looking at me across what was left of our chickens, and speaking with the same confidentiality and grimness that he usually reserved for bombing mission code words, he asked, "How do you feel?"

"What?"

He seemed flustered and embarrassed by my apparent poor hearing and using the heavy-handed mannerisms and slow speech he usually addressed the Thais with, asked me again, "How…do…you…feel?"

"Fine."

"But, uh," He looked around, "Did you examine yourself?"

I understood what he was getting at, but I was not about to make it very comfortable for him.

"What the hell do you mean, did I examine myself? Do I have dirt on my face, is my skin yellow, what?"

"No, no, no, not that. What I mean is," and then he wiped his jaw with one hand and cupping his mouth with both, he whispered to me, "Did you examine your organ?"

"You mean, did I look at my pecker?"

Bob's face went red, and he nodded his head yes.

"What the hell for?"

"Well, you did have relations with that girl last night, didn't you?"

I laughed and some of the airmen at other tables looked over at us. "Bob, I'm ashamed of you. Were you listening at my door?"

He grew redder yet. "No, I mean I saw, you know what I mean, she was in, uh, in the shower. Oh come on, you know, you know. Did you check to see if you've contacted venereal disease?"

I laughed again, and by now most of the mess hall was looking at us. "Bob, even if she was nothing but an open syphilis sore, it would take weeks before any of the symptoms would show."

"Oh, I see," he said, as he seemed to gain a little composure. "Of course, that must be awful, too."

"What must be awful?"

"Well, uh, you know, waiting around to see if you caught it."

I assured Bob that I was not planning on nervously examining myself each day until any possible incubation period had passed. And that I had taken several precautions which were recommended by Doc Dugan, the site medic. That last bit of information seemed to ease his mind considerably, but he was not through reflecting on his first, although most decidedly vicarious experience with a bar girl.

"You know what seemed strange to me, I mean, I was, well, a little shocked she walked into the shower, and, well, I guess I, well, probably stared at her. I mean, I know I shouldn't have, but anyway, you see, she didn't have, I mean I guess you should know. She didn't have much hair on her, her, her, her vagina. And well, I could see it quite well. I mean, after all, I was sitting down, and she was standing up, so, well, we were on about the same level. Well, what I mean is, it, it, it didn't look dirty. I mean I couldn't see any diseases, you know. I mean, well, wouldn't you think I should've been able to?"

"Why, Bob," I said quite loudly, turning more heads, "I'm surprised at you. Don't you know you should stand when a lady enters the room?"

Bob lived in mortal fear of the dirt and disease he was convinced was endemic to Thailand. The country, to him, was a land whose chief production item was debilitating diseases. It was, unfortunately, not particularly clean. Open sewers made the water unsafe, and even the poorer of the Thais boiled it before using. VD was rampant, even in the brothels frequented solely by the Thais—of which there were more than a few—and, like most tropical and sub-tropical areas, malaria was a constant threat. But, in no way was the country the rotten, festering sore on the face of the Earth that Bob imagined it. I once found him scrubbing the toilet seat with ammonia after one of the girls I had brought home had used it in the morning. "One of the most common means of contracting syphilis and gonorrhea," he said, nodding his head in that curious way he had of taking your concurrence for granted. Another time he pleaded with Doc Dugan for shot of penicillin because he discovered our maid had washed our sheets and switched them on the beds. Even after they had been subjected to hot water and soap, some dormant syphilis and gonorrhea germs, Bob feared, might reach out and attack him in his sleep. But Bob's fear was not limited to these two diseases. The possibilities were endless. At one time or another, I heard him express a fear that he may have come into contact with leprosy, tuberculosis, rabies, meningitis, diarrhea, pneumonia, diphtheria, typhoid fever, sleeping sickness, cholera, anthrax, dysentery, bubonic plague, scarlet fever, hookworm, and crotch rot.

November 1967

CHAPTER SIX

ON AN AFTERNOON EARLY IN November while I was making a perfunctory inspection of the hooches, Sak, the site interpreter found me and asked that I come back to the orderly room to talk to a girl who was asking about a job.

The girl, her name was Sunida, had shown up earlier in the day asking the Thai guard at the gate about getting a job. When he told her she would have to talk with an American lieutenant, she left. However, she was back in the afternoon saying she would like to see the American. She rose when I entered the room; her eyes quickly turned away when I smiled. Standing, she appeared to be tall for a Thai, about five foot two or three. Her eyes were large and brown, sweeping up gracefully to high corners, and she had the sharper nose of someone with Indian blood. Her hair was straight and black, but she wore it close to her head and did not split it over the shoulders in the fashion of the bar girls.

We exchanged wais, and I motioned for her to the chair by my desk, but she seemed reluctant to sit before I did, so I sat quickly, and she appeared to relax a little. I realized I was smiling broadly, but when I made a conscious effort to stop, I saw a look of terror in her eyes, and I smiled again. She appeared embarrassed that her feelings had been so obvious because, although pleased that I had smiled, she turned her head away, her face reddening.

The interview did not, to say the least, go well. I asked what she would like, and she said "Work please, Sir." I asked her what kind of work. She said "Work, yes, Sir. Thank you." I asked her if she could speak English. She said, "Yes, Sir, thank you." Could she read and write English? "Yes, Sir, thank you, please." When I asked her what she would like to be paid, she only looked at me again and smiled.

I was charmed, certainly, but I was also very frustrated. I said to her, "Miss Sunida, I am sorry, but we do not have any jobs right now. I will put your name on a list, and if any jobs come up, we will call you, but I wish you had told me more about what you would like to do, because it would be easier to help you then."

She smiled and said, "yes, Sir, thank you.

For good measure, I asked Sak to repeat it in Thai. When he had done so, she rose, thanked us both and began to leave. She had her bicycle at the gate, and I escorted her to it. I held it for her as she got on, and when she reached for the handle bar her hand rested on mine. Her skin was very soft but cold and wet with perspiration, and she looked away again. Before she reached the corner, she turned, smiled and waved.

For the first time she seemed relaxed. I don't think she really wanted the job, but for some reason she felt obliged to ask for it. I smiled back, raised my hand and waved, and then I continued to smile when she had turned the corner and disappeared into the tall reeds that the site access road led through.

When I turned to go back through the gate, Boon, the head Thai guard, a fellow as horny as any American, was holding his left hand up forming a circle with the thumb and forefinger, and inserting the forefinger of his right hand through the circle. He grinned and winked at me "Number one pooying, heh, Loootenant?"

Sak later told me more about Sunida. She was a teacher in Pitchit, a town fifty miles to the south, but her parents lived in Nakorn Sarang and wanted her to come home and take care of them since they were both old and poor. She wanted to come home, also, but there were no jobs in the schools in Nakorn Sarang. A friend told her to try at the American air base, so she did.

Sak said, "Now she will go back to Pitchit and send money to her parents."

"How much does she make in Pitchit?"

"Twenty dollars."

"A week?"

"A month."

Twenty dollars, why practically any job on the site would have paid her at least fifty dollars. "But how much can she send her parents out of that?"

"Obviously, Sir, not very much. She will not live well. In Thailand, to be a teacher is not such a good job."

I found myself thinking of Sunida often, and when I was in town I would scan the faces in the streets hoping to see her, but, of course, she had gone back to Pitchit, and I never saw her. When, three weeks later, the boy who worked in the library came and told me he was moving to Bangkok to go to the university, I went to Sak.

"Sak, that girl who was here, how well could she read and write English?" When he said that he thought she was very good at it, I asked why then had she been so quiet?

"Sir, she was very frightened. She had never even talked to an American before." So far he was telling me what I already knew and wanted to hear, but that I had to ask about. I asked him, if she came to work at the site, would she become less shy and would she do a good job?

"Oh, yes, Sir. She is very good girl, and she would work very hard."

"Could you find her again, Sak?"

"She went back to Pitchit." I felt something tumble about in my stomach, "But I think Sir, if I write to her, she will come back here to work," Sak grinned, "because her parents live here, and she feels she must be with them."

So Sunida came to work in the library for fifty dollar a month, and, as Sak had predicted, she adjusted well. Of course she was still very shy, and, I am sure, the first days, when the airmen crowded the library to see the beautiful new librarian, were difficult for her. Sak once found her quietly crying, the noise of a roomful of loudly talking, large Americans having overwhelmed her, but she needed the job, and she forced herself to adjust to it.

Fortunately, the job was not difficult. The library was small, and most of the reading done by the men was of the magazines, the westerns, and the science fiction. We received only a few new titles, so the job consisted mainly of filing the returned books back to the shelf. Books were something of an anathema to most of the men, so the library was thought of, for the most part, as a place to kill time.

There were some incidents. Once a sergeant, a few beers in him, while sitting in one of the lounge type chairs, reached out as she went by and grabbed her bottom. Sak, who she went to, came and told me she was quitting.

"Why?"

"I think Sir, Sgt. Hunnicut, how you say, goose her."

"Oh, for Christ's sake, what the hell's he doing in the library anyway? I don't think he even knows how to read."

Sak and I found her at the gate sitting in the guard shack. She was crying and refused to look up at me, and she was saying that she was sorry. She was sorry? It was, however, clear she should not go back to the library that day. I told her to go home and rest, not to be sorry, and Sak and I would talk to her soon. I added, "Please don't quit, you do such good work. I need you here."

By the time I found Sgt. Hunnicut, he seemed somewhat contrite. "Ah, shit, Lieutenant, I'm sorry. I di'nt mean nothin'. I was jus' sittin' there, a half dozen or so beers in me. I seen her ass go by, I grab it. I guess I thought I was home."

There did not seem to be any overwhelming reason to do much to Hunnicut. In fact, many of the other girls on the site were able to deal with the coarser instincts of the airmen quite effectively, and a hand reaching out to pinch or rub a thigh was often met with a slap and a laugh. Hunnicut, especially after what, knowing him, was probably closer to a dozen beers, could hardly be expected to make distinctions between who he could and who he could not try to pinch. However, I did suggest that he stay out of the library for awhile.

"Shit yes, Lieutenant. I don't know what the fuck I was doin' there to start with. I can hardly read anyway, you know."

After she had been home a full day, Sak and I met with Sunida at Sak's house and convinced her to return. I told her that Sgt. Hunnicut was very sorry, and I promised it would not happen again, and she quietly consented to come back. But there was a sense of depression in me when we left because I saw great sadness in her eyes. She would, I am sure, have much preferred to never go near the site again, but she needed the money badly, and it was not my words or entreaties which were bringing her back, but her need. It hurt, but she would, in her own eyes, humiliate herself for the thousand baht.

There was one other time that she nearly left, but the reasons were quite different, and I don't think Sunida was even aware of the crisis. Major Hudson went into the library looking for a cowboy novel he had spotted during one of his inspections. When he couldn't find it on the shelf, he approached Sunida at her desk.

"Yuhhav'DodgeCiteeShootout'?"

I would imagine she smiled at him and said, "Excuse, Sir, I do not understand."

"'DodgeCiteeShootout', izzuhcowboybook."

"Excuse please, I do not understand. If you would write on paper, Sir." Then she probably handed him a piece of paper and pencil, something I had advised he to do when she couldn't understand someone's request.

"No, 'DodgeCiteeShootout', wher'zit?"

"Please, Sir. If you would write."

"Neva'min' innyway."

When Hudson strode by my desk on his way into his office, he said, "Lt. Doyle, gettuhnewgirlinnuhlibrary. At wun can'tevenunnderstan' English."

I followed him into his office, but he had already sat down and was opening the mail Sgt. Sutton had placed on the desk.

"Excuse me, Sir."

"I'mreadin'uhmail."

"But, Sir."

"Lt. Doyle, I'mreadin'uhmail."

When at last he had finished his task, I began to try and convince him why she should not be fired right then. "I need her here, Sir. She's done very good work. Since she came, the entire library is in much better shape. The records are better kept, she's cut down on overdues, just about everything's better."

Most of it was a lie; the boy had been a very efficient worker. Sunida was certainly no worse, but then, the job was hardly demanding. "And," I added, "she understands English better all the time. She works very hard at it."

In the end he mumbled, "Awrigh', buhshegottuhlearnuhunnerstan' Englishgettuh."

After that, the only time he ever went into the library was on his inspection tours, and all he ever said to her was, "Hav'yuhlearnuhunnerstan'Englishbettuhyet?" and she would reply, "Yes, Sir. Much better now, thank you, Sir," not because she understood him—he was more unintelligible than ever—but because that was what I had told her to say when ever Major Hudson spoke to her. Sometimes, when I accompanied him on the inspections, as we were leaving I would look back at her; my eyes would catch hers, and she would smile.

CHAPTER SEVEN

LATER IN NOVEMBER, JOE AND I found a bungalow to share. We had both been driven to comparative stages of distraction by our original roommates. Granted, they were pests of a different nature. Bob Saunders wore you down gradually. He got to you with circular attacks. I was never convinced he was trying to drive me crazy, but his letter reading, his shock at my bar-girl friends, his sincere and mind boggling earnestness about the site's work and his general obtuseness reached a point where I dreaded going back to the bungalow in the evening and found myself spending more and more time at the bar to avoid him.

Russ Sheets was more direct in his assault. Most likely through the prodding of his girl friend Joy he kept trying to promote the decidedly erotic pleasures of her sister, Cann. Joe would arrive back at the bungalow from work, and at least once a week, find Cann there, naked in his bed. He always asked her to leave ("I had only one objection. She was Russ's idea. I prefer to pick my own.") After about four weeks, Sheets gave up on Cann, but he began to promote the fortunes of a parade of other girls, each resembling his fantasies of ornately dressed and garishly made up Oriental dragon ladies. And his own sensibilities seemed deeply offended as Joe chose, when he was carnally inclined, to bring home some of the earthier girls from the Argo Bar. More precisely, Joy, her bar girl sense of class distinction offended, would take great offense at having "her" home trespassed by such girls, and would deny Sheets her favors. This, of course, in turn would make Sheets antagonistic towards Joe.

At any rate, about the same time, Joe and I had both reached the conclusion that we could no longer live under such conditions. With Sak's assistance, we found a very comfortable bungalow close to the site for one hundred dollars a month which was high and, Joe later explained to me, included a fee for Sak's services.

Shortly after that, Ewan arrived for the first time. Joe mentioned it to me one morning as we were preparing to leave for the site, I on my little Honda which I had recently bought and Joe was going to wait for the bus. The heat was already beginning to settle in for the day; a fine film of perspiration had already formed on my skin. "Jim, tonight there's a girl coming from Bangkok to live with me. Her name's Ewan, and she'll probably stay for a few weeks. You don't have to do anything special or act differently. I just wanted you to know she's coming. Later at lunch, I asked him for more information about her, "I mean you never mentioned it as a possibility. I'm just kind of curious about it."

Joe separated the wet globules of bread from our regular Monday meat loaf and then ate the remaining shreds of hamburger. "I met her when I was first stationed in Bangkok four years ago. She was just starting work as a bar girl, and I was one of the first Americans she had been with. I guess she liked me. Anyway, since then she has always come and visited me for a few weeks at a time whenever I've been stationed in Thailand. At first, she said she wanted to live with me all the time as my teeloc, but I vetoed that idea pretty quick, and so now she comes around every now and then. I just got a letter from her a day or so ago. I didn't mean to keep it a secret. I didn't know if she was coming and if so, when."

So she came to live with us, and I think I've mentioned this before also. That evening when I arrived home, she was there, and I'll get back to it very shortly. Late in the afternoon, Joe left for home, and I went to the club with Joe Gallo and Harry Simpson, two of the other controllers, and with whom I shared a tenuous and light hearted friendship. During our second beer or so, at least sometime before we began playing poker, Simpson had asked me if I still shared a bungalow with Bob Saunders.

"No, Joe Stacy and I have a place now. Why?"

"Oh, I don't know. I was just wondering what the hell he had?"

"Had? Nothing that I know about, except maybe a cranial cavity. Actually, I'm not sure I know what the hell you're talking about."

Gallo sat down at our table, returning from the pin ball machines. "'I don't know what the hell you're talking about.' That's all I ever hear you say. Typical admin officer."

Simpson ignored him. "Well, Saunders was in seeing Doc Dugan about something today. I saw him coming out of the dispensary as I was going in. Doc wouldn't tell what Saunders was there for, but he kept laughing. I thought it might be worth knowing."

"I put ten dollars of fucking quarters in that goddamned one-armed bandit, and all I got was three goddamned cherries."

I looked over at Gallo. "Cherries? In Nakorn Sarang? You wouldn't know what to do with them"

"Fuck off, pencil pusher."

Simpson waved his hand in front of me. "Hey, has Hudson ever said anything to you about what they're going to do with Saunders?"

"Not that I've been able to understand. Again, however, I must ask, why?"

"Hell, he's about two months overdue in qualifying. Sheets is afraid the little twerp is going to cost him his bronze star."

"What's his problem?"

Gallo broke back in. "What's his problem? Shit! That clown couldn't eat spaghetti and breathe at the same time." He paused and apparently considered his remark. "I don't know if that makes sense. I'll have to work on that one. What I mean is if

Saunders thinks he's said the wrong thing to a pilot, hw gives him a new heading. He had some silly son-of-a-bitch heading for Hanoi the other day before Capt. Stacy grabbed the mike."

"That's bad, right?"

Simpson picked it up. "Now you're catching on. You'll be a war hero yet. The fact is though, Saunders is an embarrassment to the whole place. Hudson was in asking Sgt. Reade if there wasn't some sort of regulations that could be used to cover up Saunders, some way they could use him for something else. One goddamned thing for sure, he'll never get qualified as long as there's any work to do here."

Gallo shook his head and wondered, "I'd like to know who that little bastard's angel is. He's got to have one somewhere because someone's sure protecting him. Nobody can be that incompetent and survive without one."

I decided it was time for a change. "One thing for sure, he hasn't got the clap."

Gallo stopped and stared at me. "Now what the hell are you talking about?"

"Harry started this off by asking me if I knew why Saunders was in the dispensary. I said, it's for sure he hasn't got the clap. What's the matter, can't you follow the conversation?"

Halfway through the poker game, down about thirty dollars and pretty well smashed, I remembered that Joe's girl was going to be there that night. "I gotta go. Joe's teeloc's gonna be there."

Gallo was rearranging the money in front of him. He stopped and looked up. "Joe's teeloc? Capt. Stacy has a girl?"

"That's what he said. Some girl he knows from Bangkok is coming to stay with him for a couple of weeks."

"Hmm, I never thought Stacy would have a girl live with him."

"Why not?"

Simpson entered the talk. "It's just he doesn't seem much like the type. You know, not a lunatic like Sheets, and not sad like Crawford and Alvarez who miss their wives so goddamned much and just want to pretend they've still got them with them."

"I don't know, just he said she's coming and she's gonna be here for a couple of weeks. Anyway, I wanna get going and see what she looks like. Good night."

"So long, form filler."

I felt a little too drunk to ride my Honda, so I took the bus. Sgt. Hunnicut was driving that night which meant we hit every pot hole on the road. By the time I got home, my stomach was in my throat, and when Joe and Ewan walked out of the bedroom into the living room, and when Joe said, "Jim, I'd like you to meet Ewan," and she raised her hands to give me a wai, I barfed down the front of my shirt.

I slept that night in my uniform, less the shirt which I had thrown into the shower after having perfunctorily mopped the floor with it. Ewan had turned and gone back into the bedroom after watching me get sick. Joe, I saw, when my eyes had cleared, laughed and called me a buffoon, before also going back into the bedroom. And I, I made my way clumsily to my room where I collapsed onto my bed and went to sleep. Sometime during the night, I got up and took off my shoes.

During the next afternoon, Joe stopped in the orderly room and said, "They ran the Green Anchor late this morning, so the goddamned recoveries won't be until after five. See if you can keep your hands off Ewan if you get home before I do."

I dusted off my Honda which had sat unused for a day and a half and went home. By the time I got there, the heat was overwhelming. Even the overhead fan on full did little to relieve me as I stretched out on one of the living room chairs, my uniform shirt open to the waist. I hoped that the evening rain would come soon bringing at least a temporary relief. I thought of getting up and taking a shower, but the air seemed to be holding me down.

"Jim want beer?" Ewan had come out of Joe's room and was standing off to one side of the room. In truth, it was the first time I had seen her. I was stunned at how small she was, just under five feet (Joe was at least six two). Her face was a very pleasing collection of nearly straight lines with small breaks on ends of them. Her mouth seemed to convey a slight hint of weariness and sorrow. She had the long, straight black hair that was the favorite of the bar girls, parted in the center, bangs in the front and hanging down over the shoulders, some of it down to her breasts. She stood leaning against the doorway, her left arm hanging straight down her side, and her right hand holding the left arm at the elbow. She wore a paisin wrapped over one shoulder.

"Oh." I looked up a little startled. The heat had made me forget that she was supposed to be there. "Excuse me, no thank you."

"Jim like Coke?"

I smiled and said, "Yes, that sounds good."

She was into the kitchen and returning immediately with the soda, also with a dish of nuts which she said she had fried that morning. Then she went back to leaning against the wall.

"Ewan, wouldn't you like a Coke?"

"Yes, please, thank you," and before I could move, she was out to the refrigerator and returning. I motioned to one of the chairs opposite me, and she sat.

I watched her sitting in the chair; her eyes did not seem to be focusing on anything. She remained entirely motionless except for the occasional lifting of the glass of Coke to her lips. There was a fine coat of perspiration on her face, shoulders, and arms in contrast to the heavy drops of sweat bursting out of my skin.

My performance the evening before, I felt, needed to be mentioned. In my mind, I fumbled to try and put together a sentence of apology in Thai. What I finally said was, "Koa-towd kop, pom mai sabai, mai-dee." Literally it means, "Pardon me, I sick bad." I combined it with some gestures of my hands that were also intended to convey my deepest apologies.

Ewan looked at me blankly for several seconds. She must have been wondering what the hell I was talking about. Then when she seemed to have put together the gist of my remarks, she laughed briefly and a faint smile lingered on her lips. She said, "Oh, mai pen rai, kah." She drank some more of her Coke and laughed to herself again which caused her to choke on the soda. When she coughed, she patted herself on the chest. Her hands had the same natural grace of a classical Siamese dancer. It was not that unusual for bar girls to have that grace, but every time I noticed it, I was struck again by the beauty and charm of their movements.

When she had caught her breath, she smiled and said, "Jim, your Thai is not so good, no?"

"No," and I smiled back. "I didn't know how well you spoke English, Ewan."

"Very good, thank you." She smiled again quickly. "It is very important in my job, you know."

"Yes," I said and then wondered if I should have said anything. Was it really good manners to talk with her about her "Job"? So I quickly expanded my apology in English. "Ewan, I'm very sorry about last night. I promise not to do that again. That was not nice."

"Jim, I say before, mai pen rai."

It's fair to say, I believe, that over the next nine months, Ewan and I became good friends. She was never verbose, but I began to feel a warmth from her, and I think she genuinely enjoyed the times we spent together during her visits when Joe was not at the bungalow. We did not often say much. She would get a Coke or a beer for me depending on how my stomach felt, and we would sit on the chairs facing one another, just sitting there. I think that all our conversations strung together might constitute no more than a long evening's talk over drinks between old friends. Yet a sense of affection and concern always seemed present.

I also saw her when I went to Bangkok, with or without Joe. She always operated out of the same bar, Max's on Patpong Road, and if I got there early, we would go to dinner, but I would return her to the bar before the crowds came. It was unsaid, but there were certainly no circumstance under which she would come to my hotel. Instead, she would introduce me to a friend of hers, and I would usually spend the night with that girl.

In fact, it was in such a way that I met a girl named Pitsommai, who, during my later visits to Bangkok, always shared the dinners with Ewan and me. Pitsommai and I also spent some close moments together, but we had a more carnal core to our relationship, and I never felt that bittersweet warmth towards her that I had for Ewan.

Of course, if I ever let myself think Ewan might really be more fond of me than of Joe, it was always quickly dispelled when he entered the bungalow. They would exchange polite wais, and then she would take him to the bedroom to help him into a robe or a paisin, and after he was seated in a chair, she would bring him a beer and nuts and, in general, ignore me. Joe, one time said to me, "The first time she came to visit me, I told her not to make such a fuss, not to wait on me like that. She stopped, but she began to pout. And slowly, each day, she'd try to sneak in another little way of taking care of me. I eventually gave up and not let her do anything she wants. I have to admit, I'm beginning to like it. I suppose that if she were here all the time, I'd be a little more insistent about it, but as it is, it makes for a pleasant break."

Ewan appeared to literally worship him. I pieced together from conversations with her and Joe, and with Pitsommai how it had all come about.

Ewan had come to Bangkok from Ayutthya when she was seventeen. Her brother, who was a taxi driver had made arrangements for a job in a massage parlor and sent for her. It was 1963 and there was first beginning to emerge a large and apparently permanent contingent of American servicemen and businessmen in the city. Her brother also found her a place to live with a group of girls from the parlor and some others who worked in bars and nightclubs. The job in the massage parlor proved to be a total disaster. She had rarely seen a farang, or white westerner, in Ayutthya, and now they were lying naked on a table in front of her and demanding things like "hand jobs," "short times," and "blow jobs". The papa-san at the parlor became infuriated with her because of her refusal to cooperate, and, in effect, told her to shape up or ship out. That was on her third day.

Back at her quarters where she spent a whole morning crying and too frightened to go to work in the afternoon, one of the other girls suggested Ewan quit the parlor and come to the bar with her that night. A girl there had more choice about whom she went with, and you got to keep more of the money. Ewan, like most poorer Thai girls, had long ago lost her virginity. A friend of her brother, some years older, had, while home on his first leave from the army, literally taken her behind the bushes. When she told her mother, there was no uproar, no screaming, no threats of vengeance. After it was obvious she was not pregnant, her mother showed her how to douche herself and insure she would not get pregnant in the future. After that, it was not unusual for Ewan and a boyfriend to spend an afternoon together beneath the palm trees.

What she had not done before was drink. On her first night in the bar, she met Joe. He frightened her at first because of his size, but early on, she became won over by his smile and good nature. Her English was limited then to a few phrases, and worse, she rarely understood anything a farang said. In fact, she hardly knew there were farangs who spoke different languages. But Joe, while never really a linguist, always had a facility for making himself understood through a combination of gesture, phrase, and physical expression. His moon-sized face, beaming, eyes stretched and turning, could reduce even the most hard hearted of bargirls to giggles.

So that night she went home with him. When they got to his room, Joe took out a bottle of bourbon and made himself a drink. She looked at it and asked for one. He made her a very light bourbon and soda, but it was more than she could handle. Within fifteen minutes, she was sick to her stomach and totally convinced she was going to die. Her skin grew cool, and her hands were wet. Joe managed to keep from laughing and helped her to bed. He put a damp towel on her forehead and covered her with several blankets. He, himself, slept on the floor. In the morning, he went out and bought her a toothbrush, gave her some aspirin, and made her some tea. When she finally became assured she was not about to meet Buddha, he put her in a taxi which he paid for, and sent her home. When she got back to the room, she found two red one hundred baht bills in her purse.

Still, she was embarrassed and frightened and refused to go back to the bar the next night. She thought about going home to Ayutthya, or, perhaps, just running away. One of the girls came back from the bar early that night and told Ewan that big man she had been with the night before had come in and asked for her. When told she would not be in, he asked the other girl to bring Ewan something; it was a small, furry tiger doll. When Ewan visited Joe, she brought the doll with her and placed it on his bureau.

The next night she went back to work, but she did not see Joe for several days. One night he finally came in, and she went right up to him and said, "Joe, I come you. You no pay." A month later, she moved her things into his bungalow, but it was not for long. Joe was near the end of his tour and was being sent back to the States. She was disconsolate and uncomprehending for several days. "What you mean, Joe? Go home? Bangkok your home, no?" After some time, Joe was able to explain in rudimentary fashion something about Air Force assignments, and she accepted his leaving, but she extracted one promise: "Ewan, I'll be back to see you someday." It was a promise he continued to keep.

DECEMBER 1967

CHAPTER EIGHT

BY DECEMBER, THE LIBRARY HAD become my favorite hide-out. I wonder if others noticed how much time I was spending there. I would drop by two or three times a day. I read every magazine in the place, every novel that was at all bearable, and what few things there were about Thailand and Asia. When shipments of new books arrived on the plane from Takhli, I was there to carry them, to open them, and, after Sunida had registered and marked them, to help put them on the shelves (the boy had done all of these things himself). I asked her if the room layout was satisfactory; maybe she would like to have the chairs and tables placed in a different pattern, or would she like to have her desk by the door? She smiled and said no, everything was fine.

One day, while on my way from the BX to the orderly room, I stopped in the library. My duties as special officer for the variety of functions I had been assigned usually entailed no more than periodically dropping in on one or another of them, sitting down with an enlisted man, or in some cases the Thai, who ran the operation, and ask how things were going. After they said, "Fine, no problems," I was free to go. So, having checked on the efficiency of the BX, I decided that the two hundred yard walk to the orderly room was more than I could handle in such heat and ducked into the library.

A particularly baby-faced airman named Hendrickson, who was off duty and in his civilian clothes, was leaning across Sunida's desk and talking to her when I came in. She did not seem to notice me, and I sat in one of the easy chairs by the magazine rack and began to go through the most recent edition of *Time.* I was all the way through the section devoted to current national news, and Hendrickson was still talking to Sunida. I stood up and yawned, replacing the magazine on the rack. I said out loud, "Oh, well, that's enough of *Time.* What should I read now?"

Settling on a copy of *Sports Illustrated,* I turned and sat back down. Hendrickson was still bent over her desk. The magazine was filled with pictures of football and basketball players, but I couldn't seem to concentrate long enough to read any of the accompanying stories, and my eyes kept drifting back to Hendrickson and Sunida. I could not hear what they were saying; they were talking very quietly, and all I could hear was a low mumble, although occasionally I thought I could hear her laughing. I looked at my watch and realized I had already spent nearly thirty minutes sitting there. What the hell could they be talking about for so long? On my way out I stopped by the desk and asked, "Is there something I can help you with Hendrickson?"

He looked at me startled. Sunida looked up and smiled. "No, sir. No problems," he said.

"Well, I saw you standing here so long, I thought maybe you were having trouble making yourself understood. You sure there isn't something I can find for you?"

"No, thanks, Lieutenant, everything's just fine." He appeared a little annoyed at my intrusion, shaking his head and looking away. "Sunida and I were just speaking to each other in Thai."

"In what?"

"Speaking in Thai, Lieutenant. That's the language here, you know." I used to notice that when the enlisted men were particularly irritated by me, they would address me as "Lieutenant" and couch their remarks with phrases such as "you know," "as you are aware," "most certainly," and "obviously," when what they had just said was otherwise rather clearly stated.

"You speak Thai?" I looked at Sunida.

"Mr. Hendrickson speak excellent Thai, Sir." She smiled.

I stood there as dumfounded as if I had just been told that Major Hudson had delivered the commencement address at Harvard. Of course, there was no real reason I should have been so shocked. Hendrickson, who was Doc Dugan's assistant in the dispensary and generally stayed out of my sight, had given every indication of being a reasonably intelligent young man.

They started to speak again, in Thai and without any hesitation.

"Where'd you learn to do that?"

They paused and Hendrickson turned slowly to stare at me, twisting his mouth slightly at the corners. "Excuse me, Lieutenant, do what?"

"Speak Thai."

"Oh, just around, talking to the chow hall girls, the guards, people in town, Sunida. You know, just kind of picked it up."

"No lessons?"

"No, just kind of picked it up."

"Just kind of picked it up?" But he didn't answer me again. Instead, he turned and went back to talking to her. They both laughed. At me?

Although Sunida smiled, Hendrickson didn't even look up when I left. All the way back to the orderly room, I was talking to myself. "She must think I really am a dumb bastard. I don't know anything more than a few stupid phrases, and then I probably don't even pronounce them right. Hendrickson has only been here a little more than a month longer than I have, and he speaks the goddamned language like he was one of them."

Back in the orderly room, Hudson wanted to know where the PACAF 7 report was. I told him, "It's the safe, Major. It's classified secret, as you are aware, and we can't leave it lying around on your desk, you know." He mumbled something which I could not make out, and then interrupted Sgt. Chance, who was initialing the center block on a pile of forms, to ask him to open the safe and find him the PACAF 7 report. Chance said, "Fuckin' A, Maj'."

I looked over and said to Sak who was sitting behind Chance, "Sak, could you teach me to speak Thai?"

So, in a fashion, I learned to speak Thai. Sak, however, did not turn out to be a good teacher. He was too intuitive in his approach and was not able to organize himself very well. In the end, my teacher turned out to be Sunida.

Several weeks after the Hendrickson affair (I imagine it would surprise both Sunida and Hendrickson to see it called that), I was in the library and approached her desk. In Thai, I said to her, "I am learning to speak your language," and she laughed.

Somewhat non-plussed, I told her that, "Sak is teaching me to speak your language," and she laughed again.

"Why are you laughing?" I asked her in English.

She smiled and seemed a little embarrassed for having laughed. "Excuse me, but I laugh because I know what you mean to say, but it is not what you say. Your, how do you say, your sound, tone, flection?"

"Inflection?"

"Yes, your inflection is not good. That is the most difficult part of Thai for farang to learn."

"Farang?"

She stopped and looked away from me. It was the first time I had heard her use the term which of course was loosely applied to all non-Orientals, but which I sensed also carried a rather derogatory tone. I was a little set back to hear Suida use it. I asked her again, "Farang? What do you mean by farang?"

When she at last looked up at me, she said, "Farang mean man who is not from Asia."

"I have heard it before and I have thought that it had a bad meaning."

She shook her head slightly and seemed ill at ease. "Sometimes, yes, but not all times. All Americans are farang, but some good farang, some bad farang."

I looked at her, and pointing my finger towards my chest, said, "Bad farang, yes?"

Her head shot up, and she began to shake it rapidly. "Oh, no. Oh, no," she said, but when she saw me laughing, she joined in.

I digress. After some more words, I asked her to teach me to speak Thai. She agreed, and even Sak was pleased, since he had only consented to do it out of politeness. I offered to pay her five dollars a week for two lessons each week. We settled on two dollars a week for the two lessons. I would go to her home after dinner on Monday and Wednesday evenings for one hour each night.

On the first night, I met her as we agreed, at the square in the village, and from there followed on my Honda, and she on the bike to her home. She was a little withdrawn when we first met in the center of town, but as we moved away from it and closer to her home, she relaxed, occasionally looking back over her shoulder to check on my progress, and when seeing me, my head encased in the hard, white crash helmet, she laughed.

I followed her back through parts of Nakorn Sarang I had never seen before. We left the tarred streets and turned down a dirt road illuminated only by lights from the small bungalows and fires along the side of the road around which gathered whole families complete with dogs, ducks, chickens, and pigs. The sound of a motorcycle in the neighborhood must have been rare because all of the dogs came out to greet me, and the children looked up and some ran alongside me and would call out. Sometimes I could hear one of them call to Sunida, and she would turn and smile and wave her hand.

At the far end of one of the streets, she stopped and told me to leave my motorbike there. She pointed to a tree, and said I should lock the bike to it. Then I followed her down a dirt path, climbed a short ladder which led to a plankway which I walked on, a little unsteadily, across a small rice paddy to an open bungalow that stood on stilts high above the water.

Inside the front room which was protected from the weather only by the long overhang of the roof, a single hanging light bulb lit the area. A low, crudely made table was the only piece of furniture, and it rested on a woven mat that was slightly larger in area than the table. At the front of the room, just under the edge of the roof was a small stone stove which contained the remaining embers of a fire that had cooked the family dinner. Also, at the front of the room, on the opposite side from the stove, was a huge clay urn filled with rainwater. On the back wall, nailed up, was a cheap blackboard with a tray containing several pieces of chalk. Written on the board were the Thai numbers one through twenty; Sunida had been preparing for our lesson On the far wall, high up, bordering the ceiling, was a color picture of King Bumiphol and Queen Sirikit. Two other rooms led off the open room, and they were each protected by curtains.

Sunida asked that I leave my shoes outside the door, and waved me to sit at the low table. Then she called out something, and an old couple appeared out of one of the rooms. The woman was extremely bent over. She wore a paisin tied at the waist, and an old gray shirt, much too big but pulled several times around her. He wore only a paisin, his chest and stomach lay bare, and there was still some firmness to his muscles, his stomach still was flat. Both wore their hair the same way, cut short and brushed straight back, and it was thick and luxuriantly white. They smiled, and I saw their teeth were red from chewing betel nut.

Sunida said, "This is my family. Father, Narong Thanom Buranaket. Mother Churai Buranaket." I rose and returned the deep wais they both offered me.

Narong Thanom Buranaket smiled and said in a slow and practiced manner, "It is great honor to have famous American soldier in my home."

I answered, "It is a great honor to be here, but I am not a famous American soldier, only a young lieutenant." They continued to smile, but shifted their eyes to Sunida. She immediately began to speak to them in Thai, and I realized they didn't speak any English, and that Sunida must have taught her father his short welcome. So I smiled at her and her fatuous compliment.

Her parents excused themselves from the room, and Sunida turned to the blackboard. "Shall we begin the lesson?" She was a most efficient teacher, not allowing anytime for diversion. For the next hour, despite my efforts, we talked of nothing but the Thai alphabet and numbers. She would even dare to snap at me when I, not being able to pronounce something or having forgotten what she had just told me, would try to pass it off with a smile. I kept checking my watch, and with exactly one minute to go in the hour, she said, "Now count one to twenty." It took me all of the sixty seconds, but I didn't miss anything since I had been somewhat familiar with the numbers before. When I finished, she smiled for the first time since the start of the lesson and said, "Dee mak, Lieutenant Jim." I waved my hand at her. "Please don't call me Lieutenant. It's silly, just call me Jim." She smiled and looked down waiting to see if I had anything more to say.

looked around the room, and at the door to her parent's room. "What does your father do?"

"You have a word, I think it means he does not work, too old"

"Yes, retired."

She nodded. "Yes, that is it. He retired. Before, he make small store, sell rice and fish. But he get too old and cannot work hard."

"How old are your parents," I asked.

She pointed to their room, and moved her hand as if signaling to each of them. "Father is in year seventy-one. Mother has sixty-seven years."

It fell silent, and I could hear the birds and the monkeys and other animals outside the small bungalow. I looked around the room, and my eyes settled on some books I hadn't noticed before beneath the blackboard. I got up and went over to them. They were in Thai but contained many English words. They were instructional books for the teaching of English.

"What do you do with these?"

She came over and took one of the books from me. "Oh, these are for my classes for the children."

"What children?"

She waved her hand towards the street. "The children here. Many people are very poor. Children must work, cannot go to school. In night, I hold class here for them. Teach them numbers, to speak English. For person to do well in Thailand, very helpful to speak English."

"Do they pay you?"

She shook her head and appeared a little taken back by my question. "Oh, no! When I teach in Pitchit, pay is very small. Now, in library, I make much money, so I not need pay to teach children."

It was silent again, and I merely stood there until she raised her hand to the blackboard and said, "Mr. Hendrickson bring blackboard for me. It is most helpful in my class."

"What?"

"Mr. Hendrickson bring blackboard for me. It is most helpful in my class." I looked at it and asked her if he said where he had gotten it.

"He say supply do not need blackboard."

I felt that it was time to be leaving, and I said so.

"You can find my home next time?" I said I could, and then I said good night. My hard mood melted somewhat when I looked back as I was crossing the wooden planks and saw her smile and wave.

The road was much darker on the way back. The fires along the roadside were mostly out by then, and the families had disappeared. Sometimes a dog would bark and chase after me, but I would easily shoo him away.

At the Hoa Far restaurant, I ordered a large bottle of Singha and some nuts and wondered if a general court martial, a dishonorable discharge, and ten years of hard labor in Leavenworth were more punishment than Airman Hendrickson deserved for stealing the blackboard.

By the time of my next lesson, I had decided not to pursue my plans to see Hendrickson in Leavenworth. Instead, I went to the BX that afternoon and purchased a small transistor radio hardly any larger than a pack of cigarettes for ten dollars and carried it that evening to the home of Narong.

The old couple came out to greet me when I arrived, and before they could retire to one of the back rooms, I signaled them to sit at the low table. There I took the radio out of my shirt, turned it on and placed it on the table. Churai Buranaket's face exploded in glee, but she kept cautiously back from the table and the radio. Narong, a little more confident of the mechanics of the gadget, slowly reached out and turned the selection dial. After a moment of silence, the tinny music was replaced by a rapid, staccato, Thai voice. Churai, who had stopped laughing when the music stopped, let out a slow, respectful "ooooh," when the voice came on. Narong positioned the radio so that it rested very squarely on the table, and, an expression of certain accomplishment on his face, slowly sat back and crossed his arms across his chest.

I gestured with my hand toward the radio, and, in the words of Thai that I had spent the better part of the afternoon learning from Sak, said, "Please accept my gift to you for having me as a guest in your home."

Narong, after a second or two of holding back, broke into a grin and began to thank me many times. Giving me a deep wai, he said, "Ko kun mak, kop. Kop kun mak." Churai looked at him strangely before he turned to her and repeated my words with a slightly different inflection. Then she also thanked me.

When her parents had gone back to their room, Sunida, who had watched all this silently and with brief smiles, very formally turned to the lesson. I could hear the radio playing, occasionally the station being changed and Churai laughing. However, once during the evening, Sunida stopped in the lesson and said almost as if I were not there, "My father could never have bought radio. Cost too much, and I would have to save money for long time. But you buy radio for my family and can buy one for self, too." It was as if she were saying it aloud so she could understand the facts better, and I certainly did not feel I was being thanked for my generosity.

JANUARY 1968

CHAPTER NINE

IN JANUARY I MADE MY first trip to Bangkok. It was to attend a conference of administrative officers from the 606th Tactical Air Control Group. The 606th TAC, responsible for radar operations for all of Southeast Asia, consisted of seventeen radar sites, eleven in South Vietnam and six in Thailand. About every six months, the admin officers of each detachment met for a three day conference. Similar conferences were held for other functions such as maintenance, operations, and security. Site commanders held a conference every three months. Naturally, with the choice of location being either Saigon or Bangkok, the latter was always the location of the conferences.

Since the request for attendees allowed for two of us, Staff Sergeant Lafayette Chance, as the orderly room NCOIC, was asked to attend with me. "Shit, Lieutenant, I hate that fuckin' place. It's thuh fuckin' clap center uv thuh fuckin' world."

"Well, in that case, Lafayette, if you really don't want to go, maybe I should bring Smiley along in your place."

"Aw shit, Lieutenant, poor fuckin' Burnett won't know what thuh fuck's goin' on there. I bettuh fuckin' go jes' to make sure we don't miss somethin' important."

So Chance and I took the C-130 to Don Muang Airport and the taxi from there to the Nana Hotel in downtown Bangkok. We checked in at the desk, and I watched a bellboy lead Chance off in the direction of his room. The next time I saw him was at the airport three days later waiting for our C-130 back to Nakorn Sarang. His face was a bright red, and he wore a pair of very dark wraparound glasses to protect his eyes from the light. When I asked him if he enjoyed his time at the conference, he said, "What fuckin' conference?" In filing my report on the conference, I noted that, "Staff Sergeant Lafayette D. (D for Delbert) Chance had been an active and effective contributor to the discussions on the problems of administrative services in a combat area."

Chance probably had the best idea. Colonel Curtis Herder, commander of the 606th TAC, who attended all conferences of all natures, opened the meeting on the first morning by pointing out the great importance of the work of the group, the profound seriousness of the communist threat throughout Southeast Asia ("These people have no respect for the things we value, the American flag, free enterprise, the Air Force, or the MPS-14 acquisition radar"), the responsibility of a good orderly room, and he closed by adding, "And if you're interested in buying some jewelry while you're here, let me most strongly recommend Jimmee's Jewelry on Suriwongse Road."

The next time we saw Col. Herder was the last morning, and he said, now also wearing dark glasses, "Men, you've all done a fine job here. Don't forget what you've all learned, and remember what I've told you about Jimmee's. This conference is now dismissed.

The rest of the sessions consisted of discussions of such subjects as "Proper Accomplishment of Air Force Form 1098," "Effective Routing of Airman Efficiency Reports and Officer Effectiveness Reports," and "Guidelines for Medals and Awards in Southeast Asia."

On the first afternoon—there being no sessions scheduled—most of the attendees headed for the Happy-Happy Massage Parlor down the road from the hotel. Joe had made some notes for me of places to go, and he even took the trouble to suggest avoiding the Happy-Happy. But I was somewhat leery of heading off by myself through Bangkok, so I headed for the Happy-Happy with the masses.

After spending the afternoon there, I hardly had enough energy to go out for the evening. The Happy-Happy was a large building with several floors of little cubicles, each with a bathtub and a massage table. But the main part of the building was like an automobile showroom. There, nearly one hundred girls sat behind a large glass window in a room which resembled a college lecture hall, spending their time watching television, knitting, and paging through magazines. Each of them wore a small blue smock which had on it a large red pin with a number—one through one hundred. On the other side of the glass sat the customers, drinking Singhas and making their selections of a masseuse and discussing the selection: "Number forty-three has good shoulders and hands, very strong;" "Fourteen looks like a goddamned dragon lady;" "Eighty-six can't give much of a massage, but what a beautiful blow job!;" "I think twenty-three stole my watch last week."

I sat down and ordered a Singha, had a cigarette, and watched the girls. It all seemed quite pleasant. I began to wonder what it was that Joe didn't like about this place. The room where I sat with a dozen or so other farangs was pleasant and comfortable. We each sat in soft chairs with arms, although like most Thai furniture, they were a little small for westerners. On the other side of the window, the masseuses presented a pleasant view. Their blue smocks stopped mid-way down their thighs. Their hair was neatly combed, generally in the straight fashion most admired by the farangs. They all seemed very much at ease as they sat there. None assumed awkward positions. I tried in my mind to think what the girls from the Argo Bar would look like behind that window. Granted, with probably no more than a few days experience, they would be indistinguishable, but my thought was of what they would look like at the moment. Some might be squatting on their heels, a spread out paisin exposing their underpants, if any had been worn. They would periodically pick their noses as casually as you or I might rub our foreheads. One might be chomping away on a rice bug, or pushing some fried rice from off a dirty banana leaf into her mouth with her fingers. Now, I must admit, such behavior often evoked a certain amount of casual charm, and I quite frequently would spend my afternoon off lounging at the Argo and enjoying the girls' light hearted if somewhat crude company. What I am suggesting is that after nearly four months of exposure to no intimate female companionship except the girls from the Argo, I was experiencing a sensation of mild euphoria as I watched the sixty or so girls (there were always about forty girls at work in the cubicles) sitting on the other side of the window—sitting there comfortably, naturally, and most importantly, gracefully. My beer was empty. I realized I had been sitting nearly an hour enjoying the sight of so many pretty girls. I ordered another beer and looked back into the showroom.

Off on one side and sitting away from the central block of girls, my eyes began to focus on twenty-nine. She was not knitting or reading or watching the television as the others were. Her eyes, large and brown and sweeping gracefully up to high corners, looked away from the window. I could see her eyelids flutter from time to time. Even sitting, she appeared somewhat tall for a Thai, five foot two or three. She had the sharper nose of someone with Indian blood. I rose and walked to the other side of the waiting room. All the time I kept watching twenty-nine. As I moved, her lovely bronzed skin changed shades.

I stopped at the edge of the room and continued to look at her. The Mama-san came up to my side and said, "You see girl you like, yes?"

I kept looking at twenty-nine and said, "Yes".

A few minutes later I was walking down a long corridor past small doors, a hint of steam in the air, following twenty-nine as she silently made her way to the end of the hall swinging in her hand a key on a large plastic holder. She reached our room and unlocked it for me holding it open so I could enter before her. When I went through the door, I tried to catch her eyes. They met for a moment, and she smiled briefly. Did her face blush? I thought so, but then my judgment on such matters is notoriously inaccurate.

It was a small room, well lit and clean. In the center was a high table, like the kind found in men's locker rooms. There was a single, straight backed chair to one side. On the far side was a bathtub, the old style that stood on legs. It did not have a shower, but there was a long, pink rubber hose with a shower head coiled and hanging from a hook near the tub. Twenty-nine walked directly to the tub and turned on the hot water. Steam began to rise immediately. She leaned over and made some quick swipes at the tub with a large sponge. Then she plugged the drain and sprinkled some bath powder into the water. The suds started to form quickly, and as the steam rose, a few small bubbles floated on it. I could smell the fragrance of the powder. The warmth of the steam and smell of the powder were extremely pleasant. The idea of a hot bath began to have stronger and stronger appeal.

As I stood there and felt the first beads of perspiration form on me, I saw twenty-nine, with a flicking motion of her hand, unfasten the top of her smock. Then, dropping her shoulder slightly, the entire robe fell to the floor. I stared at her. Her skin changed colors as the room filled with steam. She stood over the tub, watching it fill. She was very slim with small but well formed breasts. They were held in a very slight bra which she hardly needed since they were firm and stood on their own. Thin bikini style underpants hid her bottom, but through the material, especially as the pants clung to her in the heat, her firm and lovely cheeks stood there like two, ripe, tender, melons. In the front of her pants a small, dark triangle was visible. She went to the head of the tub and adjusted the water. The steam stopped rising as quickly, and she stuck her hand into the suds leaving it there and swirling the water about. She was sitting on the edge of the tub, and her body broke into the most pleasant combination of lines and curves. Her hair dropped and hung down over her eyes. Carefully, but effortlessly, she placed it back over her shoulders. She looked up at me and smiled, raising her eyes for a short moment and catching mine. I had been standing the whole time watching her, my rear end against the massage table.

She raised her hand and gestured to me. "Hang your clothes on that hook, Handsome, and get into the tub." I continued to stare at her. What did she say? What did she call me? She must have understood my look because she said it again. "Hang your clothes on that hook, Handsome, and get into the tub." She gestured with her hand to several hooks on the back of the door, then she added, "Come on before the water gets cold." Her voice was light and pleasant, but there was only the slightest trace of a Thai accent. She pronounced her works too distinctly, and her cadences were a beat out of rhythm.

I walked over to the door, stripped down to my shorts and stood there. "Everything, Honey. Come on."

As I walked back across the room in the altogether, I was hoping that my pecker would stay limp, hiding itself between my legs, but I could feel the blood flowing to it, and it began to harden and stand itself up. Twenty-nine reached out as I got near the tub and patted my rump. "Not bad, Handsome, not bad. Come on now, get in."

Now it may seem strange that as I have previously described, I had enjoyed such a raunchy and casual attitude towards sex with the girls at the Argo, and yet I was so dumbstruck and shy when in the Happy-Happy Massage Parlor. Well, sex at the Argo was about as intimate as playing doctor with the little girl next door when you are a child, and being led to massage room bathtub by number twenty-nine made me feel like nothing so much as if I were being carefully seduced by an older woman I had known all my life.

The hot water literally melted me. My body slid down into it and to keep from submerging, I hung my arms from the side of the tub. Twenty-nine took a pink facecloth from a shelf and a bar of soap from a little metal rack and began to lather me, starting with my neck and shoulders. She had strong and fine fingers. I could feel the tips of them scurrying about on my neck, and for a moment my mind ceased operations. I closed my eyes and made some sound. As she moved her hands to my chest, she said, "That's good, that's good, just relax, Handsome."

She reached down into the water for a second to rinse the facecloth, and as she did, she briefly stroked my pecker. My breathing stopped and my eyes popped open.

"Easy, Handsome, easy. Later with that." Her hands were back soaping and working on my chest sides, and I settled back into the water.

"Hey, how come you call me Handsome? I'd rather you called me by my name." She told me to lean forward and when I did, she went behind me and began to wash my back.

"Okay, so what's your name?" I told her and she continued washing my backside. Again she reached down into the water. This time she put her hand into the cleavage between my cheeks and firmly ran her soapy hand along the length of my spine. I collapsed down into the tub, splashing some water over the edges.

"Jim, that's a nice name. Here, Jim, give me your arms." She picked up each of my arms in turn and ran the warm cloth the length of them, letting my fingers drop out of hers and back into the water.

As she reached into the water at the far end of the tub and found my feet, I asked her, "What is your name?"

She ran her fingernail lightly along my instep and reached for my other foot. "Barbara".

Before she tickled my foot again, I was able to say, "But that's not a Thai name. How'd you get that?" her fingernail made a little circle in my instep, sending a small and pleasant shock through my body. She moved her hands up and was starting to work on my thighs. With each stroke, she was coming closer to my pecker and balls. She alternated from one leg to the other.

"All girls here take an American name. I don't like my Thai name." Her hands were, by then, on my balls. She held them very lightly and let the soap guide them through her fingers. "I pick name of famous movie star."

I had a full-fledged erection by then. It stuck itself up out of the water through the suds. Barbara put her hand around its base and squeezed it very firmly. The tip expanded more and grew very red. My mouth opened. She gave the muscle one upward stroke, leaving it throbbing and waving in the air. Flexing the muscles of my groin, I tried to control myself. I didn't want to come yet; I was beginning to consider other possibilities. She pulled the plug from the tub and reached for the pink shower hose. I rested my head against the back of the tub. There was a gurgling noise as the water started to drain. When I had regained some composure, although my pecker was still standing straight up, I said, "Whose name did you pick?"

She turned the spray on me. To my great surprise, it was ice cold. The first place it hit was my pecker, causing it to sag like a leaking tire.

"Barbara Streisand, she is most beautiful girl in the world."

When the cold water shock wore off, I started to rise, but she indicated I should turn over, and when I did, she hosed down my backside.

Once out of the tub, Barbara (twenty-nine) slipped me into a large terry cloth robe. The modesty of the drying process surprised me. She tied the robe in front and began rubbing it into my skin starting with my shoulders and working down. Through the terry cloth, she cupped my cheeks in her strong hands and pushed her fingers towards my balls. But before I could respond at all, she was off to the shelf from which she returned with a single towel. She opened the front of the robe and pushed it back off my shoulders. As it fell to the floor, I stood motionless not sure what reactions I was expected to be having. My pecker seemed confused as well. It had faded and was hanging limply like a still flag. She took the towel and ran it down one leg and back up the other. As she came back to my groin, she pulled the towel away and took all of me into her right hand. She fondled them momentarily and said, "Hey, what happened? Did this thing die?"

It stood up again, but she had already removed her hand and was hanging up the robe and towel. "Get up on the table, okay, Handsome?" She gestured towards the table. I noticed the arch in her wrist. "Lie on your stomach, Honey."

"Jim," I said.

"Oh, yeah, I forgot. Get up on the table, okay, Jim." She had a container of baby powder in her hand now. I got up and stretched across the table. The eroticism was fading from me. I began to think that maybe I really was going to get a massage.

Barbara had my right foot in her hand. "You relax now, Jim. Close your eyes." What the hell, so I closed my eyes and rested my head on the table. She took the ball of my foot in her left hand and pulled sharply on my big toe with her right hand, and she proceeded to do the same with each of my toes. A few of them popped as she pulled on them.

On my calves, she alternately jabbed at me with short, rapid, little karate chops and then kneaded the muscles. She had strong fingers, and I preferred the latter, but she couldn't seem to make up her mind as to which she was supposed to be doing. I thought of old fight movies, the boxer lying on the table, the fierce glare in his eyes, his trainer working on his back telling him things like, "Go right in there and get him Kid," and "Keep sticking your left in his puss, Kid." I chuckled to myself and turned my head to look at Barbara. Her hands were drumming away on my left calf, and she was staring at the wall with a vacant look. I dropped my head back down and closed my eyes.

She flexed my knees for me a couple of times before proceeding on to my thighs with her rubbing and chopping. I drifted more into my thoughts. I wondered again about Joe's list of places to go and places to avoid. I was beginning to understand why he said to avoid this place. What would she call me next; Handsome, Honey, or Jim? Joe's only recommended massage parlor was something called the ABC on New Road; he had even recommended asking for a specific girl, Lot. There, at least, the girls had Thai names, and I probably could have listened to some pleasant broken English. But, on the bright side, it was doubtful if I would have had a more beautiful or more graceful girl than Barbara. Her slightest and briefest motions blended smoothly. There was not the least abruptness in them.

At that moment, Barbara used one of those brief, non-abrupt motions to slap my ass. "Okay, handsome Jim, don't move now," With that she leaped to the table and stood on the small of my back. Somewhat startled, I started to turn over.

"Hey, what's the matter with you? I told you don't move. What? Do you want me to fall and get hurt?"

Her sharpness of tone surprised me, and I lay back down obediently. With her toes she began to knead the muscles in my lower back. The weight of her body increased the effectiveness of her rubbing. As she moved her feet, occasionally my back would feel as if it were about to collapse, and I would let out some sort of low groan, but, in all, she seemed to have a feel for our relative strengths and weights, and she balanced her weight and let it down slowly. For the first time since I had left the tub, I was enjoying massage.

When she reached my shoulders, she leaned over slightly and said, "Here, Handsome, give me your hand." I didn't bother to remind her of my name, I just carefully lifted my arm until she grasped my hand. She pulled on my arm as if it were a large lever, but always stopping just short of causing me pain. Her foot was directly at my shoulder joint. I felt the muscles in my shoulder and chest stretching past any recently exercised point. Holding my hand in the air, she repeated her toe-jerking procedure on my fingers. When one of them would pop, she'd laugh and say, "Not bad, Handsome, not bad." Then she began to rotate my arm in its socket some more, this time pulling back a little farther than before, but now my muscles didn't offer as much resistance. When she let go of my hand, the arm dropped silently to the table, and I let it lie enjoying its spent feeling as she repeated the exercise on my other arm and hand.

When that was done, I felt like I certainly must be through, but she was urging me to turn over. "Come on, Honey, roll over, there's still more to come."

While I lay on my back, she fooled with my chest and shoulders, chopping and kneading, then started to work her way down to my stomach. She paused on my belly to run her fingernails lightly over the skin. When I snorted and looked up, she said, "Hey Good Looking, so you're ticklish, hey?" She scratched my stomach and few more strokes and started for my privates. When she first started to fondle my pecker and nuts, there was an immediate reaction. The blood flowed to it and it began to rise. I raised my head for a moment, but then I thought of the three or four times she had teased me in the tub and during drying, and I actively tried to restrain myself. She took me in her hand and started to stroke it rapidly, but I was winning the battle. A full erection was eluding her. I propped my head and shoulder up on my elbows and watched her struggle with me. She looked up at my face.

"Hey, what's the matter? I thought you were a lover."

"Gee, no other girl has ever had a problem."

She pulled on it for several more seconds, but nothing happened. Her eyes flashed at me. Then she stopped stroking and leaned her head over, and, holding he mouth only an inch from the end of my pecker, she breathed gently on it. It stood straight up, the head bright and red. "There we go, Handsome. Now that's pretty."

She let go and ran over to her shelf. When she returned, I was still strong and hard. She surprised me by climbing up on the table again, sitting astride me, her back to my face. In that position, with both hands, she resumed stroking. There was something on her hands.

"Hey, what's on your hands?"

"Wesson Oil, Honey."

With that, the battle quickly ended. I made an ignored suggestion that he take her pants off, but in a matter of seconds, I was coming into a hankie she had pulled out of her pants.

Walking back up Sukhumvit Road to the hotel, I was yawning and musing on my frustrating encounter with twenty-nine. In the bar I told one of the other lieutenants at the conference about it. He seemed, rightly so, indifferent to the whole thing, but he did look up at the end of my story and say in a mildly bemused tone, "Barbara Streisand?"

Oh, yes, I did manage to go out that night. Following Joe's advice this time, I went to Max's Bar on Patpong Road. There I met Ewan and we went to dinner. After dinner, as I've said, we went back to the bar where she introduced me to a girl who I ended up spending the night with. The following night, Ewan and I had dinner again, and she again introduced me to a girl, but I didn't share my bed that night. On my third and last night in Bangkok, Ewan introduced me to Pitsommai. Pitsommai was probably the prettiest of all the girls I knew. She had large brown eyes that she used to charm unabashedly. She had a flashing mouth and possessed a sassy personality, topped off by a touch of the risqué. She was professional in her work and enjoyed it, and we came to enjoy a pleasant, carnal, and uncomplicated friendship. It was in direct contrast to the romantic and sentimental overtones that I demanded of other relationships.

One night, while I was in Bangkok on another trip, Pitsommai had made a date to meet at Max's at seven o'clock. When I arrived, I found her sitting in a booth with another man. Slightly stunned, I started for the door, but she called out to me. When she approached, she teasingly looked at me and said, "Jim, is you?" I nodded, and she ran back to the booth and stared at the guy there. Then she picked up her purse, came back over to me, put her hand on my arm and said in a very off-handed and light way, "So sorry. Pitsommai make mistake. All American look same to me." We both laughed loudly, then had a great night. From the night Ewan introduced us, whenever I was in Bangkok, Pitsommai and I spent the evenings and nights together.

FEBRUARY 1968

CHAPTER TEN

IN LATE JANUARY AND EARLY February, the news magazines and *The Stars and Stripes* began carrying a series of bloody pictures of the Tet offensive in Vietnam. One particularly gruesome photo, carried by them all, the object of much concentrated staring and silent reflection, was of an air policeman, standing on his knees, his arms hanging numbly at his sides, helmet knocked off, and blood streaking down his forehead, one thin very red line running the length of his nose. His eyes were dazed and his mouth hung open. It did not take much imagination to know that he was dying, that he would soon collapse over in a lifeless pile of flesh and bones. It was, however, the dazed look that most bothered our airmen. It was that shock in the eyes, surprise and anger: I didn't think it could happen to me, to some poor infantry jerk out in the boonies, but not to me.

For several days prior to seeing the photos, we had been receiving reports of the offensive. Radio AFTN (Air Force Thailand Network) had been, between old rock songs and sports scores, feeding us the MACV releases every hour. There was certainly no credibility in them, number counts of great American and South Vietnamese victories. The Bangkok Post had carried garbled versions of the same press releases, lines inverted, tortured syntax, and occasional references to great victories by the Thai unit, the Queen's Cobras. But the pictures finally gave a touch of reality to the whole thing, and for the first time, some of us began to feel that we were getting a true idea of what was going on and what we were, at least in some remote sense, involved in.

The most intelligent thing I heard said during those early days of February was out of the mouth of Smiley Burnett. "You know, Sir," he said as he looked up from a copy of *Newsweek*, "I sure am glad I am over here and not over there." During those days, most of us shared that view. Reflections on the morality of the war, or even on the effectiveness of it, would wait awhile, the time then was for a sense of relief at having physically avoided it. Most of the cowboy soldiers, those who strutted about as if out of some old cavalry movie, gave up their acts and just kept to doing their jobs and enjoying our spot of peace.

Unfortunately, some of us did not. Captain Gunn took to wearing his jungle fatigues all of the time. He also started wearing a thirty-eight pistol (all of the officers were authorized them and were issued them upon arrival, but even then the rest of us kept them buried deep in the recesses of our desks). Captain Sheets began sitting in the radar ops office wearing a helmet and talking as much about the site's perimeter security as about his erotic adventures with Joy. I think I preferred the latter. Too much of their time, for my taste, was spent in the orderly room in ear shot of Hudson, detailing how they would fight the war, when and if it ever came to them.

Gunn: We're fighting a war with one hand tied behind our back. It's not our boys' fault this goddamn war is still dragging on like this. It's that chicken-shit Johnson's. If he'd just unleash the Air Force, this little ol' shoot-out would be over in no time, pardner.

Sheets: Nuke'em! Fucking flatten 'em! Theat's the only thing the Oriental understands. Force!

Gunn: Bomb'em night and day. Right back to the stone age, just like Lemay says. We'll make a parking lot out of North Vietnam, Laos, and China too, if necessary.

Sheets: I understand the Oriental mind (pause), it's perverse.

Gunn: I'm ready to sacrifice. It's a necessary part of war. Work night and day. My men will keep that radar operating at any cost. I'll work a scope myself if needed. Sacrifice, goddamnit, that's what we're here for.

Sheets: The Oriental puts no value on life. They'll kill a million people and never think a thing about it. They have no sense of human decency, not a shred of respect for human dignity.

Hudson (passing through the orderly room on his way to the mess hall): IwishIwuzbac'nColumbus.

One morning, Gunn stood at one of the orderly room windows and watched the Thai workers entering through the main gate. Out loud, but to no one in particular, he said, "You know, I've heard that at Tan San Nhut during the first day of Tet, most of the workers it turned out were VC's themselves. When the shit began to hit the fan, they all pulled out AK-47's from underneath their shirts and started opening up on our boys." He turned and ran his hands through his flat-top. "Sneaky little bastards. You got to keep an eye on them at all times." Hudson, who was standing in front of one of the personnel charts, looked over and said, "Hey, howz'at?" The next morning when I pulled up to the gate on my Honda, most of the Thai employees were lined up on the outside. One of the Thai guards saluted and let me through. When I came back after putting my bike away, I could see that the guards were frisking each person before letting them on the site. Most of the mess hall girls were complaining. In the rear of the group, I could see Sunida; she seemed somewhat puzzled. Boon, the head Thai guard, a lecher and bully by nature and practice, was personally searching each of the girls. There was nothing subtle in his method.

Sgt. Puckett, the air police NCOIC was watching. "Hey, Sarge, what the hell's going on?" I asked.

"Maj. Hudson's orders, Sir. Search awll foh-reign nashunuls fower cohnsealed weapons. Maj' don't want no Tet Ohfense cOh-mitted on this heah site."

I looked back to the line and saw Sunida was about twentieth in line. I was positive I saw Boon leering over at her. I found Hudson in the mess hall trying to hold down Thursday morning's regular biscuits and gravy. "Major, are you sure you want to do this, search everyone?"

"Uh-huh."

"But Major, I'm pretty sure we're in violation of one of the Agreement of Forces regulations."

"Huh what?" He looked up with his mouth open. It was full of biscuits and gravy. "Yes, Sir," I continued. Once I saw I had him going, I continued on the same line. "We are not allowed, in any way whatsoever, to harass Thai nationals who are employees. That is, of course, without permission of Royal Thai Supreme Headquarters. I take it we have their permission, right, Sir?"

"Uh oh." He wiped his mouth with his hand thinking he had a napkin in his hand. When he looked and saw the globules of gravy on his hand, he wiped it on the tablecloth.

"If we don't have permission, Sir, then I'm afraid General Davis at Thirteenth is going to be one pissed off general."

"Shitshitshit!" I followed him up and out the door and across the yard to the gate.

"Sar'n'Puckett, 'at'senuff, 'at'senuff. 'Mergency'sover."

Sunida was next in line. I didn't take any chance with the order being carried out too slowly. I grabbed the guard's arm and pulled him away from the person he was searching.

Puckett saluted both of us. "Yeasss Sir. An' may ah say, Maj'a 't ol' Boon heah did one hail of a fine job." Boon turned and saluted us too, but I think I noticed some disappointment in his eyes.

As Sunida came through the gate, I smiled at her and wondered if I should tell her what I had done. I very reluctantly decided not to mention it. There was one other positive benefit from the morning's absurdities. As what I thought quite obvious, I had no idea if there was any such clause in the U.S.-Thai Agreement of Forces, or if there even was such a document. I was merely trying to stop the searches before Boon had shoved his hand into Sunida's crotch and so frightened and embarrassed her that she would never set foot on the site again. However, it turned out there was a clause very similar to the one I had made up in some document or another and when Hudson confirmed it, he was quite pleased with me for having informed him about it before some incident occurred. As a result, he listened more to my advice, and, best of all, for awhile at least he left me alone.

For several more weeks, reports of increased casualties kept filling our newspapers and magazines. There also was increased hostilities along the Thailand-Laos border. The weekly figure for American deaths in Vietnam seemed to settle at slightly better than five hundred; previously it rarely hit three hundred. The list of KIA and MIA began to include more and more airmen and more and more ground and support troops. When several names from other units of the 606th TAC appeared on the lists—three dead, ten wounded—the effect on the airmen's morale was profound. Men moved about the site more quietly. The bar, never any less full, became haunted by silent drinkers. Fights broke out more frequently there and all over the site. The cause were such great matters as someone taking another's seat, sitting on someone else's bed, or being accused of taking something off one's dinner plate. Papa-san from the Argo Bar even visited the site and asked Joe and I if we could arrange a meeting between him and Major Hudson. The violence was spreading to the Argo. There had been regular scenes of tables being overturned, chairs thrown through windows, bottles broken, and on and on. Joe and I assured him that we would speak to Hudson (there would have been little profit in getting the two of them together. Hudson would only be certain Papa-san wanted to make some blackmail proposal regarding the Major's supposedly secret liaisons).

Joe walked into the orderly room the next afternoon and began complaining out loud to anyone who was there. "Jesus H. Christ, I went into the fucking dispensary to get some goddamned aspirin for a headache. What a fucking line! Black eyes, cut fingers, noses, missing teeth, cuts, bruised ribs. Shit! There isn't going to be a guy capable of working here soon."

I looked into Hudson's office. As usual, he was trying to ignore Joe. The big man's confidence and obvious disregard for the Air Force frightened the commander. Yet occasionally he would lift his eyes in the direction of the orderly room. Joe moved directly in front of the Major's door. "Hell, you'd think we were in a fucking combat zone. We've got more casualties than they do at Dong Ha. And all I want is some goddamned aspirin for my hangover."

The next morning, Joe did the same thing. "Fuck it all, I just want some goddamned surgical soap for this piss-ass case of the fucking crabs I think I've got, and there's another damn line of cuts and bruises, bent noses, chipped teeth. What about us poor bastards who just get sick from having a good time?"

At that point, Chance walked in the door. He had a black eye and a bandage on his forehead above the shiner. Joe looked at him. "Lafayette, what the hell happened to you? You punch someone in the fist with your eye?" Smiley collapsed on his typewriter in laughter.

Chance threw his cap on his desk and sat down disgustedly. "Ah, fuck it, Cap'n, what thuh fuck's with this fuckin' place, anyway? I'm downuh fuckin' Argo getting' my fuckin' rocks off last night. I go uppuh fuckin' room with Nitnoy and when I come out, there's fuckin' Pivarnik. He says, 'What thuh fuck you doin' with my girl,' and then he fuckin' punches me innuh fuckin' eye." Chance fingered his brow and eye lightly. "Ow, hurts like fuckin' hell, that's what it hurts like." He picked up a pile of forms and began to place his initials in the lower left hand corner of each of them.

Joe paused at the door before leaving. "Christ sakes, it's only a matter of time before someone get killed around here." I turned and checked on the Major. He was staring at the door Joe had just exited through.

Hudson approached me at the lunch table as I was attempting to slice through some of our Tuesday gristly pot roast. He sat down and also began trying to put a not very sharp knife through the meat. He looked around the room and surveyed the assembly of patches and bruises that the airmen presented.

"Whaddyuhthinksuhproblemhere?"

"The what, Sir?"

"Uhproblem. Lookitalluhban'ages." Ever'wunzfightin'alluhtime."

"Bandages, fighting all the time?" I paused and looked around the mess hall. "Oh, my gosh, will you look at that. Well, I'll be." I looked around again. It was the wildest assortment of black eyes, cuts, patches, band-aids, and mercurochrome ever seen. One out of three airmen bore some mark of a scrape. And glum; no one was talking. "Gee, Major, I don't know. Of course, I've been hearing a lot of talk. Maybe it's true, what they're saying."

Hudson's fork stopped in front of his mouth. "Huh? What? Who' zsayin'? Whadduhtheysay?"

"Oh, you know, the regular stuff."

"Wha'wha'?"

"Oh, you know. Guys are a little tense, starting a lot of fights. That kind of stuff, you know." Hudson looked at me as if I were talking about the Trojan War.

"Sar'n'Sutton sezever'wunzdrinkin'toomuch."

"Everyone's drinking about as much as they ever drank. It's just affecting them differently."

"Whaddyuhmean?"

If he was already getting advice from Sutton, then it was time to quit fooling and start pushing my idea. "Well, what I heard is a lot of the guys are feeling a little guilty because they're over here in Thailand, and they keep seeing everything in the magazines and papers about Tet in Vietnam. They say it's eating at them, making them edgy." I watched Hudson's eyes and he seemed to be following me, so I continued. "The site's small, they keep seeing the same faces every day, some one hundred or so faces. They keep doing the same jobs, most which they could do with their eyes closed. They keep getting bossed around by the same assholes…"

"Who'zanasshole?"

I might have been going too quickly. "Excuse me, Sir, but I didn't mean anyone's an asshole. It just seems that way to the guys when they're tired and tense. And they saw that stuff about one guy catching his lunch at Monkey Mountain, and another at Don Ha. And then even one of the technicians at Tan San Nhut bought the farm. A lot of our guys knew these guys. And they all noticed that it was buck sergeants and airmen that made up the KIA and WIA lists, no senior NCO's and no officers."

Hudson stopped listening to me and began to concentrate on sawing his way through a piece of his pot roast. Finally he gave up, folded the meat several times and stuffed the whole wad into his mouth. With his jaw making slow, wide turns of the meat, he looked back at me. "Wha'wer'yuhsayin'?"

I went back a couple of points. "Everything's the same, every goddamn day. Same faces, same jobs, same place, same bosses. And they keep hearing about guys, guys doing the same kind of jobs they're doing, getting their asses blown off. They're close enough to feel guilty, they're working in the same war, but they're removed from it. They're nice and safe over here in Thailand, while some of their friends not too far away are catching holy hell. Why some of our people have even been to a lot of these sites on TDY in the last couple of months. So here they are, safe and sound, and feeling a little guilty, maybe a lot guilty. And they're getting more and more pissed off at and tired with the guy who's bossing them around, some E-7 or E-8, or some captain or lieutenant. And they can't do much about that, so when explosion time comes, they haul off and pop their buddy in the nose. Then they feel even worse."

"Iguessit'llbebackuhnormalsoon." He worked the wad of meat down his throat with a twisting motion, his Adam's apple jumping about like a fish. He got up and went for some coffee, acting as if he had discovered the problem, considered it, and solved it. When he sat back down, I started at him again. "I don't think it will be back to normal soon, Sir."

"Huh, wha'zat? Backuhnormal, wha'?" I looked at him stunned. With Hudson, you always had to consider the possibility that he had completely forgotten everything you were talking about only seconds earlier. The way his face was moving, he seemed to be chewing his coffee. His eyes were darting about through the hall; that was good. I knew he couldn't be missing all the bandages, the bruises, black eyes. He didn't.

"Yuhthinksumthin'wors'llhapp'n?"

I nodded yes. "I'm afraid so, Sir. This kind of stuff will keep up until someone gets hurt really bad, then maybe everyone will lay off, but not before something serious happens."

"Shitshitshit. Sumtin'badhapp'nz, myassizbusted. ColonelHerder'll sen'meback tuh-Saigoninnuhminute." I let him consider the possibility of his rapid reassignment to Vietnam for awhile. He rubbed his face with both hands as if he were trying to rearrange his features.

"MaybeIoughttuhclos'uhclubawhile, puttuhArgo offlimits."

"Sir, I don't think closing the club and putting the Argo off limits will do it. There've been fights all over the damned site, as many in the hooches as anywhere. Some right here in the mess hall."

But his mind seemed to have fixed itself. "Naw, I'mgonnuhcloz'uhclubannuhArgo." What happened next was fortuitous. I would have been very pleased if there had never been another fight at Nakorn Sarang, yet the one that broke out that instant delighted me. Airman Candido came through the cow line, put his tray down on a table, picked up his plate of gristly pot roast, walked to another table, and dropped in on the head of Smiley Burnett.

"You stop that fucking grinning, you happy asshole!"

Smiley, of course, did not stop the grinning (I'm sure he was congenitally incapable of stopping), but he did stand up and leap at Candido. They both collapsed to the floor in a tangle of arms and legs where they helplessly and relatively harmlessly squeezed at one another's torsos and limbs and exchanged invitations to give up amid grunts and groans. It lasted no more than thirty seconds as other jumped in an pulled the two apart. Candido went back to his table and began eating what was left of his lunch, some rolls and a very gelatinous slice of peach pie, and Smiley left the mess hall to take a shower and wash the gristly pot roast and gravy out of his hair.

"Major, you can't put the mess hall off limits."

He went back to rubbing his face. "Shitshitshit, ifsumwungetskilled, I'minnuhshithouse."

"Major, no one has to get killed, no one's got to be in the shithouse. I've got a suggestion."

"Huh, wha'?"

It was the time. "The guys need some kind of occasion to let off steam, especially at the officers. Give us some hell and not have to worry about getting in trouble over it."

I might have been going too fast for him. His face was contorting rapidly.

"Yuhwannuhlet'empunchuhofficers?"

"Oh, no, Sir. I don't want anyone punching the officers. I could get hurt that way. That's definitely not my plan, but maybe we could set up something so they could let off some steam, you know, one night where they could let themselves down, tell us off and not have to worry about it later."

"Wha'kin'uhthing?" I wondered if I should go kiss Candido and Burnett. Between their fight and the gate incident, Hudson was ready to act on anything I said.

"Well, here's my idea. This Saturday night, let the club pay for a party, pay for everything, all the booze and food. We both know the club can afford it. Let the girls from the Argo come out, maybe hire a stripper from Takhli. See, it lets the guys blow off without worrying about spending all their own money. That'll help keep them calm. But…" I watched Hudson's face. It was frozen in a contorted grimace which usually meant he was listening. "But the big thing is we have all the officers and senior NCO's attend, except for the controller on duty. They all attend in civilian clothes, and the word will be out that anyone can say anything they want to any of them, complaints, justified and justified, and they don't have to worry about any of it being held against them later. It's all forgotten in the morning. Well, what do you think, Sir?"

His face held the grimace, but his eyes were twisting about.

"Hum-uh, well, Idunno, Icouldgetinnuhlottuhtrouble."

"Major, think of the trouble we're all in if someone ever really gets hurt in a fight here. I won't even mention it someone gets killed?"

His grimace broke up, and his whole face dropped. "Shitshitshit, why'z why'z'ishaftuhhapp'nuhme?"

My plan was finally accepted about as I suggested. Joe, all of the other junior officers, and most of the senior NCO's backed me. It was better than nothing was the general attitude. Sheets and Gunn were opposed initially, but they finally came over since they were both quite confident that few complaints would be made against them. Oh, excuse me, there was one junior officer against the plan. Bob Saunders of course. "The Colonel would never approve of such an idea. It goes against every principle of military discipline and leadership."

"If," said Joe, leaning over Bob in the ops message room, "the Colonel, your father-in-law or any other colonel in the whole fucking Air Force ever hears about this party, Saunders, then I will personally throw you off the TPS-14 radar tower."

As another precaution, Bob was assigned as the controller on duty for the night. That would keep him out of the club.

Chapter Eleven

It might have really worked, my plan that is. I don't think the problems of the site ran so deep that they could not have been cured by a combination of scream therapy, free food and booze, and sex. But it's all very problematical, the troubles were cured, but in a way which none of us could have prescribed or predicted. I'm not sure if we owe our thanks to some Thai insurgents in the northern provinces, or to the overreaction of the Thai military high command. At any rate, during the middle of the party, at ten p.m., Detachment 8 of the 519th Tactical Air Control Squadron and all other military units in Thailand were placed on full alert.

The party up till then had been going much as planned. Things were just beginning to loosen up. To my own surprise, I had been the target already of several complaints. Airman Candido tore me up and down for staying in between on two many issues, for not always cutting down Hudson, Sheets, Gunn, and Sutton. "I understand this whole fucking thing was your idea. Big fucking deal! What do you want? A medal? You should something like this for us every goddamned weekend." Later, Sgt. Pivarnik stood in front of me and waved a finger in my face. "You know what the fucking trouble with the Air Force is anyway? It's shitty little candy-ass officers like you. All the goddamned time supporting the no good little bastard airmen. Those little shits have never been any fucking good, but at least we used to have officers who were real men. That's the fucking trouble with the Air Force today."

Sometime after 9:00 o'clock, Bob Saunders called on the phone asking for Capt. Sheets, but Sheets was sitting at a table with Joy and the stripper from Takhli, who it turned out was also a sister of Joy's, and he didn't want to be disturbed. "Tell Capt. Stacy to see what the kid wants." Bob told Joe he couldn't discuss it over the phone, so Joe went to the ops office. Joe returned with a strangely grim and puzzled look on his face. He first sought out Major Hudson and told him something. Hudson and Sutton left. After one of the airmen finished telling me off, Joe signaled me to the bar where he had a can of Budweiser waiting for me. "Saunders received a message from MACTHAI, we're in DEFCON 2. I've been in Thailand a total of two and half years, and I've never seen this before. I wouldn't be surprised if we go higher. Let the AP's know and tell them to go to the guard shack, but there's no reason anyone else to know yet.

The AP's slipped quietly out. The rest of the airmen were enjoying themselves too much to notice their leaving. After Joe told Sheets about the possible alert, Sheets left Joy and her sister alone at the table. Many of the airmen were dancing with the girls from the Argo as the band blared out with their imitation of the records from America. I too slipped out and back to the orderly room and my desk where from deep in the back of it, I dug out the helmet and pistol I had been issued on my first day in Nakorn Sarang. I removed the rounds from the thirty-eight and placed them in the ammunition pocket of the belt and fastened the whole thing on. At that very moment, the sirens began to wail.

I left the orderly room and ran to the large bunker which was opposite the club, and the one to which all non-operations and radar maintenance personnel were to report. The ops and maintenance buildings were protected themselves and served as their own bunkers. The ops office during an alert was to serve as the command post, and Major Hudson would be there. When I arrived at my bunker, Sgt. Puckett was already there. He had opened up the weapons storage case and was lining up M-16's for distribution. There was nobody else anywhere near the bunker, and when I looked over at the club, the door was not even open. The sirens continued to wail.

When, after nearly two minutes had passed and still no one had left the club, the P.A. system began to crackle and what had to be Major Hudson's voice came rasping through the buzzing and screeching of the loudspeakers. As best as I could make it out, he said something that translated as, "Awwwgghpht, eeeeeeeeggly, deffffffconkunnnnnnnnseeeeeeskk!" Then he repeated it and it sounded much the same. Nothing happened. The door to the club remained closed. The speakers began to crackle with a different voice and this time the message was quite clear. "DEFCON 1, DEFCON 1, uh, this is not a practice, this is the, uh, real thing, uh repeat, repeat. DEFCON 1, DEFCON 1, uh, this is not a practice, this is, uh, the real thing, uh, the real thing."

The club doors flew open and bodies began falling over one another as they tumbled out. Some fell, but they got up and ran on. The rear and side doors must have been opened because I could see shadows crashing about in those areas.

Smiley Burnett later told me that when the sirens first went off, someone announced over the band's speakers that it was the fire alarm, but obviously the club wasn't on fire so there was no sense in leaving. As the sirens continued to wail, someone else looked out one of the doors, and seeing no fires anywhere, the word was passed that some drunk was fooling around with the alarm system. Some attention was paid when Hudson was unmistakably attempting to say something, but it was not till Sgt. Sutton explained the meaning of the wailing that the idea of an alert dawned on anyone.

As the airmen crowded their way through both entrances to the bunker, Sgt. Puckett tried to distribute the M-16's in an orderly fashion. To the first man through, he handed a weapon and a clip of twenty rounds. I reached over and too the clip out of the airman's hand.

"No ammo, not yet, Sarge."

Pluckett looked at me, incredulously. "Why, Lieutenant, hoaw the main gOhnnuh dee-fend thaimselves?"

I held to the one clip and placed my other hand on the pile Puckett had made. "I don't want a drunk shooting one of our own, Sarge. After they all get in here, we'll hand out clips to the sober ones."

"But hoaw'll we tail, Lieutenant?"

"Anyone who stays awake."

That proved to be about half of the men. The rest sagged to the ground, usually fashioning some sort of impromptu pillow out of the M-16.

"Don't load your clips unless you hear shots," I said after the clips had been distributed. Puckett worried about that command as well, but I assured him that it meant no real delay and would best prevent any accidents.

About five minutes after the last airman had entered the bunker and we had distributed the weapons and ammo, there came the sound of someone moving across the walk from the club to the bunker. Puckett pulled out his pistol and edged his way towards one of the entrances, his body pressed against the side of the wall. The two Thai guards who were standing atop the bunker began chattering to us, but I couldn't make out a thing they were saying. I fingered the ammo pocket on my holster belt and wondered if I might not be wise to load my pistol. I decided against it.

Puckett's voice was high and crackly when he called out, "Hoawlt, whoo gOes their?"

"Aw, shut theh fuck up, you fuckin' ape."

I jumped out of the bunker. "Lafayette, what the hell are you doing? Get your ass in here!"

"Aw shit, quit playin' fuckin' cowboy, will yah, Lieutenant."

"Where've you been?"

"Finishin' my fuckin' drink. That pooying from Takhli is some fuckin' stripper. I'd sure like to bang'er." Puckett handed him an M-16 and a clip. Chance stuck the clip in his pocket and hung the rifle over his shoulder.

"Jesus, what is this, a fuckin' war?"

I watched him for a moment as he moved to the side of the bunker. He was dressed in his civvies, a cowboy shirt stretched across his wide stomach and chest. He opened the shirt complaining about the "fuckin' heat". On the center of his chest was a tattoo of a naked girl standing with her legs apart and her hands on her hips. Beneath was some scrolled lettering which read, "Born to Love." Lafayette saw me watching him and said as he slid to the ground, "Nice tattoo, huh? Boy, was I ever drunk when I got that. My ol' lady was fuckin' pissed."

We began to wait. Movement on the site stopped. There was the occasional sound of the air police in the perimeter bunkers making their radio checks. Other than that, for about five minutes at a stretch, the only sounds were from the jungle about us, the birds and monkeys. Of course, there was the snoring of about half the men in the bunker, and Sgt. Plukett kept trying to reach the ops office, or as he referred to it, the command post, on his radio. "Saintral, saintral, this is pOhsishun fowur, this is POhsishun fowur, kain yew give us mowur infOhmaishun, kain yew give us mowur infOhmaishun." With the phone to his ear, he kept repeating this, but getting no response. When he wasn't trying to raise them, I kept watching the dark outlines of the hooches and listening to the birds and animals. After about thirty minutes had passed, I began to feel certain there was no danger close, at least not from any insurgent groups. During that period the only disturbance came when the silence was broken by the splashing sound of one of the airmen pissing out the back entrance.

"Jesus," someone yelled, "you stupid bastard. That's gonnuh stink like hell."

"Aw, cut it out, I had to pee. I wouldduh wet my pants."

I heard the voices, but I didn't want to know who it was. Puckett didn't hear it, what with his ear stuck to the radio still trying to reach central.

Somewhere between forty-five minutes and an hour into the alert, Puckett finally did reach them. I could hear some noise coming through the other end of the radio. He put it down and looked over at me. "Saintral ree-ports gOhrilla activiteee on nowurthern perimeter of Thailand. Eff-102's at A-O-C Baingkok haive bain scraimbled." He looked to the sky, and I stupidly did the same. The moon was trying to break through some of the heavy and twisting rain clouds. "Ah shewur feel bettuh knOwhwin' thaim buhuds iz up thair."

The closest northern border to us was at least sixty miles away. It had never been reported as an area of guerrilla activity, although that could have certainly changed. At any rate I was finding it difficult to understand why we were sitting there, three score miles from any danger, rifles drawn, on full alert.

Plunkett kept occasionally trying to reach the command post. That, the sounds from the perimeter bunkers, and the birds and monkeys were the only noises. The sound of the snoring, of course, increased. Looking to the top of the bunker, I saw that the Thai guards had gone to sleep. I didn't bother to wake them. Some noise started up in the far corner of the bunker and when I checked on it, it was Sgt. Coyne, the club NCO, who had started a crap game.

I wondered what the hell was going on in the ops office. Joe later told me that Sheets and Gunn spent the whole time in their helmets and flak jackets. Hudson and Sutton rooted themselves in the message room where they anxiously waited for any change in the DEFCON status. Gunn, delighted to be back in some form of command, after having been the target of dozens of rather harsh attacks from the airmen earlier in the evening, spent much of his time pacing up and down the office, hand always on his pistol, saying something like "We've got to be prepared to sacrifice. It's a keystone of successful military operations. You must be willing to sacrifice something to obtain an objective. If we don't hear anything soon, I recommend we send out a patrol to insure the security of the landing strip. We must be prepared to sacrifice."

Most of the junior officers were assigned to sitting in front of the scopes, even though there was little air traffic. Bob Saunders, though, had been removed from them and was assigned as officer-in-charge of the nap room which was at the rear of the building. Joe said he had looked there once, and the place was scattered with sleeping airmen. Except for Bob, who sat wide awake at the far end of the room, his eyes glued to the rear door and his hand on his pistol.

At the hour and a half point, I began yawning and sat down against the wall of the bunker. The moon had won the fight with the clouds and was now illuminating the entire site in a gray glow. There were absolutely no noises by then; the birds and monkeys seemed to have given up; the crap game was over (as usual, Sgt. Coyn had wiped out anyone foolish enough to play with him. He once told me that the ledger of his own bets contained more entries than the one he kept for the club's accounts). I looked out into the grounds again, letting my eyes wander about. A slight breeze began to move some of the trees, but it didn't do much for the heat. I removed my helmet and put my hand to my head; my hair was matted down wet against my skull. I looked at the helmet. With it on, I thought, I must have appeared a ridiculous sight: slacks, loafers, sport shirt, holster, pistol and a helmet. I quietly laughed at myself. Back out in the area I could make out the ops building very clearly. Did I just see a flash of light in the rear of it?

The crack of gunfire tore across the site before my thought was complete. I jumped up and back from the bunker entrance, fumbling for my bullets. My hands shook, and I kept dropping the rounds. Sgt. Puckett dropped his radio and began yelling, "Heah they come, heah they come!" I could hear the sound of clips being inserted into the M-16's which frightened me nearly as much as the thought of someone on the outside of the bunker firing on us. And that, I assure you, frightened me a lot.

The silence following the shot was more profound than any before it. We waited. I noticed I was silently counting to myself. When I reached twenty, the loudspeakers began crackling.

"Attention in the area, attention in the area. We have been returned to DEFCON 3, DEFCON 3. I repeat, we have been returned to DEFCON 3. The alert is over, the alert is over. Return your weapons and go back to the party. Go back to the party." The voice was Joe's.

I stayed with Sgt. Puckett to insure that all of the weapons and the clips were returned. When that was finished, I headed for the ops office, stopping in the orderly room to hide my gear again in the back of my desk.

I would have liked a drink, but I wanted to find out what the hell the gunfire had been, so I didn't go back to the club right away. Smiley, who was one of the first back to the bar, told me that when he got there, the bartenders, waiters, cooks waitresses, bar-girls and band were still having a party, and it was obvious they had been going at it since the alert started. Most of them were smashed. The band was still blaring out with American rock music; both Joy and her sister were stark naked and go-go dancing on the stage. It made one feel sorry to have missed it.

I went instead to the ops office which was in chaos. Hudson, Gunn, and Sheets stood in the center of the room yelling and waving their arms about. Gunn and Sheets were still in their helmets and flak jackets, pistols on their hips. Hudson stood in the center and had moved his hands to his face where he kept twisting his features about. Joe sat at his desk, and when I entered, he greeted me with raised eyebrows. Sgt. Pol was against one wall and he saluted me. In the far corner, his face red, the only one in uniform also with his helmet still on, sat Bob.

Sheets said something about, "I will immediately develop a firearms operation course."

"It's time," said Gunn, "that some of our personnel, officers included," he looked at me and I smiled, "realized this is not a country club. We are in a combat zone, pardner." I nodded and he looked away from me.

I edged my way over to Joe and whispered to him, "Joe, what the hell happened?"

He shifted in his seat and whispered back as Sheets and Gunn kept bellowing alongside Hudson. "We had just got the word that we had been returned to DEFCON 3 and were about to sound the all clear. Little Bobby stepped out the back door to look around and he tripped on the steps. For some fool reason he reached for his pistol, and when he hit the ground, he squeezed the trigger. Luckily it didn't hit him or anyone else. But Jesus, you should've seen this place. Sheets and Gunn both start waving their pistols around, and when Hudson comes running out of the message room, he sees those two and hits the floor immediately. One of the airmen comes running in from out back and says Bobby has just fallen and accidentally fired his pistol. Gunn and Sheets just kept standing there with their thirty-eight's out and their mouths open, so I grabbed the P.A. system and made the announcement. They've been yelling at each other ever since."

I looked over at Bob. As I caught his eye, I gave him the "thumbs-up" sign and winked. He chose to ignore me and straightened his helmet.

Gunn and Sheets finally stopped yelling and started to remove their battle gear. Hudson came over to me. As he approached, he tugged at the crotch of his pants, and

I wondered if he might not have dropped a little fecal matter when the shot was fired. His voice was measured and fairly distinct. "Lieutena't Doyle."

"Yes, Sir."

"I wan' yuh tuh go onnuh TDY tuh Bangkok very soon. Fin' sum reason. Check onnuh BX supplies or sumthin'. I don't care wha'." He pointed over his shoulder to Bob. "Take Lieutena't Sanners with yuh. Get'im laid, anythin', but get'im straighten' out, 'for he drives me crazy. Please."

CHAPTER TWELVE

BEFORE ARRANGEMENTS COULD BE MADE for my mission to Bangkok, I was able to get in two more lessons with Sunida. They had been going extremely well—she proved to be a continually tough task master—and we were now conducting most of the lessons in Thai. She had decided I should first learn to speak the language in a rudimentary fashion, after which I could attempt to master its forty-four character alphabet. In any event, I was enjoying my minor fluency and felt mild ecstasy when I was able to make myself understood in some circumstances. But that is another matter. At the end of my Monday evening lesson, I smiled at Sunida and said, in Thai, "Would you have dinner with me on Wednesday before our lesson?"

She smiled instantly, her head jumping back and then paused. Her delight, I was afraid, was more with my fluency than with my offer, so before she could demure, I added, "We can meet in the village, at Tipalow's and then come here to study."

She hesitated still and looked away from me, her face turning red. I worried that I may have embarrassed her (I should have checked on the protocol with Sak). But in the end, she returned with her smile to me and said, in English, "Yes, I will meet you. Thank you very much."

We met. I, a little nervous, was at Tipalow's fifteen minutes before our date. The waiter picked a table for me, but I explained to him that I was waiting for a girl to meet me, and he gave me nicer table against the wall. He smiled when he sat me and gave me a somewhat lecherous grin, saying, "Teeloc, ching-ching?" I smiled and insisted that it was only a friend and not a sweetheart, but he only grinned. I declined to have a Singha while I waited which surprised the waiter.

When Sunida arrived, she was greeted warmly by the waiter and several of the patrons, but their faces turned blank when she declined the table offered and made her way to me. I rose and pulled out the chair for her and told her that she looked especially pretty that evening. She blushed slightly and smiled too, but she refused to look directly into my eyes.

After a few moments I asked the waiter to come over to our table, but he took his time in coming, and I began to suspect he was not very pleased to see me there with a "nice" girl. As he stood there sullenly taking our orders, I became confirmed in my suspicion. The warmth with which he had greeted Sunida had also disappeared and our service for the rest of the dinner was only perfunctory. When we left, I tried the device I best knew to elicit some smiling "thank you's" from the waiter, a big tip, but this too failed.

Yet it was not an entirely unpleasant evening. The food, despite the surly service, was still good. We had some pigeon egg soup, barbecued pork on sticks, egg rolls, fried beef and noodles, and lastly fried rice with pork. Sunida drank tea with her meal, and I had Singha. I debated beforehand whether it would be polite to drink beer in front of her, but there is nothing that goes so well with those foods, so my sensual side won out.

And we talked. We ate for nearly an hour, and despite the waiter and the kitchen staff, which occasionally peeked out to see the farang with the school teacher, we did hold a long and friendly conversation. I had previously, in my hours of talking to her in the library found most of the bare facts of her life, that she had been born and raised in Nakorn Sarang, had helped her mother and father run their small shop since she was little more than an infant. They had insisted she remain in school, where she proved to be an outstanding student. Yet without any money, it was nearly impossible for her to hope to attend any of the universities in Chiang Mai or Bangkok, and when her applications for scholarships seemed to disappear in the government bureaucracies, she felt fortunate that she was able to attend the teacher's college. Still, it was a source of great pride to her family when she left to teach in Pitchit. Also, in our library conversations, she had told me much about the many Thai customs and legends, and recommended English language history books for me to read, and, of course, with great discipline, was teaching me to speak her language. But she had never gone beyond the roughest outline of her past, or talked about the future, or, either, dared to be so impertinent as to ask me about my life. So this evening, we finally did talk, sometimes in Thai, but mostly in English, since hers was so good, and my Thai still halting and groping. It facilitated the flow of the conversation.

"What do you plan to do in the future?"

"Someday, when I can afford it, I go back to Pitchit to teach."

I was polite enough not to ask her when that might be. "Why not teach in Nakorn Sarang? Why do you have to go to Putchit?"

"There are people there, friends."

"People, friends, you have a boy friend there?"

"Oh, no, but many friends, all my cousins, men and women." The Thais use the work "cousin" broadly, often to refer to a good friend.

"You like to teach?"

"Oh, yes, very much. It is very important for Thailand to have good teachers. When I was small, if it were not for very nice teacher who worked hard with me, I would not have stayed in school. Now I would work in store or in fields. When I grow old, I would bend over and chew betel. And my teeth would be red."

"You were sorry to leave your job in Pitchit?"

"Oh, yes, very. It was very sad. Some of my cousins very mad at me for leaving, but there was no…" Her eyes and voice drifted away at this point, while I coughed slightly and then mentioned how good the egg rolls were.

"When you go back to America, what will you do?"

"Oh, I have to stay in the Air Force for two more years, then, oh, I don't know. Maybe work for a large company, maybe teach school. I just don't know, maybe I'll even go back to school."

"You don't know? You went to university, yes?'

"Yes."

"What did you study?"

"English."

"You learn to speak English?" In the university?"

"Oh, no, no, I studied English literature, you know, the great books, the stories and poems."

"Oh, so you like to write stories and poems."

"Oh, no, I'm not very good at that. I just like to read."

"If you go to the university, I think you study what you want to be so you may become something."

"Well, yes, that's true. It's just I kept changing my mind, and, well, I never gave it too much thought."

"Did you study to become soldier?"

"No, no, I just sort of became one. It sort of just happened. Anyway, I'm not really a soldier. I'm in the Air Force, and I don't expect to ever see any action." (I have noticed that when pinned down for an answer as regards my approach to life, I don't always manage to give a very impressive account of myself.) It was, I felt, a good time to talk of other things.

"What do you think of the Americans?"

"I like many, but some, some, I think, scare me."

"Are you glad we're here?"

"I am happy to have met you."

"But you wish the Americans were not here."

"Sometimes they are loud and big. I think they don't like Thai people."

"What do you think would happen if we were not here?'

"My government says Chinese and Vietnamese would come to Thailand."

"Do you believe that?"

"You know Thailand was never colony. We not like Burma, Laos, Cambodia and Vietnam. I do not think we ever will be."

"Do you like the Chinese?"

"There are many Chinese in Thailand, you know. They own most stores. They are the businessmen."

"Do you like them?"

"Some Chinese I like, but I do not like many businessmen. For many years my father must work for Chinaman to sell his rice. That is why he is poor man."

I would have liked to ask her more about her feelings toward the war and the Americans, but I sensed she was uneasy talking to me about it. She found it hard to understand that I was in the Air Force, but did not feel a part of it, and I don't think she entirely trusted me with her feelings about these matters. Certainly she would not have dared to express doubts about the war or about her own government's policies with a Thai soldier. People disappearing in the middle of the night, while perhaps not as common as in Stalinist Russia and Hitler Germany, was not an unheard of occurrence in Thailand. So for lack of an alternate subject, I turned again to the food and commented on the quality of the beef and noodles.

"You say you not married, yes?" I had said that many times, but she had never pursued the subject any farther.

"No, I'm not married."

"You have fiancée?"

"No."

"You have girlfriend then?"

"No, no one special. In fact, I'm not even writing to any girl."

"But when will you marry?"

I coughed on a noodle. "Marry? I don't know. When I meet a girl that I love, I guess. Maybe never. I never thought about it much."

"But you must marry someday, yes? You must raise family."

"Well, I guess so, but I don't know. It will just happen someday, if it's going to happen, I suppose." I began to sense that the rather haphazard structure of my life plans was proving an anathema to Sunida.

"When will you marry?" I asked.

"I think in about one year."

"One year? Who will you marry?"

"I don't know, but then it will be time to marry."

"Time to marry? Where will he be from? Will he be a Thai?"

"Oh, yes, of course he will be Thai, and he will be from Nakorn Sarang or Pitchit. I think he will be teacher, but it does not matter, just it will be time."

Our dinner was nearly through by then, and I too was drinking tea. I waved for the waiter to bring the check, and when he had done so and I was paying him, I tried to regain his friendship by highly praising the food. Sunida joined in the praise as well, but we failed to crack the grim lines of his face. As I said, even my oversized tip failed. As we walked out through the large open door, the busboy and the samlow drivers, who had all greeted her when she entered, now ignored her. She appeared to notice the slights less than I did, and when she got on her bicycle to start for home, she smiled at me and said, "Thank you, Jim, for a very nice dinner."

On my Honda, I again followed her to her home where I was greeted by old Thanom and Churai before they retired to their room with their radio. Sunida very professionally re-assumed her role of teacher and seriously and with strict discipline pushed me through my lesson. When it was over, I watched her as she wiped clean Hentrickson's blackboard and piled her books under the same.

"Sunida, you are a very good teacher. I don't pay you very much. Why do you work so hard on my lessons?"

She sat down across the table from me. "What should I do? You pay me to teach you. I have pride as teacher to do good job."

"But sometimes I don't think the Thais work as hard for a farang as for a Thai. They like to take it easy.

She laughed slightly. "Oh yes, that is true, of course. But this is different work. I am a teacher, and," she paused and smiled at me, "I was very happy when you came to me and say you would like to learn to speak my language."

Then I did something which to this day I still wonder about. Was I wrong? Was I too impulsive? Did I assume too much? I reached out across the table and softly placed my hand upon hers. I stared at our hands for seconds, several of them, noticing that my pink flesh did not too harshly clash with her lovely bronze skin. When I looked at her face, it was blank but she unhesitatingly met my eyes with hers, and we looked carefully at each other. Her lips parted and slowly smiled, and gently removing her hand from beneath mine, she said, "Good night, Jim, and thank you again."

"Good night, Sunida," and I quickly left.

It was to me, of course, a wonderful evening and I was, the next afternoon, not prepared, while I sat at my desk and checked my TDY orders to Bangkok (I would be getting the midnight train since Hudson couldn't wait for the next plane to get little Bobby out of his hair), that Sak should ask to speak to me about Sunida, and said she had asked him to tell me she could no longer give me Thai lessons.

"What?"

"Yes, Sir. She says she is very sorry, but the can do no more. She also say it will not help to talk to her. That is all that she say, Sir."

"I don't get it. Do you know anything more about this, Sak?"

He looked down and even though he said, "No, Sir," I knew that he did.

"Sak, tell me what you know. This is not fair to anyone."

"Sir, that is all she tell me," but after he paused, he looked up and continued, "but, Sir, I hear many things in town this morning. Many people say she have dinner with you at Tipalow's. They see her there. You buy dinner, drink beer."

"I drank beer, she drank tea."

"Of course, Sir, but they still say what they want. Some people say, 'Sunida is G.I. whore.'"

"What? How the hell...?"

"Sir, does not have to be true, but people still say so. Sunida, she hears this, she is very frightened. You know she has classes for children at night."

"Yes."

"I think she is afraid children cannot come to class with her again if she is seen with you."

"Oh, for Christ's sake."

I found her alone in the library, and I am afraid I greatly embarrassed her. Of course she refused to accept my pleas which she had hoped I would have had the courtesy not even to make. I first suggested that we not have dinner together again, but that we still continue the lessons, but she remained firm. Neither of us mentioned the miserable rumors that were at the heart of the matter, but we were obviously well aware of them. After nearly a half an hour of incessant entreaties, and a point where I nearly had her in tears, she agreed to continue the lessons, but in the future, they would be conducted in the orderly room, immediately after work. It was understood, but unsaid, that we should never again be seen in the village together.

But there was a piece of lead in my stomach when she left that evening, and when I went home to pack my things, and when I returned to the site to lock up my Honda and to wait for the midnight train. She had, I knew, only given in because she was afraid her job at the site would otherwise be in jeopardy, and although I would never have fired her, I did consciously let her think I would. Which I suppose goes at least a little ways to explain why I sat in the club and drank bourbon and water till eleven-thirty, when, along with Bob Saunders, I got one of the air policemen to drive us to the railroad station where I squeezed myself into an undersized compartment and immediately fell asleep.

CHAPTER THIRTEEN

"THE KING OF THAILAND HAS thirty wives and over one hundred children." I opened my eyes and looked across the compartment. The train was approaching Bangkok, and the early rays of the sun were coming through our window. Bob sat across from me, the light fully on his face and reflecting off his glasses. He looked like he had been awake a long time.

I pulled myself up in my bed. "Now where the hell did you hear that horse shit?"

"Betty wrote me about it. She saw *The King and I* on TV a couple of weeks ago." He continued to look out the window. We were on the outskirts of the city, and not unlike American cities, the area along the railroad tracks was not a particularly attractive one. Bob kept staring out the window. As we passed a shack, off which some old man was urinating, he turned to me. "Betty said that what improvements that Thailand has made—it was called Siam in the movie, but it's the same place—are because of an English lady who was hired to tutor the King's kids, but who ended up running the country."

"What the hell are you talking about?"

"She was played by Deborah Kerr." He looked back out the window.

I couldn't listen to Bob on an empty stomach. I put on my pants and went out into the hallway and down to the bathroom where leaning over the basin, I was able to brush my teeth and wash my face. On my way back to our compartment, I ordered some fried rice with egg and had some tea sent to us. Naturally, Bob didn't eat any of his, which was fine with me. I ate both servings.

By the time I got a taxi at the railroad station, it was already getting hot. As we made our way through the traffic and towards the Nana Hotel, Bob said, "It's banned in Thailand, I learned."

"What is?"

"*The King and I.*"

"For good goddamned reason."

The hotel, at Bob's request, assigned us adjoining rooms, which meant that as soon as he had unpacked, he was knocking at my door. I answered it in my underwear. He had already gotten into uniform, his 1505's with ribbons. I noticed he had added the Vietnamese Service ribbons we were authorized to wear after six months in Southeast Asia. Along with his marksmanship ribbons, it gave him a second row.

"You have a marksmanship ribbon?"

"Yes, of course." Bob seemed to ignore my amazement. He entered and looked around my room running his hand along the edges of the desks and window sills.

"Bob, are you looking for microphones?" He stopped checking out the room and sat down.

"Well, where do we go first, Jim?"

"Bob, I don't know about you, but I really don't sleep all that well on trains, especially on these Thai trains with the five foot beds. So if it's all the same to you, I'm going to rack out till this afternoon"

He appeared somewhat disconcerted. "Oh." He stood up, took his cap off and stuck it in his belt. I went to the door and opened it for him. In it, he paused. "Jim, shouldn't we get working. Isn't that what we're here for?"

"Bob, we're here for three days and two nights. The work we've got to do, I can take care of in about two hours. The rest of the time is for rest and recreation. The proverbial "R n' R." You've heard of that, right?" He nodded. "Well, I'm starting with the rest. I advise you to do the same."

"Gee, I don't think I'll be able to sleep. What should I do?"

My worst fears of the trip were beginning to materialize. "Oh, shit, Bob, I don't know. Take a tour of the city or something. You can get on one from the hotel lobby."

"But what should I see?"

I was into my bed by then. "I don't care. Any of them, the temples, the markets, TIMLAND, any of them. They're all good." With that, I rolled over and pulled the sheets up over my head. I heard the door close as Bob exited.

But I was up immediately, going to the door and opening it. Bob was waddling his way toward the elevator. I called to him to come back to my room. He closed the door behind him when he entered.

"Have you decided to come with me, Jim? I think that would be better."

"No, goddamnit, I am not going with you, but let me give you a couple of points of advice."

Bob, always respectful of such things as advice, too his cap off again and sat down.

"Bob, first, don't go wandering around town in your uniform. You'll end up paying higher prices for things, and people don't like it anyway. It doesn't do the Thais' ego much good to see a bunch of big Americans parading about their capital wearing uniforms." I winced at calling Bob big, but let it ride. "And one more thing, I'd cut out that shit about *The King and I* while you're here. That story takes place about a hundred or so years ago and any resemblance it ever had to reality is long gone. In case you haven't noticed, that picture you keep seeing everywhere, including in the hotel lobby, is of the King. His name is Bumiphol and he has only one wife, and her name is Sirikit. That's her in the same picture. He's a direct descendant of King Monkgut, who is the character in the movie. The Thais have deep respect for all of them, and will take great offense if they hear you babbling about the movie."

"I'm sure they wouldn't if they saw the movie."

"I think the general opinion of most historians is that Mrs. Leonowens had an over inflated view of her own importance and a decidedly faulty memory."

"Who?"

"Mrs. Anna Leonowens. That's the part Deborah Kerr plays in the movie. The story is based on her journals. Since her journals, a book called *Anna and the King of Siam,* a movie by that same name and *The King and I* are all disrespectful of the king, they're all banned here."

"How did you get to know all this, Jim?"

"Bob, this may be hard to comprehend, but I read about it. In books that are in our library in Nakorn Sarang."

Bob stared at me and stood up. "Oh."

After finally getting back into bed and once again pulling the covers up over my head, I tried to figure out how I was going to deal with Bob for the next two days. I couldn't keep pulling the sheets over my head. Hudson had finally dreamed up enough of an excuse for me to visit Bangkok: To straighten out administrative problems with the BX center. There were no real problems. I was not lying when I told Bob that it would take no more than two hours. Hudson managed to slip Saunders' name onto the orders, and then I had the unofficial orders repeated to me: "Get that goddamned little pain-in-the-ass laid, massaged, jerked-off, anything, but get him straightened out before he drives us all crazy." (I, in writing this, have taken the liberty of clarifying Hudson's normal garbled speech in hopes of emphasizing its urgency.) Looking back, I'm amused at Hudson's analysis of Bob's obtuseness and his proposed cure: Sex. What else could it be, Hudson must have thought, that's what I want, that's what he must want. But I am confounded by my own rapid and apparently complete compliance in the application of the analysis. Battle fatigue (the battle being the war with Hudson and Company) is the only answer. So, lying there, that morning in Bangkok, my head under the covers, I was afraid that Bob Saunders already had a running start on driving *me* crazy.

I also thought of Sunida, but that didn't help either.

Things got worse. I got up around noon, dressed and went down to the coffee shop for a hamburger and a beer. I must admit that one of the delights of a visit to Bangkok was the opportunity to enjoy some decent, simple American style food. Our regular Saturday lunch hamburgers were deadly, crashing into your stomach, and then showing up early the next morning in an unscheduled rush to the toilet. After finishing my lunch, I returned to my room and changed into my uniform. Best to get what work there was out of the way quickly. I called Bob's room and told him to meet me in the lobby. He was there when I got down. As we rode out to the BX we talked.

"Did you go on a tour?"

"Oh yes, I went to TIMLAND." TIMLAND was a Thai version of Disneyland. The letters stood for Thailand in Miniature Land. It included exhibitions of pottery making, silk weaving, lumber cutting with elephants doing the log rolling. There was a snake farm where some cobras were kept constantly enraged, and visitors were able to pet a giant python. The last stop on the tour was the theater where a performance of Thai classical dancing was followed by a Thai boxing match.

"What did you think of it?"

"The boxers fight dirty."

"Bob, it's not a matter of Thai boxers fighting dirty. That is Thai boxing. Your feet are considered to be weapons the same as your fists. Those are just the rules of Thai boxing."

"Well, that may be, but you still shouldn't kick when you fight. If they would only fight fair, I don't think they'd be very good fighters. Then anyone could beat them."

As I've mentioned before, conversations with Bob are not really worth pursuing. I should not have bothered to respond to his first statement. But then I don't learn easily. I continued to make mistakes.

"What did you think of the classical dancers?"

"Boy, that stuff is really boring. I fell asleep."

I thought of the dancers. All of those graceful curves and the arched wrists. I put my head back and closed my eyes, feigning sleep till we got to the BX.

The afternoon meeting with BX officials passed without any problems. And well it should have. There was absolutely no reason for the meeting in the first place. I thought for a moment the BX officer was about to ask, "What, Lieutenant Doyle, did you request this meeting for?" but the look passed. I think he was quite used to spending wasted hours with representatives of upcountry bases who needed an excuse to visit Bangkok.

That evening I took Bob to the restaurant in the Imperial Hotel for Kobe steaks, thick delicious slabs of beef from cattle that rumors claimed were fed on beer and hand patted day and night by some unfortunate peasant. In any case they were always huge and tender. Bob seemed genuinely overwhelmed.

"Gee, that's the best looking piece of meat I've seen since I left home. That's one thing I sure do miss over here, a good steak. Boy, oh boy, that was Betty's specialty, charcoal grilled steaks."

I suggested a bottle of wine with the steak, and Bob mentioned something about having known an Italian family once, and "they drank a lot of wine." Instead, he had a Coke. I ordered a bottle of rose anyway and drank the whole thing myself. It eased the pain of trying to figure out how I was going to carry out my orders.

Over after-dinner drinks (Bob had another Coke, I had a stinger.), I approached the subject. "Bob, would you like to take a ride over to a massage parlor, or over to a nightclub?"

"Oh, no thanks, I'm going over to the telegraph office. I've heard you can make a phone call to the States from there. I'm going to call Betty." He was correct. Some division or another of Western Union had an office in Bangkok that, for fifteen or twenty dollars, would patch in a telephone call to the States. They were making a windfall business out of the American servicemen taking 'R 'n R' in Bangkok. Regardless, I felt my hopes of accomplishing my assignment were shattered for that evening. It was going to be difficult enough, but after he had talked directly to his wife, he would be impossible.

So outside the Imperial, we took separate taxis. Bob went to the telegraph office, and I went to Max's. Pitsommai was still there, and we sat and had a few drinks. Then we went to the Lido Nightclub and watched the floorshow. Pitsommai enjoyed it, and I had some more drinks. After I had gotten sufficiently drunk, we went to the hotel. Naturally, I was incapable of an erection, and we went directly to sleep.

My phone rang at seven a.m. On my first attempt to answer it, I knocked the whole thing off the nightstand. With Pitsommai's assistance I managed to get the receiver to my ear.

"Aaoowwgh?" (Sometimes I have nightmares about growing up to be another Major Hudson.)

"Jim, are we going back to the BX today?"

"Who is this?"

"Lt. Saunders."

"Who?"

"Jim, it's me, Bob."

"What the fuck are you doing on the phone at this time of day?"

"I wanted to check on when we were going to get to work."

"Jesus Christ. We are not going to work. We're done, we've finished everything. Besides, it's Saturday. Now we rest and recreate, remember? And Bob, let me give you some more advice."

"Yes?"

"When in Bangkok, never call my room before noon." I hung up. My first thought was to go back to sleep, and I pushed my face into the pillow. But by then I was sober, and Pitsommai was there in the bed with me. She had turned her back to me and pushed her face back down into the pillow. She laughed when I put my hand on her hip and kissed her shoulder. Jesus, she had the most beautiful skin, golden and warm.

"Big, handsome American thinks he is man now, no?"

She turned and smiled at me. "Big, handsome, American need to brush teeth very much, no?"

I bounded out of bed and into the bathroom.

Later, after the love making and a short nap, we talked some. Pitsommai, like most bar-girls I knew, was very observant when she wanted to be. "Jim, you drink but no laugh, just sit, get drunk. Why so unhappy?"

Well, I wasn't going to be able to tell it to my mother, or to the chaplain, so I told her in abbreviated fashion about my "mission" with Bob. I did not tell her about Sunida, which I think was also part of the reason I drank, but didn't laugh.

"Jim, Putsommai have girl friend maybe your friend like."

"I don't think so, besides my problem is getting him to Max's to start with."

"Jim, Pitsommai have friend at Max Bar ten o'clock, s'okay? You try have your friend too, no?"

For the rest of the day, I drove myself buggy worrying about finding some way of getting Bob to Max's. We spent the afternoon lying around the pool, at least I did. Bob took some time for a tour of the Marble Temple and the Temple of the Emerald Buddha, which he didn't like because you had to take your shoes off to go inside. "It didn't seem like a very clean thing to do. Besides, someone may have stolen my shoes."

"Did you reach your wife last night?"

"Oh, yes. It was nearly midnight here when I got through. I woke her up."

"What time was it there?"

"Eleven a.m. She asked me not to call so early if I call again."

I spent a good part of the last hours of the afternoon wondering if it was best to try and find Bob a girl, or just to drown him in a canal. I was beginning to feel that I had passed the maximum amount of time one can spend with Bob Saunders without going crackers.

Naturally, when I turned to Bob after dinner (spaghetti and meatballs at Mario's on Gaysorn Road—wine for me, Coke for Bob) and asked him if he would like to stop by Max's for a drink or two, he blankly stared at me and did what I'd least expect. He said, "Okay, I've never been to a bar in Bangkok before."

At Max's, Pitsommai joined us at a table and was introduced to Bob. He took her offered hand somewhat reluctantly, but her obvious cleanliness and the smell of her perfume must have quickly won him over because he held on to her hand for several seconds, and a somewhat bemused look came over his face. He started to speak, and I could imagine him asking her where she went to college or where she worked. Of course, he surprised me.

"How do you like Thailand?" That was Bob speaking, not Pitsommai.

She looked over at me, her eyes wide and quizzical. I shrugged my shoulders, and she said, a little uncertainly, "Yes, very much, thank you. It is my home."

Bob nodded. "Yes, I thought so." Then he looked around the room. Pitsommai stared at him, waiting for him to say something more, but I knew he was done with that subject.

After several quiet moments, Bob got up to go to the bathroom. While he was gone, Pitsommai told me that the short girl at the end of the bar was her friend. If I wanted her to join us, I should go over and ask her. She had agreed to stay with Bob as long as possible, but if nothing worked out at all, I owed her five dollars. It seemed like a bargain.

"Hello, my name is Jim, Pitsommai's friend. Would you like to meet a rich American?" She turned, looking up at me and smiled. It was an extremely pleasant smile which lit up her small, round face. She laughed a little, but it was not a snicker. She had about her a very delightful exuberance which I immediately liked. She reminded me of a small child.

I can't say I thought they were getting along famously. She sat down next to Bob and Pisommai introduced everyone. "This Renu, this Jim, This Bob." Renu smiled, but I didn't feel that Bob was as charmed by it as I was.

"What kind of name is Renu?"

She looked at Pitsommai as Pitsommai had previously looked at me. "It is Thai name."

Again Bob nodded. "Yes, I thought so."

When Renu asked him if he were married, and he brought out his little packet of pictures of his wife, I leaned over and suggested to Pitsommai that we go somewhere to dance. I felt there was little more I could do at Max's.

Pitsommai and I had a fine night at the Starlight on New Road. I drank a lot, but I also laughed a lot and danced until nearly one in the morning. Even back at the hotel I had a lot of energy—something had been lifted off my back, or more correctly, I had dropped something from my back—and we cavorted in bed till the sun was coming up.

We didn't get up until after noon. I had a light breakfast sent up, and it was nearly two before Pitsommai took her leave. I gave her a "gift" of sixty dollars and told her I would write and let her know when I would next be in Bangkok. As I was putting her in a taxi, she stopped me and looked straight at my eyes. "Jim, you nice man, but drink too much." I was more touched by her concern than by the words themselves. Certainly it was not triumph of observation to note that I tended to overindulge, but to be concerned about it, now that was nice.

On the way back to my room, I stopped at Bob's to remind him that the train for Nakorn Sarang left at four p.m. There was no answer, but I didn't overly concern myself with it, figuring he might have decided to take another tour.

At three-fifteen, I knocked on his door again, but there was still no response. This time, a little worried, I called the switchboard to see if Bob had left any messages. The girl at the desk said that Lt. Saunders had checked out before noon.

I had only about fifteen minutes before I should have been leaving for the train myself. Yet in that time I queried everyone possible, but to no avail. It wasn't just that they didn't know where he'd gone, there was no one who even professed to having ever seen such a person. All my descriptions of a short, blond haired, American with glasses met with a blank stare, or shrugged shoulders. Only the desk log even indicated that he had ever been near the Nana Hotel, and it clearly showed that he had checked out at 11:30 a.m.

Traffic was very heavy, and I nearly missed the train myself, so I didn't have time to be searching the platform for Bob. He was nowhere to be seen in the first class section, but then it was a big train, and he could be anywhere on it. Besides, he was supposed to be a big boy and knew what time the train left.

By the time the train was half way to Nakorn Sarang and I had consumed two liters of Singha and plate of fried rice, I was acknowledging to myself the fact I secretly hoped that Bob had missed the train. I wondered if Hudson would be as pleased to learn I had merely lost Bob Saunders rather than have had him sexually worked over. On that thought I invited the two Thai businessmen sitting across the aisle to join me in two more liters of Singha.

CHAPTER FOURTEEN

WHEN THE TRAIN ARRIVED IN Nakorn Sarang, I was, bag in hand, waiting on the steps, ready to jump off. Eight hours on a hot, overcrowded, rough-riding train is too long a time to encourage the luxury of casually disembarking. It was midnight, and I began immediately to push my way through the crowd that always seemed to be in the railroad station, pushing my way towards the samlow stand. I reached one, gave the driver my bag, and climbed in saying, "Pan Ngarm House, hah baht, okay?" The driver, who I knew and whose name was Chan turned and smiled. I knew the five baht I offered was well over the standard rate, but by this time, all I wanted was to get home. I closed my eyes.

"Jim, Jim, wait for me." Well, Bob Saunders had not missed the train after all. I turned and saw him trying to make his way through the crowd. He had one arm wrapped around his suitcase, and with his free hand he was holding his flight cap on. He was, otherwise, dressed in civilian clothes.

"How much should I pay for a samlow?"

"Why do you have your hat on?"

"Is two baht too much?"

"That's not enough. Why do you have your hat on?"

"Isn't it? I guess not, after all, it's for two, maybe ten baht."

"What do you mean two? I'm not riding with you. And why the hell do you have your hat on?"

"No, of course not, I didn't mean that. It's for Renu."

"Who?"

"Renu, the girl you introduced me to last night," and then, shifting the grip on his bag, and releasing the lock he held on his hat, he turned and motioned to someone standing behind him. The girl stepped out of the dark towards me, and she was, as Bob said, the girl I had introduced him to the night before. Or was it the night before the night before. Confusion was setting in. I think she still had on the same mini dress that she had worn whenever the hell it was I introduced her to him, but there was a new flower in her long black hair, and she looked remarkably fresh for having just made the miserable train trip.

"What?"

"Renu has come to Nakorn Sarang to live with me."

"What?"

"I plan to bring her back to the U.S. and marry her."

"What?"

"As soon as I divorce Betty, of course."

"What?"

Bob managed to find a samlow and was loading Renu and their bags into it, instructing the driver, "House, Lt. Saunders, ten baht, chop-chop." As they started to move, he put his hand to his head to hold his cap on. Then as they were abreast of me, they both looked over and smiled.

I said, "What?"

"Oh, Jim, you know what?"

"What?"

"I forgot to pack my hat."

"What?"

"That's why I'm wearing it."

"What?"

"You asked about it."

"What?"

"See you tomorrow, Jim."

"What?" Then they were gone.

Back at our bungalow, Joe was not home, but I found a bottle of bourbon in his closet, and, after stripping down to my underwear, sat underneath the fan in the living room with a tall glass of bourbon and water in my hand. The ceiling light was on, and two geckels kept pursuing flies and moths across the ceiling. This seemed to be enough to entertain me for the first drink. On the second one, more bourbon, less water, I dug out an old copy of the Far East edition of *Newsweek*. That lasted me through the third drink, bourbon on the rocks. For the fourth one, I was out of ice by the, and I tried to read the paperback that I had with me on the train, but I couldn't make out the words. With a real effort, I could make out the clock on the wall, and noting it was three a.m., I began to wonder why the fuck I was sitting there, in Nakorn Sarang, Thailand, at three o'clock in the morning, in my underwear getting smashed.

Out loud I said to the room, "What?"

That must have at least answered some portion of the question to me because I suddenly seemed to have some plan. I was going to the Argo Bar. My pants and shirt were on the floor where I had left them, but I couldn't find my shoes, so I left in my bare feet.

Fortunately there was a bright moon that night. I looked up and down the street. There were no samlows in sight, so I began to yell for one.

"Samlow!" No response.

"Samlow! Hah baht!" A dog from across the road began to bark.

"Samlow, samlow! Argo Bar, sip (ten) baht!" A light in one of the small bungalows near the street went on.

"Samlow, yee-sip (twenty) baht!" The dog was now right in front of me making at least as much noise as I was.

I yelled for a samlow again. A man was coming out of the house and towards me. I recognized him. It was Pridi, a school teacher who's classes I had visited a few times.

"Pridi, sawadee. I need a samlow so I can go to the Argo Bar. You wannuh come along with me?" The dog was now nipping at my pants cuffs.

"Jim, you drunk. Go bed. Please."

"No, thanks. I gottuh date. D'you see a samlow?"

"No samlows now, too late. Please, go bed."

"I yelled again, "Samlow! Sahm-sip (thirty) baht!"

"Jim, please. Maybe police come, have big trouble."

The dog kept pulling on my cuff, and I fell over, hitting my face on the pavement. Lying there, with my nose resting on the warm tar, I began to consider the possibility that maybe there wouldn't be a samlow for me that night.

Pridi was gently pulling on my arm, "Jim, you okay? Here I help you go bed now. S'okay?" He helped me to my feet. The dog seemed satisfied and had returned to his place under Pridi's bungalow. With Pridi leading me by the arm, I could feel myself heading up the driveway to my bungalow.

"Wait, I'm gonnuh the Argo Bar." And turning, I headed across the street and towards the path that lead through the woods to the Argo. I could hear Pridi following behind me, but once I go into the darkness of the trees, he stopped and called after me. "Jim, Jim, no go, please. Maybe meet cobra."

Now that was something I had not thought of, and I stopped abruptly and turned to look back, but I couldn't see any light in either direction. I knew it must be shorter to go back the way I had come, but of course that would not put me any closer to the bar, and I was still intent on getting there. So I made up my mind to head in that direction and off I went. My foot caught immediately on a tree trunk or something like that and over I went plunging head first through some large ferns into mud. It was not too deep, and I was able to get back up and head off in the direction that seemed most likely to get me to the Argo. I was moving with some ease now and was pleased that I was feeling dry earth under my bare feet. At first, after falling, I was counting my steps, measuring my progress. When I reached twenty, I felt exhilarated and began walking faster; after a time, nearly running.

What my foot tripped over then, I'm not sure, but it was warm and round, and seemed to give some, so I didn't fall down directly. Rather, I began stumbling, my head and shoulders crashing ahead of me, off the path again. My knee hit the ground first, and then my torso crashed over, my face again splashing into the mug. For the first time since I had left the house, I was wondering if I might not ever get to the Argo.

However, when I felt the warm grip under my arm, I began to think I might not ever make it to anywhere again. My face was in the mud, the third time that might that I had found myself lying face down. I was not concerned so much as to when the cobra would bite—that he would bit was certain—but where would he bit me? Would it be a quicker death if he bit me in the neck, or would the arm be best? Could he get his fangs into my back? My wang? A fang in the wang? Maybe I should make an offering: Here, take my hand.

"Jim, you okay?" The warm grip was a hand, and it helped turn me over. The other hand was holding a flashlight and, in the light, I would make out Pridi's face.

I said, "What?' Drunk or sober, my response was becoming quite predictable.

"I go back, get flashlight. Come home now, s'okay?"

I was on my feet by then and wiping the mud off my face.

"Naw, I'm gonnuh Argo Bar."

I turned and quickly headed off again in the direction of the bar before my will faded. Behind me, Pridi was cursing in Thai, but soon he was alongside me, and shining the light into the path before us.

"Jim?"

"What?"

"Why you do this? I think you number one American. No like Major Hudson, no like Sgt. Hunnicut."

"What?"

"What's the matter you? Pridi never see before, Jim make noise in street. Why you do, hey Jim?"

"'Cuz Lt. Saunders is marrying Renu."

"What?" Good, now I had him saying it.

We were getting close to the street, and I could see it rising in front of us. Pridi scrambled up the bank and then reached back to help me up it. When I reached the road, I lay down on my back and closed my eyes. I could feel the adrenalin flowing from me, and even in my state I knew I would have to move quickly if were to complete my evening's plan.

"Jim, Pridi go home now, you come, s'okay?"

I pulled myself up and shook my head, trying to clear the spots from my eyes. With my hands I stretched and pulled the skin of my face, and then ran my fingers through my hair. Then I turned and headed off down the road again. There was still something I had to do that night.

"Sorry, Pridi, I'm gonnuh Argo Bar."

When I looked back, I could see Pridi running off in the opposite direction, obviously planning on going the long way back to his bungalow. I couldn't understand why he wasn't going back through the woods. Strangely enough, the Argo Bar was closed when I got there, its doors and windows tightly shut, but I immediately began pounding on the door and yelling for Papa-san.

"Papa-san, Papa-san! Open up!" There was no reaction, so I waited a few seconds, catching my breath. Then drawing up my energy, I began again. "Papa-san, wake up! I got song-loy (two hundred) baht." I pounded on the door some more, and then went over to a window and began trying to open it. Since my hand was not a very effective crowbar, I went off to look for a stick, but just then, I heard something above me, and looking, I could see Papa-san, his head sticking out a window.

"Loootenin' Jim, what you do?"

"I wan' Malee, song-loy baht."

"Malee no here. Go Maja'Hudson."

"Where's Supatra?"

"Supatra go Chiang Mai, see sister."

"Shit! Gimme any girl."

The window closed for a moment and I could hear some chattering going on behind it. Papa-san finally looked out. This time the window was open less than before.

"Have no girls, too late, go home. Please, Loootenin'."

"Any girl, Papa-san. I got see-loy (four hundred) baht."

"Wait." The window closed again and I could hear the chattering renew itself.

I sat down on the steps to wait. In the rear of the building, I could hear some movement, and when I looked around, a man was standing alongside me. He was thin and wiry and was wearing dark shorts and shirt. A short brimmed straw hat was on his head. Betel stained teeth grinned at me through a wide mouth. Thieves often stayed in the rear of the bar, sometimes offering to clean up the place for a night's rest, or if they had just robbed someone, maybe even having a girl. My screaming about how much money I had on my probably woke him, and now he was coming to relieve me of it before Pap-san brought me a girl. He reached with his right hand around to his hip pocket, and I stood up, trying to decide which way to run before he came at me with his knife.

"G.I. need samlow?" With the flashlight he now had in his hand, he swung the beam around, and it rested on a rather rundown old samlow that had been pushed back into the bushes.

As my breath came pouring out from the deepest part of my chest, I laughed weakly and said, "Kopkun kop."

"Sip baht?"

"Kop."

As I was beginning to consider this piece of good fortune (I had not yet considered how I would get home), the door of the bar opened and Papa-san was calling my name and waving me over to him. He was filling the entire opening with his body, so I couldn't see if anyone was behind him.

"Loootenin', have only one girl."

"Good, who is it?"

"No can tell, you take, pay hah-loy (five hundred) baht."

I shook my head violently. "Oh no, too much, too much!"

The door shut immediately. I was pounding on it before Papa-san could begin to close the latch, and I was screaming again.

"Okay, okay, but Papa-san, gimme bottle of Mekong, too."

When the door opened he was grinning. "Is good deal." He went over to the bar and picked out one of the small bottles of whiskey and brought it over to me. Then he waved me into the bar, and as I came in, he flicked on another light. In the corner of the room I could see a short and very fat girl who looked vaguely familiar.

Papa-san said, "Name Suripong. Very good girl." She moved out into the light, and I recognized her.

"Sawadee, Mama-san." For sure enough, it was Papa-san's wife. She broke into a big grin, her red teeth showing, and came over and put her arms around me. Her fat body was warm against me, yet I began to feel dizzy, and I reached out for the wall. Mama-san fell against me and pinned me to the wall, holding me up as my legs let go and my shoulders caved over. I could feel the perspiration cold on my face. If I did not shake the weakness of quickly, my evening would be ended, and I would not have accomplished my goal.

I called weakly for the samlow, and both Papa-san and Mama-san helped me into it. Then she climbed up into my lap. Papa-san reached over and gave the driver the ten baht, saying he would pay for the ride. With the slow, grunting starting strides of the driver, we began to move out of the driveway.

When I looked back at Papa-san, he was waving goodbye to us, my five red bills in his hand.

During the ride back to my bungalow, Mama-san kept giggling and threatening to sober me up with her breath. If I was going to do my thing for the night, I would need some of the Mekong, so I reached for the bottle in my hip pocket. It was already half empty. So much for the free samlow ride. There may be things in the future that I will be able to say taste like Mekong, but there has been nothing in my past to compare to the taste. It ripped at my throat, and landed in my stomach like fire. My eyes began to water, and my breath burst forth in long, deep gasps, followed by horrendous coughs which brought up large mouthfuls of phlegm from deep in my throat, but I managed to keep the whiskey down. It was just what I needed.

Back at the bungalow, Mama-san helped me up the stairs and through the door which I had forgotten to lock. Since I had left the lights and the fan on, it probably appeared someone was home. Joe was still not there, and Mama-san and I went straight to my room. After crashing down across my bed, I started to worm out of my clothes without getting up. While I was doing that, she left the room, and I could hear her knocking around in the kitchen. Waiting for her, my eyes kept blinking, and I was threatening to pass out, but still she didn't return. I called for her several times, and, although there was no answer, I could still hear her out there. I pulled myself off the side of the bed and was able with great effort to get out the door. She was sitting at the table drinking a Coke and pushing a large peanut butter sandwich into her mouth. When she saw me standing there stark naked, she spit the sandwich all over the kitchen.

The sun was starting through the windows, laying red light beams against the wall by the time she finally came to my bed. I could feel her large soft breasts and the fat rolls of her stomach against me, and it was warm and comfortable. But there was no possibility that my wang would respond to anything, not even when, in exasperation, Mama-san began to fondle it with both hands. It was as limp as a wet sock fresh from the washer.

"Hey, G.I.," she pleased, "what's matter you. I numba' one pom-pom."

"Mama-san," I said, with a very tired and thick tongue, putting my arms around her and pulling her up so I could look into her face, "I love you. I want to marry you and take you back to America with me." Then having done what I started out to do, I passed out.

CHAPTER FIFTEEN

A POUNDING ON THE DOOR awoke me. It was accompanied by a yelling, "Lieutenant Doyle, Lieutenant, you in there?" The voice was Smiley Burnett's. Looking to my right side, I could see that Mama-san had left, and to my right side, I could see by my clock that it was eleven o'clock.

Smiley was embarrassingly startled when I opened the door with no clothes on. That seems guaranteed to get a reaction. "Hiyuh, Smiley. Is this still Monday, or did I miss that one entirely?"

Burnett entered. "Oh, yes, Sir, it's still Monday all right, and Major Hudson is madder than all hell. Says for you to get your ass right out to the site."

"Yeah, yeah, okay. I've got to take a shower first. You've got the truck, right? So you can wait for me. Make yourself at home. I think there's still some soda and beer in the refrigerator."

The shower, which by that time of morning was lukewarm, felt great. My feet, which were black with mud, took a lot of effort to clean, but, miraculously, there were no cuts. In the other room I could hear Smiley chuckling about something. I let the water pour down over my face for a long time. I scrubbed up an especially lather over my privates and let it rest there for several minutes before turning to the water to rinse. While the shower was still running I started brushing my teeth. I rubbed them so hard my gums began to bleed. Facing the shower, I let the spray wash out my mouth. I dried off, put on my robe and went into the kitchen. Already I could feel a fine cover of sweat forming on my body.

Smiley was sitting at the kitchen table where mama-san had sprayed the peanut butter sandwich not too long before. He was drinking a Coke and there was an even broader grin that usual on his face. My shoes were on the table.

"Where'd you find them?"

Between laughs he managed to get it out that they were under the Cokes in the refrigerator. I said, "Oh," picked them up and went into my room to get dressed. I placed the shoes directly in the hot sunlight, but they were still cold by the time I put them on.

When I entered the orderly room, Hudson saw me immediately and waved me into his office. His face was flushed red, and there were unopened letters from his wife on his desk.

"Wha'thuhhell'sgoin'on?" I thought he was overreacting a little to my being late for work.

"I apologize, sir. I got kind of drunk on the train, and I just couldn't get up this morning."

He stared straight at me. "Wha'thuhhellyuhtalkin'abou'? Iwannuhknowwha'yuh didtuhLooenin'Sanners?"

"What'd I do to Lt. Saunders?" Now I can't really claim that I had forgotten all about the Bob Saunders incident. After all, I did remember that I had Mama-san in my bed as the sun was coming up, and she had been eating my peanut butter. So if I had looked into my mind for the reasons that that had occurred, or like why I had been lying with my face in the mud in the middle of the woods, or on the road in front of Pridi's bungalow, then I'm sure I would have known what major Hudson was talking about. But the cobwebs were still entrenched in my skull, and all I could say was the old and familiar, "What?"

Hudson's hands were beginning to twist, and his speech kept running together. "Goddamnit. I tol'yuhtuhget'imlaid. Tha'sall."

He sat down and began to mumble incoherently to no one in particular. He looked up at me, and I heard him say something about marriage and divorce. Then it all came back. I could see Bob's samlow disappearing into the crowd, one hand around the girl and other holding his cap on.

"You mean he's serious about that crap? Getting married, I mean getting divorced. I mean both. You mean he's already been in here to see you about it?"

Hudson looked up again and shook his head yes.

I slowly sat down and said, "Holy Christ, that fucking lunatic."

Hudson was still looking at me, and I heard him say, rather distinctly, "Lootenin' Doyle, this iz all your goddamn fault."

"What?"

Hudson nodded yes again. "I to'yuhtuh gettim laid. Now he sez he'sgonnuhmarry thuhwhore. He sezyuhknow alluhabou'it. Sezyuhintrodus'im." I looked toward the corner and noticed Sgt. Sutton had entered and was standing there nodding and stroking his moustache.

In those circumstances I somehow felt I should defend myself. "Oh, Jesus, all I did was take him out last night, or the night before last, I'm not sure when. But hell, all I did was take him to Max's Bar over on Patpong. The first girl I saw, I asked her if she wanted to meet a rich American. She said yes. I sat her down at the table with Saunders and left. The last I saw, he was showing her pictures of his wife."

Hudson spread his hands out wide in front of himself as if he were about to catch a beach ball. There was a puzzled look on his face. "But, hesez yuhknowalluhabou'it."

"The next time I saw him was last night, or this morning, or whenever. Downtown, here in Nakorn Sarang. When we got off the train." Sutton now had hands folded across his chest, but his head was still nodding. "And he had this girl with him, the one I introduced him to. Renu, or something like that."

"Renu Wangaboo..la….," said Hudson and began fumbling for a piece of paper on his desk and handed it to me. It was a letter from Bob to Hudson, requesting that "all appropriate procedures be instituted to effect his intention to marry Miss Renu Wandaungsai." I looked at it for several seconds.

"Yeah, I guess that's her. All I knew was the first name. Anyway, it was late and I was tired. He did say something about getting married, but I didn't pay much attention to him, and I went home. I figured he was just joking and didn't mean it." Now at any time, then or now, I knew what I just said was a lie. Bob Saunders always meant exactly what he said, no matter how absurd it was, which was why I had gone home, did as much damage to Joe's bottle of bourbon as I could, risked by life by walking barefoot through the woods at night, and ended up with old, fat Mama-san in my bed as the sun was coming up.

"I guess I was wrong," I said, adding the obvious.

Silence fell over the three of us in the small office. I looked back down at Bob's letter to the Major. It was perfect Bob Saunders. The language was the same as if he had been requisitioning a new pair of sunglasses. And yet, in view of Hudson's twitching face and squirming hands, and Sutton's nodding and insane mustache stroking, there was almost a certain tone of reasonableness to Bob's letter. Not, of course, if you knew him, but just in terms of the tight order of the words, and the clear organization of the paragraphs and ideas, ending with: "The early resolution of this and related matters will most assuredly improve the quality of my job accomplishment and lend credit to myself and the United States Air Force."

On that note, I was able to say, "Granted, Lt. Saunders is out of his mind, but isn't that *his* problem? If this is what he wants to do, so let him. What's the big deal? Anyway, the girl is quite pretty."

Major Hudson's response to that was to put his face in his hand and say, "Guuhhh."

"You, uh, see, Lieutenant," said Sgt. Sutton as he moved more fully into the office, "the United States Air Force, and, I would imagine, the, uh, other branches of the military, uh, while they do not forbid the marriage of, uh, their personnel and those of, uh, foreign nationals—in, uh, this instance, Thai types—does require that the various, uh, circumstances surrounding each, uh, instance of the proposed union, be fully, and, uh, professionally investigated."

I stared up at him in bewilderment. "You mean that anyone wanting to marry a Thai is harassed so much that they'll give up the idea."

Hudson's face was still deep in his hands, and he made his sound again, "Guuhhh".

Sutton's fingers were stroking his moustache, and then he held his hand out in front of his chin as if he were calming the air. "Oh, no, Sir. The purpose of the, uh, pertinent operating procedure in this, uh, operational is to insure, that the, uh, parties involved are, uh, cognizant of their alternates." Sutton paused to admire his own eloquence. "We are only concerned with the, uh, welfare of the three, uh, participants in the occurrence."

"Three?"

"Why, uh, yes, Sir. The military personnel, in this instance, uh, Lt. Saunders, uh, the foreign national, in this instance, uh, the whore, and the United States Air Force."

"War sure makes strange bedfellows, hey?"

"Excuse me, Sir?"

"Nothing, Sarge."

"Major Hudson said, "Guuhhh," again and looked out the window. Some of the hooch girls were walking by and they waved to him. "Ooooh, GenrulMartinizgonnuhhavemyass."

"General Martin, Sir? You mean *the* General Martin."

Hudson nodded. General Millicent "Marty" Martin was Seventh Air Force Commander, hence in charge of all air operations for the entire war. He had a reputation for being a perfectionist, although to some it translated as being a nit-picker. In any case, I seriously doubted if he even knew where Nakorn Sarang was.

"But what's he got to do with this? Surely he can't be bothered with items this small. Jesus, I should hope he's got something more important to worry about."

The explanation was simple. "Lootenin'Sanners' father'nlaw uzedtuhbe Genrul-Martin'saide. 'Ey're stillguhdfrens, still playgolf'nall'atshit." Hudson rubbed his face and made another noise that sounded like, "Aawugggh." Turning on his chair, he looked as directly into my eyes as possible for him. "ThuhdayLootenin'Sannersgot here, KurnulHerder callzme, jus'tuhsay 'atIhadduhfine youngofficer' "Wha'? Hesez, 'Yeah." GenrulMartinjus'call'im-tuhsayso. ThennuhKurnul tellzmeuhwholethin'."

Hudson put his hat on, then took it right off and ran his hands through his hair. "Aaawshit! Whythuh hellyuh think Idi'n't throw thuh littlebasterd outtuhhere lon'time ago?"

I looked around the room and said to the corner of Hudson's, "So General Martin is Bob Saunder's angel?"

"Shirshitshit, whyz'is havetuhhapp'n tuhme?"

At lunch that day, I did something I had certainly never previously done while in Nakorn Sarang. I sought out Bob Saunders and sat down to eat with him. He looked up from Monday's meatloaf as if there were nothing unusual in my doing so. "Hi, Jim, what'd you think of her?"

I spread some ketchup on my meat and said, "You mean, uhm, your teeloc?"

"My fiancée."

With Bob Saunders there was no use sneaking up on a subject. "Bob, are you serious about this shit? I mean do you know what the hell you're doing?"

He nodded with a casual sense of certainty. "Oh, yes, very. I've already been to see Major Hudson about it. And Sgt Chance is ordering the forms for me. They should be here on the next plane from Takhli."

I looked around the room to try and hold on to my senses. Talking to Bob Saunders while suffering a major hangover was always a discomforting business. At one of the airmen's tables, I could see Smiley Burnett energetically explaining something to the others at the table. They kept looking up from their food to glance at Bob.

"Bob, what the hell about Betty?"

He wiped some ketchup from the corner of his mouth. "Oh, I think she'll understand. We've always said that you couldn't be married to someone if you loved someone else more."

Reaching into his shirt pocket, he pulled out a letter and showed the address to me: Mrs. Robert A. Saunders, Box 3491, Bergstrom Air Force Base, Texas.

"I'm mailing this letter to her right now, telling her all about the whole thing. I'll leave it up to her what kind of settlement to make." He pulled his little frown fatigue cap out of his pocket and pulled it down on his head. "She can have anything she wants. She's really a very fine person, and I have great respect for her."

Pushing his chair back, he stood up. "Excuse me, Jim. I've got to go to the post office to mail this letter."

I caught him just outside the chow hall and began to walk along with him to the mailroom. "Bob, let's go have a beer, talk about this some. What do you say?"

"I can't have a drink now. I've got to be on the scope this afternoon." He kept on his steady way to the mailroom.

I suppose I could have grabbed the letter from him, ripped it us and then tried to talk some sense to him. But I didn't think I ever really wanted to do that. The thought of Bob's father-in-law, the Colonel, exploding in some impotent rage tickled me. And Betty, who from her letters I found to be even more dull-witted and obtuse than Bob, elicited little sympathy from me. The added twist that this affair would reach all the way to General Martin, and from there filter its unsettling way through Colonel Herder, Colonel Wolff, and finally down to Major Hudson caused in me a sensation of sweet expectation. Of course, there were some negative considerations. If Hudson's world became difficult, then mine was disrupted at some factor slightly greater than one, and since I prized serenity and tried to foster it, the specter of chaos was certainly unsettling. However, all things considered, I was hoping that Bob's affair would go on at least a little longer. So when Bob reached the mailroom and dropped his letter in the box, I felt a little elated and almost erotically titillated.

Yet, I wanted to talk to Bob more about Renu and his plans. This would answer two needs. First of all, if I was going to give the appearance to Hudson of doing my best, even if a fumbling best, to dissuade Bob, then I would have to know more, and I was still generally astonished by the whole thing and wanted to know what was going on in Bob Saunders' skull. In the back of my mind, I harbored the suspicion it was, as usual, less than met the eye.

"Well, let's have a Coke or something then."

"Okay."

There were few people in the club at that time of day. Sgt. Chance was having a shot and a beer and playing one of the quarter slot machines. Bob and I sat at a back table. I had a beer and Bob a Coke. With some frequency, we could hear Chance pound the machine and hell at it, "You fuckinn' lyin', cheatin', cock-suckin' whore." When that happened, Bob's eyes would blink and his jaw tighten momentarily.

"Well, Bob," I said, "Here we are." He nodded and looked back at me through his slightly cock-eyed glasses with an expression that I knew he could maintain much longer than I could keep saying, "Well, Bob, here we are."

I lit a cigarette and as I exhaled, I said, "Uhm, where's Renu now, at your bungalow?"

"Yes. I'm going home right after this afternoon's recoveries. Then we're going shopping. She's going to fix up the place. It's needed a woman's touch."

Such is the way the conversation went. I'd try and open up some opportunity for him to explain things, and he would close it with some quick, although not impolite explanation.

Sgt. Chance, having exhausted his supply of quarters, kicked and cursed the slot machine for the last time then he started to leave, but he saw us sitting and came over. "Hey, Lt. Saunders, I'm glad tuh hear yuh finally got yuh fuckin' wick wet."

When Chance had left, Bob turned to me and said, "I don't always completely understand what Sgt. Chance says, but it always seems to make me feel embarrassed."

I picked him up on it. "Have you done anything to be embarrassed about, Bob?"

He looked at me quite stunned. "Why, of course not. What do you mean?" He stared at me and adjusted his glasses.

"Well, Bob, I mean you've always been a straight arrow."

"A what?"

"I mean you've never messed around with the girls. You know, like you were always shocked when I brought a bar-girl home from the Argo."

"You can't mean you think Renu is the same as the girls in the Argo."

"Well, of course there are differences. The girls in Bangkok have a lot more class. They don't sit around and pick their noses, and they wear make-up and nice dresses, and they don't say 'fuck off, G.I.', but, in the end, Bob, I think you'll have to say they're all working the same profession."

"Now look," he sputtered, "you can't go around saying those kind of things about my fiancée." He stood up, but I reached over and pushed him back down into his chair.

"Wait a minute. Don't get me wrong. I don't have anything against any of those girls, and most of all, nothing against Renu. In fact, I really like Malee, and Supatra, and Nok, and all the girls at the Argo. And I like all the girls at max's in Bangkok. Prostitute is just a goddamned word that someone decided to call them. It doesn't really mean anything. I certainly don't mean anything bad by it. And I'm really sorry if I offended you."

Bob seemed to calm a little. He placed his cap on the table. "Okay, but Renu is not the same as the other girls in bars." I nodded in agreement (it was easier). "Oh, I admit," he continued, "I've changed some opinions since I've met her. She had really opened my eyes to a lot of things." He paused and looked around the room. "I mean, did you know that's not whiskey in the girl's glasses at Max's Bar? It's just colored water."

"Well, I'll be a monkey's uncle."

"Yes, and that's not all. Renu told me that when you take a taxi with one of the girls from a bar, sometimes the girls will tell you to pay more than you should, and then, later, the driver gives some of the overcharge back to the girl."

"Well, you could knock me over with a feather."

"Yes, that's true." He paused and leaned back. "Oh, and there's more, lots more. Renu has really taught me a lot. You know, Jim," and he looked me as straight in the eye as was possible for him, "I don't think I'll ever be the same. I guess you just can't go home again."

"Not until after this afternoon's recoveries, at least."

"What?"

"Nothing, Bob."

He started to get up to leave, but I caught him again by the arm and pulled him back down. "But I've got recoveries coming in."

"You've got some time yet. Look, Bob, I'm no expert, but it doesn't seem to me that you can chuck off one wife and take up a new one, solely because the new one tells you how to save a couple of baht when you're out on the town in Bangkok."

"Well, of course not. I said there was more. For instance, never buy jewelry at…"

"Bob, is it sex?"

"What?"

"Is it sex? Is that why you want to marry Renu? Bob, I don't want to seem cruel to her, but just because you've slept with a girl doesn't mean you have to marry her. She's certainly not the only girl you've slept with."

"No, of course she isn't. I am already married, you remember. Anyway, I shouldn't say this, it's really none of your business, but you seem so concerned. I did more than sleep with Renu. We had, well, we had relations."

"Yes, I gathered that, that's what I meant, and you still don't have to marry the girl because there were *relations*."

"I told you there was more."

"Like what?"

"Well, for instance, she told me that most of the girls in the massage parlors are not really masseuses, they're just…"

"Okay, okay! Now look, Bob." My suspicions about the lack of activity in Bob's skull having been confirmed, it seemed time to get on to other matters. "Look, Bob, don't you think Betty and her dad will be a little mad at this?"

"Gee, there are lots of other things I could tell you."

"Bob, what about Betty and her father?"

"Hmmm, well," Bob paused to consider. "I suppose that it will be upsetting for Betty, but then it would be even worse if I were to go on living with her, but was actually in love with Renu. It's like I said, we have promised to always be honest with each other. I'm sure she'd be just as truthful if it was the other way around." (For some reason, I found that situation hard to imagine, but then, I was finding the present situation hard to imagine even as I sat and listened to it.) "Of course, I wrote her a carefully worded letter, and I told her that I shall always have nothing but the fondest memories and greatest respect for her." He stopped.

"And what about the Colonel?"

"Oh, gee, I really hadn't thought much about him, but I guess," Bob paused to guess awhile. I conjured up a vision of the old buzzard keeling over in an apoplectic fit. Bob continued, indulging in some wishful thinking, "Gee, he does have a temper, but I'm sure, that after awhile, he'll see it was the best thing."

"Bob, what about General Martin?"

"Who?"

"General Martin, Seventh Air Force commander?"

"Gee, what would General Martin have to do with this?"

"Bob, wasn't the Colonel an aide to Martin once, and don't they still see each other fairly often?"

"Well, yes they do, but heck, I don't think the Colonel would ever mention me to General Martin. Hey, I never told you about that. How'd you find that out?"

"Never mind. The fact that I know indicated that it's rather common knowledge." Even Bob deserved some warning of the holocaust that was building up around him. "Bob, don't you realize that Hudson is madder than hell. He and Sutton are going to do everything they can to block this, and you certainly aren't going to be able to count on the Colonel to help you either."

"But why should this upset them? Isn't it my own business?"

"Bob, the Air Force doesn't like to see its personnel getting romantic with the natives. It's all right to fool around, but marriage is definitely frowned upon. It wouldn't matter if you wanted to marry the daughter of the governor of Nakorn Sarang, they'd give you a hard time. But you want to marry a bar girl."

"Well, I can understand all that if they're talking about one of the girls at the Argo Bar, or even one of the other girls at Max's, but Renu is different. You know that." (I could see myself being listed as a character reference.)

"Sure, Bob, but try and explain it to Hudson. Bob, believe me, they are going to harass you like a son-of-a-bitch, hoping you'll give up the idea."

Bob stood up and put on his cap. He stared down at me intently through his glasses. "Oh, no, I know my rights. They can't do that to me. It's not fair. I'll fight them I'm going to stick it out."

I looked up at him and thought, Jesus Christ, this stupid little bastard is going to take on the whole Air Force. I didn't think much of his cause, she was just another bar girl, and he didn't know what the hell he was talking about. But taking on the Air Force with a frontal attack, on its own terms, by the book, that was something I don't think I really ever had the nerve to do. I'd always seen myself as kind of a guerrilla fighter, appearing to go along, but creating little sabotages along the way, throwing a little sand in the gears. Of course the system always won out, but at least I made it a little more difficult. And here was bob Saunders, fool and incompetent, standing right up to it. What the hell, even a lunatic, if he was fighting the noble fight, deserved support. So I agreed to become Bob Saunders' secret sharer.

"Bob, don't say anything to Sheets or Hudson or Sutton. Don't tell them I talked to you. I'll try and help you, but let's go quietly for now, okay?"

"Okay, thanks." He paused. "Gee, it's good to know we're still friends. I was kind of worried when you moved out of the bungalow." So, a good four months of insults just went down the drain.

What I want to know is, if I willingly agreed to be Bob's accomplice in the battle, maybe even enthusiastically agreed to it, why did I sit in the club drinking beers until four-thirty, when Smiley came and got me and said that Major Hudson was madder than hell and wanted to see me again.

Fortunately for me, Hudson was so wrapped up in the one thing on his mind that he didn't notice I was half in the bag.

"Didyuhtalktuh'atgoddamsillyiddiot?"

I waited before starting to talk, trying to get my mouth primed for action, but the words were still rather slow and uncertain. "Yes, Sir, I did."

"Well, wha'suhdeal?"

"Nothing new, Sir. He just explained to me what he's doing." Hudson's hand went to his forehead, and I figured I better give him all the news. "Uhm, of course, he did send a letter to his wife telling her all about it and asking for a divorce."

His other hand went to his forehead. "Shitshitshit! Whyn't yuhstop'im?"

"He did it before I saw him." No sense in telling Hudson and Sutton that I had the letter waved in front of my face in the chow hall, and then walked across the courtyard with him and stood there while he dropped the letter into the mailbox.

"Did itgeton' smornin'splane?"

"No, Sir, it didn't get on the plane. I think he mailed it just after lunch. It's probably sitting in the mail box right now."

Hudson picked up his phone, and after a brief wait for the operator to come on the line, said, "Gimmethuhmailroom." After another wait, he said, "Gimmetheuhgoddamnmailroom, I sed."

Sgt. Sutton seemed a little concerned by Hudson's action and came over with his hand out. "Excuse me, Major, but I would not, uh, recommend attempting to, uh, interfere with the United States mail."

"Sgt. Patterson, gidduphererightaway," Hudson snapped into the phone. "'Isiz MajerHudson, whothuhhellyuhthinkitiz?"

While we waited for Patterson to come up from the mail room, I went out to the orderly room to get a drink of water. Sgt. Chance was at the door getting ready to leave.

"What do you think of this whole thing, Lafayette?"

Chance opened the door and spat into the heat. "Shit! It's like I fuckin' tol'yuh, Lietenant. You fuckin' officers dunk you dick one time, and yuh go fuckin' crazy." The beer was still in my brain, and I was beginning to get a headache, but that made about as much sense as anything I had heard since I had arrived back in Nakorn Sarang.

Sgt. Patterson entered as Chance left. He was black, young, and very bright. He was not under Hudson's command since all post office personnel were under jurisdiction of Postal Services, Thailand, which was located in Bangkok. Hence, Patterson kept just a hair short of insolence when dealing with most officers. I always felt we got along pretty well, but he certainly never deferred to my rank.

"Hey, baby, what's happening?"

I pointed to Hudson's office and said, "Rear of the room, please." We exchanged quick laughs.

Patterson entered without taking off his cap. "Hey, Maje, hey Sutton, what's happening?"

Hudson's face turned especially pained, but he went right to the point. "Lt. Sanners mailed uh letter tuhday." (Hudson always took great pains to separate his speech when talking to "colored people", as he referred to them. That included most Thais, although not site employees. In general, he avoided, whenever possible, talking to all "Coloreds". That prevented any possible trouble, he felt.) "I wan' yuh to get it out an' bring it tuh me."

"Hey, man, what? You crazy? You cats know I can't mess with the mail once it's in that box." Patterson took off his hat and ran his hand through the beginnings of an Afro. "No way, man, no way!"

Sgt. Sutton started to say something like, "See what I meant, Major," but Hudson interrupted him.

"Sar'n't Patterson, Lootenin' Sanners made uh mistake in mailin' 'at letter."

"Hey man, if that so, then why don't Lt. Saunders ask me to get the letter back for him?"

Hudson's hand went back to rubbing his forehead. "Lootenin' Sanners don' know he made uh mistake."

"Hey, baby, listen. If that little Lieutenant come to me, say, 'Hey, Sgt. Patterson, can I have my letter back?', then I say, 'Beautiful.'' No sweat, see. But suppose I digs out that letter and give it to you, and the little Lieutenant say, 'Major Hudson, and Sgt. Sutton, and Lt. Doyle, and Sgt. Patterson interfered with the United States mail,' then, baby, we is all in deeeep sheeeit."

"Shitshitshit!"

So the plan to interfere with the mail ended, but it was still three days till the next mail plane, and the letter was lying there in the mailroom like a time bomb.

Following the scene in the orderly room, I was exhausted. Not enough sleep, too much whiskey and beer, and a day full of surprises had sapped my never-too-full reservoir of strength, so I got the next bus to my bungalow. The first evening bus, the one that took most of us who lived in town home, had already left, and I got the one that took the first load of airmen into the village for the evening. There seemed to be only one topic of conversation: Lt. Saunders and his teeloc.

"What'd you say?"

"I said Lt. Saunders come back from Bangkok with the finest pooying you ever seen."

"Get out of here!"

"Your ass, your ass!"

"I ain't shitting you. Ask Candy, he seen him in town."

"That's right, seen'em at one of the tailors. Shit man, she's a regular Suzie Wong."

"No shit, too much."

"Hey, listen to this. That ain't all. Smiley says Fuzz-face wants to marry her, already asked Chance to get him the right forms."

"Marry?"

"Holy fuck!"

"Hey, ain't that little dip-shit already married. I know I seen some picture of some four-eyed bitch on his desk."

"That's right. Smiley says the little Lieutenant's gonnuh gettuh divorce."

"Sheeeit!"

"Ooooweee. Man, that cat's crazy!"

"I don't know. What would you rather have? If you seen them both, I bet you'd bet you'd take the pooying."

"Hey, I bet the old man is spraining a goddamned wrist."

"Smiley say he spent the whole day having a fit and yelling at Lt. Doyle."

"Hey, Lt. Doyle, this all true? Fuzz gonnuh really marry a slant-eye?"

I drew on my close association with Major Hudson and said, as I wiped my hand across my mouth, "Hummawauggh."

Behind me someone, someone with brains said, "You know something, that little bastard's crazy enough to go through with all this shit."

CHAPTER SIXTEEN

JOE WAS IN THE ROOM asleep when I got back to the bungalow. I stuck my head in and said his name several times, but he only continued to snore, so I stripped down to my underwear and, with a cold beer in hand, sat in the living room with the light off under the fan. I drank my beer and smoked a cigarette in the fading daylight. The landlord's children were playing behind the house, and I could hear their chatter. It was not unpleasant. Beyond that, I could hear the tinkling of some kind of ceremonial bells, not an unusual sound, but it had been a long time since I had noticed it. The birds and crickets were playing their evening songs, and I felt great waves of tension flowing from my body. Even Joe's snoring was a sedative, an even, low, purring sound.

I thought to myself: It's amazing I'm not thinking about Bob Saunders, which naturally took care of that. So my thoughts changed, and as my eyes closed, I began to have visions of Bob Saunders—yelling for me at the train station the night before—riding off into the crowd with Renu, hand on head—walking toward the mailbox, the letter in his hand—looking at me through his glasses and explaining what he had learned—calling me "friend". Then I turned to fantasy, things like Renu giving Bob a massage, walking on his back, and him with his glasses and cap still on. Around that time, or maybe just before, I feel asleep.

I was awoken by the sound of a jeep horn outside my bungalow. It was Hudson. He had also woken up the dogs which Papa-san provided for us to keep away thieves, and they were barking. When I got my pants on, I went down to the gate.

"Yes, Sir, what can I do for you?"

He did not get out of his jeep. I could tell from the red in his face he had been drinking heavily, probably alone in his bungalow. Of course, when he began to speak, my little bit of observation became hardly a moot point. I could barely understand him.

"'Id juhheahinneethin'new?"

"Hear anything new, about what?" I looked at my watch. It was eight-thirty. I figured he must have been drinking since I last saw him.

"BoutSanners, 'at'sooo." His hands were twisting, slowly in front of his face.

"No, I haven't heard anything about Saunders. I've been sleeping. What the hell can happen before the next mail plane, anyway?"

Hudson's foot, which must have been holding the clutch inn, slipped and the jeep lurched forward several feet, stalling the engine. He swung his feet around and went on as if nothing had happened, leaving the ignition and lights still on.

"Cap' nGunn seen'em inuhtown 'isaffernoon." He nodded to confirm his own statement.

"Seen them in town this afternoon? What the hell's he doing, tailing them?"

"'EesezSannerswuzbyin' eruhgol ring."

"Buying her a gold ring? How the hell'd he find that out?"

"Ee ass' duhstorekeep'"

"Asked the storekeeper? Jesus Christ, Major, is this shit really necessary? Christ, Saunders will probably forget all this in a few weeks."

"Cap 'nGunnthinks shemigh' beuh communisss'."

"She might be a communist! Holy shit!" I watched as Hudson nodded to confirm his own statement. His own "yes" man. Who was the bigger lunatic, I wondered, Hudson or Bob?

"Jus 'wannuhknowwha 'sgoin'on." He turned back into the jeep and turned on the ignition without depressing the clutch. The jeep lurched forward again. After he put the clutch in, he turned the starter motor over long after the engine had started. The grinding sound started the dogs barking again.

"Okay, Major, I promise I'll let you know what's going on. Of course, I have to know what's going on to do that, and so far, I've been remarkably out of it."

The jeep stalled once, when he let the clutch out in third gear, but he finally got going, speeding out the driveway, leaving the dust flying and the dogs barking. He beeped his horn a few times as he neared the road. Normally his propensity for horn blowing annoyed me, but in light of his condition, I thought the warning was justified.

When I got back to the living room, Joe was up, standing in the doorway in his paisin. "What the hell was that racket?"

"It was fucking Hudson. He is smashed out of his goddamned mind."

Joe went out to the kitchen and came back with a beer. "What's he drinking about tonight?"

"Aaw, this goddamned Saunders shit has got him even loonier than normal."

"What Saunders shit?"

I looked at Joe and realized it was the first time I had seen him since I had gotten back from Bangkok. "Hey, where've you been, anyway? You weren't here when I got in this morning, and you weren't here when I got up, either. And I don't think I saw you at the site, or anywhere."

Joe sat down and drank some of his beer. "Oh, fucking Sheets screwed up the assignments. I worked the night shift, and then no one turned up to work the morning rendezvouses, so I had to cover them. When I finally got off around ten, I went over and racked out on one of the empty bunks. I got up about noon and came home. When I got here, the maid was raising hell about the mess you made. Something about peanut butter. I listened to that four about five minutes and then went to bed. Been sleeping ever since. What the hell time is it, anyway?"

So I told Joe the time and the story. I included the part about my evening walk, but I didn't tell about agreeing to aid Bob. The more I told him, the more he laughed. By the time I got through, there were tears in his eyes.

"Jesus, I was wondering when this would happen. Something like this has happened each time I've been in Thailand before. Although both times it was senior officers involved. In Bangkok, some L.C. flipped his bird over a stripper downtown. He never wanted to marry her, he just kept extending his tour of duty until one day, his wife showed up on a goddamned plane at Don Muang Airport. The whole thing ended just like that. In two weeks the colonel was back in the States."

Joe went out to the kitchen for another beer, and he brought me one as well. "In Nakhon Phanom, a major from the Air Police went bananas over a waitress in one of the local nightclubs. I don't think he was married, because he arranged for her to get a passport, bought her an airline ticket, and gave her a couple of thousand dollars, planning on bringing her back to the States. He left for home and, naturally, she cashed in the airline ticket and disappeared with the two thou. I understand she opened her own house in Korat. Like I say, the only difference is their ages, younger guys usually keep themselves together. Of course, Saunders is twenty-four going on fifty."

Joe laughed some more. "The thing that really makes this funny is getting General Martin into it. But I don't envy you because Hudson's line is going to be buzzing like all hell, and that means shit for you."

Joe's little encapsulision of my situation did not really do a lot for my sense of well being. In fact, it probably wrecked whatever hope I had of getting a good night's sleep. In view of the circumstances, it seemed the best path lay in the direction of Tipalow's restaurant and the Argo Bar.

Joe agreed. "Well, since I've done nothing but sleep all day, I'd say some fun would be in order. Besides, in view of what you've got to look forward to," Joe paused to look at me and laugh, "you better have all the fun you can have right now."

I did not laugh.

At Tipalow's, we ordered the special, some six courses that ranged from fried chicken and fish to pigeon egg soup and monkey brains. The waiter, who was once again friendly to me, placed some bowls of hot sauce on the table, but we carefully avoided using them. The stuff could quite literally blow your brains out. Once, as a stupid and unpractical joke, I had soaked a dining companion's shrimp in the sauce and placed it on the unsuspecting fellow's plate. His reaction was so violent that for twenty minutes I was afraid he might pass out. In the end, he merely had to leave for home, his meal unfinished. I never admitted my part in it for fear of physical retaliation, but I did, for what it was worth, vow never to do such a thing again. And I always ate with a slight fear in me that someone might do the same to me.

To wash down the last scrapings of rice off our plates, we ordered another liter of Singha. The still hot air of the night came into the restaurant through the wide doors causing sweat to coat my body, so it seemed like the beers could go down forever. Word was that a drop of formaldehyde was used in the making of Singha to kill off whatever impurities had survived the brewing process. It was entirely believable. The first night of drinking some, sharing a few bottles with Harry Simpson, produced one of the most horrendous hangovers of my life, a sensation of having had my innards inverted and scrubbed with a wire brush. But once my body adjusted itself, I developed a real taste for the stuff and much preferred it to its American counterpart.

Joe talked some more about Bob Saunders. "You know, this foolishness gets more and more interesting the more you think about it. Saunders may be the perfect one to carry it off. Career types or senior officers like the L.C. and the Major I told you about could never take it all the way. Someday they'd have to go back to the States and then what would happen? Could you see one of those girls at the Officer Wives' Club? Shit! In truth, they'd be a damn sight better than any of the bitches there, but those old hags would assassinate the poor girls. And the husbands, every other pea brain who'd ever been anywhere near Southeast Asia would know immediately where the girl came from. There'd be all kinds of snickering behind the back, and the worst fucking part is, if the situation was someone else's, then that same L.C. or Major would be just like the others, making rotten little jokes. Those poor cretins live in houses without mirrors. But Saunders, he's like them and he's different. Like you've said, he's positive that this girl is completely different from any other bar girl. She may be, but I doubt it, which as you well know, doesn't mean I don't like her, and hence, he would make remarks about anyone else who wanted to marry a Thai. So in that way, he's no fucking different from the L.C. or the Major.

"But there's one thing he's got going for him. He is beyond a doubt, bar none, the most unconscious mother-fucker I've ever met. He could survive all that Officer Club shit. And I doubt if he even goes there that much anyway, so she wouldn't have to suffer that. Unconscious, Jesus, the silly little bastard has been here for six months and he's still not fully qualified. He can't work more than one rendezvous at a time. The only time he can be left alone on the scope is for recoveries, and he still thinks an intercept is something that happens in a football game. Yet, that stupid little shit will sit over there in the ops office and talk like a fucking combat ace about the morning's work. I never know whether to laugh or strangle him. Shit! So anyway, he could probably survive the isolation he's going to face, and that stupidity might also get him through the harassment he's going to face before he leaves here.

"Of course, you know, under another commander, things might not get so bad. Someone with a little more confidence might just let the whole thing simmer, let Saunders' father-in-law work some pressure. Goddamnit, it would probably fade away anyway. But Hudson knows the only thing that keeps him here is the fact there haven't been any personnel problems, no scandals. He doesn't have the foggiest fucking idea what goes on over in ops. We could be bombing St. Louis for all he knows. So, he'll worry himself sick over this shit, and unfortunately, he'll drive the rest of us nuts as well. You more than anyone."

To Joe's remarks, the Singhas filling up inside of me, I responded with a burp. The Bob Saunders' crisis was certainly bringing out a lot of inner strength in me.

We paid our bill, left, and started trying to drum up a couple of samlows to take us to the Argo.

"Hey, Baby, what's happening?"

It was Sgt. Patterson, walking down the street with a very pretty girl. Rumor, and that was all since Patterson kept quiet about her, had it that she had been the number two wife of the Thai third army commander, and Patterson had stolen her right from under the general's eyes.

Joe waved at him. "Hey, Pat, baby." Then he looked up the street for a samlow. "Not much, we're trying to catch a couple of samlows to take us to the Argo, have some fun." I smiled and nodded.

"Argo Bar? My, my." Patterson looked over at his girlfriend. She shook her head. "Baby, that place is nowhere. Man, I keep my feet away from there."

We finally found a couple of samlows and loaded up into them. Just as mine started to move, Sgt. Patterson came over and said, speaking softly, "Hey, man, you been all right to me. I don't want to see you catch no shit. If it helps you, man, like I could sit on the little Lieutenant's letter for a mail plane or two. No big thing, Baby."

So I had an out. I thought of all that Joe had talked about, especially the part about Hudson driving me nuts, and he would, or at least to drink, which in my case is not a far drive. And I thought of General Martin and Colonel Herder and tried to imagine what pressure they could bring to bear. Then I thought of Betty, that silly little fool, and the Colonel. I could see her weeping into a little handkerchief, and the Colonel blustering, his face looking like a tomato. That made me laugh. Then I thought of Hudson again. I saw him, his face in his hands, saying, "Guuhhh." I could see his fingers twisting before his mouth, and could hear his words becoming more and more muffled; his carefully protected world falling apart, all because of the silliest, most ridiculous person on the whole site.

I looked over at Patterson and said, "Umm, naw, Pat. I think we better just leave everything alone," and smiled.

Pat's mouth curled into a sly smile, and he winked. "Okay, Baby, anyway you want it," he said, and I slapped his upturned palms.

The time at the Argo passed quickly. For a Monday night, it was a big crowd, it not being too long past payday, and the girls were very busy. I saw Supatra when I came in, and few times after that, always coming or going through the back door. It was the same with most of the other girls. Many of the airmen kept coming up to me and asking, "Hey, it is true?" or, "What's going on with Lt. Fuzz?" to which I could only reply, "Yup," or "Just like you heard." Mama-san was working the tables delivering the Singhas and Mekongs. She took time out to come over to me and laugh. Holding her index finger out straight, she demonstrated my previous night's impotence, letting the finger sag and saying, "G.I. numbah ten pom-pom."

Papa-san eyed me a little uneasily for the first hour or so. One time when near the bar, he touched my arm and said he had another bottle Mekong for me because, "Big mistake, I give wrong bottle for you last night."

I stared at him blankly, "What bottle? Last night? Was I here last night?" He smiled and begged forgiveness, he had made another mistake, very sorry. I would have, overall, preferred that the whole night be forgotten.

Joe made an arrangement with Malee for her to come to the bungalow when things quieted down at the bar. "She'll be tired then, but I'm off tomorrow till the night shift, so we'll spend the whole day in bed. At least till it gets too hot, then maybe we'll take a shower for the rest of the day."

It occurred to me that Tuesday was a working day and I was probably going to have to listen to a lot of blabbering from Hudson about the Saunders' business. In other words, I decided to go home alone. When Joe and I went outside to get two samlows, an air police truck pulled up and Sgt. Reid jumped out.

"Capt. Stacy! Lt. Doyle!"

"What, what?"

"I've been looking all over for you two."

"What for?"

"Capt. Sheets wants you both out at the base. Capt. Sheets has called a meeting of all section heads."

"What for?"

"Because of the emergency."

"What emergency?"

"The Major Hudson thing."

"What Major Hudson thing?"

"Haven't you heard?"

Joe put his hand on Reid's shoulder and said, very patiently, "Reid, retracing this conversation, has there been anything said that gives you the slightest idea that we know what the fuck you're talking about?"

"What?"

"Reid, for Christ's sake, what the hell is going on?"

"You mean you didn't hear that Major Hudson drove his jeep into a klong and is in the hospital. He nearly drowned."

On the ride out to the site, we were able to get nothing more from Reid other than that the accident had occurred about an hour and a half earlier on the road from town to the Thai Third Army headquarters. It was by then nearly midnight.

At the site, the meeting was held in the ops office because, as was later explained, it was more secure than the orderly room. Sgt. Sutton, the only NCO there, was standing by the door as we entered. He eyed us grimly and then stepped aside to let us in. Capt. Gunn had a map of the village spread out on one of the desks and was leaning over it. A red X was marked on the road that led to the Third Army base. He did not look up. Capt Sheets was sitting behind his desk. Both of them were wearing helmets and had their thirty-eights on.

"Close that door, Captain Stacy."

Joe responded, "Russ, boy, what's up?"

"Hasn't Sgt. Reid briefed you?"

"Only," and Joe smiled, "briefly. What's the deal with Hudson? Is he all right?"

Sheets leaned forward and pulled the slide-out of his desk to lean on. Joe mentioned something about the nice, flattering pictures of Joy, and Sheets quickly pushed it back in. "Major Hudson has suffered four cracked ribs, a laceration on the forehead and several minor cuts and bruises. He is presently under heavy sedation at the natives' hospital."

"What the hell happened?"

"We suspect sabotage."

"What?"

Gunn came up to Joe, holding the map. With a red crayon, he was pointing to the X on the map. "This red X marks the area where the vehicle left the road. It came to rest at this point." He moved the crayon a few inches along the map and made a Y. "Major Hudson, fortunately, was not thrown from the vehicle. However, he did hit his head on the windshield and cracked his ribs on either the steering wheel or gear shift. Naturally he was leaning over and his head was below the water level of the canal in which the vehicle came to rest. The accident occurred within view of two Thai army sergeants, who pulled him out and reported it."

I sat down in what was normally Sgt. Pol's chair. "So where's the sabotage?"

Capt. Sheets stood up and placed one hand on his pistol. "Tell them, Capt. Gunn."

"Major Hudson was discovered, by the aforementioned Thai army sergeants, bent over, mumbling, in a state of shock."

"For Hudson that's not shock, that's normal."

Gunn glared at me, then continued. "The two witnesses stated that the vehicle suddenly swerved into the canal without provocation. They reported finding no other objects on the road. The same has been confirmed by our own Air Police. It is my considered opinion that something had been tampered with on the vehicle causing a loss of control. Tomorrow I will request the vehicle maintenance section to conduct a thorough examination of the vehicle."

"Has it ever been suggested that Hudson was just plain drunk?"

Sheets cut me off. "Doyle, the situation is deserving of a certain degree of respect."

"All I know is Hudson came by my place about eight-thirty and he could barely drive then. Reid says the accident occurred about ten-thirty, and I don't think he had sobered up much by then."

Gunn, who lived with Hudson, stepped between Sheets and myself. "I saw the Major at approximately twenty-one hundred hours. He was, at the time, in complete control of his faculties. He mentioned having visited the Lieutenant, who, the major noted, had been sleeping at the time." I looked over and saw Sheets staring at the watch and counting the numerals. Joe was now sitting in his regular chair, laughing quietly. My point of view was failing to gain much acceptance.

Sheets got up and began to walk back and forth across the room. "In light of the circumstances, and in view of my responsibility to assume command in Major Hudson's incapacitation, I have had readied several bunks in the hooches for officers and senior NCO's, so that they will not have to hazard themselves by exposure to any hostile elements in the area. Of course, however, it should also be considered that any hasty show of alarm on our part could cause panic among the natives, so I am making it optional and you may elect to stay on the site or return to your bungalows. I, for one, choose not to alarm the natives and will remain in my bungalow. But I will insist that all officers and senior NCO's who elect to remain off-site maintain the closest of watch and immediately report any unusual occurrences or the appearance of strange people."

Joe asked, "You mean like someone with slanted eyes, Russ?"

"Capt. Stacy, the circumstances are not of a humorous nature."

Something occurred to me. "Say, Capt. Sheets, Has either Takhli or Bangkok been notified of this?"

He looked at me out of the sides of his eyes. "No, I think we can adequately handle the situation."

"No doubt, Sir, but I believe there's some sort of operational order for Thailand, that except in emergency situations all injured personnel be removed to U.S. medical facilities, which would be either Takhli or Bangkok in our case." I saw Sheets' and Gunn's faces freeze. "Isn't that right, Sgt. Sutton?"

"Um, yes, Sir. I'm afraid the Lieutenant is, uh, correct, Captains. If you will recall the time when Sgt. Reid shot himself in the foot, that is the order that, uh, prevailed at that time."

Sheets and Gunn exchanged glances and both ended up staring at me. I could hear Joe laughing. When Sheets spoke to Sutton, he continued to look at me. "You're sure about this, Sergeant?"

Sutton stroked his moustache. "Uh, yes, Sir. I'm afraid the Lieutenant is entirely correct."

Gunn asked the next question. "Who's supposed to do the reporting, Sergeant?"

I broke in. "The site medic."

"I asked the Sergeant, Doyle."

Sutton pointed to me. "The Lieutenant is, uh, correct again, Sir. In this instance, uh, that would be Doc, I mean, Technical Sergeant Dugan."

When the meeting was over, Joe and I got Sgt. Reid to take us to our bungalow. Before that, Doc Dugan had been located and he made a report, which was wired to both Takhli and Bangkok. A plane was to be dispatched the next morning to pick up Major Hudson and take him to the American hospital in Bangkok.

As we were walking up our driveway, Joe asked me, "Do you know what this means?"

I had a pretty clear idea, but I thought I'd wait to hear what Joe thought it signified.

"No, not really, what?"

"If Hudson was as loaded as you say he way, then it will probably show up in the medical report. and if that's so, I imagine we've seen the last of Major Carl R. Hudson as commander of Detachment 8 of the 519th Tactical Air Control Squadron."

"Gee, that would sure be too bad, wouldn't it."

Somebody was sitting on our porch steps.

"Capt'n Joe, where you be? Argo Bar Close, I come layo-layo, wait long time." It was Malee. If Sheets had been with us, he probably would have shot her as a saboteur.

The next day, things went pretty much as expected. Takhli sent up a C-47 "Goony Bird" to pick up Hudson. It arrived at ten a.m. to take him to a hospital in Bangkok. We had him ready and waiting at the airport. One of the Thai doctors from the local hospital stood there with us; in his hand was Hudson's medical report. I said to him, "Doctor, it is very important that the medical report be in clear English. Would you like our interpreter to review it with you?"

He turned a pair of tired eyes on me, but kept his face straight ahead. "Lieutenant, I received my degree from the Indiana University medical school. The report is quite clear." Not really aware of the nature of my concern, he added, "Probably too clear."

When the air crew lifted Hudson's stretcher onto the plane, I yelled at them, "Hey, take it easy, will you? That man is still our commander." Hudson's white-bandaged head swung to look at me. His eyes glared, and I saluted.

As the plane lifted off, Gunn and Sheets were standing at attention, saluting, as was Sgt. Sutton. Doc Dugan was already walking back to his truck. Joe had elected not to change his plans and was back at the bungalow with Malee.

The reviewing medical officer in Bangkok must have been a very dispassionate and objective man. His report, a copy of which was forwarded on to Saigon and Colonel Herder, read, "Subject was heavily intoxicated at time of accident."

Our phones started ringing at five that afternoon. Colonel Herder would be flying into Nakorn Sarang for a special visit the next day. He would be accompanied by the new site commander, name to be supplied in a later transmission. The transmission never arrived, but Herder and the new commander, Major Robert L. Richter, did.

CHAPTER SEVENTEEN

WHILE IT WOULDN'T BE TRUE to say I never thought about Bob Saunders and his girl during the next four or five days, I am fair in saying I thought little about them. It wasn't until early the next week—well after Colonel Herder and Colonel Wolff had left and Major Richter was busily immersed in the job of learning everything about the site (an effort which caused much embarrassment to more than a few section chiefs)—that the Major, from what was now his office, called out to me, "Jim what the hell's this 'Request to Marry Foreign National'?" and the problems of Bob Saunders once again became a central concern of mine.

Prior to that, much else had occurred. Another Goony Bird, but not the same one that took Major Hudson away, arrived on Wednesday morning. It carried three men: Colonel Herder, first off the plane and not immediately recognizable to me since I had last seen him wearing a brightly colored sport shirt and dark glasses, and he was now fitted into a pair of custom tailored jungle fatigues, which led me to suspect he was wearing a girdle, an idea strengthened when he quickly, but stiffly, jumped from the plane and perfunctorily returned the salutes of Sheets, Gunn, Sutton, and myself; Colonel Wolff, our squadron commander from Udorn Royal Thai Air Force Base, a squat and generally unpleasant man, whose only acknowledgement of any of us was a thinly disguised look of disgust; and the man who was our new site commander, Major Robert L. Richter, thin and young—later confirmed to be thirty-five—who sharply returned each of our salutes and, at his own iniative, shook each of our hands. He did not smile, but later events convinced me that this, in keeping with the rather solemn circumstances of his assumption of command, took a concentrated effort on his part. Of course, I was at the same time making great efforts to restrain my own glee.

Colonel Herder wanted to see the jeep that Hudson had been driving and at the sound of his request, Sheets, Gunn, and Sutton began falling all over one another in getting Herder and Wolff into one of the jeeps we had come to the airport in. Sutton, due to rank, was left without a seat and was forced to return to the site in the other jeep with me and Major Richter, who seemed nearly forgotten in the excitement.

On the ride to the site, Major Richter mentioned in introducing himself, that he had been the group operations officer in Saigon for the past two months, and while he had visited most of the sites in Vietnam, this was his first trip to Thailand. Sergeant Sutton leaned forward from his seat in the rear (I was driving) and, while stroking his moustache, said, "I, uh, and I believe the Lieutenant here, and, uh, the various Captains involved in the, uh, performance of operational, uh, duties here am sure, uh, are sure, uh, Major Richter, Sir, that you will, uh, discover our methods and, uh, prescriptions to be entirely within the, uh, parameters," (Sutton said "para-mEters"), "and guidelines which are, uh, prevailing throughout the entirety of the, uh, combat zone, and you will therefore be well, uh, familiarized with their, uh, implements."

While trying to avoid the pot holes, I caught sight out of the corner of my eye of Major Richter turn and stare back at Sutton. He said, with a slightly pained and puzzled look settling on his face, "Sergeant Sutton, what the hell are you talking about?" At that point, I felt, somehow, that things were going to be getting better.

Hudson's jeep had been cleaned, but as Sgt. Bailey the vehicle maintenance NCOIC said, "It's still not running quite right Colonel, since the carburetor and fuel line sucked in a mess of mud when the jeep landed in the klong."

Colonel Herder walked slowly around the jeep as if it were a column of troops standing inspection. "Sergeant," he turned and checked Bailey's name tag again, "Sgt. Bailey, did you find any evidence of sabotage?"

"Sabotage, Sir?"

"Yes, sabotage. Was there any evidence that the jeep had been tampered with so that Major Hudson couldn't keep it on the road."

"Oh, no, Sir, no evidence of any sabotage."

Herder turned his attention to Gunn. "Capt. Gunn, didn't you tell one of my staff people over the phone that you were positive that Major Hudson's jeep had been tampered with?"

Gunn stepped forward a little, but he spoke softly and hesitantly without looking directly at the Colonel. "Well, yes, Sir. That was before we received the medical report, and sabotage seemed the most likely answer."

"But weren't you aware that Hudson had been drinking heavily?"

Gunn paused some and wiped his hand across his nose and mouth. "Well, Sir, the Major had had one or two, but I wouldn't say he'd been drinking heavily. And, of course, like any good soldier, he could hold his whiskey, so I just didn't think he had an accident without some form of provocation, Sir."

Herder shook his head and said, "Uh huh."

Colonel Wolff came forward and leaned on the front fender of the jeep. "What about the medical report, filed by the doctor here in Nakorn Sarang, which said Major Hudson was heavily intoxicated?"

Nobody spoke and Wolff said, "Captain Gunn, Captain Sheets?"

"Well, Sir," said Sheets stepping up alongside Gunn, I don't trust that report all that much. First, the doctor, as you know, is a Thai, and, frankly, I doubt his qualifications and competence. Second, he probably harbors a prejudice against Americans. And third, he was probably using a medical definition of intoxicated, and the Major was capable of handling more than his share of liquor."

Wolff slapped his hand down on the hood of the jeep, causing Sheets and Gunn to drop back the few steps they had advanced. "Oh, bullshit! I've know Carl Hudson for several years, and he's always been a short hitter. What the hell are you two talking about, anyway? What really concerns me is, was this a regular occurrence and could it have been prevented by one of you saying something earlier. Sheets, did Major Hudson regularly get drunk and drive around town?"

"No, Sir."

"Gunn?"

"No, Sir. Never!"

"Lt. Doyle?"

I nodded a short and neutral, "No, Sir." I saw no sense in making more trouble for Mumbles. He was already out of my hair.

Herder and Wolff exchanged wary glances over the hood of the jeep, and then Herder turned his head back over his shoulder to speak to Major Richter. "Bob, would you take Capt. Gunn and Lt. Doyle and wait with them in the mess hall. I'd like to see Capt. Sheets in the orderly room. When I'm through with him, he'll tell you who Colonel Wolff and I want to see next." He waved his hand in the direction of the mess hall, then signaling Colonel Wolff and Capt. Sheets, started towards the orderly room.

"Sir, uh, Colonel."

"Yes?"

"Well, uh, Sir, I, uh…"

"Oh, yes. Sutton, go on home, I'm through with you."

Over coffee, Gunn started the conversation. "Well, Major Richter, is there anything I can fill you in on while we wait?" He was holding his cup with both hands, but I could note a slight tremor in his hands, and his eyes kept darting to the door, watching for Sheet's return.

Richter seemed completely relaxed. He was obviously aware of what Herder and Wolff had planned. Sipping at his coffee and drawing casually on a cigarette, he put most of his attention on Gunn, at least for the time being. When he spoke, the words started slowly, and the last ones came clearly and rapidly, seeming to add a certain authority to whatever he was saying.

"You're the maintenance officer here, aren't you, Capt. Gunn?"

"Yes, Sir. We've had a less than 2% down time record since I took over."

Richter turned his eyes away from Gunn and asked, "What was the down time rate of the previous maintenance officer?"

Gunn hesitated, then said, "Well, Sir," stopped, drew on his coffee, then finally continued, "Well, Sir. It was about the same. Yes, Sir…As a matter of fact, it was exactly the same, Sir."

"So, you haven't improved it any, have you, Capt. Gunn?" Richter looked at poor Gunn with a cool stare.

His eyes unable to meet those of his new commander, Gunn turned them downward, and I could see his jaw starting to move, but there were no words forthcoming. I almost felt a little embarrassed for him, but Richter broke the silence.

"I'm sorry, Capt. Gunn, that was unnecessary. Less than 2% down time is a good rate for anyone." He paused. I later came to notice that in talking with Major Richter, he always controlled the conversation. When there were pauses, they were because he wanted them. When they were broken, it was usually by him, and it was never the Major who was made uncomfortable by them. It was maybe sixty seconds before he spoke. "Are you also a controller, Capt. Gunn?"

"Yes, Sir. I've got a secondary AFSC as a controller. Yes, Sir. I always told the Major, uhm, Major Hudson, that is, that I'd man a scope anytime it was needed. I'm ready to do my share to get this war over with."

The Major looked at Gunn with cool eyes and said, "Good, I'll remember your offer."

The three of us sat there in silence for several minutes; Gunn got up twice to refill his coffee cup, and the Major just sat there for minutes at a time seeming not even to move. In fact, I, too, found myself somewhat unsettled. The silence was broken by Sheets' entrance. His tan uniform was soiled by large splotches of sweat spreading out from his armpits. He bumped into another table, but still quickly got to ours.

"Bill, the Colonels would like to see you now." He jerked his hand in the direction of the orderly room. "Oh, excuse me, Major, Colonel Herder and Colonel Wolff would like to see Capt. Gunn."

"Of course, go ahead Capt. Gunn."

Gunn saluted and left. The Major smiled faintly as he returned Gunn's salute and then watched Guerrilla also stumble into one of the other tables.

Sheets, who was still standing, asked if it would be all right if he went back to operations for awhile as there were a few items he wanted to check on.

"Certainly, Capt. Sheets." he returned Sheets' salute and watched after him as Russ left, this time without bumping into anything. Again it was silent at the table, but I figured since I hadn't yet been challenged, I might as well take the initiative.

"Where were you before you went to Vietnam, Major?"

He brought his eyes up to meet mine and smiled faintly again." Germany." Without pausing, he directed the conversation back to me. "Besides being the admin officer, Lt. Doyle, what else do you do? That can't possibly keep you busy."

"Well, Sir, I've got additional duties of…" Fortunately it occurred to me that it was hardly necessary to run down the entire list. "Er, I'm in charge of all non-operational areas except radar maintenance and security."

Major Richter's eyes raised slightly, the first indication of surprise he'd yet shown. "All? Isn't that quite a bit, Lieutenant? I've never heard of such a situation."

There was no sense in trying to bullshit him, he'd find out sooner or later what my jobs were like. "Well, Sir, not really. Most of the shops kind of run themselves. I leave it more or less up to the NCO's and just drop around every now and then."

"You mean, Lt. Doyle,, that you're not working the Southeast Asia sixty-hour week?"

"Oh, oh no, Sir, I don't mean that," and then I couldn't go on any further. My face burst into a smile and I said, "Actually, I guess I do mean that, Sir. I spend about sixty hours a week in uniform, sitting at my desk, or walking around the site, but I'd hardly call it work. Hell, a lot of the time, I spend in the library, just reading." Suddenly I stopped. Had I just hung myself? If I had ever admitted that to Hudson, I'd have found myself with another idiot job in five minutes. What was there to assure me that Richter wouldn't do the same thing?

Now he smiled, and not faintly. "Good, I appreciate the honesty. I don't believe in keeping people tied to the site. It's nice to be around, in case you're needed, but it's hardly necessary to lock people to their jobs." He paused and looked out the window for several seconds before turning back to me. "What's your first name, Lt. Doyle?"

"Jim, Sir."

Gunn appeared in the doorway. He was pale white. When he spoke, his voice faltered. "Sir, Major Richter, Colonel Herder and Colonel Wolff would like to see Lt. Doyle."

"Fine. Go ahead, Jim. Capt. Gunn, sit down. I'd like to talk to you some more."

At the doorway, I could hear the beginnings of their talk.

"I understand you were in Germany before you came here, Captain?"

"Uh, yes, Sir."

"Where?"

Colonel Herder was sitting at Hudson's desk (I guess it was fair to still call it Hudson's, Major Richter hadn't even seen it yet). Colonel Wolff was seated off to one side. I saluted sharply and reported in. Herder mechanically returned my salute, but Wolff just stared at me. Nothing was said while I silently counted to ten.

Colonel Wolff spoke first. "Lt. Doyle, are you aware that Major Hudson was dissatisfied with your job performance?"

How does one respond t such a question, or a statement? The best I could say was a weak, "No, Sir." In fact I was stunned. I knew that Hudson and I had never really clicked. He was never comfortable around me, and I always thought he envied my rapport with the Thais, but I also thought he respected my competence, especially after the gate incident, and to learn he actually conveyed expression of displeasure on up the line was unsettling, to say the least.

"Well, he was. In fact, he had recommended that you be transferred to one of our sites in Vietnam. Did you know that?"

"No, Sir, I didn't."

Colonel Herder broke in. "You can stand at ease, Lieutenant. We're not sending you there. With this damn change her, we can't be sending out people who are familiar with the site."

At this point, I may have let out some air, or smiled, but I said nothing.

"Besides," Herder continued, "I've heard good things about you from other sources. You know, my group admin officer was impressed with you at the conference in Bangkok."

"Oh. Thank you, Sir."

There was another ten seconds of silence, before Wolff again broke the silence. "These are goddamned shitty times, Doyle. I want you to know that I think Major Hudson probably drove around in the bag quite a bit, and I think you were fucking lying earlier. But I only hold Sheets and Gunn responsible for not saying anything about it. I wouldn't want my lieutenants thinking they should be reporting on my majors."

You don't say anything to a statement like that, so there was another ten seconds of nothing. This time, however, it was Herder who spoke.

"Lt. Doyle, I understand you have a motorcycle."

"Yes, Sir."

"Did you know that was one of the things about you that displeased Major Hudson?"

"No, Sir." I lied about that. Hudson hated the bikes that so many of the airmen had. He regarded them as some sort of threat to his authority, and he often asked me, "Whenuh yuhgonnuhselluhgoddamnthin'?" And I would say, "Oh, I'll never sell my Honda, Major. It's like a part of me." Which he would react to by twisting his face and wringing his hands.

"Yes, he did. He thought you were irresponsible." Well, that proved Hudson couldn't be wrong all of the time.

Herder looked at me and smiled this time. "Lt. Doyle, I want you to tell all the officers that there'll be a special dinner tonight at seven o'clock in the best restaurant in town. Then get on that motorcycle of yours and get your ass downtown and set up the dinner. You pick the menu."

"Yes, Sir." I smiled, saluted and turned to leave, but Herder wanted to add something.

"Wait a minute, Doyle. Do you know Lt. Saunders?"

"Yes, Sir."

"Well make sure he's at the dinner, and make sure he sits next to me. I've heard so many good things about him, I want to finally meet him. Dismissed!"

CHAPTER EIGHTEEN

THE ENTIRE TIME I WAS notifying the other officers about the dinner, and the time I spent at Tipalow's ordering the food (pigeon egg soup, barbecued pork sticks, fried fish, vegetables tempura, chicken and noodles, Genghis Khan beef, and fried rice), there was gnawing at the back of my mind one thought: Oh, Christ, if Bob says anything to Herder about his plan to marry Renu, the shit will really hit the fan. So immediately after I had returned to the site and told Colonel Herder that the plans for the dinner were complete (I found him, Colonel Wolff, and Major Richter in the orderly room where Sgt. Chance was explaining that the personnel chart listed, "every fuckin' jerk on the whole fuckin' site and his fuckin' AFSC"), I went over to ops and asked Bob if we couldn't meet for a beer at the club.

"Gee, why would Colonel Herder want to sit next to me?"

"First, Bob, Colonel Herder does not want to sit next to you, he wants you to sit next to him. Second, when he gets back to Saigon and sees General Martin, he wants to be able to say, 'General Martin, Sir, I met that Lt. Saunders. He is one fine young officer.'"

"Oh, thank you, Jim."

I put my head in my hands and shuddered. "Bob, I am not congratulating you. I'm merely saying that I think Colonel Herder want to..., Oh, never mind."

"What I don't understand is what all this would mean to General Martin. I've never met him."

"Bob, please, listen. General Martin and your father-in-law are friends, right?" He nodded yes. "And they play golf together often, right?" He nodded yes again. "And when they play golf, it would not be unlikely that your father-in-law might say to General Martin, 'Say, you know my son-in-law, Lt. Robert A. Saunders, is going to be under your command this coming year.' Right?" Again Bob nodded yes. "And naturally, since they're old friends, General Martin, as a favor to your father-in-law, would sort of look out for you. Right?"

Bob's glasses were at a cockeyed angle, and I had the impression that one of his eyes was higher on his head than the other. He spoke. "Wouldn't that be favoritism? Gee, I sure wouldn't want anything like that. I ask only to be treated just like any other dedicated officer."

When I removed my head from my hands where I had placed it to brace myself for a sob that was working its way through my body, I said, "Bob, whether it's what you wanted or not, please believe me it's the truth. When you arrived here, Major Hudson received a phone call from Colonel Herder, who had before that received a phone call from General Martin. The message, all the way down the line, was 'Take special care of Lt. Saunders.'"

"You know, if that's true, maybe I should ask Colonel Herder to help me with the paperwork so I can marry Renu."

Shudder! "Bob, their interest in you is because you are married to the Colonel's daughter, and now that's the girl you want to divorce. Remember?"

"Oh, yeah."

At this point since I felt Bob had understood as many of the facts as he ever would, or at least as many as I was willing to try and explain, I plodded on into my plan. "Bob, remember the other day, our talk? Remember you agreed to go slowly, to let me help you?"

"Uh, huh."

"Well, at this point it's better to just go along the paper route way. Don't mention anything about your plans to Colonel Herder. And I want you to go as far as, if Colonel Herder asks you about your wife, to say, 'Betty is just fine.' Okay?"

"I'll try." I had visions of him *trying,* his brow furrowed, his glasses a kilter, biting on his tongue. Colonel Herder would think his prize lieutenant was suffering a fit.

When I left Bob at the table, I heard him saying quietly to himself, "Betty is just fine, Betty is just fine."

To say I was uncomfortable through dinner would be an understatement. The two colonels and Major Richter sat at the head of the table. Incongruously, and to the befuddlement of everyone else, but at the high command's insistence, Bob Saunders was also at the head of the table. Joe and I sat at the far end, with the rest of the gang and with Sheets and Gunn spread in between. Those two were remarkably quiet and subdued. At least Gunn was, until he had put away his fourth or fifth glass of Singha, when he brought to everyone's attention the altogether unremarkable coincidence that he and the new commander had both been stationed in Germany, albeit at different bases, and that, in admiration of German craftsmanship and efficiency, he had purchased, while there, ten cuckoo clocks.

Major Richter raised his eyebrows in the same manner he had done with me earlier in the day and said, "You bought ten cuckoo clocks?"

"Yes, Sir," boasted Gunn, "and they all work. And that's not all. I've ordered from the woodcarver in Chaing Mai ten custom made new housings for them. I recommend it for anyone who's bought German cuckoo clocks.

Herder, Wolff, and Richter all cast curious eyes on Gunn for several uncomfortable seconds, then nearly simultaneously turned away, perhaps to contemplate, like I was, the sound of midnight in the Gunn household.

However, his garrulousness did not last long. After his sixth or seventh Singha, his head began to nod, and, thanks to the superb efforts of Harry Simpson, who prevented him from putting his face into his fried rice, Gunn passed out sitting up.

The rest of the evening at Tipalow's was, except for the food, unremarkable. Of course, I did, each time I saw Colonel Herder lean toward Bob to ask a question or impart some wisdom, hold in my mouth whatever food I was chewing to wait, and, on signal from whatever the Colonel's reaction was, decide whether I should swallow it or, in horror, spit it out.

As the waiters were serving tea, hot towels, and small bottles of a glucose solution, which they claimed insured your potency, Colonel Herder bellowed down the length of the table, "Hey, Lt. Doyle, Colonel Wolff and I would like to do some partying and meet some of your fine pooyings."

Joe relieved me of some of the burden by saying, "Colonel, I believe I know just the place to go, the Mitrinakorn nightclub."

"Well, that sounds fine, that sounds just fine. I hope that everyone will join us."

However, before we were finished with our tea, Russ Sheets excused himself on the pretext of helping Gunn to his home ("He's been working real hard and he's bushed, Colonel"); and after dinner, I suggested to Bob he excuse himself to Colonel Herder claiming he was scheduled for the early shift, and he wanted to be alert. The Colonel gave him a nod of the head. Other than those three, we all headed for the Mitrinakorn, although I did remain behind a while to settle the bill with the restaurant owner.

When I was finally leaving, about ten minutes after the others had departed, I was met, out on the road, by two speeding samlows. In the first was Sheets, and in the second were Joy and her "sister," Cann.

"Where'd they go, where'd they go?"

"Who?"

"Colonel Herder and Colonel Wolff, who else, you jerk!"

"The Mitrinakorn," and before I could add, "where the hell'd you think, you asshole," Sheets had instructed the drivers to turn about and get to the Mitrinakorn as fast as "your little yellow legs can go."

When I entered the nightclub, Joe was standing at the door. The band was playing "Moon River." I expected to hear it at least a dozen more times that night.

"Where is everybody?"

"Over there, on the other side of the dance floor." Looking through the couples dancing, I could see Herder and Wolff, seated together. Resting on their laps were two of the dance hostesses who worked at the Mitrinakorn. For two dollars and fifty cents an hour the girls would sit at your table and dance with you. For an additional consideration, they could usually be persuaded to go home with you.

"Didn't Sheets get here with Joy and Cann?"

"Yeah, abut ten minutes ago. He came running through the door and went sailing up to Herder, saying, "Oh, Colonel, I've got two number one pooyings for you.' When the girls came near the table, Cann saw me and must've thought Russ was trying to fix her up with me again. She started yelling 'Oh, no, fuck you, G.I., I number one fuck, make love many generals, Cann no go with Fat Joe.' Then she turned and zipped out the door. Poor Russ and Joy went chasing after her."

"Who got them the girls they're with?"

"I was the pimp for that. I think they've already struck some ridiculous bargain for the evening." A Thai business man (the Mitrinakorn's clientele was only about twenty percent G.I.s) came by and asked Joe if he would like to join the man and his friends. Joe declined saying, "No, but thank you very much, I must get home. I have a lot of work tomorrow." He started for the door.

"You really going home?"

"No, I'm going to the Argo, where I can relax and enjoy myself. You coming?"

I told Joe I might see him there later, but I was curious to watch the group's dynamics for a while.

"Jim, they're senior Air Force officers, there's nothing interesting to watch. You've seen one, you've seen 'em all. Assholes!"

Despite this, I stayed. By the time I made my way across the floor, the band was playing a Thai song (it usually alternated, depending how many Americans were there that night, between a Thai song and an American one), and Herder and Wolff had gotten up to dance with their companions. In its proper form, the dance consisted of a line of dancers, men and women alternating positions, following about in a circle. The positions of the feet and the sweeping graceful arches of the arms, capped by the graceful lifting and falling of the hands, was said to have very beautiful, symbolic meanings. However, as Herder and Wolff performed it (my suspicions had been confirmed; Herder had been wearing a girdle at the airport. Now back in his bright sport shirt he appeared to be carrying a semi-inflated basketball around his waist), the dance looked like a bunch of drag queens flitting about on exhibition. I decided to keep my observation to myself.

As he was sitting down when the music ended, Colonel Herder called out to Major Richter, who was seated with some of the lieutenants a good twenty feet away, "Hey, Bob, you'd be smart to learn some of the native dances. It'll help you make a lot of friends later on." I winced as I watched some of the "natives" turn and cast hateful eyes upon our tables.

After he was seated and his girl was seated back on his lap, Herder spotted me seated with the other lieutenants and leaned back. "Hey, Lt. Doyle, what's that big captain's name again?"

"Stacy, Sir, Joe Stacy."

"Oh, yes," Then turning slightly in his chair, he addressed the Major. "Hey, Bob, that Stacy's a fine young officer. I'd keep him in mind if any positions open up at the site. Yes indeed, a fine young officer." At that point he turned around and nuzzled his face into the girl's breasts.

Near the end of my first Singha, Russ Sheets reappeared. Joy and Cann were with him again, and as they made their way across the floor, they were greeted by many turning heads, since the two were dressed in Micro-mini skirts, which, as if they weren't short enough, featured slits up the sides, nearly to their hips. I assumed they weren't wearing underpants. It soon became obvious there was trouble coming again, because while Russ was introducing the "sisters" to Herder and Wolff, the four girls (Joy and Cann, and the two hostesses) were exchanging the iciest of stares.

When Herder and Wolff indicated they were satisfied with their present companions, and Cann became aware she was suffering another rebuff, she blew up. Unfortunately, the band had stopped playing at that moment and her outburst was heard across the entire room in all its glorious and obscene eloquence.

"You big cocksucker, bum-fuck G.I. What'ch you think I am, anyhow? I number one fuck, ask anyone. I no go with old fat man who like ten-baht, cock sucking, mother fucking whore." Then she turned on her highly pointed heels and strutted across the dance floor, muttering some Thai words that Sunida would have never felt comfortable teaching me. When she reached the door, she turned and yelled back to our table. "Hey, Colonel, catch this, you fat slob!" And with a wonderfully practiced, theatrical gesture, she shot our group commander a highly graphic and emphatic finger.

The only sound I could hear in the next few seconds was the weak and very pathetic gurgle coming from somewhere in Russ Sheets' throat. Standing on the edge of the dance floor, he and Joy were, now that Cann had left, the only people in the entire room who were illuminated. He seemed a lonely and tired figure, and against my better judgment, I felt sorry for him.

At least a minimum of strength returned and he stumbled on in the only way he knew. Speaking over the heads of the two colonels, he asked Major Richter if he wouldn't like to sit with Joy, but the Major responded with a slow, blank, and negative nod of his head.

At this final indignity, Joy informed the rest of the audience, in Thai, that the G.I.'s were a "bunch of queers," and then to a round of laughter and whistles from the Thais strutted across the floor. The band joined in the merriment, and before she reached the door, had started to play "I'm Gonna Dance Till the Midnight Hour," which increased the laughter and screams from the tables.

Our group assumed that Joy was the butt of the laughter and joined in, but, even with my limited fluency, I knew it was all directed at us, and shortly after, I slunk out of the Mitrinakorn making sure to stay in the dark against the walls to join Joe at the Argo.

Joe thought that it was all very funny, and I had to admit to some humor in it as I related the events, but there was a queasiness in my stomach that had been there since I first saw the hate in the eyes of the Thai patrons and heard the derision and scorn in their laughter and whistles.

It took Supatra to cheer my mood at all. She came in the back door about twenty minutes after I had arrived, greeted me with a whistle, and, when closer, by grabbing my pecker.

"Captain Joe say you come by later. I go my room, make me look numba' one for you. What you think, s'okay?" She stepped back, and placing one hand on her hip, sticking her rear end in my direction, and her other hand on her head with the elbow jutting up into the air, said, "Ha, cha, cha." I laughed and said, "S'okay."

Following another hour of Singhas, Supatra came with me to my bungalow. We thrashed about for nearly an hour, but, although I didn't consider myself drunk and felt I was on the verge of it several times, I never reached an orgasm. At last, I gave up and collapsed onto my back. Supatra was very solicitous.

"S'okay, Jim. You still numba' one. S'appen to everyone. S'even happen to me. You believe that?" Then she turned over and was soon fast asleep.

I, however, did not sleep for a long time. I lay there thinking of…. In fact, I didn't know what I thought about, but I do know that each time I was about to fall asleep, I was awakened by the sound of derisive laughter.

CHAPTER NINETEEN

WHY I WAS SO PARTICULARLY disturbed by the scene in the Mitrinakorna eludes me. I know, and knew before that night, that there was a deep hostility towards us felt by most of the Thais. I even know that it extended to me: Witness the reaction against poor Sunida for only having dinner with me in public. And I certainly knew that Americans could act ridiculous in front of and abusive to Thais. (I, myself, had had my ridiculous moments, if not abusive ones, which I probably did too.) I was disturbed, hell, when I should have been elated at the ill winds that had blown towards Sheets and Gunn. Instead, I'm afraid I was distressed at having had to witness an ill mood I would have preferred only to know about, and never have seen.

But, there was little time for such reflection, and little time, as I've said, for much thought about Bob Saunders and his girlfriend. Major Richter tore into his new job with relish and also with great demands on everyone else. The two colonels had departed in mid-morning of the following day, Herder back in his girdle and showing obvious signs of distress, Wolff, his habitual mean temper showing in his face as always. Their plane had barely lifted off the runway and Richter, Sutton, and I (Sheets and Gunn were conspicuously absent from the unceremonial departure) turned to our jeep, then the Major said, "Jim, I want you to set up a Commander's call for Saturday morning. Everyone not on critical duty will be there. First, though, call a staff meeting for two this afternoon. All section chiefs, no assistants."

Sutton jumped in to say he would take care of that, but Major Richter stopped just as he was about to step into the jeep and turned on Sutton with his now familiar cold stare. "I said, 'Jim.'"

Sutton missed the Major's emphatic tone. "But, Sir, that responsibility has always fallen under the, uh, surveillance of my job description."

"Whatever you just said may well have *been* true, Sergeant, but I said, 'Jim'." Then as he climbed into the driver's seat of the jeep, he added, "I'll drive," leaving Sutton to scramble into the rear just before we pulled away.

Sgt. Sutton was able to retain his job of calling the meeting to attention when the commander entered the staff meeting. He did so, and then Major Richter, still standing at one end of the long table set up in the back room of the club, began, "Good afternoon, gentlemen. I wanted to meet each of you as soon as possible to start being able to associate your names and faces with your sections. I'll start with myself. I'm Major Robert L. Richter and for the last two months, I've been the Group Operations

Officer at Tan San Nhut. Before that, I was stationed in Germany. This is my first command, and I'm looking forward to it. I may add that I like to think I'm open about how to run things, but I will be demanding a lot of your attention, especially in these coming days. Now let's start around the room. Each of you identify yourselves, giving me your name and your section. Even if I've already met you, please give me it all again. We'll start here with Sgt. Sutton and continue around."

"Sgt. Sutton, uh, first sergeant."

"Sgt. Dugan, dispensary."

"Sgt. Kruger, supply."

"Sgt. Coyne, club."

"Sgt. Bailey, vehicle maintenance."

"Sgt. Russell, engineering."

"Sgt. Tremble, mess hall."

Major Richter broke in here. "Excuse me, Tremble, you're a buck sergeant. Now didn't I see a staff sergeant yesterday when I was in the mess hall?"

"Uhm, yes, Sir, that was Sgt. Tennyson, he's my boss."

"Your boss, is he? Then why isn't he here?"

"Well, he sent me, see."

"Yes, Sgt. Tremble, I do see that, but 'why' is my question?"

"Oh, he don't work in the afternoon."

"He don't do he? Sgt. Temble, is he still on the site?"

"Yes, Sir, he is."

"Then would you please go get him."

Tremble got up and left, and the Major signaled for the rest of the table to introduce themselves.

"Sgt. Patterson, mail room."

"Sgt. James, communications."

"Excuse me, hic, Sir. You wanted to see me, hic?" It was Sgt. Tennyson, standing at a wavering attention and saluting in the doorway, the rapidity of his appearance due to the fact he had been in the next room, drinking at the bar, which was his regular afternoon routine.

"You're Sgt. Tennyson, I take it. Could you tell me, Sergeant, why, when my orders were for 'all section chiefs, no associates,' that you chose to send Sgt. Tremble?"

The mess sergeant was still standing in the doorway, and although he was no longer saluting, he was still at attention. "Well, Sir, hic, I figgered sssince Sarjin' Tremle doessss alluh work innyway, you'd prob'ly jusht as sssoon have'im here, innyway."

Richter looked at me and raised his eyebrow. "Well, another honest man." Then turning back to the staff, he said, "Sit down, Sergeant. Let's continue with the last few of you."

"Capt. Sheets, operations."

"Sgt. Pivarnik, operations."

"Sgt. Ballard, maintenance."

"Capt. William H. Gunn, Jr., Sir, communications, equipment, maintenance, Sir. That includes responsibility for radar maintenance, as well, Sir."

"Yes, I'm quite aware of that, thank you."

There was a pause as the Major looked around the table, then stopping and looking at me again, he said, "And you, Lieutenant, you have a name and job I take it."

That cost me some of my self-satisfaction. "Oh, yes, Sir. Lt. Doyle, orderly room."

He let the meeting pause again, to reassert his presence, and then went on in his flat and unemotional voice. "Gentlemen, I'd like to say that I have not been given any, as they say, 'inside' information on any of you. I'm prepared to accept each of you on your performance. Also, this site is favorably viewed by Colonel Herder and Colonel Wolff, in spite of the events of the past week. That's behind us. Completely. I'll be around to each of your sections in the next few days. I'll expect a briefing and to be introduced to all of your people.

"Looking ahead a little, today is seven March; on twenty-five March, I'm leaving for a Group Commanders' Conference in Chiang Mai. By that time I expect to have a pretty sound idea about each of your operations. Since I'll be keeping after each of you quite a bit between now and then, and you all have your regular work to contend with, I will require, but not until after I return from Chiang Mai, a written report on your entire shop, to include procedures and work schedules. Also recommendations for improvements. You should each be thinking about it.

"Well, that's all for now."

Just before Sgt. Sutton could open his mouth to call the staff to attention for the Major's departure, Gunn spoke up. "Sir, I think I speak for every man here when I say I want you to know that we stand behind you to the man, Sir. And, of course, Sir, I want you to know that you can count on me at any time, Sir, to give one hundred and ten percent to make this the best, goddamned, radar site in all of Southeast Asia. Yes, Sir, one hundred and ten per cent!'

"Oh, well, that's nice, thank you, Captain," responded Richter, then he started to leave once again, but, he paused another split second before Sutton could get out his words to say, "As a matter of fact, Captain Gunn, it would be a great help to me if you would submit your written report to me on Monday, sort of give me a head start. Since you offered, I'll take you up on it."

From Gunn came a weak, "Oh," and Sutton finally called the group to attention, but Major Richter stopped, and while we all stood straight, said to Sutton, "Tell Tennyson to be in my office at seven-thirty tomorrow morning."

So in the days that followed, Major Richter caused a great deal of terror and panic. He asked Captain Sheets how many rendezvous operations had been handled n the month of February, which until Sgt. Pivarnik answered with the exact number—2,123—caused Sheets to stand in the center of the ops office saying something that sounded like, "Uh humma, humma, humma." The next time the Major asked Sheets something about ops—"How many intercepts did we handle last months?"—he made sure Pivarnik was not there to rescue the ops officer. In fact, he asked it while sitting across from Sheets at the officer's table during Saturday lunch. The Captain silently chewed on Saturday's regular hamburger till there could have been nothing in his mouth but a smooth paste.

"Capt. Sheets, while in Saigon I received copies of Detachment 8's monthly report, which listed these figures. I had assumed you had a hand in preparing these reports. I know them well, I suggest you become equally familiar with them."

The same was repeated in many other offices, but neither was Major Richter above citing someone for a good job; in particular he was impressed by Sgt. Patterson in the mail room, Joe with the operations training program, and Doc Dugan in the dispensary. Doc, in fact, was a direct contrast to Sheets:"How many cases of VD last month, Sir? Eleven doses of Gonorrhea, two cases of the shanks, six treatments for the crabs, two cases of non-specific, and one possible syphilis. We're waiting tests on that now. I'll let you know as soon as they're in."

So my days were filled with work, or a form of it following Richter about the site, answering his stream of questions about my areas (I thought I conducted myself well), and watching, with concealed delight, as he embarrassed a number of the thorns in my side. And, as I noted a while back, I was not prepared when early the next week, he called out to me, "Jim, what the hell's this 'request to Marry Foreign National'?

Sgt Chance said that at the sound of those words, he had looked over at me and saw my head rise from whatever I was reading on my desk, but that my face stayed where it was, and I had the look of an old and very troubled hound dog. I believe it. For the previous four or five days, I had been enjoying having little to think about other than the workings of the site. And, of course, I didn't have to anticipate or expect anything from or about Bob Saunders. Naturally, I had been fooling myself, and now I had to face it.

"Um, I believe, Sir, that Lt. Saunders wants to marry a girl he met in Bangkok."

Richter didn't look up from the form. "It says something about a 'divorce pending.'"

"Uhm, yes, Sir, he's going to divorce his wife back in the States."

"This girl he wants to marry, what do you know about her?"

"Um, I believe he met her, I mean I know he met her at Max's Bar in Bangkok. She's living with him at his bungalow now, Sir.

On this the Major looked up with a raised eyebrow, "He's divorcing his wife to marry a bar girl from Bangkok?"

"Um, yes, Sir."

Richter shrugged and made a short laugh, then signed his name in the blank that said, "Noted and forwarded." "That's his problem, not mine." And after he handed the form to me, he asked, "Isn't Saunders the one who Capt. Stacy said is having difficulties getting fully qualified?"

"Yes, Sir." I turned to leave, but after a short debate in my nervous mind, I elected to tell Major Richter the entire story. "Sir, there are some other things about the Saunders' situation that I think you ought to know."

The Major was already examining the next paper in the pile on his desk and did not bother to look up. "You mean that Saunders' father-in-law used to be General Martin's aide and they're still good friends and that Colonel Herder is very interested in seeing that Lt. Saunders is well taken care of."

"Um, y-y-yes."

"Colonel Herder told me all about the various relationships of Lt. Saunders. Of course I don't think he yet knows anything about this marriage and divorce business, does he?"

"No, Sir."

He looked up at me now. "I assume it's out of fear of Colonel Herder and General Martin that nothing has been done about Saunders' performance to date."

"Yes, Sir."

"And I assume that the piece of paper in your hand,: and he paused to point briefly at Bob's request, "caused a great deal of fear and trembling for my predecessor."

"Yes, Sir."

"Well, that's tough shit. Saunders is going to qualify or a report will be filed on him, and his 'request' will be sent along the chain just like anyone else's."

After several bewildered breathes, I finally said, "Yes, Sir," again and started out the door.

"Oh, Jim, just a minute." He was looking directly at me with his hands calmly folded into one another on the top of his desk. "Jim, don't think I'm some brave and naïve fool. It's just that I've got an angel of my own, and it's a pretty powerful one."

CHAPTER TWENTY

BOB SAUNDERS' "REQUEST" WAS RETURNED to the orderly room from Takhli's personnel office twice in the next two weeks. Each time, it was because of some bureaucratic nonsense: "Requestee Failed To Initial Form In Space 7b;" Or, "Line, *Additional Considerations* should be capitalized: Example; ADDITIONAL CONSIDERATIONS." Bob, a believer in the efficiency of the Air Force, did not correctly interpret the returns as the first signs of the Air Force's resistance to his intentions. He was undaunted and would continue to plug away in his fashion. In this respect, he was the perfect opponent of the bureaucracy, because Bob was the ultimate plodder, he was never discouraged by its plodding and could match it plod for plod forever. In the back of my mind there was the distressing image of Bob returning to the U.S. in late July when his tour ended, still trying to get his "Request to Marry Foreign National" past the Takhli personnel office.

The visit of the chaplain was not so easily dealt with. He had to at least be talked to. His office must have been one of the first notified when such "requests" came in, on the assumption, somewhat shaky in foundation, that a few words from one's spiritual counselor would soon dissuade a good American boy from wanting to involve himself in any permanent way with one of the natives. The Reverend "Swede" Svenson, Captain, Chaplain Corps, United States Air Force, had no sooner entered the orderly room, after having been met at the train and brought out to the site by Sgt. Sutton, then he asked if he couldn't meet with Lt. Saunders.

While waiting for Bob to be located and brought to the orderly room, Swede sat down in front of my desk, grinned (an unsettling and constant habit of his), and said, "I always love to get up here to NSG, great bunch of guys up here." That was his sobriquet for everyone, "great guy". For more than one, "great bunch of guys." That is except when referring to the pilots at Takhli (a group that I, at least in partial agreement with Joe, often found to be an obnoxious group of egomaniacs and fools), who he referred to a "a great, great bunch of guys", and, of course, the Wing Commander and Vice Commander at Takhli, occasional fliers of combat missions (usually those "special" ones, the wings of their F-105's loaded down with 1600 pound bombs till the tips nearly touched the ground before flying off to bomb the shit out of some swaying, bamboo bridges along the Ho Chi Minh Trail), who Chaplain Svenson always called, "a fantastic pair of super guys."

When I looked up at him, I saw he was about to speak some more. Through his grinning mouth, from beneath a bulbous, red nose (a physical sign that he spent many hours alone in his hooch, guzzling some kind of booze in order to avoid coming to grips with the strange place he had been plunked down in, where the men spent half their off duty time screwing the natives, and the other half drinking and talking about it), he said, "Well, Jim-Boy," (another irritating habit, adding "boy" to one's name), "What'd you think about the Super Bowl, hey?"

I tried the Major Richter approach. I kept my eyes on my desk, as if something there were demanding of my attention, and tried to speak in a very off hand manner. "Yeah, really something, Chaplain."

"Hey, Jim Boy, don't be so formal, you don't have to call me Chaplain."

"Okay, Captain Svenson."

I couldn't help but look up on that one. His face was grinning in a very uncertain manner that made him look about the room as if searching for some assistance.

He found it. "Hi, Chaplain, boy am I sure glad to see you. I need your help with a problem," said Bob as he entered the room.

"Hi Bob Boy, don't be so formal. You don't have to call me Chaplain." Within a few minutes they had left for the mess hall where they could talk.

As the door closed behind them, Lafayette looked up from a stack of file cards he was initialing in the upper left hand corner and said, "You know, I don't think thuh fuckin' chaplain's even gotten over what happened on that fuckin' picnic."

Svenson, like his fellow chaplains at Takhli—Parson, another Protestant (called Parson Parson) and O'Brien ("Pat" of course), the Catholic—was in the habit of making monthly visits to Nakorn Sarang in his enfeebled efforts to rescue our otherwise ignored souls. On the occasion of one of Svenson's visits, Sgt. Sutton, at the chaplain's urging, made arrangements for a Sunday picnic. The regular bus runs into the village were cancelled, and, instead, the bus was loaded with two clean garbage cans, filled with beer and ice and several coolers of sandwiches, sole slaw, and macaroni salad. Then, with Sgt. Hunnicut having volunteered as the driver, and all the seats filled with off duty airmen—many of them accompanied by girls from the Argo—the bus headed off towards the hills, where about twenty miles away, there was a series of waterfalls and an idyllic little pond. I decided not to go, but was at the site when the bus rolled back in, in the early evening. those who had not passed out and were still sober enough to sing were completing their umpteenth chorus of "Roll me over, lay me down and do it again, do it again." In the front of the bus, centered around Chaplain Svenson, were two airmen and Sgt. Sutton, countering with "Rock of Ages." First off the bus, Chaplain Svenson, with delirious eyes and nervous grin, said to me, as we watched the others stumble or be carried off, "What a great bunch of guys!"

On his next visit, Svenson brought with him a roll of movie film he had taken on the day of the picnic, and invited everyone to view it in the theater one afternoon. He must not have watched the movie himself previously. They were all of the airmen cavorting about in the water, splashing one another, eating sandwiches, drinking beer and soda, and, since the movies were soundless, appearing to have had a lot of good, clean fun. Sometime during the afternoon, Svenson had walked around to the opposite side of the pond and taken what he announced as, just before it flashed on the screen, "my panorama shot." It was initially an attractive enough bit of footage. With his high-priced Japanese camera and his super range finder, it was very clear indeed. Svenson again called out, "I couldn't even see it this clearly when I was taking it. What a great bunch of guys."

Suddenly, as we watched the splashing of the water and the sight of divers leaping from the rocks, someone yelled out. "Hey, lookit Hunnicut over there," and all eyes focused on the lower right corner of the screen, where Hunnicut, behind some rocks and trees and therefore hidden from the other bathers, but not from the camera's eye, was very unmistakably engaged in a bit of carnal exercise with one of the girls. The audience erupted into the obscenity that it was more comfortable with: "Hey Hunnicut, couldn't you have taken your shoes off?" "Who is she, Sarge?" "Hey, that looks like Capt. Sheets' girl," "Hunnicut, you got the ugliest ass in the whole goddamned Air Force," "Very unusual effect, Chaplain. What setting did you use on your camera?"

Poor Chaplain Svenson sat stunned, his face frozen in a painful nervous grin and his eyes flashing about until Sgt. Sutton reached over with his pocket knife and slit the film as it fed through the projector, then stood up, turned on the lights, and said, "Uh-oh, the film has, uh, destructed. I guess that's the end of the, uh, entertainment."

After the airmen had left the theater and Sgt. Sutton was rewinding the remainder of the film, Svenson, his composure apparently intact, said, "Gee, that's really too bad about the film. I hope it can be fixed. I had some great shots of the guys singing on the way back. They're all such a great bunch of guys."

I would have liked to listen in on the conversation between Bob and the Chaplain. It must have been the ultimate in two people working at absolute cross purposes. The Chaplain re-entered the orderly room just as Lafayette, in response to a request from Takhli's personnel office for the third or fourth copy of one of our airman's APR, let loose with, "That fuckin' NCOIC down there in fuckin' personnel is the dumbis' fuckin' jerk innuh whole fuckin' Air Force," so I'm not exactly sure what the Chaplain's especially uneasy grin was in response to.

Chance apologized. "Oh, I'm sorry, Chaps. If I'dduh known you was ther, I'dduh said fuckin' nothin'. Ah, shit, I'm sorry again. I bettuh jus' keep my fuckin' mouth shut. Shit!"

Smiley Burnett, his hand over his mouth to stifle a laugh, stood up, put on his cap, and raced out the door. On his way out, he collided with Sgt. Sutton who was entering.

"Uh, hiya, Reverend. All though there? Now, would you like to see the, uh, new chapel we have, uh, erected behind the movie screen?"

Svenson seemed delighted to be distracted from the performance being put on by my orderly room staff, but he was not quite through with the Bob Saunders' business. "Oh, yes, that would be really swell, Sgt. Sutton, but do you think I could use a phone to make a call first?"

Sutton made a sweeping gesture with one arm, apparently to indicate that the chaplain had the run of the whole place and said, "Uh, of course, please do, Reverend."

Svernson's entire face turned a bright red, thereby matching his nose, and seemingly embarrassed at not having his request understood immediately, added, "Gee, could I use a private phone, please, Sgt. Sutton?"

As Sutton escorted the chaplain into his own office, Svenson said, "Oh, great, gee, yes, that's just wonderful, swell, thank you Sergeant." When Sutton came back out of his office, he closed the door and placed himself squarely in front of it, sentry fashion. After stroking his thin moustache several times, he seemed to realize that neither Chance nor myself were about to storm the door, and he began to stride about the room.

I couldn't hear much of the conversation. Svenson's voice was very muffled (I suspect he kept one hand over the mouthpiece) and, of course, I didn't want to appear too inquisitive what with Sutton nervously pacing about the room. But the call took quite a time to be placed so it probably was beyond Takhli's exchange, and at one point I heard the chaplain say, "Yes, Colonel, that's exactly what I told him." There was a click of the phone being replaced in its cradle, followed by a silence of more than a minute, before the chaplain came out of the first sergeant's office, his composure restored, albeit a bit tenuously.

"Well, so the guys built a new chapel, hey Sgt. Sutton. Gee, that's great, just wonderful. What a great bunch of guys, great bunch." Actually, the chapel had been built by a local Thai carpenter using funds provided from Takhli's chaplain office. I doubted if more than five or six of our "great bunch of guys" even knew where the chapel was.

After Svenson and Sutton had left for their visit to the chapel, to be followed, I hoped, by a long tour of the site, it occurred to me that I had not heard the Chaplain refer to Bob as "a great guy." It was a significant omission. Bob's version of their conversation provided some explanation.

"I think the chaplain's on my side now."

"Why do you say that?" I asked.

"Well, he seemed to agree with me, and I agreed with him, too."

"He agreed with you?"

"Yes, he told me that marriage is a matter of trust and fidelity. That you have a tremendous obligation to the person you love."

"And?"

"I told him I agreed with him. So then I told him that's exactly why I wanted to marry Renu, because she is the girl I love the most."

"So, what'd he say?"

"Oh, he agreed."

"He did? You mean he said 'yes'?"

"Well, not exactly."

"What did he do?"

"He nodded his head, like this," and Bob began to shake his head up and down rapidly. I didn't bother to suggest to Bob that the chaplain may have been on the verge of a fit. All I did was say, "Oh."

Bob spared me any description of the two of them discussing the sexual aspects of the situation. Their conversation, he said, ended on another note of agreement.

"So, the Chaplain said to me, 'Well, my son, you will give a lot of consideration to everything I said, won't you?' And I said to him, 'Of course, Chaplain.' Then I told him that he'd been a great help to me, how just talking to him always seemed to help things, and how I knew things would work out for Renu and me now that he was on my side."

"And he nodded in agreement again, right?"

"Gee, yes, how'd you know?"

"Just a guess."

"Oh, Jim, something else happened later, something I don't think I understood."

"What was that?"

"Well, when I went back over to ops, Sgt. Reade said something to me which puzzled me."

"What'd he say?"

"He said how was my talk with Cecil B. DeMille?"

CHAPTER TWENTY-ONE

FOR THE MOST PART, BOB kept Renu away from the site. I was never sure if he did so out of respect for her, or just because he didn't care that much for the place to start with. He never was one to come out to the club at night, even before he brought Renu to live with him, and while he probably would have liked to go to the movies, the usual raucousness of the theater (a lot of drinking was done in there, and that generally incited a constant and frequently obscene dialogue between the audience and the screen) discomforted him. Of course, if it were permissible for Renu to enter to the ops office and the dark room, Bob would have taken here there, since he admired those places. As he would say, standing on the top dais and surveying the three levels of equipment, "It makes a man proud to be where the action is." But, as Bob was the first to point out, the rules and regulations would not permit her to enter there. So, in the first weeks following Bob's "engagement" and Hudson's subsequent departure, I saw little of Renu. Bob and she spent their evenings at his bungalow. She would shop during the day, and under Bob's careful eye (there would be no dog meat consumed in his home), she prepared meals, and then they would listen to music, or talk, even occasionally go to a movie in the village, or they would do whatever it was that such couples did.

Bob and the Air Force having settled into a sort of trench warfare, and Major Richter quietly and efficiently picking up the reins of command, my life settled down itself. I tended to the many forms that Lafayette prepared for my signature, made leisurely walks around the site to "supervise" my many areas of responsibility, drank more than was necessary—although not with the same intensity that I demonstrated only shortly before—and I concentrated on my Thai lessons. The first ones to be held in the orderly room were unproductive and uncomfortable, but after the initial awkwardness of the situation had faded, Sunida's efficiency and dedication as a teacher returned.

A benefit of this new arrangement that I had not foreseen was that I could then ride with Sunida to town when the lessons had ended. I was at first reluctant to suggest it, in view of the possibility of reviving the unfortunate rumors, but the implications were not as severe as the two of us dining together in the village. After all, most of the village knew she worked at the site and understood her reasons for it; and, if the two of us left work at the same time, and rode in the same direction, then it would be foolish not to ride together. So, on nights when I felt like going directly home, instead of drinking at the club, Sunida and I rode home with each other—I putting on my Honda alongside of her in first gear.

She always rode so effortlessly. In the great heat of Nakorn Sarang, she had only the finest film of perspiration on her skin, and I was covered with large beads of sweat even while riding my motorcycle. The light from the setting sun with its reddish tint, more than ever made her skin glow. It was all I could do to keep my Honda upright. But at times, we did manage to talk, although generally not about much.

But that wasn't always true.

"I like Major Richter," she said to me one evening, shortly after we left the site.

"Good, I'm glad. It makes work easier."

"I understand when he talk. That is most important thing for me." She looked over and smiled briefly.

"Yes, I like him much better, too." So far it was just another conversation, the kind we routinely indulged in on the ride home, but that I enjoyed because I was able to stare at her.

When we had reached the airport and moved onto a paved road, with her eyes straight ahead, she asked, "How is Lt. Saunders?"

"What?" (Here we go again.)

"How is Lt. Saunders?" She was still looking ahead.

"Oh, he's okay, I guess. Why do you ask?"

She blushed slightly, or was it just the light from the sunset. "I am told he want to marry Thai girl. Girl from Bangkok. She is very pretty, yes?"

"Well, uh, yes, she is, I guess. Yes, he says he's going to. But, I didn't know you knew about it."

She appeared to be watching some children at play along the side of the road, the side away from me. "It is small town, I hear many things, but I thought Lt. Saunders had wife in America."

"Yes, he does, but he's divorcing her."

"Excuse me, I do not understand."

"Divorce, it means he's ending the marriage, so he can marry Renu."

"Renu, that is the girl's name?"

"Yes." She had looked briefly at me when she said the last thing, and I continued, "What do you think of this?"

"Oh, if he is happy, then I am happy for him."

"But what do you think about him marrying a Thai, is that good or bad?"

"It is fine if everything will be all right, but I think there will be problems."

"Like what?"

"They cannot live here. Lt. Saunders is not kind of farang who can live in Thailand. He misses America too much. So they will live there. I think there are many Americans who do not like to see American marry Thai. It will be hard for her."

"That's true. Are there other things?"

Since we were outside the driveway to my bungalow, we stopped riding and paused for a moment. This time, she blushed without a doubt. "Yes. She is girl from bar. If that is known, it will be very hard for her, I think. In Thailand not good. In America, maybe more bad."

Just as she rose to push off again on her bike, I held her back with a question. "Sunida, could you marry a farang?"

She took her foot off the pedal and turned and faced me. She didn't smile, but there was genuine warmth in her face—or maybe it was just the deepening sunset (I've never been one to understand such things in a woman). After some time she said to me, "Yes, I think I could marry farang, but I could not leave Thailand. Maybe visit America sometime, but I must live in Nakorn Sarang or Pitchit."

I only stared at her, I think with my mouth open. After several seconds, she looked away from me briefly, and when she returned her eyes, she was smiling in a light way. She rose off the bike pedals to pull away from me, and when she waved, I said, "Oh," and stared after her till she was indistinguishable from the others in the street.

By then the Honda had stalled and rather than start it again, I walked it up my driveway and parked it under the bungalow. All the time I pushed it up the driveway, I tried to avoid thinking about what I might have just said. While I was physically involved in putting the bike away, I could manage it, but by the time I had climbed the steps to the porch, I could no longer keep from confronting it, and I thought to myself, "Holy Christ, I think I may have just proposed to Sunida, and, even more amazing, she may have in a fashion, accepted."

For some time I stayed on the porch and stared into the sunset. The setting of the sun in Thailand on days when the sky was relatively clear, was a truly beautiful event. Red beams of light would make their way through the patchy and turbulent skies and cast their rosy glows on the trees and bungalows. Standing and leaning against the rail of my porch, I watched the sky to go through a series of convolutions and permutations that even without being a very literate or romantic person, I found symbolic of the unstable nature of my life. I had never thought of the word "marry" at any time when considering Sunida, but without any stretch of the imagination, one could say I had just asked her to marry me. And she had answered in no less definitive a manner, that yes, she would within certain conditions. Just as the sunset seemed to be losing its attractiveness in a mass of clouds, it suddenly burst open again and drenched the porch in a flood of crimson light. Of course, those conditions she had set forth (hell, I had nearly two years to go in the Air Force, even after my tour in Thailand was over) certainly complicated things. Until then, I had not even thought about marriage with anyone, and I was trying to come to grips with a nearly firm acceptance of a proposal that had blurted out of me before its meaning was even clear in my mind. What the hell would I do in Thailand for a living? Was it even possible? Would the

Thai government let me stay? Standing there on the porch, I found myself wishing I would step back thirty minutes in time and eliminate those words from my life so I could properly consider things without the pressure of what I thought I had just said.

"Sawadee, Jim."

I turned and it was Ewan. She stepped out onto the porch letting the screen door close behind her. Her paisin was hung over one shoulder and her long hair was piled on her head so that her neck would be open to the breeze. The sun's light cast her skin in deep, rich bronze.

"Where Joe?" It was her regular opening question, to clear the air as to why she was there. I should always understand that she was first and foremost interested in him. Once understood, we could talk in our normal fashion.

"He's at the site. I think he said he was going to stay and see the movie." Joe was, for the most part, as ignorant as I was of Ewan's arrival and departure schedule. "Do you want me to go out and tell him you're here."

"No, he come soon, s'okay." She waved her hand and I watched its graceful arch. As she turned to go back inside, she asked, "How you be, Jim?"

I thought about Sunida and the great puzzle clunking about in my brain and said, "Oh, about the same as always."

"Good. You like beer? I get." I nodded yes and went through the door to find Renu sitting in one of the rattan chairs. Had I entered the room and found my mother sitting there, I could not have been more shocked, so even after she had risen and given me a more than polite wai and said, "Sawadee, kun sabai dee loo," I could no more than manage a weak, "Oh."

Of course there was nothing really surprising about finding Renu there. She and Ewan were friends, and when Ewan had arrived on the afternoon train, and found Joe not yet home, she sought out Renu, and now the two of them were sitting in my bungalow chatting about I don't know what—Nakorn Sarang, perhaps—as I entered after having possibly just proposed to the site librarian.

I did eventually recover my composure, or whatever it is that passes for it in my mind, and after Ewan explained the obvious to me, I changed into a paisin (I, like Joe, had come to find these robes the most comfortable outfit in which to wait out the heat) and sat down to talk to the girls.

I opened the conversation with the remarkably perceptive and witty, "Where's Bob?"

She smiled (it was the same beguiling child's smile that I remembered from the night in Bangkok) and said, "He work night. Bob say be home maybe twelve midnight."

"Oh." (It seemed to be replacing "what" in my vocabulary)

Ewan came into the room with my beer and said, "I bring letter from Pitsommai." With that she ducked into Joe's room to return with a perfumed blue envelope. It was addressed to Mr. Lt. Jim Doyle. I suggested that I read it later, but the girls insisted I open it immediately, so I did. It was short and written in a neat and slightly unsure hand. I quote in its entirety:

> Hello handsome G.I. Jim. Tee hee.
> I miss you too much. When you are gone, I no butterfly.
> Stay home every night. Tee hee. When you come see me?
> Write letter to me please. I can read the English.
> You are my favorite man.
>
> Love, your friend Pitsommai
> P.S.: Do not drink too much

I was touched by the words. I could imagine her leaning over the paper (it was decorated along one border with pictures of frolicking little lambs sporting blue and pink ribbons around their necks) alternately chewing on one end of her pen and then carefully and laboriously forming the foreign letters. The image made me pause and reflect on Pitsommai for some time; naturally, my fantasy eventually made its way into her bed.

When I finally looked up Renu was looking at me and giggling, and Ewan was nearly laughing—her normal bittersweet smile having spread into wide grin. The cause of their laughter was a bulge in my paisin, the result of an erection I had conjured up. I crossed my legs and reached for my beer.

Renu was wearing a short, jumper style dress. While I sat there trying to pretend I wasn't embarrassed, she pulled her legs up so that she was scrunched in the chair. It was a charmingly coquettish move, the type I associated with movies starring Nancy Kwan and France Nuyen.

When I felt sufficiently comfortable with myself I spoke. "So, you're going to America."

She again made her little girl's laugh, and with raised eyebrows said, "Oh, yes, that is what I hear."

"You don't believe you really will?"

"Oh, maybe," and then she shook her head in a light pleasant way, "but I think I will stay in Thailand."

"You mean, you may say no to Bob."

Her face became quickly serious and she looked directly at me as she said, "Oh, no, no. If Bob want to go America, I go."

"But you said you think you will stay in Thailand."

"Yes, I do."

"But, I, uh, I don't understand. You said…" At this point my words trailed off, and I turned to Ewan. When she saw my eyes, she seemed to understand and turned to Renu and started speaking very rapidly in Thai. I couldn't keep up with her talk, but I know she started by saying that I was confused, and I heard her say "America" several times, and Bob's name was mentioned.

Renu looked back at me when Ewan finished. She continued to mile. "I mean I not think Bob will take me to America, but if he want, I go."

"But he says he wants to marry you, he says so."

"G.I. say many thing. Bob is G.I."

"You mean you don't believe him. You think he's lying."

She shook her head vigorously. "Oh, no, Bob no lie. But I think he will change mind."

"So why did you come here? If you don't really believe he'll marry you and take you to America, why'd you come?" I was getting a little excited and was beginning to speak rapidly. Renu looked at me with a puzzled expression for a moment, but Ewan broke in again and said something. Then Renu turned back to me.

"Because Bob is nice to me. Never yell, never hit. Ask me what I want. He buy for me. you say, I think, he very thoughtful."

"Bob is?" Such ideas are enough to cloud one's brain. Bob Saunders thoughtful? You couldn't even call Bob Saunders thoughtless. Thought was not a quality that entered one's mind when considering him.

"Yes, very."

"And just for that, because he's 'thoughtful,' because he's nice to you, you will marry him and go to America if he want you to?"

She answered, "Yes," so quickly and so sharply that I was left speechless for several seconds. I noticed Ewan seemed to be laughing.

"But do you love him? Does he love you?" I asked.

"He say he love me."

"Do you love him"

Renu and Ewan caught each other's eyes, and Renu nodded her head before continuing. "Yes, if you like, I love him."

"No, not if I like. I mean if you're going to marry him and go to America, you have to be in love, right?"

"I say before. Bob is nice to me. No yell, no hit. Buy me things, very thoughtful. Because he is nice, I will be nice and do what he want. I *do* like him. He is cute, like, what you say, teddy bear."

A teddy bear? "I think I'll have another beer." I had two, one without leaving the kitchen, the second I brought back to the living room.

Joe came home a little after eight. "I was going to stay for the entire movie. It was one of the James Bond jobs. Problem was the shipment must've gotten screwed up, and we ended up with two first reels. At Takhli they're probably showing two second reels. On top of that, Hunnicut was sitting next to me, smashed. He passed out early in the movie. By the time the titles came on for the second time, he was snoring like a bandit."

Ewan had risen to greet him with her customary wai, and, with a pleasantly surprised look on his face, Joe returned it. When Renu also extended a wai, Joe smiled and said, "The future Mrs. Bob Saunders, I presume." It reminded me how little attention Joe paid to Bob. It was nearly a month since Bob had returned from Bangkok with Renu, and this was the first time Joe had met her.

"Well, the sun's down. Why don't I shower, then we'll all go to the Hoa Far and eat." I liked the sound of the idea immediately, but Renu began to speak rapidly to Ewan, and without any hesitation Ewan told Joe that she had already bought some meat, rice, noodles and vegetables to cook for all of us. It seemed agreeable enough, and then I realized I had heard Renu saying that she could not go to a restaurant without Bob.

After the girls had gone downstairs to the kitchen (it was a room separate from the rest of the bungalow, although the refrigerator and dining table were upstairs in a room I normally referred to as the kitchen) and Joe had showered and changed into his paisin, the two of us sat in the living room, drinking beers and waiting for our dinner. For a while we talked about the general panic Major Richter was causing on the site with his requests for detailed reports on each section. Joe had spent the better part of the day briefing Sheets on how operations worked. Sheets had conducted it as if he were checking on Joe but like many other section chiefs, he was scared about the report he was supposed to have ready for major Richter upon the commander's return from the conference he was presently attending in Chiang Mai.

But when Joe came back to the living room after going for another round of beers he changed the subject. "You know, I figured Ewan had bought some food for a meal. She usually doesn't put her hair up if she figures on going out again that night, but I suggested it to see what Renu's reaction would be. I was impressed. She's not just another bar girl, she has come sense of appearances. She wouldn't want to embarrass herself or Saunders by being seen in town with someone else."

I agreed. "Yeah, that's what I thought too." Then after some silence, and as the pungent smells of beef frying in oil with scallions, garlic, and peppers wafted its way into the living room, I mused out loud, "You know, I wonder what she sees in someone like Bob. I'm not trying to say she should be with someone like me, but I can't figure out what the hell she sees in that turkey."

"None of them, not even Ewan or Pitsommai, are looking for the same things we're used to being concerned about."

Joe paused. I said, "Oh?"

Looking across the room at me, he laughed and continued. "Oh, don't worry, they recognize a lot of the same romantic images we do. There's not a bar girl, or for that matter probably any girl in all of Thailand that doesn't skip a goddamned heartbeat when they see Paul Newman in a picture, but what I'm saying is this, when it comes to who they want to live with, they'll take the plain jerk who doesn't beat them, is kind to them. Saunders shares our stupid, silly romantic ideas. He probably thinks Renu is the prettiest girl he's ever seen. Jesus, you remember the picture of that dog of a wife he used to keep on his desk. So now, he had a little pooying, a regular Siamese doll, and he can't be nice enough to her. And if he's nice to her, she feels she should be nice to him. He's in love, and she's devoted."

"Hey, come on. Look at Russ Sheet's tee-loc. Every time he turns around she's banging half the base and most of the Thai third army. It's the same with most of the other hired wives I can think of."

"Wait a minute. Don't misunderstand me. The coldest goddamned thing in the world is still a whore's heart, but there are always some exceptions. Ewan, when she's back in Bangkok, has got to make a living, but when she's here, she feels a responsibility to be faithful to me because I treat her decently."

"But, Jesus, Joe, anyone can see she's in love with you."

He drew deeply on his beer. "Don't get your terms confused. We're talking about two different worlds. I'm sure there's some real affection on her part, probably even what we'd call love, but that's developed very slowly, over better than four years, and it's not what she makes her decisions on. At first, she just felt she wanted to be nice to me because I had been nice to her, and she wanted me to continue to be nice to her. Most of these poor girls don't get treated with much consideration very often. When they are, they're appreciative."

"And what about you?"

"Me?"

"What do you feel?"

"Oh, shit, I'm in love with her, of course. I have been since shortly after I met her."

Now that was a shock to me. I mumbled something about getting another beer and went to the refrigerator. As I stood in front of it and reached for the cans, it struck me how poorly I had read things. I had always had the situation reversed; Ewan certainly, to me, had always been deeply in love with Joe, and he, being cynical but kindly, had treated her with gentleness and consideration out of respect and general decency, but not out of what one would normally consider to be love. Yet if this new state, new to me that is, was true then what the hell was Joe going to do about it? He had already told me he wasn't planning on staying in the Air Force. That meant the end of free tickets to Thailand. Was he going to marry her and take her home, or would he find a way to stay here and marry her?

"Jim, unfortunately nothing will happen. there's no way Ewan could ever come back to the U.S. with me. She'd never be able to stand it. It would be horrible, can you imagine her settling down in Missouri? She wouldn't last two years before she'd be begging me to send her back to Bangkok. Or she might start hitting the sauce. Whatever, she couldn't stand it. And how could I stay here? What would I do, run opium? I suppose I could get a job with Air America or some other CIA cover, but can you imagine having to spend much time with those lunatics and clowns. It'd be worse than the Air Force. Those fucking assholes really believe in themselves. Besides, I want to get completely away from the goddamned United States government and what they're doing over here.

"So, anyway, there's no way for Ewan and me. I'm going to send her some money, so she'll have some independence. In four or five years, we've talked about having her, as they say, retire. I'll send her a lump sum—who knows, I might even take a vacation and come over and bring it to her in person—and she'll get out of the business. It's not too difficult to buy your way out of your own past over here, and she might even settle down to a fairly respectable Thai family life. Of course, that'd be the end of everything for us; no more letters, no more money, no more visits."

There wasn't time to reflect on the sadness of what Joe had just said. We were interrupted by the girls coming up the back stairs, carrying two platters. One, steeped with rice covered with the fried beef I had smelled cooking, let off the richest and most edible of aromas as it was placed on the table. The other, heavy with cut mangoes, bananas, and lumyi—a grapelike fruit—was placed in the refrigerator to stay cold till we had consumed the rich beef, vegetables, peppers, scallions and rice. To add to it, Joe reached into the back of the refrigerator and came out with a well-chilled bottle of Mateus he had been saving for such an occasion. Actually, we often hid bottles of Mateus in the back of the cooler—for some "special occasion," as we like to say—but they were usually consumed late in the evening as a nightcap to what had been a distinctly less than "special occasion." Our pleasure, in this instance, was heightened by the experience of seeing a bottle through to its intended use.

The meal of course was a delight, and as we sat, sated, nibbling on the fruit and sipping the last of the Mateus (in truth, Joe and I had drunk most of it. Ewan and Renu, after sipping small portions early had switched to the water our maid had boiled and placed in the refrigerator), and the delightful exhaustion that follows such a meal draped itself over me, I found myself amused and beguiled by an endless mirage of Thai women, and at the center of them were four special ones: Ewan, mysterious and soft; Sunida, shy and beautiful; Pitsommai, sexy and lively; and Renu, childlike and precious. I no sooner focused it in my mind before it was gone, and I was back at the table, raising glass to mouth for the last of the wine.

At eleven Renu said it was time for her to start home and asked if it would be all right if she took some of the left over fruit so she would have something for Bob when he got home at midnight. Since I knew from past experience that it was unlikely there would be a samlow around at that hour, I offered to take her home on my Honda. She declined saying she was frightened by motorcycles. Instead, I sped into the center of the village and found Chan, my favorite driver and asked him to come back to my bungalow with his samlow. Back at the house I offered to walk Renu to the end of the driveway to wait for Chan.

As we walked down the way, I, back in my pants and shirt I had put on to ride into the village, and Renu in her short dress and carrying a bag of fruit, there was a hint of coolness in the air. It was still several weeks till the Water Festival, the holiday which celebrated the return of the rainy season, and in this time of relative dryness, the evenings could be quite cool and pleasant. However, the Thais found them too chilly. Renu was shivering, and I took off my shirt and placed it over her shoulders. She accepted it without embarrassment, looked up and smiled, and kept on her way toward the road.

"Bob say you learn speak Thai."

"Yes, I'm trying."

"Could you speak Thai, please?"

"Yes, of course. But you must speak slow, or I won't understand you."

She smiled and spoke back to me in a moderately paced voice. For the rest of our wait, we spoke in Thai.

"Bob has told me that you are being very helpful to us."

"I am just making sure that he does what is necessary to bring you to America with him."

"It is very nice of you, and I thank you for it."

"Oh, you mean you do want to go to America."

"Yes. Why do you not believe me?"

"Well, you said before you did not think you would really go."

"Yes, I said I do not think so, but I do want to. And, I think if you are a friend of Bob and you will help us, I think I will go.

"Thank you. If you want to go, I will do everything I can to help. I hope you will like it."

She looked down the road. The samlow was not yet in sight. When she turned back to me, there was a quizzical look on her face. "You do not like Bob, do you, Jim?"

I hope in the dark she couldn't follow my eyes, because I think they betrayed me. My voice did too because, for a second, I broke into English. But I managed to finally speak in Thai. "No, that is not true. He is not a good friend, like Joe, but I like him. Does Bob think I do not like him?"

"Oh, no. He thinks you are his best friend." (I shuddered) "But, I do not think you like him too much. I remember you told Pitsommai you wanted a girl for, as you say, a 'dummy'. I said I would go because she was my friend, and I would do her a favor."

"I thought you liked him."

"I did. Even that night he was very polite and very kind. When I asked if he wanted me to go to his hotel with him, he was very surprised and said no. But I said it was all right if he did not take me with him, but it was also all right if he changed his mind because I thought he was very nice. Then we went to a nightclub. We danced. He is not a good dancer. We had some drinks. We talked a lot. I told him many things about girls in Bangkok and how to save his money."

"Yes, he told me about that."

She smiled and went on. "Later, he asked me if I would still go to his hotel with him. He said I was the prettiest girl he had ever known, that I made him feel very nice, and he did not want to go to hotel alone. I said yes, I would go. When I woke up in the morning, he was sitting on the side of the bed. He was all dressed. He said he wanted me to come to Nakorn Sarang with him. He said then we would get married and later go back to America. At first I thought it was very funny, and I laughed. But he said he was not joking. He wanted me to get up and go to my home to pack my things. He kept saying this. Soon, I began to think maybe I will go to Nakorn Sarang. I did not think he really meant to take me to America, but I had not been to Nakorn Sarang, and Ewan said it was very nice. It seemed like a chance for a vacation."

I could see Chan peddling his samlow up the road. He would be to us in a few moments. "You came here for a vacation, but now you want to marry Bob and go to America."

"Yes. I thought when I got here Bob would change and start to be like other G.I.'s. I thought he would become mean and want me to do everything for him. When he started being like that, then I would go back to Bangkok. But he always stays the same. He is always very kind, always thoughtful. At first, when I said I wanted something, he would buy it for me. Now, I do not say I want things because I do not want to waste his money. He is not very handsome, not like you," (I blushed at this outrageous flattery) "but he becomes very cute the longer you see him. He is like teddy bear."

"Yes, you said that."

"At first I thought I do not dislike him. It is all right to spend time with him. But then I started to like him. He is always so good to me that I want to be good to him. He kept saying he wanted to marry me and take me back to America. I began to think if he will do that, I will go because I do not think I will ever meet another man who is so kind. But if he changes his mind, that will be all right too. I will have had a nice time in Nakorn Sarang and will go back to Bangkok. When he said you were going to help us, I thought it might really happen because Ewan and Pitsommai have said you are a nice man. Then tonight I met you and talked to you. Now I think, yes, I will go to America because Jim will help Bob and me."

Chan and his samlow were alongside us by then. I was badly tempted to grab Renu and kiss her, but I restrained myself and settled for firmly grasping her hand as I helped her into the seat. While doing so, I said in English, "Everything is going to be all right." When I turned to Chan to give him ten baht—five for coming out to my bungalow and five for taking Renu home—I was met with a rogue's admiring leer, and I realized immediately what he was thinking. After all, what would I think if I saw some guy putting a lady into a cab, he bare-chested, and she wearing his shirt? I declined to say anything for fear of embarrassing Renu, and it was more than likely fruitless, anyway. I waved goodbye and for the second time in the same evening stood at the end of my driveway and watched until the girl (girl who I had never more than touched her hand) disappeared from my sight.

Back in the bungalow, Joe and Ewan had retired to their bedroom. The door to the room was closed, the fans were all on high, and Joe had placed a transistor radio in the living room turned to a program of Thai music. They were all effective bafflers of the sound of their lovemaking. As I sat alone in the living room drinking beers, the slight tremor of the house was more noticeable than any sounds.

After I had finished my third beer, and as the hands of the clock merged to signify twelve midnight, and as I realized Bob Saunders was returning to his home and Renu, I began considering making a trip to the Argo Bar. Fortunately, my eyes began to sag with drowsiness at the same time, and remembering the outcome of my last late night visit to the Argo, I wisely elected to go to bed.

Just before the last holds on my consciousness gave out and I dropped into a deep and boozy sleep, I thought of Sunida and our talk, of Joe's words, and of Renu. I think I heard myself say out loud, "Jesus Christ, I don't believe it, but I'm actually jealous of Bob Saunders!"

MARCH 1968

CHAPTER TWENTY-TWO

WHEN MAJOR RICHTER RETURNED FROM the Commanders' Conference in Chiang Mai, I alone met him at the airport. The days of our large greeting parties—exchanging formal and grim salutes—seemed to have gone by the boards. I, out of force of habit and a slight sense of apprehension towards the Major which he carefully allowed me to retain, did rigidly salute, but he casually waved at his forehead as he stepped down off the C-47's ladder and asked, "Well, anything I should know immediately, Jim?"

As we walked to the jeep, I mentioned a couple of items—things like newly arrived supplies—but didn't see fit to mention that I may have proposed to the site librarian. After all, Sunida and I had not, since the night we rode home together, mentioned the subject. I, of course, was hesitant to for fear she would laugh at me, and Sunida, it was apparent, had the good sense to view the entire conversation as a hypothetical exercise. At least that's my impression of her reaction, since she said nothing about our short talk and yet was still warm and friendly to me. We had had one subsequent lesson after which I elected not to ride into town with her but claimed I was going to stay and watch the movie. Actually, I stayed and drank beers for several hours before going home to a solid sleep. Oh, yes, the lesson was marked by Sunida's strict professionalism, so there was nothing said then.

Major Richter and I sat in the jeep and watched the old Goony Bird clear the end of the runway. After it had and as I was starting to let out the clutch, he turned and said, "Well, Jim, we're going to win the war."

My foot slipped off the clutch, and the jeep and I both coughed. I started the vehicle up again and said, "Pardon me?" even though I heard him perfectly clearly and knew exactly what he meant.

"We're going to finally win the war." He spoke, as always, calmly and without any false emotion. "Colonel Herder had all of us together this morning. He told us about his most recent meeting with General Westmoreland. I'm sure it was a large briefing, but the Colonel seemed to prefer letting us assume it was a face-to-face encounter. Anyway, Westmoreland's back in Washington right now with President Johnson making his recommendations in response to Tet. Two hundred and six thousand more troops for Nam alone, and he wants to start bombing everything that moves in the North. That's where we come in. If his recommendations are accepted, and it's about a ninety-nine percent certainty that they will be, then we're going to be very busy here. Whereas up to now, we've been working with morning strikes only and then sitting around waiting on recoveries, from now on we'll be working with three and four sets of strikes a day. It'll be months before our manpower need catch up with us, so we, the controllers at least, will be working our asses off. As soon as we get back to the site, I want you to get all the controllers together in the ops office, plus Capt. Gunn and yourself. Let me know as soon as you get them altogether."

I listened numbly and said, "Yes, Sir." The meeting was easy enough to arrange. By mid-afternoon, the entire group had been assembled, and the Major and I started the short walk to operations. "You know, Jim, this may amuse you and besides as the admin officer you probably ought to know this. As the meeting was ending this morning, Colonel Herder asked me to wait and when the others were gone, he went into a tirade about Lt. Saunders and this stuff about his divorce and marriage. He said he didn't care how I did it, but he wanted this 'silliness' as he put it, ended. Said General Martin had called him several times about it, and the General says it *will* stop immediately. I didn't say anything, but can you believe it? He was actually more excited about this damn foolishness than he was about the other news. I found it hard to even believe he'd take the time to talk about it."

Like the Major, I too found it hard to imagine anyone, let alone Colonel Herder, mentioning the two items in approximate breaths. And I was equally puzzled that Major Richter should take this opportunity to bring it up with me. But then, as if to prove my own ability to consider the monstrous and the ridiculous in the same moment, I said, "What are you going to do about it, Sir?"

He kept looking straight ahead and continued to walk to the ops building. "Nothing, goddamnit! He talked to me about two subjects. I have to think he trusts my judgment about which I choose to concentrate on. Of course, I feel the war has somewhat more immediacy."

The answer satisfied me, and we entered to meet the waiting group. Major Richter repeated practically word for word what he had told me as we rode in the jeep. When he came to the part about "bombing everything that moves in the North," Gunn blurted out, "Hot damn!" and Sheets answered, "We ought to nuk'em." Richter paused sharply and turned his cold eyes on the two of them. There was a period of silence, and the two of them nervously averted the Major's eyes, but I sensed beyond their fear of the Major, and nervously restrained beneath their surfaces, some explosion of joy in each of them.

At the end of Richter's words, there was complete silence. I slowly moved my eyes about the room and watched the quiet, thoughtful faces of the eleven men in the room. Only Richter, Gunn, and Sheets were even in their thirties. I think only Bob Saunders of the others was thinking of making the Air Force a career. Each of us was somewhere in our mid-twenties. Joe, the oldest was twenty-eight, and Campbell, the newly arrived second lieutenant, might have been only twenty-two. How, I wondered, how had we at such young ages, found ourselves on the far side of the world contemplating our remote and bloodless participation in the widespread destruction of a land we would probably never see. The first to break the silence, naturally enough, was Gunn.

"As I said, Major, I'm willing to make any sacrifices necessary. Even work as a controller again."

"Yes, I remember that offer, Captain, and as you will remember, I'm a man who takes people up on their offers. I'll expect you to start re-qualifying on the scope tomorrow."

Gunn blinked his eyes. "Tomorrow?"

"Tomorrow."

Joe waved his hand and began to speak. "Excuse me, Sir, you said we're going to bomb everything that moves."

"Those were General Westmoreland's words, Joe."

"That means there'll be no distinction made between military and non-military targets, or civilian and non-civilian?"

Sheets burst in, "Every little bastard north of the seventeenth parallel is a Red and deserves whatever he gets."

Richter ignored him and spoke to Joe. "I'm afraid at this point, Joe, such distinctions have become lost." After a few more silent moments, the Major ended the meeting. "This was a warning of what to expect. General Westmoreland is expected back within the week. We should get our orders to go to work right after that. Enjoy yourselves while you've got the time." Then he turned directly to Sheets. "Capt. Sheets, I imagine your report on operations is on my desk along with everyone else's. Of course, I think you realize this development makes yours already out of date. Would you please review it and draw up new plans to handle the types of schedules we're now talking about." And as we were all getting up and starting to leave, he said, "Oh, yes, could I please see Capt. Sheets, Capt. Stacy and Lt. Saunders right here after everyone else leaves."

I couldn't understand what such a meeting could be about. If it were regarding Bob's "family problem" then why was Joe included? In any case, it didn't last long. Not more than five minutes after I had returned to my desk and begun signing a pile of forms that Chance and Burnett had prepared for my signature, Major Richter came through the orderly room, went into his office and instructed me not to disturb him for the rest of the afternoon while he went through the section reports.

But in the early evening at the bar, Joe told me about the meeting. "Major Richter wants Bob Saunders qualified for full level operations by the time this heavy bombing starts. He says he hasn't pushed it till now because the schedule's been light enough to leave the little jerk to night duties and noncritical operations, but now he needs every man able to perform all operations. If Little Bobby isn't ready when the bombing starts, then he gets his sweet ass shipped off to Saigon where they can lose him in a staff job, and we'll get sent to us a competent body. The Major holds Sheets responsible for Bob's failure, but he wanted me there as the training officer. Also, he wants me to draw up a new training schedule for the nitwit, Saunders, that is."

"Is there any way you can do it, get him qualified?"

Joe drew deeply on his beer and slowly shook his head negatively. "None. No hope. He know all the stuff, he passes all the tests and simulations, but you put him on the scope in a stress situation and he just about swallows the mike. He can't talk to a pilot in a demand situation. I'm afraid that in a week or so whenever the shit starts to hit the fan, poor Bob will find himself on the way to Saigon."

Suddenly the full implications of it came on me, and as the thoughts clarified in my tired, dull brain. I spoke them to Joe. "You know, it really just came to me, but Major Richter has very cleverly taken care of two problems with one stroke. He's going to get rid of one incompetent controller, and he's also going to be rid of the sticky problem of what to do with the son-in-law of a colonel who happens to be an old friend of General Martin and who wants to divorce the colonel's daughter to marry 'brand-X'. And he's going to do it in such a way that Saunders won't ever be able to say he's being harassed because he wants to marry a Thai. But everyone knows that with Bob in Saigon and Renu here or in Bangkok, they'll never be able to manage the enormous red tape and more than likely the whole thing will fade away." I turned to Joe and watched him slowly nodding his head. "Jesus Christ, what am I going to do about this?"

Joe turned to me with arched eyebrows. "What the hell do you mean, what are you going to do? What do you give a shit about it for?"

I fumbled a bit. "Well, Jesus, I like her. You do too. That's what you said the other night. I'd hate to see her disappointed."

"Disappointed?"

"Well, yeah. She wants to go to the States, she wants to marry Bob, that's what she said."

"Shit, she'd be equally happy going or staying. In fact, if she doesn't go, she's saved one major agony; having to spend part or all of her life with Bob Saunders. How can you wish that on anyone?"

"But she likes him, he's nice to her. You know, maybe she's just what he needs. Maybe she'll improve him."

"Oh, Christ, you are hopeless. Bob Saunders never changes. He is always Bob Saunders. Sometimes, when his wants and needs are mildly compatible with someone else's, then he can be mildly pleasant for that person, if that person's wants and needs are basically simple."

"But…"

"Oh, shit, Jim, stop it!"

We sat glumly finishing our beer at the end of which I debated whether or not to have another or to seek out Bob and help him prepare for qualifying. My dilemma ended when Joe signaled Manee the bartender to bring us two more. I lofted the fresh glass to my mouth and let thoughts of Bob Saunders fade away.

Sgt. Hunnicut approached and stood next to us at the corner of the bar. "Good evenin' Cap'n Stayzee, Lootenin' Doyl'." He gave us a very crooked smile and tried to focus his eyes on both of us at the same time. It was painful to watch his pupils dilating and contracting. He leaned forward on the bar, resting his weight on both elbows, but before he completely settled in, he stood up straight again and removed his cap sticking it into his hip pocket. He was obviously trying to present a favorable impression to us, and I suspected, it still being a day till payday, he was planning on hitting us up.

"Yeww gennelmen certainlee look ver' hannsum 'is evenin'."

To which joe beamed, "And so do you, Sarge, so do you."

After a few moments of an uncertain quiet, and Hunnicut obviously convinced he had complied with all necessary formalities, the sodden sergeant made his pitch. "Egscuze me, but could eith'uv yew gennelmen see lennin' me twenny-five dollerz?" To emphasize the sincerity and good intentions of his request, he rose off his elbows and presented himself before us at an off-kilter attention. "It would allow me," he added, attempting to further influence our decision, "to ennertain sum aquain'anzes." To this he winked in an assurance to our carnal natures that he meant he wanted to do some more drinking and then go to the Argo.

After some theatrical deliberations, during which I confessed to having only ten bucks on me, Joe reached into his wallet and peeled off two tens and a five which he handed to Hunnicut.

The sergeant ceremoniously placed the twenty-five dollars on the bar top squarely before him rigidly aligning the bills to the arm rest then called for the bartender. While Manee was coming forward, Hunnicut once again turned to us, and with propriety and formality dripping from his voice, asked, "May I have uh priflidge uv buyin' yew gennelmen uh drink?," a request we had neither time to accept or refuse since he turned to Manee and told him to bring two beers for "uh two finis' officerz innuh whole goddamn Air Forzze." On being served, we raised our glasses to him and thanked him for his generosity, after which he packed up his change and headed for the poker game in the back room.

After Joe had remarked about Sgt. Hunnicut's commitment to good manners, he turned and asked, "You're the personnel expert, can I get my extension over here rescinded and apply for separation at the end of my regular tour in August?"

"No, I don't think so. You could anywhere else, but over here paper work is slower and there's more red tape than even back in the States."

"I didn't think I could. Fuck it! You know, we'll never get out of this fucking war just because it would take too much paperwork."

"Why do you want to leave early? That shit this afternoon bother you?"

He didn't answer immediately. "I guess so. I guess it's all starting to get to me, all the stupid shit we keep doing over here. I've been here off and on now for nearly five years. It was all assistance and training back in Bangkok in '63. Then it became a little more and a little fucking more. Now we're the whole goddamned act. Now we're going to bomb 'everything that moves'. Wonderful, fucking wonderful."

"You don't think it'll do much good, huh?"

"Of course it won't. Nothing ever has. I got drunk once with an asshole Air America pilot down in Bangkok. The son-of-a-bitch had been in the Air Force, but he'd gotten out so he could make more money. At least he was honest about his goddamned motives. Sometime during the night he said he was positive that in the end the North Vietnamese would win, that there wasn't a fucking thing we could do about it. So, anyway, he had devised what he called the 'piranha plan'. He'd fill up a whole shitload of C-130's full of piranha fish and dump them in the rice paddies of North Vietnam. Since they couldn't farm the rice, they'd eventually starve to death. I was laughing when he told me about it, but after today I wouldn't be surprised to hear that's next in our bag of tricks."

"I'm afraid, Joe, you're going to be stuck here through your extension. You going to be able to handle it?"

"Oh, yeah, I always do what I'm told. What the fuck, I just can't see risking Leavenworth for it. I'll just up my intake of sauce and send some more money to McCarthy. Who knows, maybe he'll really become the goddamned president, and we might be able to cut out the horseshit."

"You been sending money to McCarthy?"

"A little, twenty here, ten there. I'm not really too crazy about him, but he's the only guy making any sense about the war."

About an hour later when I suggested we go into town for something to eat, Joe said, "Go ahead, I'm going to stay out here and drink some more. Maybe I'll get into the poker game and check on how ol' Sarge is doing with my twenty-five. Besides, Ewan went home this morning so I'm in no hurry to get to the bungalow." I left him there and rode my Honda home. I showered and changed and went to Tipalow's where I enjoyed a leisurely meal and polished off two liters of Singha.

Through the meal and while slowly sipping at my beer, I wonderingly pondered three things: The news of the stepped-up bombing and Joe's reaction to it; the new developments in Bob Saunders' situation; and Major Richter. The latter absorbed much of my thoughts. I was coming to realize that my lingering apprehensions of him had some foundation. I certainly shouldn't have been shocked that he seemed in favor of escalating the war, he was, after all a career officer, and people with contrary ideas didn't seem to be sticking around long in those days; but it was the coolness with which he announced it that bothered me. He was either deeply troubled by the bombing, or he was a cold mechanical robot who never considered the human costs. I feared it was the latter. He was intelligent, shrewd and cold, and he was always one step ahead of everyone else. Yet, he had always seemed fair and open with me. In the old jargon, he was a man who said what he meant and meant what he said. He had been appreciative of my honesty in describing my jobs and had never sought to load me with more work just to maintain an appearance of being busy (for that he also struck me as particularly enlightened). he had also been won over by Sgt. Tennyson's honesty on the afternoon of the first staff meeting, telling the sober and contrite NCO the next morning that, "If the mess hall really runs best with Tremble running it, that's fine, and I don't want to change things, but in the future, why don't you attend the staff meetings and bring Tremble with you, okay." Even Sunida liked Major Richter, and for what better reason than he spoke clearly. I wondered if my initially favorable reaction to him only because his predecessor had been so incompetent? No, that wasn't fair to Richter, even now he had never lied to me. but the "fair and open" were in doubt. He had, just that morning, curiously thrown me off guard about Bob Saunders while leading me to believe he couldn't and wouldn't be bothered about such matters, he had in fact carefully planned his action and was at that moment about to take it. I'm sure he suspected I was in sympathy with Bob and Renu and so he had misled me slightly. He knew I'd soon find out about his plan, but that wasn't important. What he was really doing was telling me that he knew what I was doing, and he was going to beat me anyway. Perhaps he was not quite so scheming, but he had definitely been signaling something to me.

The worst part was I felt entirely helpless. When Bob failed to qualify, there could be no arguing. He must go to Saigon where he would be stuffed away into some staff job and hopefully forgotten. Of course he could still go ahead with the paper work, but I doubted if the passions could stand the physical separation; and Renu was unlikely to understand the Air Force's machinations and would assume that Bob, like all G.I.'s had changed his mind. If- if if if - Bob could qualify, the marriage plans could be saved, but Joe, who should know, said there was no chance of such an occurrence. Yet, maybe, just maybe, if I worked very hard with Bob and convinced him of his need to really push himself during the next week, then just maybe, he might be able to do it.

I left Tipalow's determined to seek Bob out the next morning, sit down with him and persuade him of my plan. As I turned the corner and headed past the movie theater which was just letting out (a Thai sub-titled version of *The Sound of Music*), I nearly ran over Bob and Renu.

Over his initial objections ("Gee, it's kind of late, and I'm on the early shift tomorrow. It's very important that I be on my toes"), I persuaded them to join me back at Tipalow's for another Singha, which meant Singha for me and Cokes for Bob and Renu. ("Jim, I think you should know they put formaldehyde in their beer here") I asked the waiter to bring us a plate of fried nuts which Renu immediately began to happily munch on, but Bob refrained from even that.

"I asked how they enjoyed the movie.

"Oh, is my favorite movie. See three time Bangkok, now see again."

Bob added, "Well, it's very realistic and also true, but my favorite movies are westerns or war movies with John Wayne."

A couple of weeks earlier, I had sat through the first half or the same movie after which I had to leave and go to the Argo to avoid death from sugar poisoning. But all this is incidental to the reason I insisted they join me at the restaurant.

When I asked Bob what he thought about the morning's meeting, he started, then leaned so he was slightly behind Renu and began gesturing with his eyes and his jaw in her direction. He added emphasis by rigidly pointing at her with an extended finger which he kept very close to his chest. When he seemed convinced that I understood we couldn't discuss such highly classified information as the United State's intention to wipe North Vietnam off the face of the world while in Reny's company, let alone in such a public place as Tipalow's, he finished his hearty pantomime by pressing one solitary finger to his tightly sealed lips. I nodded to indicate my agreement but immediately went on to say, "What I meant was, what do you think your chances of qualifying within a week are?"

Bob paused, blinking, during which time I suspect he was considering whether or not discussion such a subject would constitute a violation of security. When he had sufficiently eased his mind, he unhaltingly said, "Oh, no problem, I could qualify tomorrow," and then, perhaps to allow that others did not share his supreme confidence, "but Capt. Sheets and Capt. Stacy recommend that I wait till sometime next week. They want me to receive some more training."

"Bob, Joe and I talked for quite a while tonight. He's definitely under the opinion that you won't be able to qualify."

Bob seemed stunned and hurt by my reference to Joe's flat denial of Bob's hopes. I may have been unnecessarily harsh, but I was convinced Bob needed shocking. His composure returned momentarily. "Well, Capt. Stacy and I reviewed my training records. On my last two written exams I scored 100%. I don't know what more he could want."

"He said you choke up when you talk to a pilot, no matter how well you do on your written tests."

"Oh," and then he apparently dismissed the entire question with a wave of the hand. "Jim, there's no problem there. I've had some problems in the past. I've been too demanding of my own performance. You know what a perfectionist I am. but, now when the chips are down, you can be sure I'll be equal to the task." Sitting up straight in his chair, he aligned his always slipping glasses and fixed his mouth in a grim little line. Such tough talk could not be made while comfortably ensconced over Cokes and nuts. It required some rigidity of physical position as well. However, almost instantly, his glasses began to slip again, and I once again was struck by the illusion that one of his eyes was higher on his face than the other.

Of course I was not convinced by Bob's incredible confidence, and I felt he must understand more of the implications. "Bob, you realize, don't you, that if you don't qualify, you're on your way to Saigon, don't you?"

Renu's eyes flashed. "What? Bob go Saigon?"

He raised a hand to her as if to try and calm the troubles I had just cast before her, and then leaning back again, he tried to indicate to me by silent gesture that I shouldn't speak further on the subject, but I went on. If it was t all possible, I was not going to let Bob Saunders delude himself on this item.

"Bob, you've got to face it. If you get sent to Saigon, and most of the people involved here think it's likely you will, then your's and Renu's hopes are in serious trouble."

In Renu's eyes I saw some bar-girl cynicism surfacing, mixed with a little disappointment. I wished I could also take the time to explain to her that Bob may be sent to Saigon for reasons more or less beyond his control, but if Bob could be convinced of the gravity of the threat there might never be reason to have to explain it. At the time, I did not see any irony in my being so concerned about this awkward nincompoop.

My last point was lost on him. "Gee, what do you mean by that? I could be filing the same papers from Saigon as well as from here." While I thought of but chose not to mention, the unlikelihood of Renu understanding such points of refinement (I doubted if Bob and she had ever had the conversation she and I shared while we waited for the samlow not too many nights before), Bob went on to say that, "Of course, that's no problem anyways, because I'm going to qualify without any problems."

My eyes were beginning to water, and my mind was rapidly becoming dopey from the long hours of beer drinking, eating, and confronting the impenetrable skull of Bob Saunders. I, with resignation, let the conversation descend into silence, and when they had finished their Cokes and got up to leave, I was relieved. However, as I rose simultaneously with them, I felt I owed Renu some further explanation and said to her, in Thai, "Renu, do not worry. There is very little chance Bob will go to Saigon. He and I will make sure it does not happen."

She seemed reassured, which at least is what I took her light and gay smile for, and she said, "Kop kun mak, Jim, kop kun mak."

Bob seemed not all disturbed at the sight of another man saying something to his fiancée in a language he understood not at all and seeing her react with a charming smile and a warm, effusive thank you. I regarded this phenomena with curiosity. Bob's naiveté was nothing if not incredibly—there is not another word—naïve.

Not willing to deal with the ribaldry of the Argo Bar, and not ready to confront the dark and lonely desperation that was waiting for me in my bed, I stayed at Tipalow's and drank my way through two more bottles of beer until nearly one a.m., when the owner started turning out the lights and asked me to leave. I drunkenly and painstakingly guided my motorcycle along dark streets back to my bungalow. As I was climbing the stairs, I could hear Joe snoring his way into the sleep of the dead or the sufficiently smashed. There was a light in the kitchen, and when I checked it, there sat Mama-san from the Argo, again chewing a thick peanut butter sandwich, and washing it down with a bottle of Coke.

"What the hell?"

She looked up and grinned at me exposing her betel stained teeth which were liberally covered with peanut butter. When she had cleared her mouth sufficiently to speak, she said, "Sawadee, Lootenin." I winced at her familiarity as she went on. "Captahn Joe, kee-mao mak mak, no can pom pom," and she pointed in the direction of the sharp and regular snoring.

I could say no more than, "Oh," and started out of the kitchen, leaving her to eat and drink as long as she was fit, but she called after me, suggesting she share my bed. "Hey, maybe Lootinin Jim pom pom Mama-san, numbah one, hey," but I declined, saying, "No, mai mi, kop," and raising a limp index finger to show the expected response of my sad and misused organ.

In my room, I spread myself across my bed and quickly fell into a deep and dreamless sleep.

CHAPTER TWENTY-THREE

THAT HAD ALL BEEN ON Thursday, March 28, 1968. The major returned from Chiang Mai with the message that the United States had determined it to be in the best interest to do everything in its power to reduce the landscape of North Vietnam to rubble. Joe reacted to it with a fit of depression that would leave him in a drunken, snoring unconsciousness while a strange, old woman chewed peanut butter sandwiches in our kitchen. And an apparently irresistible march of events was destined to place Bob Saunders in Saigon, Renu in Bangkok, and both of them returned to the lives they were living only five weeks before, before I, at a risk of five dollars, had introduced them to one another.

The weekend, in contrast, passed quietly. Joe continued a mild drunk through Saturday, leveling off on Sunday to sipping gin and orange juice and never removing himself from our front porch. On Monday morning, he went quietly and uneventfully to work. Bob was scheduled for work most of the weekend (I dropped into ops several times and on each occasion he assured me he was using the time to prepare himself for qualifying). Major Richter spent most of his time efficiently going through the section reports and making occasional comments to me regarding their content: "Jim, do you realize that a number of our section chiefs could be described as functional illiterates." And I put in fairly busy days at my desk Friday and Saturday, got mildly bombed the second night, and, although I visited the Argo and joked with several of the girls, I spent the night alone. On Sunday, while Joe beat off the pain with gin and juice, I raced my motorcycle up to the falls, not to recall the Svenson/Hunnicut affair, but only to rid myself of the site. There, I splashed about in the pool for several hours. Then, in a small village even beyond the falls, I bought several bottles of Singha for some of the other patrons of a roadside inn. My limited fluency was lost on them—their country Thai and my city Thai bearing only minor similarities—and our communication was restricted to periodically raising our glasses in celebration of my generosity and their good company.

APRIL 1968

CHAPTER TWENTY-FOUR

ON MONDAY MORNING, APRIL 1, 1968, the orderly room staff gathered around Sgt. Sutton's transistor radio to listen to a "Major" address by the President of the United States, Lyndon Baines Johnson. Sheets and Gunn had joined us, confidently expecting the President to announce the plans we had been privy to since the previous Thursday, and they wanted to be in Major Richter's proximity when the news became official so they could demonstrate again their great enthusiasm. The Major remained in his office, but the radio could easily be heard there. Of course I should mention that Nakorn Sarang is located twelve time zones ahead of Washington, D.C., and what we were preparing to listen to was the now famous speech of March 31, 1968, in which Johnson announced a halt to the bombing north of the 19th parallel and also that he would not seek re-election.

When the bombing halt was announced Gunn threw his bush hat to the floor and yelled, "Goddamnit, just when we had 'em on their knees, the chicken-shit bastard lets 'em up."

Sheets was genuinely stunned and said in a hollow and tired voice, "Maybe he'll let us nuk'em, just once."

Gunn kicked his hat across the room and said, "Goddamnit, when are we going to get a real man for a President and not one who's afraid to do a little ass kicking?"

Sheets, still stunned said, "Just one bomb, that's all it'd take, just one of those babies."

Upon hearing that Johnson wasn't going to run again, I leaped from my chair and let out a joyous cry of "Yea!" to the amazed and puzzled stares of both Gunn and Sheets. I sat back down to indulge in my own glee while the two loony captains exchanged their own views on what they would do if they had their druthers: Gunn, of course, would bomb them and bomb them and then bomb them some more, "Flatten 'em, that's the answer," while Sheets kept rhapsodizing on how a blast of nuclear warfare was the only way to deal with the perversities of the Oriental mind, "those sick little gooks."

Once he was sure that the speech was over, Sgt. Sutton looked up and said, "I expect this, uh, development will, uh, inflict severe and wide-spread, uh, ramifications on our yew emm deee."

Smiley Burnett gave no special reaction, he just continued to grin, and Lafayette Chance, after thumbing through his desk calendar turned over to me and said, "Hey,

Lieutenant, guess the fuck what, I got less than four fuckin' months to spend in this fuckin' place."

When Major Richter came out of his office, Gunn picked up his hat which he had continued to kick around the room as a demonstration of his great resolve to "win" the war, and said, "Major, I want you to know that my offer to do anything, absolutely anything still goes, Sir. You can count on me when the going gets tough." Since the going was obviously going to be something less than tough, I found Guerrilla's offer slightly superfluous.

"I'm sure you would, Capt. Gunn, but it won't be necessary."

"It won't? You mean you don't want me to qualify?"

"That's right."

"It is?" Sheets echoed this query and then in unison they said, "Why?"

"I'm sure that you are aware, Capt. Sheets," said the Major, staring with his cold eyes directly at the operations officer in a manner that meant, in fact, he was sure of no such thing, "as the ops officer, that all of the targets for sorties handled by our radar are north of the nineteenth parallel."

"Oh, yes, of course, but what…"

"And that, in the future, because of this order, we'll be only monitoring the occasional aircraft that pass overhead."

"Well, yes, certainly, but what…"

"Which means that we are, in other words, out of work."

He turned and, on his way to his regular morning coffee break, headed out the front door. But he paused briefly to say, "Oh, yes, Capt. Sheets, as I'm sure you're also aware, there's no longer any necessity for Lt. Saunders to qualify. He can go on as he's been going."

CHAPTER TWENTY-FIVE

BOB SAUNDERS, DESPITE THE FACT the limited bombing pause prevented him from manning a desk in Saigon, became one of its most constant critics, "It takes away a lot of the fun of being here, not being able to work real close on such an important thing."

In this respect, he was drawn closer to the worlds of Sheets and Gunn, able to sidle up to them while they kept up their nearly continual harangue against the cowardice of the nation's civilian high command. At times, the subject came close to replacing sexual innovation as the operations officer's favorite topic. Of course, the subjects frequently became confused: "We need someone who's not afraid to shove it to them, slap it to 'em. Fuck 'em, the little bastards!" Anyway, wherever the two captains gathered to exchange examples of what they would do if they only had the chance, whether in the ops office, the orderly room (a favorite place because it was in earshot of Major Richter's desk), the bar, or the mess hall, they often found themselves accompanied by the short, blond figure of Bob. He rarely said anything, his participation was generally limited to affirmative nods at points where he deemed his seniors required emphasis: "Carry it to them, Pardner, hit them where it hurts, right in their own back yard," would say Gunn; nod would go Bob. For variety—maybe every fourth or fifth time agreement was required—Bob would give the thumps-up sign, although he would occasionally botch it by clenching his hand too quickly and catching his thump in a fist, so he appeared to merely be punching at the air, like a shadow boxer. Yet while Bob's concurrence was always accepted by the two (sycophants themselves, they could not discourage pandering), neither Sheets nor Gunn became in any way sympathetic to Bob's romantic entanglements. In fact, when he was not present to be offering his agreement, he was often referred to as the "gook lover," or the "gook fucker," epithets more often than not coming from the mouth of, with unconscious irony, Sheets.

Unfortunately, also because of the bombing halt, the two loonies had more time for their harangues since we were, as Major Richter had predicted, out of work. Any hopes the more hawkish of our personnel may have heard that President Johnson's speech had been an April Fool's joke were dispelled when the morning's planes returned that afternoon, and never flew again. Never flew our way again, that is. Our location and equipment had eliminated us from any participation in what turned out to be the increased bombing of southern Laos and those areas of North Vietnam below the nineteenth parallel. So for the rest of my stay in Nakorn Sarang, there was little for our crews to do; occasional reconnaissance flights passed through our control, and training was conducted there, but that was the extent of it. I felt light-headed, overtaken by a certainly unwarranted sense of moral relief at averting a more direct connection with wholesale slaughter. Unwarranted, but I made do with it.

Major Richter, after taking time the morning of the President's speech for coffee, returned to his desk and his own self imposed task of familiarizing himself with every function on the site. He never expressed any disappointment at not having a hand in "flattening 'em", to use a Gunn term, and I doubt if he felt any either. He once said to a pro football player who was visiting us on a USO tour, and who was expressing a ferocity worthy of our babbling captains towards all communists, "Why don't you just talk about football. That's what you're here for, isn't it?" The Major regarded himself as a professional military man, not a philosopher, and he obeyed the commands of his Commander-in-Chief. It was not an altogether immoral or amoral system, certainly much preferable to other reactions I have noted, and the major moved back into my god graces, or at least my trust (whether he was in or out of either I'm sure was never any concern of his).

In those first days of April, I was exhilarated by a sense of control of the situation; things seemed to be going more or less as I would have them. My spirit of confidence was even carrying over to the matter of Renu and Bob. The crisis of his qualifying had been weathered. With Bob scheduled to depart in less than four months, I began for the first time to envision the two of them leaving together. On 15 April, as the Air Force would have me say, this illusion was shattered. The Takhli personnel office returned Bob's request with the following message: NO ACTION TAKEN. REQUEST MUST BE SUBMITTED AT LEAST FOUR MONTHS PRIOR TO REQUESTEE'S SCHEDULED DATE OF EARLIEST RETURN FROM OVERSEAS.

"But I did submit it more than four months before I'm supposed to go home," I heard Bob say into the telephone.

He turned to me with his hand clasped over the receiver so Takhli's NCOIC of personnel couldn't hear him and said, "Sgt. Sestokas says a request is not considered submitted until it reaches CBPO with all entries correctly entered."

He turned back to the phone and then back to me to complete the sergeant's words, "And our, or my request was initially and then," (he paused again to wait for the NCO's words), "...subsequently conveyed with errors of both omission and commission. Uh huh, uh huh. Therefore, it had not prior to the date in question, been submitted."

To all of this I kept up a nodding of the head. I had heard it all before from the very same Sgt. Sestokas, when I had called immediately after finding the "no action taken" request in the mailbag from Takhli. The sergeant had routinely and with a very bored tone, conveyed the exact same words to me. They carried a sense of finality which I was learning to recognize in bureaucrats. Sometimes the maze of the system is used to scare one off, and when it is, you know it by the tone of the voice, often a strident hostility, but when the system has cranked a piece of paper into a corner from which there really is no return, then you know it too: Calmness, assuredness, boredom. They have beaten you and they know it, and there is no longer any reason for hostility. Such was Sgt. Sestoka's voice that morning.

When Bob had finally assured himself (it was one of the few times he had not unconditionally accepted my word) that I had given him an accurate report on the situation, he turned to reviewing his alternatives which meant he looked at me and said, "What do we do now, Jim?"

I could think of nothing, so I said, "Look, let me check on some things. We'll meet for lunch to talk about it." As soon as I said it, I began to question my sanity. Friday's fish sticks were going to be rough enough to eat; Bob might make them totally indigestible.

"Check on some things." For the month and a half since I had returned from Bangkok with, unknowingly Bob and Renu, it seemed I had done little but check on some things. Bob's life and its problems (Bob's life was a problem) had taken up more of my time than my own life. I had reached a point where I started to identify my own peace of mind with how Bob was managing things. Given Bob's natural abilities and tendencies, such was not a peaceful or fulfilling means of judging one's self-contentment. And, on that morning I had already made a date to have lunch with Bob in a little more than an hour's time. My first inclination (and oh, how I wish I had followed it) was to give up the whole project, tell him it was useless, drop his plan, and go back home to Betty. Still, I remembered Renu, and I was sure she truly wanted it to happen. I also harbored the optimistic opinion that all of this might turn Bob around a corner and make him into a relatively human person, this despite Joe's warning that any such nonsense was just that, such nonsense.

I spent the next hour, sick with anxiety, preparing for my lunch with Bob. Today, to admit such looniness is difficult. Nevertheless, it was real and I did it. First, I went to the library where I could use the phone and be unheard (Sunida, with her great courtesy, would never think of listening to someone talking on the phone). There, I called the Judge Advocate's Office at Takhli. Capt. Ellis, a cynical son-of-a-bitch who hated the Air Force and took a particular delight in getting obviously guilty—the more guilty the better—airmen acquitted, advised me in complete violation of lawyer-client relationships, that Bob's divorce action could not possibly be complete by the time he went home. Betty was not so much contesting it as ignoring it, and there would have to be an eventual confrontation. Since there were few items involved (they had no children and little property, save for a color television and a Mustang convertible), the matter could be, once back in the States, quickly resolved. But that brought to me one very significant fact: There was no way Bob and Renu could marry before leaving Thailand. I asked Ellis if he had told all of this to Bob. "Of course," he said. (When I later asked Bob why he hadn't told me, he said, not in wise-guy fashion, but in his never-to-be imitated total innocence and unconsciousness, "You didn't ask me.") Ellis quickly tried to minimize the problem. "Look, none of this is any goddamned problem. Get the babe a passport. As soon as this dipshit gets his divorce completed, stick the babe on a plane. She gets to San Francisco, they go get married. Nothing to it."

Nothing to it the guy says. He doesn't have to lead Bob by the hand through the whole goddamned thing. I must have been out of my mind, but I was somewhat relieved to see it wasn't impossible. The most frightening aspect was that it wouldn't be complete before Bob left Nakorn Sarang. That meant I might have to see him when I got back to the States. Sob. "Hey," said Ellis just before I hung up, "one thing I got to know. Are you slipping it to this babe?" An indication of my lunacy was I was offended and shocked by his question. I stammered, then hung up.

Sak informed me that a passport would be easy to get. In Thailand, everything was easy to get for a few baht. I relayed this information to Bob during lunch. He took it all with a passivity that I found particularly annoying. I had just spent the morning pushing my stomach through a series of emotional flip-flops, and he sat there and accepted my account as if it were of no more concern to him than my telling him I had just signed thirteen forms requesting new supplies of forms. He did say, "I knew we'd work things out." We he said. During the afternoon, my stomach growled and grumbled and belched forth gas, enough so even Chance would occasionally stare at me. I'm not sure if it was the fish stick or Bob Saunders.

It had been incredibly hot day, and Joe and I headed for the club at five o'clock. On days like that, there were no lazy evenings spent lounging about the bungalow waiting for the sun to descend. We would go directly to the air conditioned bar and gasp as we drew on the clear, swift pleasure of a cold Budweiser. There would be no many-tiered meals eaten with sighs at Tipalow's, but instead the munching of a greasy hamburger form the club's grill. And talk. Not diatribes or even confessions, but merely long, lazy, and meandering conversations with even changing participants. Joe started it off that night, speaking to a table of us, a mixed group of junior officers, middle grade NCO's, and airmen. "Now, I'm not saying things haven't been slow over in ops the past two weeks. Shit, we haven't run a green anchor in that whole time. Of course you all realize that's classified, and I can count on each of you not to repeat it, right? But I'll tell you one thing we've sure been running a lot of lately, fucking intercepts. And you know why?"

There was general agreement as to our ignorance.

"Because Udorn won't take them. Since the so-called 'bombing halt' they're busier than all hell. They're handling all the reconnaissance traffic, and their equipment reaches into the areas of lower North Vietnam and Laos where ours doesn't. So they don't have any time for fooling around with foolish training operations like intercepts. But the pilots in the 102's got to get their goddamned training time, so they fly anyway and train with us. Of course, the fact that we're out of the range of MIG's doesn't make any difference to them. Just because, in case of MIG attack, they'd have to work with Udorn or NKP doesn't deter them, they're going to get their training time. Shit, I've done more intercepts in the last wto goddamned weeks than I did in three months at NORAD, and that's North American Air Defense Command."

We all added some equally ridiculous examples of Air Force bureaucratic incompetency and foul-up, each tale bringing loud guffaws and cries of, "Jesus Christ!", or, "Would you fucking believe it?" After several hours, the group had dwindled to only Joe and me. Without any particular urgency or considerable forethought, I began telling Joe about the day's developments in the engagement of Bob and Renu. Joe, in his usual manner when I chose to talk about, just sat and listened, but when I expressed a feeling of distress over the matter, he broke his normal pattern to say, "Jim, you are becoming one of the silliest bastards on this whole goddamned site."

"What?'

"Why the hell are you letting yourself get upset over anything that happens to that happy asshole?"

"Well, I guess, I mean…"

"He is the thickest skulled jerk I have ever met, and in the end, he will not even so much as say thank you. Is that the kind of guy you want to help out?"

"Yeah, I guess I know that. I think I do it for Renu."

"For Renu? Why?"

"Well, to help her get to America, I guess."

"Why?"

"Well, wouldn't it be better for her, you know, a better life?"

Joe turned and faced me directly. He put his beer down on the table and spoke very deliberately. "Did it ever occur to you that she might be better off not ever going to America, that her life as it is here in her own country such as it is, might be the best thing for her? That just possible *these people* might like living here better than they would like living in America?"

No, it hadn't, and even Joe's words didn't significantly sink into my own thick skull, but I often think of them now and wish fervently that I had paid heed to them.

The next mail plane brought Bob notice of his next assignment. He would go at the end of July to Hamilton Air Force Base just north of San Francisco. It is generally regarded as the Air Force's choicest assignment. At the end of the month, I received word of my next assignment: Davis-Monthan Air Force Base in Tucson, Arizona. Not a bad place, but certainly not San Francisco. It was another indication of the addled state of my brain that I was not in the least envious of Bob's good luck, but saw it as a sign that things were going my way again.

My way. I thought things were going my way because San Francisco possessed the largest Oriental population of any American city and that would make Renu's adjustment easier.

MAY AND JUNE 1968

CHAPTER TWENTY-SIX

MAY AND JUNE TURNED OUT to be good months. At the site that is. I well know that, in early June, Robert Kennedy was shot and killed while celebrating his victory in the California primary. In fact, he died on the day I arrived in Bangkok for the second administrative conference of the 606th Tactical Air Control Group. The mood of the meeting was alternately glum and cruelly joyous. The younger officers and NCO's were, nearly to the man, genuinely distraught (I was numb with shock and stunned beyond any sense of anger or revenge. Following the April assassination of martin Luther King, Jr., this second murder made me helplessly aware of the great distance I was from my home, physically and emotionally. Following Joe's example, I had started sending small contributions to Gene McCarthy's campaign, and I had continued to do so after Kennedy had announced his candidacy. But it was out of spite—outraged that he should let the Minnesota poet do all the dirty work—and I sensed the real hope lay in the hard-nosed Massachusetts-New Yorker. I could not imagine the Quixotic McCarthy bringing the whole thing off, and saw, wistfully, down the road, a successful merger of the two campaigns. That was now gone, and I felt adrift at sea.) On the other hand, most of the senior officers and NCO's hated the Senator's guts and were, quietly for the most part, delighted. Some however could not contain their glee. At the hotel's bar a master sergeant from one of our Vietnam detachments cried out, "And if that fat-ass baby brother of his shows his face in public, we'll blow his goddamned head off too!" I sadly report that since the man was significantly larger than me, I did not bodily attack the bastard, but limited my response to yelling, "Shut your fucking mouth, you stupid son-of-a-bitch!" Even at that, I was only saved a pummeling at the ox's hands when one of his cronies pointed out, "Hey, Sarge, don't hit the fucker, he's a goddamned lieutenant. You don't want to get in trouble for assaulting a fucking officer, do you?" The irate master sergeant stomped out of the bar complaining, "That's the goddamned trouble with the Air Force today, too many fucking officers like that." I had heard such words before.

The Thais were (those I saw, that is, the ones in the streets, the shops, the hotesl, bars, restaurants, and night clubs) at least visibly more saddened than I was. They were very romantic believers in the Kennedy legend. Joe, who was stationed in Bangkok for the last three months of 1963, remembered another example of it. For days following the assassination of John Kennedy, to see Thais walking the streets, their faces streaming with tears, their throats and lungs wracked by sobs, was not an uncommon sight. Only a week later, the Prime Minister of Thailand, Sarit Thanarat, passed away of liver failure. There was a state funeral and many long and portentous official eulogies made, but Joe saw no wet eyes, heard no sobs. There was not the slightest odd beat in the life of the city. And this was all before his successors began a discrediting of the deceased strongman with a series of revelations regarding his harem of nearly two hundred minor wives and a stashed-away fortune of over two hundred million dollars.

More to the point, the three days I spent in Bangkok following the assassination of Robert Kennedy were sad ones for myself and those with me, Pitsommai, Ewan, and Renu. Renu had followed me by a day (Bob didn't come as he couldn't get either an excuse for TDY or leave approved) and our plan was to take care of much of the paper work involved in getting her to the United States in the fall. It couldn't be handled from Nakorn Sarang since one could not make the small bribes necessary through the mail. Thai bureaucracy is even more stultifying and ponderous than our own, and the system is a maze of small and officially unimportant clerks who can forever lose whatever application you are making unless their palms are sufficiently greased. The bribes required are not outrageous and are openly accepted (they are widely considered to be a quasi-legitimate part of the clerk's income). So my hours away from the conference were filled with chasing about the city with Renu, waiting in lines, watching her fill out form after form, and then handing over one hundred or two hundred baht to one clerk after another (the price was high since an American was involved, but it also kept us waiting less time in line, as the greedy clerks recognized the opportunities for larger pay-offs and speeded us ahead of their countrymen). In the evenings, the three girls and I had dinner, after which Ewan went to Max's to work (a bar-girl's life did not permit her to take days off in mourning for an American senator), Renu went to the house she had once shared with several other girls, and Pisommai and I would go to a movie or directly to my hotel. The more cynical will suggest that Renu took advantage of her days apart from Bob Saunders to make some extra baht by plying her former trade, but I, at the risk of being termed a hopeless romantic, doubt it. Renu and I returned to Nakorn Sarang on different trains, she with a passport in hand.

Yet, separating the private from the public, May and June were good months. I found the hours spent chasing about Bangkok in pursuit of Renu's papers to be warm ones, just because of her company. She was perfect at accepting assistance. When around her, I found my instincts were always to help. She could exude an aura of helplessness (a completely alien quality for a bar-girl—such a breed does not exist) that made it joyous to aid her. When we emerged from our last office, she with her passport, and got into a taxi, she sat staring at her own picture and smiling the most outrageous and perfect smile I've ever seen. She kept saying, "I am going, I am going, I am really going." She closed the passport and clasped it to her chest. Then she looked up at me, still smiling and with tears running down her eyes, she said, "You did it, you did it, because of you I am going. I am so happy." She took my bicep in both hands, squeezed tightly, threw her face against my shoulder and said, "Jim, Jim, Jim, Jim, oh Jim." I put my other arm around her shoulders and pulled her to me (as physical as I ever was with her). At that moment I remember thinking I would have been happy protecting her for the rest of my life.

There were other things that made them good months. The Air Force's majority lists came out in mid-May. They list promotions from captain to major. If a candidate twice fails to make the list, he is discharged from the service. A name conspicuously absent from the list—for the second time—was that of Captain William H. Gunn, Jr. "This is the reward I get, after the sacrifice, the sacrificeSSS! I've laid on the altar of service to my country," moaned Guerrilla, as he paced back and forth across the orderly room, where he had come to recount the glories of his soon to end career. "I was commandant of my ROTC class at Abilene Christian College. I've never had anything less than an outstanding OER. When I was a controller, I devised a new procedure for rendezvous, and that's still the way we do it over here. I was a general's aide for three years. Ol' Steel Ass Stevers said I was the finest young officer he'd ever seen. I'd give him a call, only he kicked off a couple of years ago. Liver went on him. Just my luck. Hell, just you look over that maintenance shop. Damn, there's never been anything like the perfect record I've gotten my people to come up with. Oh well, the hell with it." At this point he would gesture in the air with a wave of surrender and plop himself into an empty chair. "What's the use? I'll just go on back home, back to Sweetwater, be like the rest of the don't-give-a-shit chicken-ass lily-livered cowards back there rioting and marching. Complainers. Guess I'll be a school teacher, something even a woman can do."

Once I interrupted him, asking, "Don't you get a pretty generous separation allowance, something like eleven or twelve thousand dollars?"

He stood up nearly to attention and spat out the words, "What do I care about that? I love my country. I'm no goddamned mercenary. I've sacrificed for my country. Besides, it's thirteen thousand, six hundred forty-nine dollars…some pennies thrown in. BUT I DON'T CARE! Just give me the chance to sacrifice. Lay my life on the line for my flag. I'm not afraid, not like a lot of these candy-assed, sugar-tit-sucking sissies you see coming up today." Then, waving his hand weakly in resignation, he turned and headed out the door. "Well, one thing, I've still got my pride. I know what kind of a job I did. Damn fine! I can hold my head high, walk tall, be a man! There aren't many who can say that."

It wasn't entirely unmoving. He had a certain élan, and even if I didn't care much for his opinions, I acknowledged him a sense of drama previously unnoticed. However, when he returned to repeat the act that afternoon, the next morning, the next afternoon, and again and again, my appreciation of the theatrics rapidly waned and he was, once again, just a boor.

Major Richter also observed Gunn's performances with diminishing patience. The first time he was present for one of them the Major silently listened without as much as looking up from his desk. For the next couple, he did look up, and once even came and stood in his doorway, while Gunn recalled the "highlights" of his sadly, less that distinguished career. When the act continued into the fourth day, the Major walked out into the orderly room, his hat on, stopped to say, "Captain, why don't you meet me over in the chow hall for a cup of coffee," then went out the door. Gunn still had enough bearing about him to realize it was not an invitation, but a demand, and quickly followed.

They were gone for nearly half an hour. I didn't have the temerity to spy on them, so I contented myself with nodding a weak affirmation when Sgt. Sutton came out of his office and said, "Boy, imagine what a rough, uh, deal the, uh, Captain's got, huh? Jeez, he's certainly had a, uh, distinguished record, huh?" Lafayette and Smiley could do no more than ape my mild concurrence, and shortly Sutton left on one of his endless inspections of the hooches.

Chance looked up when the door closed. "Shit!" Our dumb fuckin' first shirt must be the only shitbird on the whole fuckin' site believes a word that crazy fuckin' Captain ever says."

When Richter came in, he gave no indication of what had happened. But I turned and watched when he sat himself at his desk. Looking down, he shook his head once, like he had water in his ear, snorted, and then picked up a report and started to read.

Two days later, I entered the orderly room in the middle of the afternoon and found Capt. Gunn telling the story of his unfortunate military career to a new airman who was processing in. That evening Major Richter asked me to have a drink with him. It wasn't all that uncommon a thing for him to do; it didn't always signal something. He was normally a silent drinker. He'd raise his martini, say, "One less day to go," then finish it at a good pace, tap my arm, say, "Well, time for a cold shower," and leave. After a time, as I grew less intimidated by him, I found his silence friendly, and it was not unpleasant to share a very, very quiet drink with him. Yet, that evening, when he asked me to stop for a drink I sensed he had something to say. I was not wrong.

"I'm calling Colonel Wolff in the morning. I want Gunn out of here as soon as possible. He's only got a month to go in-country anyway. They can find something for him to do in at Udorn where he won't be disrupting the whole goddamned site. Christ, he'll have half the airmen going over the hill if he's allowed to sit around here and babble like he's doing. As soon as I find out where he's going, I want you to get on the phone with whatever admin officers are necessary to get him on his way the day before yesterday. Okay?"

I added an unnecessary, but polite, "Yes, Sir."

"Yesterday I took Gunn over for coffee. I told him he had to get a grip on himself. That no matter how bad it seemed, it wasn't the end of the world. I also told him that what with personnel shortages, he'd probably be asked to stay on as a Captain. If he makes it to sixteen years, then they can't throw him out and more than likely, he'd make it. He sat there listening to me nodding his head like he understood everything I was saying. When I finished, he started in telling me about all the sacrifices he's made, about all his medals, and his outstanding OER's. I had to tell him to shut up or ship out. I thought he at least understood that. Then today there he is, telling some new airman how the Air Force screws you over, You know, when I first heard he didn't make it, I felt sorry for him. I was going to let him relax for his last month. The poor guy has to come to grips with a big failure. But Jesus, this is more than I expected. He's exhausted my sympathies. There are always some guys who get screwed, don't make it when they should, but in his goddamned case, the system worked perfectly."

With a toothpick, he picked the olive out of his glass, popped it in his mouth, gave one chomp, and swallowed it. "Well, time for a cold shower. Oh, yes, have Capt. Sheets assign one of our controllers as the maintenance officer until Gunn's replacement gets here. I'm sure they can spare a man."

I did some of my best work and poor old Guerrilla was on the train the next night heading for Takhli and a plane to Udorn where he was being assigned for thirty days as something called, "Plans and Records Storage Officer." A final sacrifice.

That was in May. June was just as good. The Major and I had taken to, on occasion, having more than one drink together, and would even at times go to town for dinner and continue drinking. He never became verbose (when he spoke, it usually had to do with work, and his words were obliquely requests, warnings, and sometimes threats. For instance, I learned from him one evening that Bob Saunders was still a prime concern of Colonel Herder, and hence of General Martin, and I took his words as a hint my part in Bob's folly was not unnoticed: "Colonel Herder called me today, just talk about Lt. Saunders. He said, 'Goddamnit, Richter, that little bastard keeps going ahead with this thing. Do you suppose someone's helping him out? I don't think the little bastard's smart enough to handle it himself.'" It was shortly after my return from the conference and word that Renu had successfully applied for a passport must have reached the States. The Major's words came abruptly and were never amplified upon. My questions were ignored, and I learned not to ask them.). Yet, as I've mentioned, his stillness was not unpleasant, and I enjoyed his company. On the night I'm particularly remembering, we were at the Mitrinakorn nightclub. The atmosphere was much different than the night when I left it sick at heart. Major Richter had been stopping there frequently (it was for one thing air-conditioned) and his quiet nature was appreciated. some local businessmen joined us at our table. They brought with them their "second" wives, and shortly after sitting down insisted that we also have girls, so two of the club's prettiest hostesses were brought out for us. They were chatty and amiable, but I never enjoyed their company like I did that of the girls from Max's Bar, or even those of the Argo. At the end of an hour, they would lean towards you and say in a very pleasant tone, "You like I stay your table?" and if you did not want to put out another two-fifty and said, "No," a blank look would instantly descend across their faces and they would abruptly and coolly rise and leave you. They were, I guess, the traditional cold-hearted whores, and I was, unless quite drunk, unsettled by their company.

That night, I was not drunk and I remembered clearly seeing one of our air policemen in uniform, enter the club. He stared about in the darkness and I, realizing he had to be searching for the Major, waved to him. "Major, could you come out to the site immediately? You too, Lieutenant?"

Major Richter got up without asking anything and we headed for the site as rapidly as the streets, crowded with people and animals would permit. Crossing the runway, I noticed there seemed to be more light than normal rising from the base. When we turned the corner, I realized the emergency parimeter lights were on. Major Richter said, "Jesus Christ, we're in DEFCON ONE!"

At the gate, Capt. Sheets, in helmet and flak jacket, M-16 over his shoulder, was yelling, "Let this vehicle pass! Let this vehicle pass!"

We drove through, and Major Richter stopped his jeep in front of the orderly room. I went in to get my helmet and pistol. While in there, I heard major Richter ask, "Capt. Sheets, what's going on?"

"We're in DEFCON ONE, Sir."

"I can see that. Why are we in DEFCON ONE is my question."

By then I had pulled my gear from the deep ends of my desk, put them on and headed for my bunker. Halfway across the area, I heard Major Richter yell to me, "Jim, Jim!" When I turned to look, I saw him waving me back. "Come here, and put your stuff away."

The Major and Capt. Sheets were both in the orderly room when I got there. "Put your gear away, Jim. There's no alert."

"No alert?"

"No. It seems our security officer here overreacted to some incident and without authority, called a DEFCON ONE."

It turned out that a young Thai airman, drunk and in civilian clothes and without identification, had decided he was tired of the rice wine (a horrible sour brew) he had been drinking in his home and preferred American whiskey. So he was going to go to the site's club. That was not a crime. A provision in the establishment of the club was that the Thai airmen have access to it. The problem arose when the young man, who had come out to the site by the back road, decided not to go around to the gate, but to climb over the barbed wire fence. Even at that, he might have made it, had he not cut himself on a barb and cried out, awakening the Thai Guard. The airman was fortunate not to have been shot. Numerous animals had been when their cries interrupted the slumber of our not-so-vigilant guards. Sheets, who was in the club at the time of the incident was notified and asked to come to the guard shack, where the intruder had been brought. At the time the AP came to get him, Sheets was, Smiley Burnett related to me, in time to the music, pounding his shoe on his table, a table upon which Joy was dancing and making gestures which indicated she was preparing to strip. Upon reaching the guard shack, being told what had happened (it had not yet been discovered who the intruder was), and seeing the by-then passed out violator, Sheets surmised the site was under attack and told Sgt. Puckett to sound the alarm for DEFCON ONE. The AP sergeant, undeterred by regulations that stated such security postures can be initiated only by Thai Supreme Headquarters, sounded the alarm. By the time the Major and I had been found and brought out, the airman's identity had been discovered, and he was recognized as a threat to nothing more than the guard shack floor on which he had barfed.

From his desk in his office where he had gone to check on the specific wording of the regulation on alerts, Major Richter said, "Capt. Sheets is about to instruct Sgt. Puckett to return us to DEFCON THREE."

Sheets, obviously chagrinned and shaken, but still garbed in helmet and flak jacket, went to the door of the Major's office and said, "Excuse me, Sir, but I don't have authority to do that. Sir, only Thai Supreme Headquarters has authority to change a DEFCON status."

Major Richter slapped his desk and stood up, but by the time he spoke, he had control of his voice. "Captain, would you prefer that I notify Thai Supreme headquarters that this site is presently in DEFCON ONE because its security officer mistakenly and idiotically and in violation of all regulations ordered it? Then they could order us back to DEFCON THREE. Is that what you want?"

Sheets smiled, but it was hardly one of pleasure, and I felt a queasiness in my stomach seeing such a look on a man's face. "Well, no, Sir, but I just, uh…"

"But what?"

"Well, sir, I just believe in doing things the right way, and the regulations state that…"

"Capt. Sheets! Shut up!" The Major had yelled; it was the only time I had ever heard him do so. "Never mind about telling Puckett. I'll do it myself. Capt. Sheets, how would you like to spend your remaining month in Thailand as the Plans and Records Storage Officer in Udorn? I understand they'll soon have an opening."

"Um, uh, well, I, uh, don't think, uh…"

"Well, that's too bad, because that's where you're going to spend it."

Sheets, after standing without movement in the center of the orderly room for some time, at least till the site had been returned to its regular DEFCON position, finally took off his combat gear, went to the club, got Joy, and took the next bus to town. As the bus slowly went through the gate, I could hear Joy yelling, "Oh, no, no way, Russ. No way Joy go Udorn. Number ten town. No way, no way!"

In the morning Major Richter made his call to Colonel Wolff, and by the afternoon. Russell Sheets, Captain, United States Air Force, was on his way to Udorn Royal Thai Air Force Base. Some days later, Major Richter said to me while he sipped his martini, "You know what Colonel Wolff said to me when I called him about Sheets?"

I looked at him and waited, knowing a reply wasn't needed.

"He said, 'I'm surprised it took you this long to ask to get rid of those two jackasses.'"

To further confirm that June was a good month, Sgt. Sutton went back to the States at the end of the month. It was not as dramatic a departure, his tour was merely completed, just like a normal person's would have been. He was replaced by another master sergeant, whose name was Barton, and who turned out to be quiet and, most importantly, competent.

JULY 1968

CHAPTER TWENTY-SEVEN

SGT. LAFAYETTE CHANCE WAS SCHEDULED to rotate back to the States at the end of July. On his little desk calendar, the date July 28 was circled with a large red marking. On the previous page, the 28th of June was also brilliantly marked. However, in this case, the markings were the letters "PCOD". On the morning of July 1, when I entered the office, Sgt. Chance was sitting at his desk, his head resting on his hands, staring the calendar.

"Morning, Lafayette."

"Yeah."

There was no plane scheduled in that day, so in effect, it meant a no-work day. I immediately settled into reading a novel I kept in my desk. Sgt. Barton came in a few minutes later.

"Good morning, Sir. Good morning, Chance."

"Hey, Sarge."

"Yeah."

Smiley Burnett was leaving for home in a few days and was going through an endless series of good-bye parties, so he didn't get in until nearly nine. Even by then, he was still a little pale, and he winched whenever anyone spoke. After he had been there for almost ten minutes, he turned in his chair and spoke to Lafayette.

"How you doing, Lafayette?"

"Yeah." Chance was still seated as he was when I came in, his head in his hands and staring at his calendar.

Major Richter was in Bangkok on a make-work trip, enjoying a few days break, so we had as full an office as we were going to have. When I came to a chapter break in my reading, I got up, stretched and slowly walked around the room. I stood at the front door for awhile and watched the sky. We were heading into the heart of the rainy season, and I could see the day's first downpour approaching in the shape of large, dark clouds. Despite the dark sky and the swirling winds coming ahead of the rain, the thermometer outside the door was already approaching one hundred degrees. I thought of my next assignment in Arizona where the heat but not the rain would still be part of my day. I turned and started back to my desk. Lafayette was still there, staring at his calendar. He hadn't even started to go through his regular pile of forms. When I looked down at his desk, I noticed he had not turned his calendar page since the 28th. The red letters, "PCOD" stood out. I laughed.

"Lafayette, don't tell me you missed your pussy-cut-off-date?"

He didn't look up. "Ain't fuckin' funny, Lieutenant."

I held back from laughing out loud. "Well, how'd it happen?"

"Aw, fuck. Last night, I'm sittin' over thuh fuckin' club, havin' uh fuckin' beer. I start thinkin'. What thuh fuck am I gonnuh do for uh fuckin' month. Sit aroun' my fuckin' bunk, beat my fuckin' meat?" He still sat at his desk, staring ahead at his calendar. "Uh guy could go fuckin' nuts doin' that. Fuckin' A. So I figured, what thuh fuck, I'll jus' go down uh fuckin' Argo 'n sit arun'. Maybe I can get uh hand job, or sumthin'."

With this, he picked up the momentum of his story by straightening up and turning around. "I shouldduh had my fuckin' head examined. Anyway, wouldn't yuh fuckin' know it, in comes little fuckin' Nitnoy. I ain't seen her in at least uh fuckin' month. She been down uh Takhli, tryin' tuh go fuckin' big time. She sees me, screams, 'Lafayette, my number one teeloc,' then she grabs my fuckin' pecker. Goddamnit!" Chance began to shake his head back and forth, and then he shuddered and cursed to himself.

"Thuh next fuckin' thing, I'm up in her fuckin' room, an' I'm goin' at it like a fuckin' champ. Shit, I got fuckin' rocks in my head. My balls'll probably fall off the day I get back to thuh fuckin' States. Then what's my ol' lady gonnuh say?"

Smiley was grinning faintly. It was all you could expect from him on a day like this. I sat down at my desk and returned my attention to Lafayette. "Is it that much of a worry? You haven't had much trouble, have you?"

"Naw, I been fuckin' lucky, I only had four or five fuckin' doses uh thuh clap." With a sense of great doom, he added, "So far."

"Four or five doses! Jesus, Lafayette, did you get them all from Nitnoy?"

"Aw, fuck no. At least I don't fuckin' think so." He raised his hand and began counting on his fingers. "Lemme see. I know I got it once in fuckin' Takhli. Down there, you get it, jus' fuckin' shakin' hands with uh girl. Then I got it that time you let me go tuh Taipei. That was worth it though. Then one night I got fuckin' drunk and went down to ten-baht alley. Fuck! I don't even remember getting' laid. An' then I gave thuh fuckin' stuff to Nitnoy, an' when I finally rid of it she gives it fuckin' back to me. Iz'at four or five times?"

"Four"

"Oh, yeah, thuh fifth fuckin' time is thuh one I'm workin' on right now." He shivered in his seat. "Aw shit, Lieutenant. I can feel those fuckin' little clap germs crawlin' all over my poor pecker right this fuckin' minute.

In time, Lafayette got out his pile of forms and began stamping them in the upper left hand corner. Smiley Burnet felt better, and his normal color and grin returned. Sgt. Barton emerged from time to time to review the personnel cards of new airmen, something I never saw Sutton do. By nine-thirty, the first storm of the day had passed, and I went over to the mess hall for a cup of coffee. I brought my novel with me and stayed there about a half an hour. Pap Pai, my favorite mess hall girl kept teasing me and suggesting I was reading *Playboy*. I returned by saying that I didn't like *Playboy* anymore because they didn't have any pictures of Thai girls in it. I wasn't kidding. When I left the mess hall, I wandered around the site making my usual perfunctory visits to the areas that were nominally under my control. Noticing that the dark clouds of the day's second downpour were forming about eleven o'clock, I headed back toward the orderly room.

When just outside the office door, I looked toward the gate. A taxi drove up and stopped, and Master Sergeant Ballard jumped out and ran through the gate. He nearly knocked over the guard in doing so, and one of the air police called out and told him to take it easy. I guessed he was late for work, but he seemed overly upset about something. His uniform was already soaked with perspiration. When he saw me, he began yelling, "Lieutenant, hey Lieutenant, hey Lieutenant Doyle!"

"Easy, easy, Sarge. What's going on?"

He stopped in front of me to catch his breath, and took his hat off. His hands were shaking and waving in front of his face. I told him again to calm down. "Lieutenant, you know that girl, you know the one Lt. Fuzze's, I mean Lt. Saunders' teeloc. You know the one he says he's going to marry. You know, you know."

"Yes, Renu. She is his fiancée."

"Yeah, her. Renu. That's her. That's the one. Well she just got killed."

I felt the first drops of the rain plopping down on my head and on my shoulders, and I stared straight ahead into Sgt. Ballard's eyes. He continued to gasp and look about. I heard myself say, "No," and then, "What do you mean?"

Ballard didn't seem to be noticing my face very much and was missing what I am sure was an expression of total shock. I could hear him talking. "Just what I mean, Lieutenant. I mean she just got killed. I saw it and I came right out here."

The rain was really coming down by then. I could feel the wet working its way through my uniform. Ballard moved out of the rain and onto the little porch in front of the orderly room. My face followed him and I looked up at him, standing there one step above me. "How do you mean, I mean, I mean how?"

"Jesus, Sir, you better get out of the rain." When I didn't move, Ballard went on. "I was down town waiting for our bus, when there comes up this big commotion over by the railroad and somebody says someone got hit by a train. I push my way over there and some guys from the hospital have just gotten there. So I look over everyone's head and I see her. It's her for sure, I mean she's the best looking girl in town, so I'm sure I'll recognize her. Her face ain't even bloody, but her skin is already turned kind of gray. And Jesus, Sir, her lower half, it ain't hardly there anymore, at least not so much that you can really tell. The guys from the hospital cover her up pretty quick, and I can hear some of the people around the place saying something about 'farangs'." I guess they knew she was the Lieutenant's teeloc. Anyway, I figured I better get out here and tell someone about it."

I was soaking wet by then. The water was running down in front of my eyes, and I could barely make out Sgt. Ballard on the porch. "Jesus, Lieutenant, you better get out of the damn rain."

I felt the water building up in my shoes. The rain was so heavy and the wind so strong that even Ballard, standing on the porch was getting drenched. I could hear myself screaming, "No!" I could hear it again and again. It was like a sound coming from somewhere else.

Ballard seemed to take a step towards me. "Yeah, honest, Lieutenant, it's the truth. Now come on, get out of the rain."

I kept screaming, "No" over and over again. I could feel my face contorting, and my fists clenching. There were no conscious reactions that I can recall, no thoughts that really were considering the possibilities of Renu's death, only an overwhelming rage which seemed to be attempting to defeat the facts of death by overpowering it. I ran onto the porch and grabbed Ballard by the collar and pulled on him, screaming, "No, no, no, no!"

Ballard got his hands on my chest and pushed me backwards, breaking my hold and crashing me into the water that had formed in front of the porch. "Jesus, Lieutenant, I didn't kill her, all I did was tell you about her. She ain't even your teeloc."

Like a dog, mad with rabies, I stood in the water on all fours and great spasms shook through my body. I tried to focus my thoughts, but it was impossible. The image that Ballard had described was locked in my mind. I could see only her face and a bloody, pulpy mass beneath. I shook my head and screamed. When I looked up, I saw that the entire orderly room crew was now in the doorway watching me. I saw them, but it meant nothing to me, no more than a blank wall.

In front of me I saw the butt can, full of sand and hanging from a little white stand. When I took the can in my hands and began swinging it above my head, they all stepped back into the orderly room. As I kept swinging it around over my head, I began yelling again, but this time I was saying, "I'll kill them, I'll kill them." I remember it all, and yet at the time, I didn't seem to realize anything I was doing until I was already doing it. When I finally let go of the bucket, I aimed it at the bulletin board next to the porch. It hit, shattering the glass in the front of the board and the wet sand stuck itself across the duty lists and official announcements. The entire board shook on its legs, but it survived the blow. The bucket bounced halfway back to me, and as I watched it roll itself to a stop, I felt all of the energy drain from me, and I sat myself down in the water. The rain continued to pour down over me, and I honestly don't know if I was crying or my eyes were just burred from the rain water.

I remember hearing steps and when I looked up one of the air policemen was coming near me. He had his nightstick in front of him, held between both hands. Behind him, I could see Boon, his nightstick also out.

But the first one to reach me was Lafayette, and then Smiley. I could hear Lafayette say, "Get away you fuckin' assholes. Get thuh fuck away." And then to me he said, "Easy, Jim, easy. It's okay, easy now, it's over. Relax." He had his hand on my shoulder, and Smiley was pulling my knees up and urging me to put my head between them.

Behind those two, I could hear the air policeman saying, "Jesus, what a nut, it wasn't even his girl. What's his goddamned problem?"

Lafayette stood up and went over to the policeman, and in a voice I guess he thought I couldn't hear, said, "Shut your fuckin' mouth, you stupid fuckin' ape. Anybody with any fuckin' brains knows Lt. Doyle cared more about that girl and that stupid little bastard in ops."

When my breathing was nearly normal again, Lafayette and Smiley helped me to my feet, and Lafayette said, "Come on, Lieutenant, let us help yuh over tuh thuh fuckin' dispensary. Get Doc Dugan tuh give yuh some fuckin' dry clothes and let yuh rest some."

So with Lafayette D. Chance on one side of me and Smiley Burnett on the other, I made my way across the center yard and into the dispensary where Doc got me out of my wet clothes, put me into a bathrobe, gave me two white pills and a cup of water and told me to lie on the bed where I fell asleep.

CHAPTER TWENTY-EIGHT

RENU WAS DEAD. IT WAS true. It had happened much as Sgt. Ballard had tried to tell me. She had been at the railroad crossing waiting for a train to pass. As usual, before long a good sized crowd had amassed and pushed forward to scurry across the tracks as soon as the last car was by. Exactly what happened next was quite unclear, even in the Nakorn Sarang police report. When the crowd grew larger and more impatient as the train slowed, some shoving started. It was back from the front and away from the tracks where Renu stood, but it spread quickly and suddenly there was screaming and several people in the front of the crowd, Renu included, were pushed toward the train. A young man crashed against the side of one of the passing freight card and was pushed back, his head cut and his shoulder broken, but Renu fell between two cars and was knocked down onto the tracks. She was dragged about a hundred feet up the track bed before her body was kicked out from under the wheels. By then, the doctor assured me, she was dead. Her face, as Sgt. Ballard said was unscathed. There had been a laceration on her scalp, but it bled down the back of her head. Her body, however, was completely crushed from the chest down. There was little else in either the police or hospital report. No one else had been hurt. The boy was released from the hospital several days later and went back to school. The engineer had been aware of nothing. The train came to a regular stop two hundred yards up the track, and when the engineer looked back, he saw the crowd running along by the side of the train. It was over an hour later before he found out exactly what had happened. Some of the crowd, it was said, did not even chase after Renu's body, but calmly went on their way when the crossing was cleared.

But that was all something I learned weeks later. I woke up in the middle of the afternoon. My first thought was that it had only been a nightmare, but the Air Force issue robe and the surroundings quickly convinced me that it was true. The rage had all passed, and I wearily sat myself up on the side of the bed. Doc Dugan looked in when he heard me moving about.

"Feel better, Lieutenant?"

"Yeah, kind of sleepy, but not too bad." I wiped my eyes and looked out the window. The sun was out and steam was rising from the ground. It must have rained again. I got up and walked out to Doc's office.

"Say, Doc, just to make sure, that stuff about Lt. Saunders' fiancée is all true, I guess."

Doc looked up at me and nodded. "Yeah, afraid so. Sak called down to the hospital after Chance and Burnett brought you over here. It's all true, I'm afraid."

"What bout Lt. Saunders, where's he?"

'Went down the hospital with Sak to make some positive identification. I wouldn't worry about him none, he seemed pretty calm."

I realized I was standing there in a hospital bathrobe talking to the site medic. In other words, I became aware that I was a patient. I wondered if I was able to leave.

"Say, Doc, am I free to leave, or am I under some kind of care?"

"Shit, Lieutenant." Doc laughed and put his feet up on his desk. "Shit, what the hell you talking about? You think I'm supposed to fill out some big goddamned medical report every time I give aspirin to some guy, or someone needs to take a nap. Your uniform is hanging back there. It should be dry by now."

I looked over and saw my uniform. It had even been pressed. "That's it? Nothing more?"

"Jesus, Lieutenant. Can't you just make it easy for everybody and go back to work. Don't make them explain a lot things that it makes them uncomfortable to talk about."

So I got dressed and left. In the orderly room, the attitude was much the same. I felt I had at least perfunctorily thank Chance and Burnett for helping me, and when I did, I got an embarrassed grin from Smiley and Lafayette said, "Aw, it was fuckin' nothin', Lieutenant."

Sak came in around four o'clock, but Bob was not with him. Sak said that they had made identification of the body, but since there were no formal relations between anyone here and Renu, there was nothing else they could do. The hospital would notify whatever next of kin there was and any arrangements would be handled through them. I asked where Bob was.

"Lieutenant Saunders go by bungalow. Say not feel bad, but he finish work, go bungalow, rest." I decided I'd go visit him as soon as I could get away.

But first I went to the bar with Joe. As usual, my first drink was a beer. By that time, it seemed like I was into my third full day since morning. The first day had been that time until I met Sgt. Ballard. My fit and waking up comprised the second day. And there I was, beginning a third one. The news of Renu's death had spread quickly, and by the time I had woken in the dispensary, everybody on the site had probably heard. Of course, they had also probably heard about my crack-up. That seemed likely in view of the quiet in the club when I entered, and the number of stares that I was the object of. Anyway, the cold beer tasted great, and I had another. Through the first one, Joe and I stood silently at the bar.

As I sipped at the second beer (the first one I had guzzled), I said to Joe, "You know, I was just beginning to believe that the whole thing was really going to work out. I mean, I was beginning to be convinced that Bob was going ahead and getting the divorce, and really would marry Renu." I shook my head.

Joe didn't say anything. In fact, he seemed to be almost completely ignoring me. I drank at my beer for a while longer and then started talking again. "You now, it's strange, but as closely involved as I got in this whole thing, I can't say I ever got so I liked Bob. Oh, he's harmless enough, and you can't get yourself worked up enough to really hate him, but I never got to feeling that I like him."

Joe continued to sip at his beer, and he had bought some nuts and was munching on them. From time to time his eyes glanced at me so I knew he was listening and I went on. "Still, even though you know, I feel kind of sorry for him. She was probably the first thing he ever felt any passion about in his whole goddamned life, and now she's gone. Not that he ever showed it, but Christ's sake, to do what he was really doing, he must of really loved her."

Joe nodded or at least moved his head in some sort of motion making it appear to me as if he were nodding, but he still didn't say anything. The noise, which had stilled when I entered, was now back to normal, and we could have well been completely alone for all the attention that was being paid to us. I was finishing my third beer by then, and I ordered another one. They tasted very good and seemed to ease something that had lodged itself between my shoulder blades.

I picked up my ramblings again. "Jesus, I meant to get on over to Bob's bungalow. I really ought to see how he's feeling. The whole thing's probably troubling him more than he realizes."

"Stay seated and drink some more goddamned beer," said Joe as he broke his self inflicted silence. "You need the beers and relaxation more than that stupid little bastard needs to see you. I guarantee that nothing is troubling that cavity in his head where his brain is supposed to be."

So I stayed at the club drinking beers with Joe, easily convinced to by some grating sensation in my stomach that told me no matter how much I thought I should stop over and visit Bob, I didn't really want to. My mood lifted some and we talked about a number of totally unrelated subjects; college football, our families' expectations of us, sex, pro football, drinking, books, our last assignments, pro basketball, Chinese food, sex, gambling, whatever happened to Major Hudson, baseball, movies, music, sex, nightclubs, Thai beer, the war in Vietnam, politics and the likelihood of contacting leprosy during our stay in Nakorn Sarang (a bar girl in Takhli had been found to be suffering from a contagious form of the disease, the incubation period being from three to ten years). Of course, a number of times I mentioned Renu, not with a comment, but just in bewilderment or confusion, such as, "Jesus, I just can't get used to the idea," or "Damn, it just doesn't seem right, I mean why her?" Joe didn't respond to any of these remarks and waited for me to move on to something else before he would rejoin the conversation. Some time after my tenth or eleventh beer and two or three hamburgers, I, with a sigh, noted that I really had better be getting on over to Bob's.

Joe, resigned to my insistence on visiting Saunders, wearily waved a hand and said, "if you insist, go on."

I got the next bus, (I was in no shape to ride my cycle), stopped at my bungalow to change, waited out a thunderstorm, and then got a samlow to Bob's. On my way, I picked up two banana leaves full of fried rice in case Bob had not had anything to eat. I never learn.

From the road, at the end of the driveway that led to Bob's house, I could hear music and see lights. At the gate, which was locked, the noise was so loud that he couldn't hear me when I was yelling to get his attention. I had to wait for the music to end, and then I yelled out his name. I hear the stereo being clicked off and his little silhouette appeared at the window. I couldn't see his face because of the light coming from behind him, but I was afraid he might have been crying while sitting there getting drunk and trying to overwhelm himself with stereo. He saw me quickly and said he'd be right down to let me in.

As he approached the gate, he said, "Hey, Jim. What's up?" as he fumbled on his key chain (it must have contained fifty keys—there weren't that many locks on the entire site) I could see that he definitely had not been crying.

I held out the fried rice and said, "I brought some food along, in case you haven't eaten," but he looked at me somewhat puzzled and told me that he had heated a can of Dinty Moore beef stew on his hot plate. So, as was usual, and I don't know why I had really expected different, I ended up eating both helpings.

At the top of the stairs, Renu's clothes were piled off to one side. they were considerable and included all the items that Bob had paid local tailors to make. He said that Sgt. Barton was coming by the next day to pick them up for the site's clothing fund. I tried to imagine some poor rice farmer's wife draped in one of Renu's miniskirts or the Ao Dai with the slit up the leg nearly to the hip.

Other than the pile of dresses there was little sign of disruption around the place. Bob must have been working at his desk, the lamp being on. The stereo was silently spinning away, and Bob turned the music back on, but not as loud as before. The sound shifted from music to a voice with the slightest hint of an Oriental accent telling us that the next sound we'd hear was that of a locomotive. It was the stereo demonstration record that came with the components. Bob explained that it was the only record he owned as of yet. I looked around the room. It had been nearly eight months since I had left, and I had not stepped foot in the bungalow since. I saw that my old room was empty.

"What happened to Campbell? I thought he lived here."

"Oh, he moved out about a week or two ago. There's a new lieutenant coming in next week. I guess he'll live here. I'll only be here another four weeks so that'll finish up the year."

In the refrigerator I helped myself to a beer and sat down. I was a little reluctant to bring up any delicate subjects, but he seemed to be quite in control of things. "So what're your plans now, Bob?"

He opened a beer himself and looked around the room. "Until the new officer gets here, I'll probably use that room for storage myself. I'll be sending my whole baggage next week, so after that, I won't need the space."

I drank several more beers as I pursued the same line of questioning to much the same results. Since I was attempting in my rapidly increasing drunkenness to be, above all, sensitive to the situation and therefore avoiding any direct mention of the incident that was my sole reason for being there, I was always met with one of Bob's inane responses and his blank expression which indicated he could either sit there in silence or answer my questions, in either case, forever. For me, all of my circumspect working did nothing so much as force me to even more vividly consider the death of Renu, and I was becoming, inwardly at least, hysterical again. At long last, after opening another beer, I turned on him and yelled, "My God, Bob, what the hell are you going to do about Renu, about your life, about everything? Jesus, you've been sitting there like nothing has happened today."

I stared at him and waited for some flinching, a tick to at least pass across his face before answering, some indication of having been jogged into considering the inconsiderable. But, of course, none did, and he answered as unhesitatingly as always.

"Oh, I just finished writing to Betty." He rose and went over to the desk where the lamp was still on, picked up a letter and brought it over to show me. As I was sensing a great wave of déjà vue drape itself over me, I could hear him saying, "I told her what had happened and, certainly, that there would be no need for the divorce now."

Of course he was quite mad and why I kept expecting a change I don't know, but instead of just shaking my head sadly and leaving, I chose to discuss it further.

"But Bob, how can you be considering such a thing when your fiancée was just killed?"

"Well, Betty is my wife."

"Your ex-wife!"

"No, it's not quite final. Tomorrow I'll contact the lawyer at Takhli and stop the whole thing."

"But, Christ, man, Renu, your fiancée, the girl you were in love with is dead. You don't just move onto another romance the same day."

"I've told you that I've always had the greatest respect for Betty. It's just that I loved Renu more. Now that Renu is dead, Betty is the girl I love the most, so, of course I should be married to her."

"You think she'll have you back, just like that?"

"Why, of course. You remember I told you Betty and I always agreed that you couldn't be married if you loved somebody else more. Well, now, since Renu is dead, I don't love anyone more than I love Betty."

I was screaming by then. "But grief, for Christ's fucking sake, show some goddamned grief, man."

He blinked, the most I would ever get out of him. "Well, yes, I did fell bad when I heard the news, but I believe there must be a reason for everything that happens, and we've got to look to the future and act like adults."

Renu's image was starting to dominate my mind; one arm hanging straight at her side, the other bent at the elbow and the hand resting on the other elbow; her dark hair split and partially falling over her shoulders and down across her breasts; a red flower in her hair and a wistful, slight, and child-like smile barely formed on her lips. I slid onto the chair and when I lifted the beer can to my mouth again, I found my face was wet from tears, and I noticed I was whimpering. I could hear myself making blubbering sounds. My tongue was thick and my lips twisted over themselves. I couldn't even understand my own words. I didn't know what I was trying to say. Then, while I was still crying, Bob Saunders helped me to my feet and into the room that had once been mine where I collapsed on the bed and cried myself to sleep.

CHAPTER TWENTY-NINE

I AWOKE WHEN THE SUN first threw its light on my face. The fan was not on, and my body was already soaked with sweat, but my mouth was dry like baked sand. I sat on the side of the bed and tried to cough up some phlegm to wet my mouth, but all I did was gag. My throat must have been dry halfway to my stomach. Bob kept no boiled water in his refrigerator, so I had to drink straight tap water. I intended only to gargle, but once the water was in my mouth, my muscles by reflex swallowed. In three or four days, I estimated, my bowels would be belching out something the consistency of bad chowder. When I finally looked at my watch, it was ten-thirty. Bob was not there, neither was the pile of Renu's clothing. That meant Sgt. Barton had already been there. At least, at the site, they'd know where I was. I went back to the room I'd slept in, my old room, thinking there must be something I should pick up before I left, but I'd slept in all my clothes. Bob hadn't even seen fit to take my shoes off. I stared around the room, but there was nothing, only the bed with its bare mattress and equally bare pillow. The bureau and the locker were empty, their drawers and door slightly ajar. Since my head was beginning to ache, and Bob had no aspirin in the medicine chest (and no juice or soda in his refrigerator), I decided to leave and get a quick samlow home where I could better deal with my hangover.

At the stairs I paused to look at the spot where Renu's clothes had been piled. There was nothing, in fact there was no indication that a pile had ever been there. That thought caused me to look back around the living room to search for some sign of Renu. There was none. Impossible, I thought and started to search the room more closely. I had no idea where to look. I hadn't been in the goddamned house for eight months. There was nothing of hers in the living room. On Bob's desk, nothing. Even the letter to his wife was gone. On the far corner of the desk was something that jolted me, a picture of Betty. It was enclosed in a gold plated frame and signed across a bottom corner: "With love Forever, your loving Wife, darling, Betty." The redundancy and ill-placed capitals were worthy of Bob himself. I wondered if the damn thing had always been there, for Renu to see, but I found the frame and glass were free from dust, unlike the rest of the desk, so it must have been put out the night before. Against my better judgment, I began rifling through Bob's drawers in hopes of finding a picture of Renu. What the hell, the guy used to read me love letters from his wife, there could be nothing he would object to my seeing. I was right, there was nothing, nothing at all. Some pencils and pens, a few baht coins, some paper clips, a packet of stamps, a copy of "A Pocket Guide to Thailand," issued by the Department of Defense, two small batteries for a transistor radio, some rubber bands, and two sets of captain's bars (even with the nearly automatic promotions then in effect, I found it presumptuous of Bob to plan ahead so confidently), but no picture of Renu. I opened each drawer twice; the first time I only glanced in, but the second time I pulled them all the way out and ran my hand through them, leaving all of them open, nearly falling on the floor. When I was through, I slapped the top of the desk and yelled, "Damn!" I flashed my eyes about the rest of the room. For Christ sakes, how the hell could someone live in a room for nearly eleven months, share it for at least four months with a girl, and still leave it so devoid of any sign of habitation.

I went into the bedroom. The small bureau with the large mirror had nothing on it save Bob's electric alarm clock. There were none of the small bottles of make-up and lotions, or little jars of powder that Ewan always brought with her and which I assumed Renu would also have. To my surprise, there were two pillows on the bed, and I grabbed and sniffed at them both, but there was no smell of perfume in either of them. Bu this time, I was getting desperate. Renu had hardly been dead twenty-four hours, and I couldn't find the slightest sign of her having ever lived. I ripped back the sheets from what had been their bed, hoping maybe to find some blood, or at least the musty smell of their love making, but again, there was nothing. I sat down heavily on the bed, my hangover overtaking my senses. The heat was causing me to sweat heavily again, and I felt very weak, so I laid myself back down across the bed.

Lying on my back on Bob and Renu's odorless bed, staring at the motionless fan against the ceiling, what seemed like a great idea entered my wimpy brain. The hospital. It was between Bob's house and mine. I'd stop there and view Renu's body. A last sight, at least. In the lobby of the hospital I saw the doctor who had filled out the medical report on Major Hudson.

"Doctor, stop, please. Do you remember me?"

He viewed me with the same tired eyes, but he did turn and speak. "Yes, of course I remember you, Lieutenant. What do you want?"

"Doctor, the girl, the one hit by the train, Renu Wanduangsai."

"Yes, the bar girl."

"Could I see her?"

"Of course not, Lieutenant. You are not related. And, if I am not mistaken, she was not even your...your..."

"No, you're right, she wasn't, but couldn't I see her."

"No, it is impossible. Her container has been sealed. It is being sent to Bangkok this afternoon."

"To Bangkok? To whom?"

"To her mother."

"Her mother?"

"Her mother, Lieutenant. Even such girls have mothers."

"I didn't know. She was never mentioned."

"Such a girl would not have been proud to have her mother meet you."

"She was a nice girl, she really was."

I felt a shame coming up in me, and I may have been about to cry. The doctor must have noticed the pain in my face. He put aside his distaste for me. "Yes, yes, I am sure she was. I am sorry. Still, it is impossible to see the body." He turned and started away, but he stopped and spoke again. "Lieutenant, are you feeling all right?"

I waved my hand in front of my face. "Oh, yes. Okay. Just a little upset. I'm okay, thanks."

"You look very pale, your eyes are very red. You haven't shaved, your clothes are dirty and messy. Go home and rest." This time he turned and did go, leaving me alone in the hospital lobby, from which I also turned and left to go home.

It was well after one in the afternoon when I reached the site. I had gone back to my bungalow, eaten some dry cereal, cleaned up, changed into clean civvies (my work day was already shot, and the Major was still in Bangkok, so what the hell), and got the early afternoon bus. The Takhli plane had been in earlier in the day, so my desk was piled deep in paper.

"What's all this shit?"

"Hey, Jim, I mean Lieutenant. How the fuck are yuh?"

"Okay. What's all this shit, Lafayette?"

"Aw, jus' some fuckin 1098's, some fuckin APR's and OER's, some fuckin' supply requisitions, an' my request for fuckin' medical leave.:

"Medical leave?"

"Yeah, I'm sure my fuckin' pecker's gonnuh fall off any fuckin' minute. I wannuh go tuh Bangkok, see uh real fuckin' doctor."

"Lafayette, you go to Bangkok, you'll spend the whole time in a whorehouse. What the hell good is that?"

"Naw, hones'. I'm through with fuckin' pooyings."

"Request denied. Has Lt. Saunders been in here?"

"Shit, I knew yuh was gonnuh fuckin' say that.": Chance broke out of his normal deadpan to answer my question. "Hey, yeah, he was. Yuh ain't gonnuh fuckin' believe what he did."

"He called the lawyer in Takhli."

"He called thuh fuckin' lawyer at Takhli."

"He's going to cancel his divorce."

"He's gonnuh cancel his fuckin' divorce."

"Because his wife is the girl he loves the most."

"Because his fuckin' wife is uh girl he loves uh fuckin' most."

"Now that his fiancée is dead."

"Now that his fiancée is fuckin' dead."

While I formed my papers into a neat pile and stuck them on the far corner of my desk, Lafayette watched me for any reaction to the news he had just given me. I gave none, only asking if he knew where Sgt. Barton was.

"I think he's downnuh fuckin' library."

On my way out the door, I ran into Smiley. He stopped me with his hand on my arm. "Hey, Lieutenant, how are you? You okay, huh?"

"Yeah, fine."

I didn't find Barton in the library, I found him in the BX, but when I entered the former, Sunida rose and came out from behind her desk. "Oh, Lieutenant Jim, you are feeling better, yes?"

I wasn't anxious to talk to her at the time. "Oh, yes, I'm fine."

"Good, I am happy. I was worried when I hear you are sick."

"No, I'm okay, honest."

"Also, I am very sad when I hear Miss Renu is dead."

"Yes, very sad."

"Lt. Saunders, he is very sad I think, yes?"

"No, he doesn't…I mean yes, yes, very sad."

"And you, I think you like her too. I am very sad for you too."

"Yes, I mean thank you. Yes, I'm okay."

"I waited for you last night."

"What?"

"I wait for you. For lesson. You were sick, I think."

"Oh, Jesus, I'm sorry. Really, I'm very sorry."

"Tomorrow, you will be there?"

"Yes, tomorrow, for sure."

"Oh, very good. I talk to you. I have something for to tell you.

"Okay, good. Hey, I'm sorry, really. See you tomorrow."

When I finally found the first sergeant, we went to the club for a beer. "No uniform today, Lieutenant?"

"No, the day's pretty much shot. I wasn't feeling well this morning, couldn't get up. But I guess you know that."

"Yes, Sir. You're okay now though, I hope."

"Fine, thanks. So you already picked up Renu's clothes and turned them over to the clothing fund?"

"Yes, Sir. Lt. Saunders and I took one of the trucks and went down and picked it all up. I asked you how you felt, but you said you just wanted to sleep."

"I spoke, huh? I don't even remember it."

"She sure had a lot of beautiful clothes. I can't imagine what they'll do with some of that stuff. If my wife were smaller, I might've been tempted to send some of it to her."

"Look, Sarge, was there anything else you picked up? Pictures, letters, personal stuff, anything like that?"

"No, nothing, Lieutenant." After several seconds silence, Barton turned to me. "Since you slept there last night, I guess you must have talked to Lt. Saunders about his plans."

"Yes."

"Then I don't blame you for getting so drunk."

"He told you, huh?"

"Yeah, I have to admit, I don't see much beauty in these people over here, and I never thought too much about his plans in the first place, but, goddamnit, I couldn't believe him when he was talking this morning. Is he all there, Lieutenant?"

"Oh, he's all there, there just wasn't much there to start with."

About four o'clock I found Bob and also brought him to the club for a beer. He seemed more intent in discussing the lack of activity in the air war. "Another slow day. You know, Jim, it's really a shame that after all the really great things we accomplished before the bombing halt, to let it all go to waste."

"Forget that shit! Look, Bob, didn't Renu have any personal items? Didn't you have a picture of her? I looked all around, but I couldn't find anything."

As I suspected, Bob was totally unconcerned that I had searched his bungalow. "Oh yes, she had some letters, and some knick-knacks, and I had a picture of her. I threw them out this morning." He said it in the same tone he might have used when talking about some old beer cans.

I could feel the blood rise in my face, and I must have yelled, because some of the airmen turned to stare at us when I said, "You what?"

He explained to me very calmly once he straightened his glasses which had slumped on his nose when I yelled, that, yes, he had thrown them out because they weren't his, and he couldn't use them. And when I asked what about the picture of her, why had he thrown that out, he said, "Well, it just didn't seem right for a happily married man to have a picture of another woman, especially if she was dead."

I turned away from him and clenched the edge of the bar. "You mailed the letter to Betty?"

"Oh, yes, it went out on this morning's plane."

"And you figure she'll understand. There'll be no problem?"

"Oh no, none. You know how I've always said we agree about how important it is to live with the one you love the…"

I stopped him by raising my hand, but I refrained from looking at him. "I understand you already talked to the lawyer at Takhli?'

"Yes. He said, 'No problem'. So it looks like everything's going to be all right."

I buried my face in one hand and turned my back to him. I ordered another beer, but when I tried to raise it my mouth, my rage was so intense, I spilled some of it. I heard Bob order another beer as well. As usual, he was oblivious to my mood. In time I calmed down, but I still refused to look at him. Several minutes elapsed before he spoke. I think he meant to be conciliatory, but I wasn't ready to accept it and certainly not to accept what he said.

"You know, Jim, I think things have worked out for the best."

"Get out of here," I said, still not able to turn to face him.

"I mean, I don't think Renu would have been really happy in America. These people are best off in their own country."

On that I turned and yelled, "Get out of here!"

"Jim, what do you mean?"

"Get the hell out of here!"

"Jim, gee…"

"You little fucking asshole, get the hell out of here before I kill you!"

The bouncer, an ape of an airman named Cole, aroused from his normal catatonic state by my screaming, was starting over to us.

"Gee, Jim, I haven't finished my beer."

"Then take the fucking thing with you," I yelled as I poured the rest of the contents of his glass down the front of his shirt.

Bob, after a brief moment of shock, said, "Okay, Jim. I don't think you're feeling well." He turned and left.

Cole, who Bob passed on his way out the door, continued over to me. He spoke with deliberateness of a drugged grizzly bear. "Yuh know, Lootinin, if that wuzz innyone else, I'dduh had tuh throw yuh outtuh here."

"Yeah, thanks, Cole. Hey Manee, bring me a shot of bourbon, quick." The bourbon really straightened me out. I went back to the men's room and puked. Then I came out and tried it again, this time managing to hold it down.

Joe and I next talked in the bar, but it wasn't for nearly another hour. I had had two more shots of bourbon, but then went back to drinking beers. I even had the foresight to put down two hamburgers, so I was only mildly bombed by the time Joe joined me in holding up the bar.

"You didn't get drunk enough last night?"

"Sure, but that was last night. This, as they say, is a whole new day."

"Wonder Lieutenant came back to ops about an hour ago. The front of his uniform was soaked. I take it that was your work?"

"Uh huh."

"What was the particular thing he said that earned that?"

"I don't want to talk about it."

"That's a switch."

"That asshole is unbelievable."

"I hate to say I told you so."

"You know what he had the goddamned nerve to say?"

"You said you didn't want to talk about it."

"I changed my mind. That little bastard said..."

"Stop. I don't think I really need to hear it. I can imagine. Besides, it doesn't do you any fucking good to go over it again. Say, did you ever see Gale Sayers when he was at Kansas?"

Joe wasn't able to get talking about football or any other sport, but he did keep me from talking about Renu and Bob (but not from thinking about them). When the second evening bus was about to leave, Joe got up to get it.

"Where are you going? I thought we were going to get drunk?"

"I forgot to tell you, Ewan is coming tonight on the train."

"Does she know?"

"Yes, I sent her a telegram yesterday. She sent a telegram which I got today saying she's coming here."

"But they've shipped Renu's body out this afternoon."

"I know. Ewan made the arrangements. I guess she just wants to get out of Bangkok for awhile. Look, why don't you come and meet her with me. We can go and get something to eat."

"Naw, I'm going to stay here and drink some more."

"You ought to come. There's something I didn't tell you."

"Huh?"

"Pitsommai's coming on the train with her."

"Wha...?"

"So why don't you come along?"

Now I might have normally been pleased by the prospect of such a visit, and it might seem reasonable to assume that I would look forward to the solace which Pitsommai and I might reasonably commiserate each other with, but, as was my habit when events whose meanings were elusive overtook me, I sought not understanding but oblivion. So, assuring Joe that I would catch the next bus and more than likely, if the train from Bangkok was its usual forty minutes to an hour late, be at home when he and the two girls arrived there, I intently pondered where in hell I could go so they couldn't find me.

After another half hour of drinking in which I managed to guzzle two more cans of Budweiser and ward off an attempt at conversation by Doc Dugan with a series of garbled responses such as, "uh uh" and "uh huh,", I left the bar, went to the bike rack where I started my Honda 90 (the motorcycle which I normally had the good sense not to drive when I had been drinking), drove it out the gate, across the runway, past the airport, past the road which turned into the heart of the village, drove it for nearly forty-five minutes in the fading light, on past the waterfalls where Sgt. Hunnicut had been the unwitting star of a blue movie, past there till I had arrived at the small roadside restaurant where I had drunk Singhas on a Sunday afternoon nearly four months before.

The establishment there was obviously not regularly frequented by farangs because I was immediately recognized and welcomed by the proprietor who flashed me a toothy grin (a red toothy grin) and, ducking into his ice chest, came up with a liter bottle of Singha and placed it on the crude table at which I sat. I took a long swallow of the cold beer and then let out an exaggerated and hammy "aahhhhhh!" The papa-san laughed and shook his head affirmatively to signal his pleasure at my delight in his wares. By raising the bottle toward him, I indicated he should join me, which he immediately did. Through the rest of the bottle we saluted one another with each swallow, the proprietor saying, "Tee numg farang," and I countering with, "Dee, dee mak kop."

The news of the return of the generous farang spread quickly through the tiny hamlet and before we finished our second liter, we had been joined by several other villagers whose faces were vaguely familiar from my previous visit, and shortly thereafter, we were joined by a group of newcomers, none of whom I recognized. It made no matter, I welcomed them all, and I particularly welcomed their uncommunicative presence. There was nothing I had to do but keep paying for the Singhas and to smile as I responded to their never ending salutes to my generosity. At the height of the festivities, our numbers reached perhaps fifteen then it dropped as a few of the group staggered off to their poor homes already feeling the headiness of the rarely affordable brew, but we settled in with a group of ten to celebrate, as long as possible, my happy return. The proprietor, having mysteriously disappeared for several moments returned bearing a plate of rice and a bowl of noodles which he managed to convey to me through a series of elaborate physical gestures were his contribution to our party. We all then drank several toasts to his good character which he acknowledged by taking long draughts of beer and letting out, when through, not bad imitations of my stagey "aahhhh," which brought great laughter to the entire group.

I wish I could say I enjoyed this night like no other I spent during my year in Thailand, but as much as much as I was occasionally caught up in these poor farmer' high spirits and as much as I laughed, when there were rare quiet moments, my troubled mind returned to Renu, and I found myself—more and more as my drunkenness increased—holding back tears. Of course in such instances, I would raise my glass and signal the beginning of another toast.

Fortunately for my funds, the small restaurant's supply of Singha became exhausted before my wallet did. Laughingly and drunkenly, we all passed around the empty bottles and holding them over our glasses for extended periods of time, let out great cries of cheer when a few drops of beer would finally tumble into our cups, but that meager reserve was soon gone, and it was time to take my leave. My group of friends all saw me to the edge of the road, where, as I tumbled over when first attempting to start my Honda, they roared with laughter, but quickly jumped to my aid, and, like a many-limbed machine, dusted off my motorcycle and me. The proprietor made some gestures, like closing his eyes, putting his hands alongside his head and snoring, while pointing alternately from me to the rear of his restaurant, which I took to be an invitation to spend the night, but I declined the invitation with a shaking of the head and a donning of an expression which I was positive conveyed a reassuring impression of sobriety. Of course it would have convinced no sober mind of any such thing, but there were none there, and I shortly left my friends as they gave me long choruses of "Sawadee, sawadee, sawadee," to which I answered, "Sawadee-dee-dee." It got my last laugh of the night.

The sun was down (I had no concept of time, but in recreating the scene, it seems likely it was shortly after ten) and there were no street lights that far from Nakorn Sarang, but fortunately the road was quite straight and untraveled that late, so despite my drunkenness, I managed with some concentration to hold the road. Of course, convincing myself I needed to rest, I stopped at nearly every little inn along the road where always put away another liter of Singha. In these places I was not the gregarious host I had been on the other side of the falls, but now I sat in silence while drinking my grog and inhaling deeply on cigarettes. By that time, I had successfully drowned my own remembrance of why the hell I was drinking so much and no longer able to bring to mind visions of Renu, I did not threaten to cry, but, rather while I sat and drank and smoked in gloom that I accepted as routine, I decided I wanted to get laid.

Again, I have no idea what time it was when I arrived at the Argo, but I would estimate that my many stops along the road from the falls made the normal forty-five minute journey stretch into an hour or more, so it must have been after eleven-thirty when I parked my bike outside the bar's doors, staggered to the bar, not really cognizant of the very small crowd present, and told Papa-san to give me a bottle of Mekong (it was time for some serious drinking) and a girl.

"Oh, Lootenant, kee-mao mak mak."

"Cut the shit, Papa-san. Jes' gimme uh girl."

"Malee no here, go Takhli. Suptra mai sabai. All girls have poochai."

"What'd yuh runnin' here? Uh whorehourse, right? Then gimme uh fuckin' whore." I slapped the bottle of Mekong he had sold me to the top of the bar.

Suddenly Lafayette Chance was at my side. Beside him I could see when I turned, Smiley Burnett. "Hey, Lieutenant, where thuh fuck yuh been?"

I turned and smiled foolishly and as I poured some Mekong into a glass, said, "Hey, hey, Lafayette, howz abouttuh little drink? You too, Smiley."

"Just a Singha. I never touch that fuckin' Mekong. No shit, Jim, me and Smiley and Cap'n Stacy been lookin' all over thuh fuckin' town for yuh. Where thuh fuck yuh been?"

"I bennuh Hanoi."

"No shit, Cap'n Stacy's all fuckin' worried about yuh."

I met wi' Ho Chi Minh. He'z uh very nice guy."

"For Christ's fuckin' sake."

"Ol' Ho sez on't worry 'bout nuthin'. Jes' keep 'ose bombs 'n letters comin' folks. He Smiley, yuh know what I'm gonnuh do, I'm gonnuh ge' laid." With that I turned back to Papa-san and renewed my demand for a girl.

In an appeal for some degree of sanity, the sometime Thai Army master sergeant turned to my chief clerk. "Oh, Sergeant, please, I try tell him. He too kee-mao. No have girl, some no here, some already go G.I."

"That's thuh fuckin' truth, Jim. Look around thuh fuckin' place. Yuh see any fuckin' pussy here?"

I drank some more of my whisky and lit a cigarette which I tried to coolly drag on as I surveyed the nearly empty room. In the far corner were two other airmen whose interest in my spectacle seemed to be the only thing that was keeping them there. Other than that and our little setting of four at the bar, the Argo was empty.

"But I wannuh gettuh piece uh ass."

"Aw, com'on, Jim. Why don't yuh let me and Smiley fuckin' take yuh home?"

Suddenly I was inspired. "Hey, Papa-san, where's Mama-san?"

Before the owner could answer me, I heard Smiley spitting a mouthful of beer across the bar. "Mama-san in back, Lootenant, but I think she sleep."

"Christ, you're outtuh your fuckin' mind, Jim."

"Hey, Papa-san, I got song-loy baht and I jes' wannuh go up her room. Com'on, go 'n get'er."

"This is thuh stupidest fuckin' thinkg yuh ever did. Cut thuh shit, will yuh, Lieutenant?" Lafayette had his hand on my shoulder and Smiley was still coughing from having choked on his beer.

"Naw, Sargge, she'z really uh good fuck. Yeww oughttuh try'er sumtime."

Papa-san left the bar and quickly returned to acknowledge that his avarice had won out and indeed I could repair to his wife's room. Sgt. Chance wearily accepted his defeat, and, in fact, found it mildly acceptable. "What the fuck, he can't kill himself up there. Smiley, you stay thuh fuck here. I'm gonnuh take uh couple uh fuckin' samlows over and get Cap'n Stacy, let'm know we found thuh crazy fucker."

While Chance waited in the doorway for the one samlow driver who was there to go and chase down another so there would be one for Joe to ride in, I raised my glass to him, and saluted. "Good idea, Sarggge. I'll drink tuh'at."

"What thuh fuck. He might as well go up there. Thuh silly bastard won't be able to gettuh fuckin' hard-on anyway."

Chance was wrong. I had driven a drunken hour or more with little more than that one thought on my mind. My adrenalin was flowing. Shortly after Chance had left and I had finished one drink, I mixed another with the last of my Mekong, making it a very long one, filling the glass with soda and adding a slice of lemon, and then noisily climbed the stairs and entering Mama-san's room. By that time I had a full-fledged erection. The lights were on and she lay in bed with the sheets coyly pulled up to her chin. She giggled when she noticed the bulge in my pants. "Oh ho, Loootinin can do, can do!" Encouraged by my apparent ability to perform and envisioning I suspect her first real hope of sexual activity in quite some time, she dramatically pulled back the sheets as if she were spreading some carnal feast before me.

I was not discouraged by the rolls of soft and wrinkled flesh, and after taking a long swallow of my drink, I began to strip and throw my clothes about the room. When Mama-san saw my wang sticking out of my dark crotch, she began a long series of "oooh's" and "aaah's" and, with her hands, kept signaling me to speed to her bed. I took my drink with me and, sitting on the edge of her bed, took a long swallow to brace myself. Before I could turn, she had grabbed me by the neck and pulled me down onto her waiting flesh.

She began to push and shove at my body, instructing it; she placed my arms around her back, pulled my face into the nape of her neck, and locking her own large thighs around my hips, she used her hands to press my startled root against her entrance. I had planned on at least a minimum of foreplay, but she was immediately crying "Layo-layo," as if she could no longer stand the passion, but of course she was actually frightened that my ability and willingness to copulate would soon vanish, and she would be left with another limp and sad sock. Within moments after entering her bed, she had managed to cram my wang into her musty mouse hole.

I was not, however, able to complete the act. My erection did not wane (waning wang?), yet no matter how much I thrashed about, and no matter how much I was encouraged by Mama-san (she kept crying out, "Oh, I come, I come," and the, "Oh, I come again, I come again," and finally, "Hey, when you come, when you come?"), I never approached an orgasm. When, at long last, I rolled onto my back, letting out a long gasp of surrender to failure, she, after also catching her breath, reached over and patted my now sagging organ, saying, "Nice try, Lootinin. Maybe next time." I reached for my glass and, in one gulp, finished my drink.

Smiley was waiting for me when I returned to the bar area, after I had dressed while Mama-san douched herself over a large Earthen jar of water (a precaution which was most certainly unnecessary) and had suggested that I, too, might want to wash myself. I declined, then eager only to get to the bar and order another drink which is exactly what I did.

Smiley, who had obviously during his evening's search for and guardianship of me consumed more than a few Singhas and was himself quite smashed, said, "Ho'd it go, Jin?"

I gave him a foolish and lecherous wink, and said, "Great, yeww oughttuh try it yerself," which brought an unusually shy and embarrassed grin to his face.

The two other airmen had left probably shortly after I had taken my act upstairs, and Papa-san, in an economy move, had turned off the fans. "Say, Smiley," (I was attempting to be cordial) "Arn'choo suppoz' tewbee goin' home soon?" When he replied that he was leaving the next day, I said, "Oh, well, hava nicesh trip."

As I bolted large mouthfuls of my drink (a blend of Mekong and soda, heavy on the former), I began to sense a nausea creeping over me. I waved at Papa-san and signaled him to turn the fans back on, which he reluctantly did, but it was too late. My stomach began to shake and pound. Capping my hands over my mouth, I ran for the back door. Smiley, in his own inebriation, must have thought I was attempting to escape and followed after me, but he arrived only in time to be witness to my retching and heaving of the day's consumption into the stinking floor toilets just outside the back door. The combinations of sight and smell were too much for him, and I was wiping my mouth with my handkerchief, poor Burnett began making his own generous contribution to the Argo Bar's sewer system.

Smiley, who was not as accustomed to self-inflicted punishment and ridiculous behavior as I was, fell asleep on the bar when he returned; I had another drink. I sipped at that one, letting the well-diluted Mekong ease its way into my much maligned stomach. While sitting there, it occurred to me that what I needed was a nice ride around town on my motorcycle.

Papa-san, undoubtedly delighted to see me go, made no effort to dissuade me. The bike started on my second kick, and, as I sat on the seat, blinking my eyes in a useless attempt to clear them, I revved the little 90cc engine to its limits. The roar (at any other time a whine, but in the early morning a roar) of the pipes must have awakened Smiley, because I hear him yell, "Hey, Lieutenant, don't!" just as I was about to release the clutch.

The sound of the gears catching and Smiley's yell are the last things I remember of that night. Joe, who was approaching with Lafayette in their samlows, said I came out of the Argo at full throttle. My Honda left the ground, propelled by the lift of the Bar's driveway, when I reached the road. It landed halfway across the street and then continued in a direct course till it left the road and descended into the waist deep klong on the opposite side, where both I and my cycle disappeared from view in the muddy water. Joe and Lafayette waded in themselves and pulled me, unconscious, back onto the dry pavement, where, when I began to snore, they knew I had merely passed out. The motorcycle was destroyed.

Four days later, my pecker began to ache and when I went to the latrine and took it in my hand, puss came out of the tip. I had the clap.

CHAPTER THIRTY

THE CLAP IS NO GODDAMNED fun. It's cured easily enough—Doc Dugan shoved two large syringes of penicillin into my ass, one into each cheek, and gave me a jar of tetracycline pills to take, sixteen days worth—but, Jesus, you're not allowed to drink during that whole goddamned time. Since on Saturday, when I first began to, as Lafayette said, "burn," I had been mildly loaded for five days and fully expected and looked forward to continuing such consumption indefinitely, Doc's prescription was hard to swallow (nothing else was; I had been varying the nature of my drinking, one night, gin and tonics, the next beer, followed by bourbon, and even wine). I considered ignoring Doc's advice but a brief contemplation of possible consequences (frightening visions of sterility, blindness, horrible festering sores, the smell of rotting flesh and insanity—surely the most likely in my case) quickly dissuaded me, and I went on the wagon. It was the best thing that happened to me.

On the morning following my crash—Wednesday—Major Richter returned to Nakorn Sarang from his TDY in Bangkok. He found me just leaving the dispensary, for the second time in three days. Joe and Lafayette had picked me up off the street and loaded me into a samlow in which they transported me to the site and deposited me into one of the dispensary beds after treating me to a cold shower. The Major, having been met at the airport by Joe and quickly brought up to date on events first saw me as I exited from our mini hospital dressed in my uniform which Joe had brought out to the site for me. From a distance, I probably didn't look too bad, although I winced at the bright sunlight and failed to salute his jeep, but when he got me in his office and saw the blood which had accumulated in the whites of my eyes, noticed the paleness of my skin and the dark bags around my eye sockets, and was faced with the vapidity and vacuousness of my mind, he was genuinely concerned for me.

He had called me to his office shortly after returning. When he learned Renu was dead, Joe later told me, he stopped walking towards the jeep, turned to Joe and said, "Oh no!" As they were getting into the jeep and Joe said that Bob was taking it all very well and was in fact cancelling his plans for a divorce, the Major made a weary smile, the type that says, "I'm not surprised, but I'd been hoping...," then he said, "but I bet Jim is very upset." When I entered his office (this time I did salute), he immediately waved me to a chair.

I sat.

"How do you feel, Jim?"

"Uhhh, umm, uhride."

"Excuse me?"

"Okay."

"Jim, I hope you know I'm very sorry to hear about the girl."

"Uh huh."

His small smile appeared on his face. "But don't you think it's a little strange that it's you I should have to offer my sympathies to?"

"Uh huh."

He recommended that I get rid of my motorcycle and I, in my fashion, agreed. (The bike had been rescued from the klong that evening by the Air Police, but the engine and carburetor were so clogged with silt they required a complete overhaul). He allowed that he would eventually tolerate me on a regular bicycle, but suggested I stick to riding the bus and samlows for the near future, and I agreed.

"I understand your, uhm, girlfriend is here."

"Uh huh."

"Would you like a few days off? You and she could go to Chiang Mai, or to Bangkok. Get away."

"Uh uh."

"Lt. Saunders is all right, I gather?"

"Uh huh."

"Jim, I don't entirely understand what you're feeling…"

"Uh huh."

"…because I've never been able to understand how you could be so taken with this girl and yet seem to be helping her to marry another man…"

"Uh huh."

"…but I'll grant you your feelings. However, Jim, I gather you've been pretty much inoperative for the past two days…"

"Uh huh."

"…and that can't continue."

"Uh huh."

"Jim, you're a decent sort of young man, you're fairly bright…"

"Uh huh."

"…and whether you care about it or not, you're not a bad officer."

"Huh?"

"You can't hide yourself with booze. Someday you've got to face whatever it is that's eating at you."

"Uh huh."

"Since you don't want to take my offer for a couple of days off…"

"Uh huh."

"…I'll expect you here tomorrow morning ready to work."

"Uh huh."

"Today, spend the rest of the day lying down in the dispensary. I'll have Chance bring you some chow."

"Uh huh."

"That'll be all for now."

I got up to leave but stopped in the doorway.

"Um, Major."

"Yes?"

"Thanks."

Lafayette brought me my chow—Wednesday's fried chicken—and, surprisingly, I was able to keep it down. Most of the afternoon I spent in a dreamless near sleep (Doc closed the door on me and went about his work). My brain was as remote and detached as the planet Pluto, and even my inner self-contained conversations consisting of little more than a series of "um's" and "uh's" and "huh's". Towards the end of the afternoon, my mind began to un-muddle, but I couldn't control it, and it insistently kept focusing on images of Renu, or even worse of Bob (who, by the way, did not stop in the dispensary to see how I was). I didn't like it and started wishing for a drink, despite having made a promise to myself while talking to Major Richter, that I would lay off the stuff. Doc Dugan woke me from this inner conflict.

"Lieutenant, you have a visitor."

It was Sunida.

She shyly entered the room and approached the bed. I was lying on top of the covers with my uniform still on, although I had managed to get my shoes off. When I saw her, I sat up and swung my legs over the side of the bunk. The hospital style bed was high and my legs hung there, the feet not touching the floor. It made me feel small, even childish, and I was embarrassed.

She smiled and said, "Kun sabai dee loo?"

I managed to say, "Sabai dee", but when she continued to speak in Thai, my brain couldn't even pick up the sounds let alone click over into understanding them, so I had to ask her to speak English. I was embarrassed again by that, and then I was even further embarrassed when I realized I had the shakes. I controlled my hands by latching onto the edge of the bed and locking my elbows, but my head continued to tremble.

"I came to see you, for I do not think you will go to lesson tonight."

I could no more than mumblingly acknowledge her since she was completely right; I had entirely forgotten about it.

By then she had sat on a straight back chair several feet in front of me. Her knees were held tightly together and turned to one side. On top of them, she had placed both of her hands and she seemed to be squeezing the one in the other. She looked at me when she spoke, but when her words stopped, her eyes each time returned their gaze to her hands. I should have thought that strange. We were long past the stage where we couldn't face each other's eyes.

"You remember, I think I say I have something to tell to you."

"Yes." (I hadn't)

"I have good news for me."

"Yes?"

"I come to tell you for you are my very good friend, and I want you should know."

I knew what was coming. She must have felt very uncomfortable, coming to tell me when she knew I was distressed. Yet she would have found it unconscionable for me to have heard it from someone else.

"I am to marry." she paused to wait for some response from me. I tried to smile, but I'm not sure if I did. When I continued to just sit there, she went on. It came out in a spurt, as if she decided it was best to tell it all and have it done with.

"I am to marry with the teacher in Pitchit. His name is Praphat. Nickname 'Pat'. He is my friend long time. I tell you before I think I marry teacher in Pitchit. He come to see me. He receive promotion, is that right word?" I nodded. "In Pitchit, he is, I think you say, 'senior teacher'. Now he will come to Nakorn Sarang. Will be principal. I am very lucky. I will teach at school."

"You're going to leave the library?"

"Yes, now I can have job at school." She smiled reluctantly at her acceptance of the nepotism. "I am to marry in September. I leave library last day August. Pat and I would like very much for you to be guest at wedding."

I rubbed my eyes with both hands. It seemed like I was crying and I wanted to check, but they were dry. I held my hands together n front of my chest and stretched my fingers. I could feel my face forming into a grin. It changed to a smile and, at long last, I spoke. "I'm sorry. I wish I could, but I leave Thailand the last day of August. I'll leave Nakorn Sarang four days before. I'll spend one day in Takhli and three in Bangkok."

"Oh, I am very sad. Pat will be sad, too."

"She stood up to go, and I got down off the bed to walk across the room with her.

"I know I must tell you this. I know you are very sad since Miss Renu die. You are my very good friend. I am very sad for you. But I am very happy in my life. I think maybe my good news will help you. I hope you are happy for me." Her shyness had left and she said this to me very directly, her hands relaxed, her, her arms folded across her waist, her elbows cradled lightly by her fingers.

When we reached the door, I summoned up some of the decency the Major had claimed to recognize in me, extended my hand and said, "I am very happy for you. Mr. Pat is a lucky man. It makes me happy to hear this. Congratulations."

She took my hand as if she were going to shake it, but then she put her left hand on as well and just stood there for several seconds not shaking mine at all, but only gently holding it. When she let go, she placed her hands together well up in front of her face and gave me a vastly over-respectful wai. She turned and left.

I watched the door close, and when I was convinced it would not open again without my aid, I turned, went back to the bed, and sat down. Now a tear did really form and drop from my eye. It ran down the front of my cheek and stopped at my lips. I had, of course, lied to her. It didn't make me happy to hear about; I'm not that decent.

I was still sitting on the edge of the bed when Joe came by and said, "C'mon, it's time to go home." When I was leaving the dispensary, Doc Dugan stopped me, handed me a small container of pills and said, "Lieutenant, take one of these before you go to bed, and lay off the booze. You'll sleep better with these, and you'll feel better in the morning." Doc's advice to the contrary, before I got the bus, I stopped by the club and bought a quart of gin, went from there to the BX and bought two quarts of tonic. At the end of the driveway to our bungalow, I hired one of the neighborhood kids to go into town and buy me a half dozen limes.

Joe, wisely, made no effort to talk me out of the gin but he did try and promote the joys of the four of us going into town for dinner. I expressed no interest, in truth, I didn't even respond to the line separating the rational feelings of why you "like" someone and the wholly lunatic emotions that pass for "being in love". You either are or you are not. In the case of Pitsommai, I unfortunately was not.

What I did do was to climb the stairs, at the top of which she met me and asked if I was okay. I forced a smile, said I was, and went into my room. She followed me and found me with my shirt off. I looked coolly at her for two or three seconds, thinking for a moment that she might cry, but she didn't. Instead she stepped forward, put her arms around my waist and laid her head on my bare chest. I didn't move more until she told me she had been very worried about me, then I patted her once on the shoulder, shifted away from her and said, "Thanks."

After I had put on a paisin, I went to the refrigerator, mixed myself the first of several mild gin and tonics, took it into the living room, and parked myself for what I fully expected to be the rest of the evening. Pitsommai, shaken by my rebuff but trying to be understanding, sat alongside me and Joe and Ewan opposite me. Joe joined me drinking gin, and the girls drank iced teas. There were attempts at conversation but I warded them all off with a series of "yeahs," naws", "uh huhs", and "uh uhs". After nearly an hour's time (and three drinks for me), Ewan became the first to give any outward sign of irritation with me. She had been watching me with her usual noncommittal eyes for some time, and a deep anger, if not hate began to rise in them. Eventually she rose and casting her by then cold, cold eyes on me, announced she was going for a walk. At any other time I would have been very upset with myself and would have immediately apologized. Instead, I chose to ignore her and slumped myself deeper into my chair letting out a sigh of exhaustion and a remark to the effect that "I hope it fucking rains soon."

Joe put up with me for longer than I deserved, most likely out of fear that I might do something drastic to myself, but he finally tried once more to talk me into going to Tipalow's for dinner. I said, "Nope," and got up to make another drink. Joe took a few minutes to change clothes, called Ewan back to the house, asked me once again (I grunted and shook my head), and left. Pitsommai chose, over Ewan's objections, to stay with me, and act of concern I chose to reward by ignoring completely—except when she went out to the road and hired one of the kids to go and get us two banana leaves of fried rice, which I acknowledged by accepting and eating, but never by thanking her for. I stopped even asking her if she wanted more tea when I refilled my load of gin. She sat and watched as if I were a critically ill patient and she a nurse with no other concern than to monitor my life signs.

Sometime after nine o'clock, before Joe and Ewan had returned and due to the booze and general havoc I had heaped upon myself for the previous three days, I found myself sufficiently dopey to go to sleep. I pulled myself up from the chair and went into my room without a word to Pitsommai. I heard her follow me again, but I kept my back to her, took off my paisin and hung it on a hook.

"Jim."

I turned and stared at her. She looked terrible, tired and drawn and sadly confused. Still, I said nothing more than, "What."

"Jim, I…" She shook her head from side to side. "What you do?"

"Gonnuh bed." I reached and pulled back the covers.

She started to cry. She made no attempt to hold back; she didn't even raise her hands to wipe away the tears that had burst forth and were running down her face.

I could only plead, "Pitsommai, stop."

"What you think? You think I have no feelings?" Deep, heaving sobs interrupted her words, and she continued to cry freely.

I spread my hands wide, then dropped them uselessly at my sides. She had finally gotten to me, but even then I could offer nothing more comforting than, "I'm sorry."

She came to me and placed her hands on my shoulders and put her face flush on my chest. She cried harder. She must have been holding it in since she arrived the night before, and I, of course, had since then given her even more to cry about. "Jim, Joe send word Ewan. Say Renu dead. I cry for my friend. Joe say you very sick. Tell Ewan come Nakorn Sarang, bring Pitsommai. I come. Why you be mean?"

"Joe told you to come here?" (Why hadn't I guessed it?)"

"Yes, I come when I hear you sick."

We went to bed and she placed her head on my chest where it stayed for most of the night. She sensed my coolness, the deadness in my soul, and offered no suggestions that we make love. She cried some more and the tears lay on my chest like drops of blood.

I woke up very early, even before the sun cane up. I got some orange juice and, while sitting on the porch watching the sky in the east turn red, I began again to think of Renu and Sunida. I tried to force myself to think of Pitsommai but without being conscious of the twists in my mind, I kept drifting into mist reveries of the other two. When my alarm rang and I returned to my room to look at Pitsommai, seeing her sitting on my bed, her golden skin so sharp against the white sheets wiping the dried tears from slightly puffy eyes, I knew I must ask her to leave. It would be unfair to keep her there. I felt the melancholy again overtaking me; by evening I would once more be glum and terse. I liked her too much to put her through another such night.

She reluctantly agreed to accept my gift of a hundred dollars and take the train to Bangkok, then to Patthya, a resort city on the gulf of Siam, for a vacation; but I don't think she ever really understood my lame reasons for why she couldn't stay with me. Before Joe and I left for the site, Ewan decided to go with Pitsommai. She even professed to accept my apology about the night before. Joe and I put the girls on the afternoon train. We had come down to the village during lunchtime, then we rode in a taxi back to the site.

"I guess," said Joe during the ride, "Pitsommai told you I asked her to come up here."

"Uh huh."

"You know, I sent that telegram the same day Renu died, while you were sleeping in the dispensary. If I'd known how fucking ridiculous you were going to act, I wouldn't have put either of you through such shit."

I nodded. When we reached the site and were going through the gate again feeling I owed him some explanation, I said, "You know, Joe, I didn't mean to act like this, I mean really, I don't, but, Jesus, I don't know, I just don't know."

Joe had to get back to operations for some training exercises, but he stopped to say, "Look, Jim, I'm not much on giving advice, but you better straighten yourself up pretty damn quick because you're wearing pretty fucking thin on a lot of people here." He didn't have to say who.

Nevertheless, by the end of the afternoon, my mood had turned as irresolutely downcast as the previous day, so I went to the BX, bought a case of beer (my stomach was sufficiently tender so not to consider anything hard), stopped at the library (Sunida had already gone for the day), where I "borrowed" some magazines; went home and plopped myself down again in the chair and spent the rest of the evening sipping beers and turning pages till about ten when I roused myself from the seat and dropped myself on my bed. I did the same thing the next night, except I drank light bourbon and waters. Joe said nothing to me on either night, the second night leaving me alone while he went to a movie.

So when my pecker first started to ache on Saturday morning, I assumed it was only my urinary tract rebelling against the assault I had placed it under. Standing over the urinal holding my sore wang in my hand, and staring at the drop of puss that had just risen from its tip, I was incredulous. "What the hell? What the hell?" Then as it dawned on me, I began to laugh, and kept laughing, louder and louder till an airman entered the latrine and saw me standing in front of the urinal, my pecker in my hand, laughing at the top of my voice.

For five days, the length of my bender, I had not considered the future. Even the purchases of the means of destruction—gin, beer, whiskey—were not planned actions, but responses; like what a cow does in a pasture, she eats the grass, I imagine, without considering eating it. I did not tolerate the future, my thoughts were only of the past, and even then, I dealt only in images, not ideas. My consideration of the consequences of leaving untended my clap-ridden pecker was the first time since Monday morning that I had thought of the future. Those first visions of coming days were exceedingly grim and entirely related to the future of my carnal implement, but sometime late Saturday, when the penicillin had worked its first task and the puss stopped dropping from the end of my wang into my spotted underpants, I began to envision the prospects of all of me. They were not pleasant (my mood was if anything grimmer) and I was unable to sleep. after several hours of swatting at innumerable bugs, real and imagined, I remembered the pills Doc had given me, and rising from my sweat-soaked bed made my way to the medicine chest where I gulped down one of them and chased it with orange juice. Even before I made it back to my mattress I was feeling its effects; a general numbness over all of my body. I was asleep soon after stretching across the bed.

Sunday morning began brighter, physically and emotionally than any of its five most immediate predecessors. The house was bright and with all of the fans going the air was still comfortable. My stomach, having been put through cruel torture since the previous Monday took advantage of the break in the attack and cried out urgently for food. It had to make do with tomato juice and some dry cereal. After a cold and delightful shower, I headed for the site where with good fortune I was able to share breakfast with the chow hall girls. It was their routine after the regular breakfast shift was over to take advantage of the kitchen's extraordinary facilities and concoct an overwhelming meal of fried rice, eggs, noodles, assorted chopped vegetables, and sometimes finely chopped pork. It was a constant wonder to watch these eight or nine tiny women good-naturedly consume a giant, over-flowing platter of the delicacy. On this particular Sunday morning, I offered to assist them in their task, and was welcomed not unwarmly.

One of the girls, a wisp of a woman named Papai, who might well have shared a distant kinship with Smiley Burnett because her face was constantly graced by a warm and engaging countenance, teased me about my enthusiasm for Thai food. In her own tongue, she said, Lieutenant, what will you do when you go home and can't have Thai food? I assured her and the others who were smiling and listening for my response that in America I would certainly be able to find an abundance of rice. She giggled and the others followed suit.

"But it is not Thai rice."

Try as I might, I could not convince them of my opinion but it certainly didn't affect anyone's enjoyment of the meal. My repeated declining of their offers to liberally sprinkle hot sauce over my plate provided laughter throughout breakfast. I would raise a hand to my throat, hang out my tongue, pop my eyes, and gasp for breath in a demonstration of what would happen if I took their offer.

Following breakfast and feeling more elated than I had for a period of time longer than I cared to measure, I went to the mailroom where I picked up a letter from my mother. It had lain there for several days, days during which I concerned myself more with drunkenness and the welfare of my genitals than with news from home. My mother expressed the hope that, when I arrived in Arizona I would meet a "nice girl". "Dear Mom," I began composing my nest letter in my head, "I have met several 'nice girls' here in Thailand. Unfortunately, they are both unavailable to me. One is dead," (I did not add she was someone else's fiancé), "and the other has, amazingly, chosen to spurn my advances and will soon marry a runt—he probably wouldn't reach my shoulder—of a school teacher. A native to boot. They will live the rest of their lives in relative squalor, at least compared to the wonderful abode the Air Force and I would have provided for her. So, dear Mom, I have met the 'nice girl(s)' you are constantly wishing for me. I don't expect to ever meet any more of them."

I never actually wrote such a letter let alone mailed one. Before the next mail plane left I would compose my regular weekly report on the weather ("It rained a lot"), my health ("I'm feeling great". My current malady certainly did not need mentioning), and my expected travel plans ("I'll stop home for a couple of days leave before heading to Arizona"). Yet the mental composition of the never-to-be-inked letter as I walked to the orderly room in the increasingly uncomfortable heat (turbulent rain clouds by then dominated the skies), brought back to my mind images of my two "lost loves."

The orderly room was empty. It was, after all, Sunday. I turned on the air conditioner and sat at my desk determined to see what insights a sober mind, one unencumbered by the cobwebs of a hangover could bring to bear on recent events. It was incredible.

Certainly there can be no satisfactory explanation of accidental death. Renu most likely crossed those very tracks a half dozen times a day each day she had lived in Nakorn Sarang. And, while I never confirmed this suspicion, a check of local records would have probably turned up several previous such deaths; and no doubt others have died there since. To have blamed the accident on Thai corruption or ineptness would have been easy, and untrue. In New Canaan, Connecticut, near my home, a stretch of railroad track crosses a local road, and there, yearly it seems, a person or two meets his end. Such fates that bring together in one spot the machines and person which conspire in an irrational and accidental death defy explanation, and I cannot ascribe to them any meaning. Some may, but I cannot.

Yet in the clearness of mind produced by a pleasant breakfast on an unacidic stomach, I was able to deal with the future. Certainly we were all somewhat diminished by Renu's death. What else could we be when denied her innocent charm, her contagious good spirits, and her delicate beauty? But in the cool logic with which I found myself viewing the future, one inescapable fact was there: She had never been mine to lose, no matter if she were still alive, it was not I who would live with her and make love to her. I could not even as I once dreamed of protect her. In that respect my life had not changed. My failure in those immediately past days to give thought to the future rested on one great misconception; I could not bear to think of what life would be like without Renu. While in fact my future never included her. The loss was Bob Saunders' to bear. I felt a sense of rage ignite within me when I reminded myself of how Saunders was "bearing" the loss, but I was able to force myself to think only of my future (again I attribute this ability to my second day of sobriety). In all, it was not a pleasant reconciliation of my emotions, but it did provide me with the ability to again view the future, if a little sadly at least with some degree of tolerance.

And what of Sunida? Those deprecatory remarks made to myself when composing my mental draft of the letter to my mother already shamed me. If her announcement had come at any other time (and yet her concern to tell me herself, not to have me hear it from someone else, was greatly appreciated), I am sure it would have caused me no great trauma. After all, I had been fairly warned of its imminence, and should have rightly welcomed it for the joy it would undoubtedly bring her. But coming when it did, at the time I was rather reluctantly recovering from the shock of Renu's death, it provided me with an additional excuse (sub-conscious but no less real) to wallow some more in my grief (self-pity is more appropriate). Of course I was jealous, but I had been that since the day months earlier when I began realizing she and I would not marry—indeed, could not marry—and someone else would share her life. I had,

I acknowledged been jealous of Praphat even before I knew his name, but it was an irrational jealousy and this cool clear morning of my mind, I could deal with it.

So sobriety a secondary result of the infection that had lodged itself in my privates probably kept me sane by on that Sunday providing me with the chance to think clearly. Oh, yes, I also made a resolution regarding Bob Saunders. Following the example and advice of Joe Stacy, I resolved to ignore him.

CHAPTER THIRTY-ONE

IGNORING BOB SAUNDERS, AS MY narrative hopefully demonstrates, is easier said than done. especially after having made oneself so available over so long a time. Since he was heading back to the States at the end of the month, only one day before Lafayette Chance (the proximity of their return dates caused the sergeant much distress while waiting for his orders: "Shit, Lieutenant, if I get put on the same fuckin' plane with that four-eyes fuckin' little jerk-off across the whole Pacific fuckin' Ocean, I may go AWOL."), Bob spent much time in the orderly room with one question or another concerning proper procedures. They were, without fail, simple, bordering on moronic in nature, but I, taking not the least pains to answer them, directed the twerp in the direction of others, "Sgt. Chance'll handle that," or "Give that to Happy," ("Happy" being the nickname we had assigned to the stone-faced nineteen-going-on-fifty-year-old airman named Harold Herpsmann who had replaced Smiley Burnett). Then, feigning business elsewhere, I ran out the door.

Still, against what most surely would have been an analyst's advice had I been seeing one, there was an occasion when I actually sought out the little dimwit. Calculating the time from when he mailed the letter to Betty informing her it was no longer necessary to get a divorce to when it was most likely she could write back, I approached him the morning following the arrival of the mail plane which I figured carried her reply. It was outside the chow hall as he was returning from breakfast. I figured the still cool morning air would protect me from a possible hysterical reaction.

"Bob."

"Oh, hey, hi Jim. How are you feeling?"

"Yeah, fine, fine. Hey, look, I, uh…" I had planned on being very direct asking my question, getting my answer and leaving, but a subconscious resistance to talking to Bob Saunders (and a very commendable subconscious resistance I should note) immediately began strangling my vocal chords, and I lost the initiative of the talk. Bob, hardly out of force of personality, picked it up.

"Gee, you know, I was kind of worried about you. Did Sgt. Dugan ever say what you had?"

I gave in to him, and let the talk ramble. "I've got the clap."

"Oh."

While I was thinking to myself I had at least shocked him, he again demonstrated he had not lost the talent to completely confound me. "You know, there was once a time I thought I had some kind of venereal disease."

"Huh, what?" At that point, my original intent in approaching Bob was gone from my mind, and I stood befuddled once again by this short, blond, pudgy, four-eyed, spouter of inane words.

"Yes, I didn't think it was, er, gonorrhea or, or syphilis, but I was quite sure I had something. I was afraid it was something peculiar to Thailand, something there wasn't a cure for."

"When was this? You mean you thought you caught something from Renu?"

"Oh no. By then I'd learned my lesson. During the time she stayed with me, I took all recommended precautions."

"You mean it was when we shared the place? The time you asked Doc for the penicillin because the maid switched the sheets?"

"Oh no. Anyway, after I found out the maid boiled water to wash our clothes and sheets in, I was okay. No, this was just after you moved out. Remember Lt. Crawford came and moved into your old room?"

"Was he the next one?"

"Yes, well one night he brought back a girl from the Argo. I think it was the same one you used to bring back a lot. What was her name? She had light brown skin, brown eyes and dark hair. She was kind of small."

"That certainly narrows the field."

"She also had kind of buck teeth."

"Supatra."

"Yes, I think that's it. Well, Lt. Crawford brought her back. I think they were both a little bit drunk or something because I heard them come in and they were laughing. Then the next thing I knew, she came running into my room. She didn't have anything on, and I, well, I…" Here Bob sputtered, his face turning red. "…I, er, didn't have anything on either. It was very hot that night and I had taken all my clothes off so I could sleep better. She shouted something when she saw me, then she jumped into the bed and pressed herself right against me. She squeezed me a couple of time before I could get away and out of the room."

I leaned against the outside wall of the chow hall to keep from falling down laughing.

"Well, of course I was afraid she might have infected me in some way. When Lt. Crawford took her back into his room they were both laughing a lot. I took a very long shower. But, of course, that was with cold water. So, the next day, I got Airman Hendrickson to give me some surgical soap, and I went down to the showers on the site and I took a long hot shower. I did that three times a day for three days. I wanted to make sure I had gotten all the germs off me."

"And on the third day, your skin began to flake."

He turned to me with his most amazed stare filtering through his glasses. "Why yes, how'd you know? Did it ever happen to you?"

I assured him no it hadn't happened to me, but that the combination of surgical soap and hot water, especially the very heavily chemically treated stuff on base obviously would dry one's skin.

"That's exactly what Sgt. Dugan told me. I mean, he also told me I didn't have any kind of venereal disease."

"You went to see Doc for the flaking?"

"Oh yes. I was very concerned. He gave me some kind of ointment, told me to cut down to one shower a day and go back to using regular soap. The heavy washing may have caused my skin problems, but I still think it saved me from some other horrible disease. It was a very close call."

I wanted to roar out loud—it had suddenly come back to me how Harry Simpson had told me about finding Doc laughing to himself after Bob had visited him—but I held off by faking a coughing spasm and claiming to have swallowed the wrong way.

Bob said I should drink some water and then started off to ops. It dawned on me how I had lost the conversation, and I called him back. "Hey wait. Did you get a letter from your wife yesterday?"

"Yes, of course."

"Well, what'd she say?"

"Oh, you know, the usual. She's starting to pack, and she's getting our other stuff out of storage. Getting ready for the move, you know."

"She is? I mean just like that? She didn't say anything about Renu?"

"Oh yes, she said she was glad I had my problem worked out and not to worry about her. Said she was getting along just as always, planning our move and that kind of thing."

"Your problem…?"

"Yes, you know, it's kind of funny, but that's what she always called it. She never mentioned Renu's name, and even when I didn't write as much as I used to, she kept writing just as much, and she just kept writing like nothing was different."

"She did?"

"I guess she always knew things would work out for the best, just like they did. the Colonel gave her a lot of good advice, told her to 'stick in there,' and a lot of stuff like that. She and the Colonel are going up to San Francisco in a couple of days to look for a place for us to live."

"That's it, nothing more to it, just 'your problem' is worked out?"

"Yes, she's amazing, really an amazing girl. I've said it before and I'll say it again, I'm a lucky man to have her."

This time I left him there. I very abruptly walked away from him. I was enraged. At the orderly room I turned left and toward the bar. No matter it was barely eight a.m., I was going to demand Sgt. Coyne open up for me. He would have too, but I remembered I was still under Doc's medication and my visions of the most horrifying results of a rampaging dose of clap were still active in the recesses of my mind, so I stopped outside the door of the club and tried to catch my breath. For a few terrible moments I was petrified, scared to nearly shaking, frightened of what I would do without being able to drink in relief of my frustration.

Sober is best I discovered again. It came to me. I walked over to the civil engineering shop and asked the airman there if he had a roughly four foot section of two by four. He went to a wood bin in the rear of the shop.

"Would three and a half feet do, Sir?"

"Yes, just fine. Thanks."

I took it and left the shop. No, I did not go and crush bob Saunders' skull, but I did go to the rear of the building and there pound the two by four on a huge rock until the board splintered. It would have done me no more good to have used Bob's skull; it was harder than the rock. When I brought the shattered piece of lumber back and threw it on the pile, the airman said, "Feel better, Sir?"

"Much better, thanks."

That evening before we went to town to eat, I told Joe about my talk with Bob. He smiled, hell, he laughed. "I hate to keep saying this, but didn't I tell you so. That asshole never knew it, but there was no way, no matter what, that he would have married Renu. The old man would have never allowed it, even if it meant he had to physically restrain them."

I was beginning to agree with Joe.

"The old man had finally gotten a husband for his silly little girl and he wasn't going to let any fucking gook bar-girl mess it up. He'd keep putting the pressure on, and one day Bob would wake up and say he'd changed his mind, he wanted to stay married to Betty Fucking Boop. Oh, yea, somewhere along the way, the old man would tan Bob's ass good, figuratively if not literally at least. And he'd also say to him, take him aside like, and say, 'Son, I know a man needs to relieve himself now and then. Hell, he wouldn't be a real man if'n he didn't, but Son, it don't do no good to worry the womenfolk about it. Believe me Son, I relieved myself plenty of times when I was over there in the middle of all those Orientals, but I never went and got Betty's mommy upset about it. Okay, son?' And then he'll give Bob a big wink, like this."

When Joe squeezed his right eye closed in an exaggerated gesture, I began to laugh. "Yeah, but," I cried in between laughs, "Bob'll think he means he shouldn't tell Betty when he goes to the bathroom."

When, on the morning he was to leave Nakorn Sarang, Bob called and asked if I would meet him for lunch, I could not, despite our absurd most recent talk, refuse.

"So we met once again across the fried chicken," I said.

"What?"

"Never mind."

Neither of us spoke, I because I had nothing to say to him, and he, well who could know? But finally, as we neared the end of our chicken (it was Wednesday and the chicken was not as good as it used to be now that Sgt. Tremble had rotated and Sgt. Tennyson was forced to really run the chow hall), Bob spoke.

"I just wanted to say goodbye."

"Goodbye."

I suppose he was trying to focus his eyes on me, but it was hard to tell with his ill-fitting glasses.

"Jim, I've been thinking…"

"Impossible."

"…about all we've been through together…"

"I thought you just wanted to say goodbye?"

"…and what it's meant to both of us."

"Goodbye, Bob."

He laughed. "You're always so funny, Jim."

"Yeah, a real riot."

"It's been a tough year…"

"Would you accept so-long?"

"…what with, well, what with everything."

"You've really got a way with words."

"But all in all, I think we can say…"

"I think I hear Major Richter calling me."

"…that we're both better people for what we've been through."

"Yeah, better people."

He stood up. "Jim, I've got to go. One of the AP's is driving me to the airport." He held out his hand. "Be sure to call us when you pass through San Francisco…"

"What should I call you?"

"Betty and I would both love to hear from you or to have you over for dinner."

I held out my hand and let him shake it; a final insulting gesture seemed both unnecessary and useless. Besides, he was leaving. I would be momentarily rid of him.

As on the day we met, he started to salute me then caught himself and went out of the chow hall to the jeep waiting for him at the gate.

The jeep sped down the dirt road toward the runway. Before it disappeared around the corner and into its own cloud of dust, I caught a view of Bob, bouncing along in the passenger's seat. He was holding his cap on with one hand and with the other he several times adjusted his glasses. He was leaving Thailand after having spent a year there, and it looked the same to him as it did the day he arrived. To him it would always be the Inscrutable East but only because it never occurred to him to scrutinize it. When I heard the C-130's engines roar, I got up from my desk and watched as the huge, camouflaged transport lifted itself above the bushes and swamp grass that separated the site from the airstrip, watched it till it was no more than a pinprick in a cloud.

Lafayette had gone to meet the plane. He said he wanted to pick up the orderly room papers, but there turned out to have been another reason. "Hey, Lieutenant, I want you to meet my fuckin' replacement, Staff Sergeant Eldridge P. Dickens. Ol' Eldridge an' me was together in fuckin' Texas. Ain't it a fuckin' fact, Eldridge?"

"Fuckin' A. Howz'it fuckin' goin', Lieutenant?" They even bore a certain physical resemblance, a hard squatness and I wondered to myself if sometime thirty or so years before, Mrs. Chance and Mrs. Dickens had not shared dalliances with the same travelling salesman.

"Hey, where do I fuckin' put my stuff?"

"C'mon, I'm jus' fuckin' leavin'. You can have my fuckin' bunk and fuckin' locker. I'm leavin' this fuckin' place tomorrow."

"Good fuckin' deal."

From there they went to the bar and then to the Argo where Lafayette introduced Eldridge to Nitnoy. The next morning before he left for the train to Takhli, Lafayette informed me that, "I got ol' fuckin' Eldridge all straightened the fuck out. He knows every fuckin' think I know about thuh whole fuckin' place."

I saw him to the train where we both assured one another we would write, false promises, but still made with affection. On the platform steps he turned and confided to me, "You know, I fuckin' lucked out. That fuckin' dose uh thuh clap I was worried fuckin' silly about, I never fuckin' got it. Couple uh days ago, I went n' got uh blood test. Checked out fuckin' A number one. Feelin' fuckin' great!"

"Sure, but I bet you fooled around last night."

"He grinned, then shrugged his shoulders. "Yeah, but what thuh fuck?" The train whistle blew, Lafayette pulled himself aboard and disappeared into the passenger car.

I turned, went back through the station, got into the jeep and headed back to the site, and on the way realized that of all the people closely involved in my life there, I was the next to leave.

AUGUST 1968

CHAPTER THIRTY-TWO

IN THE DAYS BEFORE I left, during the month of August, little happened. I guess I should say little happened to me. Perhaps among the ninety-nine others or so at the site, perhaps in that new group of lieutenants and airmen arriving (July and August being times of heavy uprooting in the Air Force), perhaps among them there was one who was experiencing his own particular story. He may someday also sit down to try putting it on paper, and when and if he does, I hope he better understands what happened.

Well, a few things did happen.

I met Sunida's fiancée. He moved to Nakorn Sarang shortly before I left and Sunida asked me to have dinner with the two of them at his home. It was a well built plaster and wood structure, with luxuriant hardwood floors, glass-paned windows with screens, and overhead fans in all the rooms. It was on the grounds of the school and went with his position there. Sunida's parents would come to live with them and have two full rooms to themselves on one side of the house. Praphat's parents, retired school officials, lived in Bangkok in approximately equal comfort I was told. Praphat, or Pat, was, as I predicted, a little guy, only an inch or two taller than his fiancée. He was then of an indeterminate age (I don't like to think of myself as a racist, but in the back of my head I kept hearing myself saying, "I can never tell how old these people are"), somewhere between twenty-five and forty. He greeted me ebulliently, first with a wai midway up his face, and then with a firm and convincing handshake. He beamed and told me in clear and distinct English that he was very happy to meet me since his wife-to-be had spoken so well of me. I returned that I was extremely envious of him and then watched as Sunida blushed and turned away. We spoke alternately in English and Thai. He complimented me on my fluency and I complimented him on his (his English was infinitely better than my Thai). There was a sense of relief in meeting Pat. He was confident in his position and obviously proud in a Thai fashion of Sunida. He was a very substantial man, a man with ambition and talents (ambitions and talents which I felt extended beyond heading the local school) and worthy of Sunida's attentions. I had been afraid she might be marrying only because it was "time" to marry.

Something else worth noting happened only a few days before I left. In fact it was the day next-to-the-last supply plane from Takhli I would ever see arrive (the one after that I would be on as an outward bound passenger). Sgt. Dickens was going through the orderly room mail when he looked up and said, "Hey, we got a new fuckin' UMD." The news was hardly startling, but several minutes later he said, "Hey, Lieutenant, you ain't gonnuh fuckin' believe this, but we ain't authoriz' no fuckin' admin officer no more." This brought the rest of us—Happy Herpsmann, Sgt. Barton and myself—to our feet, and we all gathered around Dickens' desk to pour over the seven or eight pages of the new personnel lists and to run our fingers up and down the computer print-out type searching for something that read, "OFF ADMIN 1/LT 7024," but there was none. Major Richter then came out of his office and thoughtfully inspected the UMD.

"Well, Jim," he said as he turned and handed me the document, "it looks like you were one of a kind."

I did have one other meeting with Sunida. The day before I left Nakorn Sarang as I was crossing the central area of the site, trying to clear up some last pieces of work, she came out of the library and stopped me to ask if we couldn't meet and talk for a while after work. We had discontinued my Thai lessons at the end of July (I didn't feel I'd have much use for the language in Arizona) and, consequently, we hadn't the opportunity to talk in the last month. I was to attend the last of a too long series of going-away parties that night, but I said I'd love to meet her.

We spoke in English.

"You leave Nakorn Sarang tomorrow, yes?"

"Yes."

"I shall miss you."

"And I shall miss you, too. I would have been very lonely here if not for you."

"Thank you. I have learned much from you."

"Ho, ho, not as much as I've learned from you."

She stopped the talk with a movement of her eyes. "You have learned to speak Thai from me, but from you I have learned many other things, things that will be important for me in all my life. Before I know you, I look at people wrong. I think all American is the same; too big, too rich, too loud. but you are nice to me and to other Thai. I hear sometime you act like other Americans. At first I do not believe, but then I hear again. I think maybe is true, but still you are nice to me and to many people. So I think you can be many things. Other American can be many things too. Yes, is true I learn. Mr. Hendrickson is nice to me, bring things for my class. Others too. But you are first, you are most important. I am sorry I was bad to you time we have dinner. I let other people make me do wrong thing."

I raised my hand and waved it inconclusively finally rubbing the back of my neck with it. "I'm glad to see other people besides me don't always have control of their lives either. Anyway, you know I've learned a lot about the Thai people from you."

She smiled lightly, disarmingly. "They say we are very mysterious, I understand. What do you think?"

"Well, yes, I guess so."

"Are we more mysterious than Americans?"

I laughed. "Well, yes, but I've spent all my life with Americans, so maybe I just know them better."

She turned away and then immediately back to me. "Sometime I am sad for you."

"You are, you mean because of Renu, because she died?"

"No, that is over. Do you remember night we had dinner at restaurant: We talked. You did not know what you would do. You did not know when you would marry. Then I did not know what I would do too. But now I know. I will marry with Praphat soon. I will teach at the school, have many responsibilities I think you say. But you still do not know, and I am sad for you because I am so happy in my life."

I smiled. "I'm happy for you too, but don't be sad for me. It's hard for me to make decisions here so far from home. When I get to America I'm sure things will get better."

"Good. I hope so, because you get old."

"Old?"

She laughed at my reaction to the word. "Oh, I no mean you soon need cane, or lose hair. I mean it is time for you to do your work, time to have wife. I think you need wife. You are kind and thoughtful. You be good husband, good father. Wife will be good for you. You not be so lonely. That is reason I am sad for you. I think you are lonely."

I sputtered and when I regained enough composure to look at her again, I said, "Do you remember the night we rode home together?

"Yes, the night we stopped at your house, in front."

"It's funny but I thought for awhile I had asked you to marry me that night. Did you know that?"

She didn't look away as I had thought she would or blush as I had also thought she would. "Yes, I know, but I did not think you mean to say it. I think American say, 'slip of tongue.'"

"That's exactly right, but what did you think? Did you think about it?"

"Yes, but I think he must ask in right way. You say, he must think before he act."

"What would you have said then?"

"Then, I not know. But now, of course, I would say 'no'. But I think I say no then too. you are man who miss your home too much. Must live America. I too. I must live here in Thailand.

"But you did think about it, about marrying me?

"Oh, yes, very much I think about it."

After a few moments during which we exchanged addresses and I promised to write first, she started to leave. "Wait just a minute. I have a gift for you, for you and Praphat, a wedding gift."

I reached into my desk and brought out a transistor radio. We laughed and even listened to some scratchy music for a few seconds before she opened the door. Without my offering it, she reached and picked up my right hand in both of hers and actually squeezed, I mean really squeezed, enough so when she let go there were white marks where her fingers had been. Then she raised her hands before her face. I did the same.

"Goodbye, my very good friend, Jim."

"Lao kuhn, my very good friend Sunida."

I watched her go through the gate and down the road till the point it turned through the tall grass. Then I sat down at my desk and, beaming, said, "She actually thought about it. Well, I'll be."

The going away party that night was an orderly room affair with Major Richter and Joe thrown in, but it was a pretty dead one. We had our usual fine meal at Tipalow's (this had been a distinguishing feature of all of the last week's parties and consequently I had gained nearly five pounds as I stuffed myself each night afraid I might never have another chance at such concoctions). I was presented with a teak wood carving of a person bending over so far his head was literally "up his ass." Along the base of it, the staff had had imprinted, "Typical Admin Officer." I laughed and said, "I accept this in the spirit in which it is given, I hope." They tried to dead pan it, but only young-old Airman Herpsmann managed to hold it. Even Major Richter finally flashed a large grin. But something was missing; it takes no great brain to realize it wasn't a real orderly room party without Lafayette Chance and Smiley Burnett. Happy Herpsmann was certainly no Smiley, and although Eldridge Dickens bore many resemblances to my former chief clerk, he was, after only a month's familiarity, just a guy who said "fuck" a lot.

The next morning Major Richter took me to the airport to put me on the plane to Takhlii (Joe was planning on meeting me in Bangkok so he dispensed with any goodbyes at Nakorn Sarang). As we rode over, I said, "Sir, could you tell me one thing?"

"Maybe."

"You said you had a big angel. Who is it?"

He laughed, or snorted. "Okay, I don't have one, but I learned if you act like you've got one, then everyone assumes you've got one and treats you like you got one because they're so frightened. So I guess you could say my angel is fear."

At the plane, the Major wished me well and expressed a wish to see me apply myself. I said, "What, you mean in Arizona, in missiles?"

"I mean," he said, "in life." That was just before we shook hands, and I climbed onto the C-130 and found a place for me and my duffel bag next to the site's empty supply containers.

Joe wasn't able to get to Bangkok until the morning before my scheduled departure. My first two days and nights there were quiet. I checked into the Grand Hotel and got a suite for Joe and myself, but I avoided Max's Bar since I couldn't bring myself to see Pitsommai. During the days I went sight-seeing and did some shopping (some jewelry for my mother and a camera for myself) and in the evenings I enjoyed a good meal and even went to two nightclubs where I paid for hostesses to sit with me, but I didn't take any of them back to my room. There I slept fitfully and woke early each morning to watch from my balcony as Bangkok's streets came slowly to life. A sadness at leaving the country was overtaking me, and I felt helpless in the path of onrushing events.

When he showed up the next to last morning, Joe changed my pace immediately. Of course I knew he would see Ewan that night which meant I would have to see Pitsommai. To assuage my guilt for my treatment of her, I went with Joe to the Bangkok BX to buy her some nylons. As we checked out of the store, each carrying some four pairs, the woman behind us in line—I imagine the wife of an American colonel whose rank she felt gave her the right to remark in a more often than not disapproving manner on whatever she wanted whenever she felt like it—said, "I don't think you young men are buying those nylons for your wives. I think you're buying them for some Thai (a thick breath of contempt whistled through her teeth when she said "Thai") bar girls."

Joe, without the slightest hesitation, turned and said to her, "You're wrong both times, you old bag, we're buying them to pull over our heads so we can rob a fucking bank!" We left her sputtering at the check-out counter clacking sounds coming from her shaking mouth. It was the single incident which turned my mood around.

At Max's, Pitsommai greeted me warmly. She squeezed my hand and kissed my cheek when I gave her the nylons. The four of us ate a spectacular meal at Nick's No.1, then went to the Sani Chateau for the floor show. After we returned to Max's for several nightcaps and, finally, the four of us clambered to the suite at the Grand where we nearly equally shared a bottle of Mateus before adjourning to our rooms. I earlier said Pitsommai had greeted me warmly, but by the end of the night some professional detachment was evident in her behavior. On several toasts to my imminent departure, all enthusiastically joined in, except her; though she raised her glass, and drank from it, there was a perfunctory note to it. Naturally I should have expected nothing more. I had sent her packing when she had come to offer solace in a difficult time, and I had, only in the most previous day, avoided her. I should have welcomed the detachment. I shouldn't have wanted any difficult departures, but I'm afraid that's exactly what I wanted, and I was a little dispirited by her treatment of me.

We all rose early the next morning to enjoy a huge breakfast delivered to our suite. I was hung over and tired, but it was still a very pleasant morning. When Pitsommai and I stood up to go to the airport (she had agreed to ride there in the taxi with me) to catch my ten a.m. flight, Ewan stopped me at the door, pulled my head down to her, and kissed me flush on the lips. It was the only time we had ever touched. Joe gave his huge smile and said as he extended his hand, "Jim, it's been a remarkable experience. See you in six months."

On the taxi ride to Don Muang Airport, I slide my hand onto Pitsommai's lap and left two thousand baht in crisp red bills. She smiled lightly as she placed the money in her purse. At the front of hotel I had taken several pictures of her so I was not surprised when the taxi stopped at the huge converted hangar through which the G.I.'s were processed, and I said leaning over to her, "Pitsommai, I will always remember you," that she said, "Don't forget send me picture."

My plane, a Saturn charter airlines 707 was inexplicably on time in taking off. When I boarded I managed to get a window seat, and as the huge aircraft raised itself from the Earth and gained altitude in a circling pattern, I pressed my face against the window and searched out Bangkok's rapidly disappearing face for familiar landmarks like the Royal Bankok Sports Club, Wat Arun, or the Chakri Memorial Bridge, but the yellow haze from the exhaust of the city's impossible traffic soon blurred out my view. The, leaning back in my seat, I once again fell asleep.

Due to the time difference and the International Date Line (I have never yet been able to calculate it quite accurately), I arrived at Travis Air Force Base in Fairfield, California, fifty miles east of San Francisco, at around two p.m. on the same day I left Bangkok. Some of the passengers, as they got off the plane, kissed the runway. I had no such inclination and, bone-weary, went through customs, got to a phone and made a reservation on a late flight from San Francisco to New York. Then I got a bus to the San Francisco Airport. All this so I found myself sitting in the airport bar by ten p.m. waiting for the one a.m. flight. There I did a dumb thing (what else?); I called Bob Saunders.

The idea had come to me as the bus was crossing the Oakland-Bay Bridge, and I looked out across San Francisco Bay towards the area north of Sausalito where I figured Hamilton Air Force Base must be. By the time I reached the Airport, I was so nervous with anticipation I could hardly keep my drink down. The information operator gave me his number then I paused and breathed deeply before dialing it. Betty answered.

"Good evening, Lt. Saunders' residence."

I held the receiver with one hand and with the other I provided support for my forehead. I spoke hesitatingly and with a deeper than normal voice. I don't think I was trying to disguise it, but then what do I know.

"Um, yah, is uh he there?

"Yes, he is, May I say who's calling, please?" She had a grating cadence to her voice and a tone of unreality like a recording.

I really mumbled my next words, "Um, yeah, it's, uh, Jmmm, uhm, Doyl'."

She let loose with a shrill squeal that popped my ear away from the phone. "JEEEEEM DOYYYYLE!!!! OOOOOO!!!! Is it reaaaly yewwww????"

After cleaning out my ear with a finger, I confirmed my identity with a brief, "Um, yeah."

"Geeeee. Oh, wow. I just can't belieeeeve it. Where are you?"

"Uh, San Francisco."

"OOOH, nifty! You just have to come over. Bob will be so excited."

"Uh, yeah, I bet."

"Of course, I mean after all you did for him. You know, with 'his problem' (she said that like my grandparent's generation discussed sex) and all. I mean, you know, the way you helped him clear the whole thing up."

"What?"

"Oh, yes, I mean you were just marvy."

What?"

"Now let me get Bob. He'll be sooo excited."

I heard her put the receiver down, and I heard her call for him saying that he'd "never guess who's on the phone, Jeeeem Doyle!" but I didn't hear any response from him. It was turning out to be even worse than I thought it would be. I, whose sole purpose in the whole goddamned "problem" had been to try and rid the little runt of the screaming asshole who had just put down the phone and try and wed him to poor Renu, I was now in their frightened, pathetic little imitation of a home, I was now the ONE who helped clear up the "Problem". I thought I would vomit.

Bob picked up the phone and despite the fact he knew who was on the other end and that he must have been at least a little excited about talking to me, said, "Lt. Saunders speaking."

Raising my free hand while the receiver was still pressed to my ear, without saying a word, I terminated the connection. Outside the booth on my way back to the bar I began laughing—not a loud roar, but chuckling. I continued it all the way through to my plane; but I think I would have rather cried.

EPILOGUE

IN FEBRUARY OF 1969, SIX months after I returned to the U.S., Joe came home, by then a private citizen. I flew from Tucson to Kansas City to meet him, and we spent a boozy four days recalling our year together. Joe brought me up to date on events at Nakorn Sarang. Major Richter had left in January and been replaced by someone named Hanson, an officer who Joe felt was cast more in the mold of Hudson. By early February, not long after one Richard M. Nixon became president of the United States, the site began running Green Anchors again, an indication that all bombing restrictions had again been removed. And there were increasingly circulated rumors that the equipment at other radar sites was to be upgraded and Nakorn Sarang to be closed. On the personal side, Joe had seen Sunida and her husband several times, and she always mentioned that she had received several letters from me. Supatra from the Argo Bar had become engaged to Sgt. Pivarnik, the operation's NCOIC who was entering his third consecutive year there, and Joy, Capt Sheet's old girl had resurfaced along with her *sister* Cann as co-Mamasans of the Ooo-La-La night club in Takhli.

Along into our second or third night of reminiscing, I told Joe of my abortive phone call to Bob Saunders. He laughed loudly at my noisy imitation of Betty Saunders' telephone manner. From there I drifted off into a mildly drunken reverie of thoughts and images of Renu and the whole damned business. I had for the past six months been suffering a series of dreams of tremendous frustration. They all in some way concerned Renu and Nakorn Sarang. In each of them some resolution would be near at hand, and suddenly I would find myself unable to move, incapable of the least action. I would wake my jaws tight as if wired together and grating and straining sounds coming from my throat. That night at the bar in Kansas City as I spoke with Joe, many of these nightmares were coming back to me, and my thoughts wandered carrying my speech along with them. Joe listened quite attentively (I think he felt that if six months later I was still carrying these traumas around within me, he owed me his attention) as I went on. It wasn't intended as a summary, but I do recall saying:

"Now I'm not saying that it was our fault she's dead. I mean, for Christ's goddamn sake, none of us were down there pushing her onto the damn tracks. It was just a goddamned accident. And if anything, it was the Thai's fault for not having more damn safety procedures; but anyway, it's none of our faults. Shit, I guess I don't even blame Saunders, that stupid little bastard. But I do know one goddamned thing, that if we hadn't been there, I mean if the whole goddamned United States military hadn't been there, then

I would of never had to take Saunders to Bangkok, and he would of never met Renu, and she would of never come to Nakorn Sarang, and then sure as shit, she'd still be alive today."

Here I made a clucking sound, the result of my throat muscles contracting to suppress a sob, then I went dreamily on. "I don't know, Joe. Jesus, I still think of her a lot, dream about her and stuff. She was so sweet, so pretty, so little, so helpless, and now she's gone, dead. And I can't help thinking sometimes, it *is* our fault, my fault, I really mean."

Joe waited for my words to settle and then when he was sure I was through, he spoke. "You're right about everything except blaming yourself that much. Remember, you were really trying to help her out. Things just didn't work out that way, it just didn't work out right. It wasn't your particular fault. Shit, there's a whole lot of things in that poor part of the world that just aren't ever going to be the same again just because we, and I mean the whole goddamned United States, were there. And there's damn few of the changes that are any damned good. Our intentions may have been good, but we just never knew what the hell we were up to or even how to do it. We were a bunch of clumbsy intruders."

* * *

So now, about a year after I began writing this confused memory, Sunida is still in Nakorn Sarang where she and Praphat are the parents of two children—there may be more by now, our correspondence had dwindled to about one letter a year. Joe is still in Kansas City where he works for a public relations firm. He has made that sad trip back to Bangkok to say his final goodbye to Ewan. He thinks she is now married to a Thai Army captain and raising a family. Pitsommai, Joe learned during the trip, was still at Max's bar, but she had saved quite a bit of money and was planning to open her own restaurant. I am living in New York and writing copy at an ad agency, and Bob, despite the fact I received that recent Christmas card from him, I don't know where he is because he neglected to include a return address, but he appears to be prospering (I am afraid he shall out-prosper us all).

It was of course his card that spurred me into putting this story to paper. And now that I am nearly done, I realize how little I actually understand about that time. As if I understand a lot about any time. I miss them all, badly - Sunida, Ewan, Pitsommai, of course Renu. Hell, I even miss Supatra. I miss many of the airmen, at least Lafayette Chance, some of my fellow officers, in some ways Major Richter. Yet, the recurring and painful emotion that sometime overwhelms my thoughts and often plagues my sleep is, *I should have done so much more, not that I am sure what, but, oh my soul, I should have done so much more.*

August 1975

238

ABOUT THE AUTHOR

JOHN HARRINGTON WORKED IN THE magazine business, primarily in the circulation and distribution area, for most of his business life. He served five years in the US Air Force, stationed in Texas, Thailand, and Arizona. He originally wrote "The Year of The Lieutenant" in the mid-1970's, not long after leaving the military. It was not a good time for fiction related to the Vietnam War. A few years ago, he began working on it again. He lives in Rhode Island, with his wife, Eileen, and near to his son, Jim, his daughter-in-law, Amy, and his two granddaughters, Elizabeth and Olivia.